The Shape of Desire

Ace Books by Sharon Shinn

MYSTIC AND RIDER
THE THIRTEENTH HOUSE
DARK MOON DEFENDER
READER AND RAELYNX
FORTUNE AND FATE

ARCHANGEL
JOVAH'S ANGEL
THE ALLELUIA FILES
ANGELICA
ANGEL-SEEKER

WRAPT IN CRYSTAL
THE SHAPE-CHANGER'S WIFE
HEART OF GOLD
SUMMERS AT CASTLE AUBURN
JENNA STARBORN
QUATRAIN
TROUBLED WATERS
THE SHAPE OF DESIRE

Viking / Firebird Books by Sharon Shinn

THE SAFE-KEEPER'S SECRET
THE TRUTH-TELLER'S TALE
THE DREAM-MAKER'S MAGIC
GENERAL WINSTON'S DAUGHTER
GATEWAY

The Shape of Desire

SHARON SHINN

ACE BOOKS, NEW YORK

THE BERKLEY PUBLISHING GROUP
Published by the Penguin Group
Penguin Group (USA) Inc.
375 Hudson Street, New York, New York 10014, USA
Penguin Group (Canada), 90 Eglinton Avenue East, Suite 700, Toronto, Ontario M4P 2Y3, Canada
(a division of Pearson Penguin Canada Inc.)
Penguin Books Ltd., 80 Strand, London WC2R 0RL, England
Penguin Group Ireland, 25 St. Stephen's Green, Dublin 2, Ireland (a division of Penguin Books Ltd.)
Penguin Group (Australia), 250 Camberwell Road, Camberwell, Victoria 3124, Australia
(a division of Pearson Australia Group Pty. Ltd.)
Penguin Books India Pvt. Ltd., 11 Community Centre, Panchsheel Park, New Delhi—110 017, India
Penguin Group (NZ), 67 Apollo Drive, Rosedale, Auckland 0632, New Zealand
(a division of Pearson New Zealand Ltd.)
Penguin Books (South Africa) (Pty.) Ltd., 24 Sturdee Avenue, Rosebank, Johannesburg 2196, South Africa

Penguin Books Ltd., Registered Offices: 80 Strand, London WC2R 0RL, England

This is an original publication of The Berkley Publishing Group.

Text design by Laura K. Corless.

FIRST EDITION: April 2012

Library of Congress Cataloging-in-Publication Data

Shinn, Sharon.
The shape of desire / Sharon Shinn.—1st ed.
p. cm.
ISBN 978-1-937007-17-1
1. Shapeshifting—Fiction. I. Title.
PS3569.H499S49 2012
813'.54—dc23 2011041164

PRINTED IN THE UNITED STATES OF AMERICA

10 9 8 7 6 5 4 3 2 1

To Susan Austin

Because you're right:

It's long past time you had a book dedicated to you.

The Shape of Desire

CHAPTER ONE

It's around two in the morning when I hear a rustle and bump in the kitchen, and I sit up in bed. I've left the light on over the stove for the past few days, since I've been half expecting Dante to show up. Still, you never know who might have come in through an unlocked door. I get up quietly, throw a robe over my T-shirt, and grab the cell phone in case I need to call 911. Then I creep down the hallway until I can peer into the lighted kitchen and determine whether what awaits me in the other room is a murderer or a lover.

It's the lover. Dante is standing with his back to me, drinking orange juice straight out of the carton. His black hair is greasy, tangled, and halfway down his back; he is shirtless, and I can see the pattern of his ribs through the roughened layer of skin. I wonder what creature he has been this time, and for how long. Where he has been staying, what he has been eating, if he has been in danger.

For a long time, I don't speak. I simply watch as he finishes off the juice and then opens the refrigerator door again. He's clearly ravenous.

He rips open a package of cheese and consumes half the brick in two bites, still rummaging through Tupperware containers and wrapped serving bowls to find something to assuage his hunger. He actually grunts with pleasure when he finds the roast beef I defrosted and left on a plate on the bottom shelf. Setting the plate on the kitchen counter, he closes the refrigerator door and uses both hands to peel back the Saran Wrap, rolls a thick slice of beef, and eats it like a hot dog. He's halfway through the second piece before he stiffens all over and swings around to stare into the darkness of the corridor where I am hiding.

Just for a moment, I get the chance to see his face in full-on feral intensity. My God, he is so beautiful. Beneath the grime and beard stubble, his skin is marble white; his deep-set eyes are a dense and impenetrable brown. His mouth is full and heavy, his cheekbones deliberately planed. Black hair sweeps back from his forehead in a theatrical fall. He could have been an actor, a model, a muse, some rich woman's companion, if only his life had been a little different.

If only his life had been completely different.

"Maria?" he says in his low voice. It's not hard to imagine that voice dropping a few notes, losing its consonants, and coming out as a wordless growl.

He must realize that I am the likeliest presence to be standing a few feet away in the dark; but he sets his plate down, frees his hands for combat, and continues to stare in my direction. Until moments like this, I think that I would like to see him in one of his alternate forms sometime; but I always realize, in those few seconds before he recognizes me, that I really wouldn't. I am not afraid of him now, but I might be if I saw him in some other guise.

I step out of the shadows. "Yes, it's me," I say. "You look so thin."

He glances down at his chest, bare except for a necklace made of a leather cord holding a single key. Indeed, he's much leaner than I like. And I see a new wound cutting through the thin, dark mat of hair on his chest. The cut has already healed, though not long ago. Sometime in the past month, Dante has been in pain and in peril.

He lifts his gaze again and smiles at me, an expression that always reminds me why, despite everything, I love this man so much. "It's been a tough few weeks," he admits.

I come closer. "I see you found the beef," I say. "There's frozen pizza if you need some carbs."

"Maybe later," he says. "Protein's better for now."

This close, I get a pretty strong whiff of what I mentally describe as *new Dante*, the creature he always is when he first arrives. There's dirt and sweat and garbage and urine and some indefinable animal odor—the sort of scent that surrounds a zoo on a hot day. It doesn't bother me as much as you might think. I want to get closer still, throw my arms around him, press my mouth against his, remind myself of his shape and his strength. He's always the one who holds back at first. I'm never sure if it's the wild instincts making him shy away from human contact—or his human instincts shunning his animalistic side, and trying to shield me from it at the same time.

He glances from my face to the plate of roast beef and back to my face. It's clear he's trying to determine if he's eaten enough to get him through the next few hours. "I need a shower," he says, obviously deciding more food can wait. I step in his path as he heads for the doorway.

"I need to kiss you," I say, holding him in place with my hand against his chest.

"Maria—"

"Just . . . a kiss."

He holds utterly still as I stretch up and touch my lips lightly to his, but beneath my hand I can feel his heartbeat kick up a notch. I press in a little harder, just enough so that his mouth responds to mine, and then I step away. I'm smiling; he's not.

"There are towels and clean clothes in the bathroom," I say. "Want me to make you a meal?"

He's watching me with those unbelievable eyes. At times like this his expression is the most haunted, most unreadable. Is he sorry that he has disrupted my life so completely? Sorry he cannot exist beside me through ordinary days like an ordinary man? Sorry that he cannot stay away? Not sorry at all, merely roused to a passion he refuses to act upon until he has restored himself to some self-imposed level of civilization? Or is he simply still hungry and thinking of nothing more than food?

"Don't cook," he says, his voice even lower, throatier. "I'll come rummage some more once I'm out."

I nod and turn away to straighten up the little mess he's made. I don't hear him leave but I can tell when he's gone. Even when he's wearing shoes, which he isn't at the moment, he moves almost without sound. The only reason I know he has left the room is that I miss him already.

I busy myself in the kitchen for about ten minutes, putting away the meat, rinsing off some apples, making sure the sliced bread is out on the counter so he'll see it if he comes hunting for more food later on. But I can't stand being in the kitchen when he's somewhere else in the house. I lock the outside door, turn off the light, and feel my way down the dark corridor toward the bathroom. The door is open just enough to allow a little light and a lot of steam to escape.

I untie my robe, yank my T-shirt over my head, step out of my panties. I leave all of these lying in the hall as I push the door open and step into the hot, foggy bathroom. I can see his silhouette, dark and blurred, behind the translucent glass of the shower door.

When I push it open and step inside, he spins around as if he is a woodland creature startled by a predator. Water sloshes over both of us, kicked up by his feet before it can swirl into the drain, streaming down from the nozzle overhead. It is almost too misty to see, but there is no missing Dante. I scoot carefully across the slippery porcelain of the tub, lifting my arms to twine around his neck. I can smell the toothpaste on his breath as I kiss him again. Water and soap make our skin slippery as our bodies come together. He is no longer resisting me; indeed, his arms close around me, hard, and he kisses me with a furious desire. The water continues to beat down on both of us as we make love in the shower until all the hot water is gone.

It is the first time I have felt fully alive since the last time I saw him.

I know Dante will sleep all day, so I go into work, even though I obviously didn't manage to get much rest the night before. Still, I hate to waste one of my few remaining vacation days moping around the house, waiting for him to get up.

I work as an accountant at a midsize firm in Eureka, Missouri, about forty minutes outside of downtown St. Louis. The company provides Web design and marketing support to regional businesses as far away as Arkansas. There are about twenty of us scattered throughout two stories; the creative people have offices on the top level, while the nuts-and-bolts people like me populate the ground floor. Still, it's impossible to work in such a small place and not be fairly well apprised of everyone else's business.

Today, all the gossip is about one of the secretaries, who came in with what looks suspiciously like a bruise under a heavy caking of foundation. It's not the first time. We all suspect she's being abused by her husband, but whenever someone tries to approach her on the topic, she refuses to speak to us, on that subject or any other. There are several of us who feel like we're failing her as friends and human beings, and we constantly debate what we should be doing for her. I have seen up close the effects of domestic violence; I know how badly such a situation can end. But I have no more clue about how to help Kathleen than anyone else does.

The office manager drops by my desk around ten, just as I'm yawning over the same spreadsheet that I've been staring at for the past half hour. She perches on the edge of my desk, which is something of a feat since her clothes are exceedingly tight and her skirt is exceedingly short. She's a well-endowed, fiftyish woman with garishly blond hair. She looks like she should be serving coffee at a diner and wearing a name tag that identifies her as PEARL or JOLENE, but, in fact, her name is Ellen. I simply love her.

"Well, I stopped to talk to Kathleen for a few minutes this morning and asked how she was doing. Said I thought she looked kind of unwell, and wanted to know if she needed anything or wanted to talk about anything," Ellen says. I always mentally fill in the pauses in her speech by imagining her taking a drag on a cigarette. She says she hasn't lit up in more than a decade, but you can tell, by the hungry way she watches other smokers, that she still wants to.

"Did she tell you to mind your own business?"

"Her expression said, 'Fuck off, bitch,' but you know Kathleen. Not the swearing type," Ellen replies. "She just said she was fine, a little tired, and then she started going through her mail."

"We're all going to feel terrible someday when we learn she's been murdered by her husband."

"Nah, Ritchie's too chicken-shit to kill her. He'd rather beat her up for the next thirty years than try to break in a new rag doll."

"Even if you got her to talk to you, even if you got her to leave him, she'd probably just go back to him. What's the statistic about the numbers of abused wives who return to their husbands?"

Ellen shrugs. She's said before that she doesn't care much about statistics, she cares about stories. Every time she says it, I think, *You'd really love mine.* "And even if she left him, even if she got a divorce, there's no saying that he wouldn't track her down and kill her anyway," she points out. "Happens all the time."

"You're depressing me," I say, "and it's not even ten in the morning yet."

She laughs and pushes herself away from my desk. "I'm going to go make a few calls. I've got a friend who's a social worker. Maybe she'll have some ideas about how I should talk to Kathleen."

"But if it won't do any good—"

Ellen shrugs. "She's gotta live with him. I've gotta live with myself. I have to try." At the door, she turns back. "You feel like going out for lunch today? I left my brown bag at home on the kitchen counter. The cats are gonna have a field day with the tuna salad sandwich."

I hadn't had time to make lunch, since I'd waited till the last possible moment to get out of bed, so I'm delighted by the suggestion. "That would be great! Come get me whenever you're hungry."

We end up at a wannabe Friday's two blocks over. It serves mediocre food but it's only a short walk away, which makes it a popular choice with those who work in our building. I order a hamburger, causing Ellen to give me a knowing look.

"You must be having your period," she says. "You only eat meat about once a month."

I laugh and nod, although, in fact, I am midway through my cycle. It's true that I rarely eat meat, but that's because of Dante. I'm not always certain what animal shape he will take when he's away from me. What if he has chosen to become a pig or a cow? I can't stand the idea that someone could slaughter him and turn him into a Big Mac or a BLT. Only after I know he is alive and human again—only when he is at home in my bed—will I abandon my vegetarian diet.

Ellen and I have just given our orders when we're joined by Marquez, a copywriter in the creative department, who simply saunters over and pulls up a chair. Besides Ellen, he's my closest friend at the office. He's a soft man with a paunchy stomach, a doughy face, a gentle voice, and an endearing smile. He makes no secret of the fact that he's gay, though

I think he's between relationships at the moment; he isn't very forthcoming with the details of his love life. He is, however, perfectly willing to discuss everyone *else's* love life, a topic that Ellen and I also find endlessly fascinating.

After we speculate about Kathleen for a few minutes, we turn our attention to Marquez's boss, an icy, regal woman with striking good looks who keeps her dark hair short and blunt and never wears anything but black.

"As God is my witness, I think she's having an affair with Grant Vance," Marquez says. Grant is a good-looking African-American who handles customer relations and has never, as far as I've determined from personal observation, been in a bad mood.

"Grant Vance is young enough to be her *son*!" Ellen exclaims.

"Really?" I ask. "I'd guess he's thirty, but how old is Caroline? Forty?"

"*My* age, and I turned fifty-two last year," Ellen says.

Marquez is nodding at me when I look skeptical. "We had a party for her two years ago. The big five-oh," he says.

"Well, so what? Men date younger women all the time."

"I don't care who sleeps with who as long as they don't want me to watch it on TV," Ellen says. "But I would never have picked Grant and *Caroline*."

"What makes you so sure?" I ask Marquez. "I mean—he's such a puppy dog. Big and friendly and goofy. Caroline's like Cruella de Vil's mean older sister."

"Caroline likes to order men around," Marquez says cynically. "I think puppy dogs appeal to her. She can train them."

"Turn them into pit bulls," Ellen says with a snort. Caroline is about the only person that I have ever heard Ellen admit to disliking. In general, Ellen is so entertained by the antics of the human race that she enjoys everybody's company.

"But are you *sure*? She's married, isn't she?" I say.

They each give me a look of derision. "What world do *you* live in?" Marquez demands. "Married people have sex *all the time* with individuals who are not their spouses."

"She just seems so cold and dispassionate," I say. "I mean, not the kind of person who would *want* an affair."

"Sometimes it's not about sex, it's about power," Marquez says.

"People always say stuff like that, and I don't know why," Ellen replies, just as the waitress brings our food. "Sex is pretty damn good all on its own without having to be about anything else."

I would have laughed anyway, but the look on the waitress's face makes it impossible for me to stop giggling. Marquez is grinning. None of us speak again until the girl leaves, giving us one last disgusted look before she marches away. She's about eighteen; I think she's repulsed by the notion that anyone as old as we are might still be indulging in carnal acts.

"But you never told us," Ellen says, speaking around a mouthful of food. "Why do you think Grant and Caroline are getting it on?"

"He licked her face," Marquez says.

I almost choke on my burger. "He *what*?"

"They were in her office. You could tell they thought the door was closed, but it never latches quite right and it had swung open a little. I was spying on them," he admits, "because I just had a funny feeling. They've been hovering around each other. She calls him into her office five times a day. He gets this look every time she walks by. I just sensed something."

Ellen snaps her fingers, eager for him to get to the good part. "So? They're alone in her office, you're spying, the door opens, and–"

"And I *see* them. She's just standing there, with her hands down at her sides. He's about a foot away from her, with his hands at *his* sides, like she's told him not to touch her. And he leans in and he *licks* her *face*. He sticks his tongue out and he laps it along her cheek. Long and slow, like he's trying to draw out the whole experience. He does it a couple of times, like maybe she's spread honey on her skin and he's trying to get it all off. And then she turns her head, and he licks her *other* cheek. Just the same way."

"I think I might lose my lunch," Ellen says, but she chomps down on another French fry.

"I think it's kind of sweet," I say.

They both turn to stare at me as if I am the stupidest woman on the planet. "Explain to me how and in what possible context *sweet* could apply to this situation," Ellen says.

I shrug. "Maybe Caroline wanted him to do something to prove he felt affection for her. Something that wasn't actual, you know, sex. Something that would demonstrate tenderness."

"Something that was creative," Marquez says with a grin. "Something that would get her hot but didn't involve him grabbing her boob."

Ellen tosses up her hands as if conceding a feverishly contested point. "Whatever. Like I said, I don't care who does who as long as I don't have to watch."

"I *like* to watch," Marquez says.

"You're a pervert," Ellen tells him.

"But I wonder if they do more than licking," I say. "I mean, it would be kind of *sad* if he never got to touch her."

At their incredulous expressions, I feel compelled to add, "Well, if they really love each other. I mean, she's clearly a controlling bitch and he's in way over his head and there is no *way* this can end well, by any objective measure. But wouldn't it be nice if they could have a few moments of real happiness together? You know? If she's in a loveless marriage and he's lonely and somehow they come together as kindred spirits and they have really great sex and there's *something* in their lives, even for a short time? Don't you think that would make it okay?"

Marquez reaches out to squeeze my hand where it lies on the table. "Sweetie, you really are a romantic, aren't you?" he says.

Ellen snorts. "She's delusional."

"I just think there are all kinds of definitions of love," I say. "There are all kinds of reasons we're drawn to people. Maybe there's something in their relationship you don't understand—something that makes it really precious to them. You shouldn't judge."

Ellen's tone is acerbic as vinegar. "Once I've talked to my social worker friend about Kathleen, I'll ask if she has time to come in and speak to *you*," she says. "I think maybe *you* might be in a situation that you need to discuss with somebody."

For the briefest of moments, I picture that conversation: *"My boyfriend is a shape-shifter. I only see him a few days a month, when he's in human form." "And how does that make you feel?"* I think Kathleen has a better shot than I do of making any counselor understand what she's experiencing.

"I'm not uttering any disguised cries for help," I say, making my tone match Ellen's. "I'm just saying a nontraditional relationship might have benefits that aren't immediately apparent to *you*."

"Uh-huh," says Ellen. "Well, anytime you want to talk about it, you just let me know."

I sigh and roll my eyes in an exaggerated fashion. It's time to change the subject. "Hey! Did anyone see what Gage Jackson was wearing today? Was that supposed to be a *tie*?"

It's always possible to distract Marquez with the topic of fashion. "He called it a cravat," he replies. "Pretensions of British nobility, anybody?"

We finish the meal in pretty good spirits and leave the waitress a healthy tip. Ellen tips more heavily than anyone I know, usually making some comment like "Because her life is clearly so much more awful than mine" or "Because if I had to wait on scumbags and dickheads I'd be poisoning their soup and spitting in their beer." Today she says, "So she can buy a new pair of thong underwear and impress her boyfriend with her youth and beauty. *While they last.*"

Marquez and I are both grinning as we follow her toward the exit. The waitress is standing by the front desk, and she joins the hostess in thanking us for our business and wishing us a pleasant day. Just as Ellen reaches for the door, Marquez leans over and licks her left cheek. Over the explosive sound of Ellen laughing, I'm sure I hear the waitress gasp.

I'm smiling, too—it's pretty funny—but I'm not doubled over in mirth as Marquez and Ellen are. I don't think I'm in a position to question anyone else's definition of love. I'm not prepared to mock; I'm not willing to recoil in horror.

I'm almost thirty-five years old and for close to half of my life I have been in love with a man I cannot introduce to my family or my friends. People feel sorry for me; they try to set me up on dates; they think I might be a lesbian too shy to come out of the closet. They wonder if I'm simply off, strange, missing some essential component of affection or desire.

They don't understand that what I have is so precious, so intense, such an *essential* part of my life, that I would not give it up for any inducement. If I tried, or if someone forced me to, I truly believe I would die.

When I get home, Dante is up and dressed and shuffling around the house with that dazed look that means he hasn't been out of bed very long.

"How was your day?" I ask as I toss my purse and jacket to the couch. The living room is just to the left coming through the door, so the couch is handy.

Dante doesn't actually answer, just comes over and envelops me in a hug, rubbing his face in my hair and clutching me to his body as if he just wants to remind himself of my weight and scent. I love these moments of exploration. I feel both absolutely connected to him, as if we have been lovers since the beginning of the world, and delighted by the wonder and unexpectedness of his presence in my life, as if we just met the night before but instantly recognized each other as soul mates.

The tension and the arguments will come later.

"My day was very dull," he says into my skin as he nuzzles my neck. "I slept until noon, got up to eat, slept until four, got up to eat, used your computer to check my accounts, and then watched TV for about an hour."

It only takes a few moments of thought to realize it would be very hard for someone who is only human a few days a month to hold down a job. Which means it is difficult for him to earn money or afford health insurance or pay for a car or actually *buy* anything. But what does he need? A few pairs of jeans, some T-shirts, a fresh pair of New Balance shoes every couple of years? I can buy all those things for him.

But he doesn't want me to. He wants to be my lover, he says, not my gigolo. Anyway, he has his own money, funds his mother accumulated and left in separate accounts for Dante, his brother, and his sister. I'm not sure how much cash he could scare up if he needed to, but he has enough for his needs. I know some of it goes every month, through an automated payment plan, to pay for his storage shed near the Highway 44 exit that leads to my neighborhood.

He wears the key to that shed on a cord around his neck. I know that's the first place he goes every time he returns to town, every time he returns to his human life. I'm his second stop.

"That doesn't sound like such a bad day to me," I say. "Sleeping and eating and watching TV. Actually, it sounds pretty ideal."

"And having a beautiful, sexy creature come home to you at the end of the day," he says. "That's the best part."

We stand in the living room and kiss for a while, which is extraordinarily pleasurable. I know we will make love again tonight, but right now there's no urgency about it. We're still reconnecting; we're remembering what it feels like to be in another person's arms, *this* person's arms. He rubs his stubbled face against my cheek. I slip my hands inside the waistband at the back of his jeans. God, the feel of his smooth flesh against my fingers, the warmth of his breath against my forehead. I've *missed* this so much. Only now, when I can feast again on sensation, do I let myself admit how long I've been starved for contact.

I stretch up to kiss him on the mouth. "So what do you want to do tonight?" I ask. "Go out? It's Humphrey Bogart night over at the university."

Dante loves old movies. If it's black-and-white, he's seen it. Noir, screwball comedy, World War II films, weepy Bette Davis dramas. My tastes tend to skew more toward romantic comedy—and Technicolor—but I'll watch anything with him. I was one of the first people in my area to get cable, just for TCM.

"Not tonight, I think. Not yet," he says.

He's often a little skittish on his first days back, uncomfortable around people and clumsy in public. I've watched him at restaurants as he studies the table, as if reminding himself what silverware is for. He can't stand to use a straw. And he can't tolerate small, crowded spaces, like movie theatres on an opening weekend or sports bars when the home team is playing. When we do take in a movie, it's usually a matinee the day before the playbill changes or a French film showing at an art house.

"I've recorded a bunch of stuff on the DVR," I say. "Let's see if there's anything on the menu that sounds good to you."

An hour later, we curl up together on the couch, eating pizza in the flickering dark. We've reached a deal: We'll watch an hour of *The Sopranos*—which he loves and I hate—followed by an hour of classic old comedies like *The Mary Tyler Moore Show*—which he also likes, but not nearly as much as I do. And then we'll alternate again. Once the pizza is eaten and I've done up the dishes, we stretch out on the couch, entwining more completely. My back is to his chest, his arms are around me, and an old afghan knitted by my grandmother covers both of us. I watch James Gandolfini order some hapless cohort to get whacked, shutting my eyes before the scene can play out. My fingers close over Dante's and he kisses the back of my head.

I cannot remember ever being so happy.

CHAPTER TWO

There are two more days in the workweek and I force myself to go to the office both days, even though I am missing time with Dante. He sleeps most of Thursday, but by Friday morning he's restless and energetic, and I know he won't be confined to the house for long. I can hardly stand the thought that he will be roaming the streets, visiting parks, browsing through stores, *existing*, while I'm in some other part of the city. But I also can't stand the thought of having absolutely no time off for the rest of the year, and I just have two days left. And it's only September.

"I'll see if I can work through lunch and come home early," I tell him, as he gives me a lingering kiss good-bye. "Think about what you might want to do this weekend. We could drive out to the wineries. Or go hiking. The weather's supposed to be beautiful."

"We need to go see Christina," he says.

I stop with my hand on the door, turning to stare at him in surprise. Christina is his sister, and I can't remember the last time we visited her, though I think he gets in touch with her every time he's in human form. She lives outside of Rolla, about ninety minutes southwest of my house in Eureka. As far as I can determine, his brother has *no* permanent residence.

"She sent an e-mail," he adds. "She wants to see us. And William."

The advent of e-mail has made it exponentially easier for Dante to run his life, and he set up a Hotmail account ages ago. Now and then, while he's gone off in some animal shape, and I'm worried sick about him every single minute, he has a chance to shift into human form, find a library or an Internet café, and send me a quick note to let me know he's all right and thinking of me. I *live* for those messages, random and far too rare.

"Is something wrong?" I ask. "Is she sick?"

He shrugs. "I don't know. There was just a message in my in-box saying she wanted to see me when I was around. I e-mailed this morning to say I was here. She suggested we come over Sunday."

"And William will be there, too?"

Again, he hunches his shoulders. "You never know about William."

"Okay," I reply. What else is there to say? "Well, let me know if there's anything you want to do on *Saturday*. Love you. See you later."

There's an accident on Highway 109 and no easy way around it, so I have plenty of time to sit in my car and think. I don't know much about Dante's siblings—truth be told, I don't know as much about Dante as I would like. It's amazing how completely I have allowed him to dictate the parameters of our relationship. I accept what he tells me. I rarely push for more details. I never insist on proof that what he tells me is true.

In the past fifteen years, I have never once seen him transmogrify into a different form. I have only his word for it that, when he leaves me, he is something else entirely—something that a sane person would never consider to be credible. There have been times when I entertained doubts, of course, as anyone would. But as the years have passed and his story has not varied, and what I have *experienced* of his life seemed to tally with what he has *told* me of his life, I have come to believe him. Mostly. With only a faint shadow of uncertainty now and then . . .

I think it was meeting Christina and William ten years ago that really won me over. Because they all told the same tale, or variations on it, with no theatrics, no lurking twinkle, no indication that they were merely waiting for me to swear I believed them before they cried out, "Fooled you!" Of course, they all could have been subject to the same hallucinatory hysteria, victims of an insane parent who whispered to them from infancy that they were different, they were special, they closed their eyes at night and dreamed they were dogs and sheep and bears, but the dreams were real . . .

And yet, when they discussed their habits of changing, how it felt and when it happened, they seemed merely to be discussing their lives. As my cousins and I might talk about how our skin reacts to a different moisturizer, how the hair on our legs grows thicker in the winter, maybe because we forget to shave. Dante and his siblings never seem to be trying to convince me of anything. They never seem to be pretending.

Although they share a certain family resemblance, they're very different, both in attitudes and shape-shifting rituals. By the time I met Christina and William, I had finally learned a few details about Dante's own situation. During the first years of his life, he didn't change forms very often—maybe for one or two days a month. He couldn't remember the first time it had happened, which he assumed meant that he had been changing shapes since he was a baby. It was never scary; it was never strange. It just was.

From the beginning, he had had little control over what animal he would become or when the transformation would occur. He had learned to recognize the symptoms that preceded the event—the day before it happened, he would feel a buildup of pressure at the back of his head, and lights would begin flickering at the corners of his eyes. These signals proved vastly useful once he decoded them, because he made sure he was never sitting in a classroom or visiting a public space on the day he would become something else.

He never described to me the exact mechanics of transformation, though he said the process tended to be quick—five or ten minutes at the most. When he was a child, he usually turned into a small animal, such as a cat or a rabbit. As he aged and grew, acquiring weight and muscle mass, he became somewhat larger creatures, like beavers, goats, deer, and foxes. Once he attained his full adult height, he said, he was never again a creature weighing less than fifty pounds. These days when he changed, he found himself to be a wolf, a collie, a mountain lion. Mostly, he said, he took on an animal shape that was suitable to his environment.

Mostly.

"So you might turn into a bear when you're walking the streets of a major city?" I asked him one day.

"I try not to be in an urban area when I think I'm going to change."

"Maybe you should. Maybe if you always stayed in town, you'd never turn into anything except a German shepherd or a Labrador retriever."

He had not answered that. I filed the suggestion away as something to mention again if the time ever seemed right.

Something else happened as he grew older: His periods in animal form became longer and longer, until he was only human about half the time—and then even less. These days, he's in the shape of a man only about one week out of every month. I live in absolute terror of the day he changes into another creature and never changes back.

"That won't happen," he once told me.

"But how do you know?"

He'd laughed. "Because I'll be dead before then."

"What?"

He'd shrugged and given the most minimal answer, clearly sorry he'd brought it up. "Shape-shifters tend not to live very long lives. Too much wear and tear on the body, maybe. Or too much time in the form of animals that die much sooner than humans do. If I spend half a month as a collie, well, that's a much bigger percentage of a dog's life than it is of a man's life. It ages me."

"Then don't be a dog anymore," I said urgently. "Be a— Be a giant sea tortoise! They live for centuries! Slow down the process. Reverse it!"

I hadn't been kidding, but he'd laughed. "You have no reason to believe you'll live any longer than I will," he teased. "You could go in a car accident—or a plane crash. You could get cancer or meningitis. A gas leak could cause your house to blow up. Anything could—"

"I get the point! I could die! But the *probability* is that I will live to eighty or so. And you're telling me that your probability is significantly less—"

He'd shrugged again. "I'm saying I don't know. I'm not going to worry about it. I can change my shape but I can't change my destiny. I'm at peace with whatever happens."

I wasn't, of course. I fretted about that conversation for days, for weeks, until I finally realized that my anxiety did nothing but irritate him and exhaust me. It was clear I couldn't change him; I couldn't even change myself.

Christina and William, though born to the same set of parents, seem to be governed by an entirely different set of rules. William, who is five years younger than Dante, has always been animal more often than he's been human, and he's never been anything except a dog or a wolf. He claims to be able to decide when to shift between states, which raises the very interesting question of why he is so rarely human. There is a permanent wildness to his face that always reminds me of *new Dante*. If you didn't know William was a shape-shifter, you'd think he was one of those children raised by feral animals in a cave somewhere, not rescued by man until he was ten or twelve years old. You get the sense that he has learned to mimic human behaviors but that they will never be instinctive to him. He left home when he was fifteen, and it is rare, these days, that his siblings know exactly where he is.

By contrast, Christina is the most normal of the three. Younger than William by three years, she's always human, except for two or three days a month; those days are usually associated with her menstrual cycle. According to her, if the need is great enough, she can resist changing, even when her body longs for transmogrification. Like Dante, she experiences useful symptoms that let her know alteration is imminent. She can make sure she's locked in her house, away from shocked strangers and prying eyes, when she allows the metamorphosis to take her. The shapes she takes are varied, though she has never been explicit about them, at least not with me.

Their mother had been a shape-shifter, too, more like Christina than William and, from what I can tell, gifted with a preternatural patience and tranquillity. She died the summer Dante graduated from college; I never met her, which I regret to this day.

Of their father, never a word is spoken.

There might be stranger families in the world, but I have never been able to imagine what they might be like.

Work is endless. I actually nod off during the staff meeting my boss holds right after lunch, when my coworkers and I are all at our dullest. Fourteen of us are grouped around a conference table meant to hold ten, and the temperature inside the room must be close to eighty. Kathleen is sitting near the head of the table, taking notes by hand. The bruises on her face have turned from purple to a greenish-yellow, still visible under her makeup. She is wearing a new ring on her right hand, a star sapphire flanked by diamonds.

"That sumbitch gave it to her last night," Ellen whispers to me when I draw her attention to the new jewelry. "She was walking around this morning showing it off to everyone. 'See what Ritchie bought me! Isn't it beautiful?' I said, 'Kathleen, honey, why'd he get you something so nice? Is it your anniversary? I *know* your birthday's not till February.' And she said, happy as you please, 'We had an argument Monday night and he just wanted to say he was sorry.' And I said, 'Well, sugar, maybe next time you ought to let him carve your face open with a butcher knife. Then he'll owe you a *car*.'"

I put a hand to my mouth to muffle my laugh. "What did she say then?"

"She told me I was a stupid bitch and to mind my own business."

"No, she didn't."

"Well, she just turned around and walked away, but I knew what she was thinking."

"Maybe he'll be nice to her for a while."

"Well, then, happy days for sure."

When the meeting *finally* comes to its conclusion, we all jostle toward the door, and I find myself unexpectedly falling in step beside Kathleen. Almost before I know the words are forming in my mouth, I say, "I've been admiring your ring. Is it new?"

Her face lights up. She extends her right hand so I can see her fingers. "Isn't it beautiful? My husband gave it to me."

I don't know how to answer. I finally say, "I'm sure he loves you very much."

Ellen is behind me, so I can't see her face, but I know she's rolling her eyes. The thing is, he probably *does* love her, in a tortured and unhealthy way. The question isn't whether she loves him back, but whether she *should.* The question is: Is he *safe* to love?

Dante wants to go out to dinner, even though it's Friday night, which means restaurants will be crowded. We pick a small place with outdoor seating that's airy and open enough to keep Dante from getting edgy. Although it's mid-September, the days are still fairly warm, and the heat lamps strategically set up around the perimeter of the patio keep the area perfectly comfortable at night.

"Can I get you anything to drink?" our waitress asks. She's about twenty-five, pretty and buxom, with shiny brown hair pulled back in a ponytail and lipstick that looks so much like bubblegum I wonder if it came with a miniature comic wrapping.

"How about a beer?" Dante says.

She reels off the selections and he picks some kind of heavy Irish stout. I ask for lemonade. Dante makes a face at me as soon as the waitress leaves.

"I'm not going to get *drunk*, you know," he says. "You don't have to choose nonalcoholic beverages so you can be the designated driver."

He loves to drive; whenever he's in town and we go anywhere together, he automatically slips behind the steering wheel. I'm usually nervous for the first fifteen minutes, wondering if his fine motor coordination has deteriorated during his travels; but, so far anyway, he doesn't seem to have lost a jot of his competence.

"I don't feel like drinking," I say. "Alcohol messes up my sleep patterns, and I haven't gotten much sleep this week as it is."

"Well, I'll only be around a few more days," he says. "You can catch up next week."

He says the words so casually; he must have no idea how they lacerate my heart. "You'll make it through Sunday, won't you?" I say, trying to joke. "Otherwise, I guess I'll have to drive you out to Christina's. You can sit in the front seat with your head sticking out the window."

He gives this sally a brief smile. "I ought to be good through Monday at least. I guess we'll see."

"Last time it was eight days. The time before that, ten days."

He nods. "So Monday or Tuesday sounds about right."

"What are you going to get to eat?"

"I was looking at the steak tartare."

I'm silent. I always find it disturbing that he likes his meat so rare. It makes me think about how he must eat when he's in animal form, catching small creatures and devouring them raw. No wonder shapeshifters have a short life expectancy. God knows what kinds of toxins they absorb with their strange diets.

"Or the sushi," he adds.

"Maybe you should have a salad," I say. "You know, get some greens. And some fruit while you're at it. You don't want to develop scurvy."

He gives me a look filled with mockery. "Heartworms, more likely," he says. "Rabies. I don't think it's malnutrition that's going to do me in."

"Don't *talk* like that," I plead. "It makes me so sad."

"I'm a realist. You're a romantic."

"Well, maybe I am. Indulge me, just for tonight. Don't talk about death. And don't eat uncooked food!"

The waitress returns to deliver our drinks and take our orders. "What would you suggest?" he asks her. "My girlfriend thinks I should eat something healthy, but I want something that tastes good. And has a lot of calories."

"Our specialty is beef stew," she says. "It's got vegetables in it, is that healthy? But it's really hearty. Most people can't eat the whole bowl."

He folds his menu and hands it to her. "I bet I can. Let me have the stew. And some bread. And another beer."

I'm the one who gets a salad, though I've already lost my appetite, as well as any inclination to talk. But silence never bothers Dante. I suppose that's because he lives for weeks at a time without exchanging words with anyone. He leans back in his chair and looks around at the other diners with idle interest.

I always wish I could tell what he's thinking when he studies strangers in this way. Is he wondering if they, like he, conceal shocking secrets even though they look so normal? Is he wishing he could try on their ordinary lives, if only for a day or two, if only to see what he's missed all these years? Is his wolf brain or his cougar brain wondering what they would taste like if he ripped out their throats and began munching on their flesh for dinner?

I hate that such thoughts even cross my mind. I never voice them. But every time I see Dante grow as still and focused as a predator, his eyes on some stranger across a room, those terrible images fill my head.

The food is good, and Dante does indeed manage to polish off the whole bowl of stew. And a third beer. I eat most of my salad, split a dessert with him, and take the car keys from his hands as we leave.

"You remember the rule," I say, keeping my voice light. "More than two beers and I drive."

"I remember," he says amiably enough.

The alcohol has made him amorous, though. During the entirety of the short ride home, he sits half turned toward me, his left hand resting on my leg, his fingers curled around the inside of my thigh. I love to feel the weight of his hand, not moving, not stroking, simply *there*, a silent statement of intimate connection. Of possession, perhaps. It comes as no surprise to me that I feel as if I belong to him.

We're barely inside the door before he takes me in his arms, kissing me hungrily and pulling at the straps of my dress as if he cannot wait for the thirty seconds it will take me to undo the ties and buttons myself. I cling to him, suddenly desperate to feel his skin against mine, though our feverish kisses impede both of our efforts to undress. We break apart long enough to shed our clothes in a tangled pile just a few feet from the door, and then we're kissing madly again.

Moving in tandem like mating dragonflies, we've taken a few steps toward the bedroom, but it's too far away and the need is too great. His erection is between us and we rub against each other, moaning in low voices; and then he is inside me, half lifting me in his arms, as he thrusts and pulls back and thrusts again. I feel my fingers biting into the flesh of his shoulders; I must hold on to him with all my strength or get flung into the void. While his hips work, he plants breathless kisses all over my face, but not as if he is even aware he is kissing me. His mouth against my skin is just another form of speech, an expression of desire, as involuntary and absentminded as a gasp of pain or pleasure.

I come and then he does, and we both fight for air, holding tight to each other as our bodies recollect themselves and our souls filter back inside our skin. He sets me on my feet and I am keenly aware of the cool hardwood floor beneath my soles, the slick sweat that greases my stomach and his, the sharp scents produced by both of our bodies. There is no odor in the world that replicates the smell of sex. There is no rapture that can match it.

A half hour later, we are lying face-to-face in bed, both of us having showered and brushed our teeth for the night. Neither of us has bothered to put on nightclothes, and we lie side by side in that drowsy, companionable state of affection that usually follows lovemaking. We are engaging in the light foreplay we didn't have the patience for earlier, though I don't think it will lead to another bout of sex. He is running his hand idly up and down the curve of my hip and leaning in now and then to kiss me. I am working my fingers into the knotted muscles of his back and neck, pausing now and then just to caress the ridged surfaces of his chest. He is thinner than I like, but in top physical shape.

His body is that of an athlete preparing for a marathon session of training.

My hand tangles in the cord around his neck and I tug on it gently, which obligingly brings his mouth down to mine. I am still holding the strip of leather when he lifts his head, and now I examine it more closely. There's a little light spilling in through the window—enough for me to see that this isn't the same cord he was wearing when he returned a few days ago.

"This is new, isn't it?" I ask, rubbing the pieces of leather together so that the key twirls in a heavy dance.

"Yeah. Picked it up this morning."

"What was wrong with the old one? Was it starting to fray?"

"It was too short."

It takes me a moment to work that out. He'd been wearing the same cord for the past five years; the key had lain against his chest just at the breastbone. What has suddenly made it insufficient?

And then I realize: The cord is perfectly fine when he's in human shape, but not when he turns into an animal. It is still around his neck, of course—it is the only thing he is determined to never lose, though he does try to keep a pack of small supplies with him that he can carry even when he is in animal form. If the cord is too short, he must be changing into bigger and bigger beasts.

If he becomes an animal whose neck is too thick, too burly, he might be strangled by his single link to his human soul.

"Dante," I breathe.

He rolls onto his back and the strap slips through my fingers. "Don't get all fussy on me," he says.

I sit up. *Fussy* is not nearly desperate enough to describe how I feel. *"Dante,"* I say again. "Tell me what's happening to you."

He kind of shakes his head against the pillow; his hands make a small gesture of fatalism. "This last time, I was some pretty big creatures. A bear for at least a week. I could feel the cord tight against my windpipe, though it didn't hurt and it didn't bind. But I've been moving through Kansas and Colorado a lot over the past few months. What if I turn into a buffalo? What if I turn into a moose? That band wouldn't be long enough."

I pull insistently on the key. "This one wouldn't be, *either*!" I exclaim.

"Maybe not," he says. "I think I'm going to buy a bungee cord, or maybe just some industrial strength elastic, and sew the leather to that. Give myself some room to expand."

"But a buffalo—I mean, what's the collar size of an animal like that?" I say, trying to dial back my anxiety. Or, at least, to *sound* like I've dialed it back.

"Pretty damn big," he admits.

"Maybe you should think of a different plan," I say. "Wear it around your wrist."

"I'd lose it the first day I changed," he says.

"Your waist?"

"Thought about that," he says. "Maybe. But there's bound to be a similar problem. I mean, anything small enough to stay around my waist will turn into a tourniquet on a big animal."

"Yeah, but at least you won't *choke to death* in the first five minutes of transformation," I say. "If you had to, you could probably claw it off before it did any substantial damage."

"If I was a wolf or a big cat," he agrees. "But buffalo or bison? Not so sure."

"What about wearing it as part of your harness?" I say. That's how he carries the pack with him most of the time—the harness slips over his back, shoulders, and stomach, leaving his limbs free no matter what shape he assumes. The pack holds only the barest essentials: a twenty-dollar bill, a debit card, and a pair of slick running pants folded into the smallest possible shape so he has *something* to cover his nakedness when he resumes his human body. While he's gone, one of my daily tasks is to check his bank account to make sure he hasn't lost his backpack and a stranger isn't making purchases with his card.

Whenever I see new account activity—usually the purchase of running shoes and a sweatshirt—my heart always lifts. *He's himself again; he'll be back with me soon.* That isn't always true, of course. Sometimes he's hundreds of miles away and human for just a few hours, but he still needs to buy clothes if he's anywhere he might run into other people.

He shakes his head again. "The backpack I can afford to lose. The key I can't. I've got to be able to figure out a way to keep it on me all the time."

"Dante." I swing a leg over him and straddle his hips, then lean in very close, my hands on his cheeks, my eyes staring into his. "Dante. You can afford to lose the key. You don't have to go straight to the locker whenever you change. You just have to get somewhere that you can call me. I'll come to you, wherever you are. I'll bring everything you need."

He turns onto his side, trying to dislodge me, but I tumble over with him, landing so that we are still face-to-face. My leg is still wrapped around his waist, my palms are still on his face, though he has grabbed my wrists as if he wants to pull my hands away. But he doesn't.

"I cannot simply rely on you," he says, speaking the words clearly and precisely, as if to make sure that *this time* I actually understand. We have had this conversation dozens of times before. "What if you're sick? What if you're out of town? What if you simply don't want to come get me?"

"I don't think—"

He raises his voice to drown me out. "What if you're *dead*, though God knows I hope you live to be a hundred? What if you've gotten tired of me and you've taken up with some other guy and he doesn't think it's such a hot idea for you to go charging out in the middle of the night on an errand you can't explain?"

"You know that won't—"

"I trust you, Maria, with my secret, with my life, with my *soul*, but *no* human being can be everything else to another one. If you're the only thing I can count on, the time will come when I need you and you won't be there." Now he puts his hands on my cheeks, and draws me in so our foreheads touch. Our wrists make *X* shapes on either side of our faces. "Just as there have been times you've needed me and I haven't been here."

"I've never complained about that," I whisper. "I've never asked you to give me more than you can."

He kisses me, very gently, on the mouth. "And I won't let you try to give me more than you should," he says quietly. "I have to be able to do some things for myself. I'll think about the key. I'll work it out."

"I love you," I say.

He kisses me again. "I know," he replies. "My life would be nothing if you didn't."

Saturday we run errands and eat lunch out and take a short hike through Babler State Park, which is only about twenty minutes from my house. The exercise puts Dante in a good mood, and so he's willing to entertain an idea I had while I lay beside him the night before, unable to sleep.

"What about a *backup* plan?" I ask. "You'll still have the key with you in some fashion. But just in case I'm not dead or sick or on an airplane or married to someone else when you come back to town, what if we buy a prepaid cell phone and bury it somewhere that you can get to easily? And then if you lose your pack and your key, you can dig up the phone and call me."

He gives me a look filled equally with fondness and derision. "And you don't think the battery will have worn down during the weeks I've been gone?"

"We'll buy one of those special chargers," I say triumphantly. "You use a couple of AA batteries and a connector cord to recharge the cell phone battery. I bought one after my power went out last time."

He looks intrigued. "That might work." Then he has a thought. "Of course, why couldn't I just bury a spare key to my locker instead of the cell phone?"

I stare at him blankly and then burst out laughing. "Well, you could, I guess," I say. "But I think we should get the cell phone, too, just to reward me for coming up with such a clever idea!"

It's a plan that pleases both of us because it offers a couple different kinds of insurance; it also makes him feel independent and allows me to feel potentially useful. We spend the rest of the day shopping for the items we need and getting a copy of his key made. Then we take our new waterproof box back to Babler, a place that's easily accessible to Dante, whether he's human or animal, and that I can get to with a short drive.

The question quickly becomes: Where can we bury the box so that Dante can find it again, but no one else is likely to come across it by accident? The site has to be memorable enough for him to find it again no matter what the season, so trees can't be the only markers. And Babler is almost nothing but trees. A few two-lane roads connect the main entrance to the RV parking spaces and the picnic areas and a few other paved spots, but mostly it's just one big forest cluttered with scrubby underbrush beneath the heavy spreading branches of the trees.

The day is warm and spectacularly beautiful, and the park is beginning to put on its autumn finery. A few maples are showing red—one or two leaves waving like bloody hands from the vibrant green throng covering most of the branches. The tops of the sycamores look as if someone has sifted cinnamon over them from a low-flying plane, while the honey locusts appear to have accidentally dipped some of their northwestern branches into a bright vat of yellow paint. They are now trying to shake off the color in random, intermittent droplets of brilliance.

We leave my car in one of the RV spaces and plunge into the woods, following a narrow path. It's tangled with roots and vines and deep, eternal piles of rotting leaves, old gumballs, and fallen branches. Squirrels skitter around us, alert and lively. Hawks glide overhead, soundless and patient. I hear Dante take a deep breath; I think he is inhaling nature.

"These are the days I wish I could shape-shift," I say in a quiet voice. "To be in this world—among all this beauty—at the most basic, essential level. To be *part* of it, in ways a human can never be."

"Trust me," he says, his voice wry, "it's easier to appreciate it in this shape. When you're an animal, you're not admiring the scenery or noticing the pretty flowers. If you're a predator, you're trying to hear or smell your dinner. If you're prey, you're always looking for the next hiding place. There are only two things you think about—eating and staying alive. Maybe only one thing, since you eat to stay alive. There is no"—he pauses to figure out exactly what he wants to say—"aesthetic sensibility."

Maybe I should be annoyed at his pragmatic response, but instead I laugh. "Way to destroy my idealistic view of nature," I say.

He's grinning. "It's like everything else," he says. "The better you know it, the less idyllic it seems."

I take his hand and squeeze it. "Not you," I say soulfully, exaggerating the sentiment so he'll think I'm kidding. "The better I know you, the more wonderful I think you are."

"And the better I know *you*, the more delusional I think you are," he replies. "But it turns out I like that in a woman."

I let go of his hand and punch him lightly in the arm. I've lost his attention. He's pointing ahead and a little to our left, where there's a low wooden bridge over an almost invisible stream. The bridge looks sturdy enough, but neglected; if it had ever been painted, all the color has worn away, leaving a dingy gray behind.

"How about here? Or a few paces away in one direction or another?" he asks. "This ought to be easy enough for me to find again."

I glance behind us, because I'm not at all certain *I* could find the spot again. The trail is so poorly defined that I'm not even sure I could get back to the car if I was here on my own. Fortunately, Dante never gets lost. I don't know if it's because his animal instincts stay with him when he's in human form, or if it's because he's just one of those people who is always able to orient himself.

"Looks good," I say. "Let's bury our box and get back to the car. I think it'll be dark in about an hour."

He laughs, looks around, and counts out twenty paces directly north of the bridge, or what I imagine is north. Then he drops to his knees and clears away the leaves and rubble to get to the dirt below. I've brought a trowel, but I let him do the digging while I hold the package. "I didn't know you were afraid of the dark," he says.

"Well, I'm *not*, when I actually know where I am," I retort. "But I'd hate to try to find my way back to the park entrance after sunset."

"Don't worry, I know exactly where we are," he says. "*And* how to get back. I'd think you'd be more concerned about running into a coyote or a bobcat."

I look around even more nervously. I've been so focused on our mission that it hasn't even occurred to me to wonder if we're in any danger. But, of course, coyotes and bobcats are common in Missouri. "Aren't we too big for them to attack?"

He lays aside the trowel and reaches for the box. "Generally speaking, yes, but if there were a pack of coyotes—or if the cat was really, really hungry—"

"Stop it. You're scaring me," I say.

He laughs again. The box fits neatly in the space he's hollowed out, and he begins filling the hole with earth. He's made it pretty deep to discourage wild animals from going to the trouble of digging it up. "This isn't really the season for them to attack humans," he says in what is supposed to be a comforting tone. "Deep winter, now, you'd be a little more at risk. They'd be hungrier by then. But this is a season of easy pickings, so you don't look as tasty."

"I feel so reassured," I say. "But couldn't you defend me if a coyote showed up? Or a *wolf*? Couldn't you turn into a wolf yourself and fight it off?"

He's kneeling on the ground, tamping down the dirt, but now he looks up at me with a troubled expression. "That's not the way it works," he says. "I can't just *summon* the will to transform. And I can't choose what I want to be."

The tone of my voice is halfway between defensive and placating. "I just thought. Some natural instincts might assert themselves if you were in danger. You know, like fight or flight. If you need to fight, maybe your body doesn't just shoot you up with adrenaline, maybe it turns you into a creature that knows how to rumble."

He wipes his dirty hands on his jeans and stands up. His features are collecting into a scowl. "Always, with you, the most romantic interpretation," he says, his voice edged with anger or sarcasm or maybe both. "'How lovely it would be if my boyfriend would turn into a werewolf to save me from danger! I would swoon in his arms from gratitude.' But it doesn't *work* that way."

I am close to losing my temper. "Well, how would *I* know how it works? You never *tell* me anything. You don't want to *talk* about this part of your life. Everything I've ever learned about your—your alternate existence I've had to chisel out of you by asking questions you don't want to answer. Maybe I do romanticize it! But I want to understand it. I want to understand *you*. And all you want is to keep your secrets."

His lips are pressed firmly together, as if he is holding back angry words. He turns his head so he's staring at the tree line instead of me, as if he's afraid his hot gaze will burn through my skin. "When I'm with you, all I want is to be human," he says tightly. "I don't want to *think* about and *talk* about and analyze my animal nature. You think I'm being secretive, but I'm just trying to *be*." He swings his head around to look at me, and it's true; his glare is fiery enough to scorch. "Let it go."

For a moment I stare back at him, fifteen years' worth of protests clamoring on my tongue. *Let it go? I've done nothing* but *let it go! I've believed your impossible story without a shred of proof! I've designed every detail of my life so that it accommodates yours. I have loved you without conditions, trusted you without reservations. All I want is to know you better. All you want is to keep your distance.*

"Well, then," I say. "Let's go back to the car before the coyotes find us and dash all our hypotheses to the ground."

CHAPTER THREE

Both of us are in better moods Sunday as we drive out to Rolla, though what seems to keep us in charity with each other is saying as little as possible. So we don't talk much during the drive. We spend most of the time on Highway 44, but close to our destination we exit onto a two-lane county road where the median speed seems to be seventy miles an hour. Dante is focused on getting ahead of every slow-moving family car and farm vehicle we encounter, which can be challenging as the road winds and dips around blind hills and corners and once clatters over a narrow, ancient bridge scarcely wide enough to accommodate a sedan.

I don't watch. I turn my head and gaze out at the gently rolling Missouri landscape, its densely bunched covering of trees making a slow-motion transformation from emerald to garnet and topaz. It is as if someone has caught a freeze-frame image of the instant a hillside has caught fire. Flames have been halted in their leap from branch to branch; gold has crystallized halfway on its journey to orange. In a couple of months, every tree will be bare, stripped to a mute, stubborn brown. It will be hard to even remember the color green.

We pass farmland, some of it still high with crops waiting to be harvested, some mowed clean and tilled down to the soil. We pass grazing cattle and a few lazy horses. I am tempted to speak. *Were you ever a cow? Have you ever been a horse? How about a pig?* But I would rather keep the peace than find answers to my questions.

I think about what might lie ahead of us at Christina's house. Rolla is a small town with a population of somewhere around twenty thousand, probably best known for being home to the University of Missouri campus that specializes in engineering. Christina lives a good ten miles outside of the city limits, in the house that used to belong to their mother. She works as a secretary for the local school district, a job that seems to pay well, to be recession-proof, and to afford her enough flexibility that she can take a day off whenever she needs. I know she comes to St. Louis on a fairly regular basis, because she talks about events she's attended and restaurants she's gone to with college friends who live in the city. Not once since I've known her has she gotten in touch with me on those visits.

I wonder if I would think she was odd even if I didn't know her secret; I suspect I would. She's got Dante's same dramatic coloring, but she's more delicate. You think you could probably snap the bones in her arm just by applying a minimum amount of pressure. She's almost always smiling in a way that strikes me as artificial, which makes me wonder what she's really thinking, and her laugh is high and tinkling. She flutters like an indecisive butterfly. I think the people in the school district must find her exhausting to be around all week. Then again, maybe she is more relaxed and natural around them. Perhaps I only see her at her worst, around her brothers. Perhaps she tries too hard to charm them—or to charm Dante, at any rate.

She seems to have a closer relationship with William, despite the fact that he is human so rarely. From what I understand, her house is the place he returns whenever he wants to reenter the world of men; it's where he keeps his clothes and his few possessions. *She* is his storage locker, his emergency cell phone, his key. If William has made any other long-term connections over the years, I have never heard about them.

I remember the first time Dante told me about his siblings, granting details like much-begrudged diamonds. "William and Christina and Dante Romano," I had said, because I still liked to roll the Italian surname off my tongue. "Why do *you* have the weird first name?"

That had actually made him laugh. "My mother had a thing for the Rossettis."

I had laughed, too, though the name had meant nothing to me at the time. But I committed it to memory and tracked down a reference room staff member the next time I was at the library. This was in the days before easy Internet search engines, and finding arcane information often required determination and assistance.

"I need to know about the Rossettis," I'd said, not sure if that was a place, a family name, or some other category. "Specifically, any of them who might be related to Dante, Christina, and William."

As it happened, the reference room staff member was a specialist in twentieth-century literature, so she had to do a little research. But the first world biographical resource she pulled out listed "Dante Gabriel Rossetti" and described him as a painter and a poet. From there it was pretty easy to amass a history of the flamboyant, charismatic, and deeply flawed artist who was my lover's namesake, and learn stories about his brother and sister as well. I found myself drawn to the painter's vividly hewed, richly detailed canvases, at least from the early part of his career; I found the endless late-stage portraits of his mistress much less appealing. And none of his poetry ever spoke to me, though I struggled through as many volumes as I could.

Christina Rossetti was harder to like. She had led a bleak and restricted spinster's life after experiencing a couple of severe disappointments in love. Most of her poems were morbid and resigned meditations on death. She seemed to spend her whole life preparing herself for the grave.

Except . . .

One poem is full of anticipation and delight; one poem is nothing but metaphors of elation. I've read it over and over again, memorizing it without even intending to. Today her heart is a singing bird, she says in convoluted Victorian language. Today she wants to dress up in peacock feathers and fur. And why?

Because the birthday of my life
Is come, my love is come to me.

Somehow she had known, this woman who had renounced love for religion, who had died a virgin, who had lived long enough to see almost everyone she cared for pass away. Somehow she had gotten it right . . .

I still feel that way, every time Dante walks in my door. *The birthday of my life / Is come, my love is come to me.* It took a depressed British lady poet to put my emotions into words.

William Rossetti survived his brother and his sister, and led the most ordinary life of the three. Given what I know about my own Dante and his siblings, it seems to me this is the ultimate joke. Or it would be, if any of this was funny.

Christina lives in a well-maintained one-story white clapboard house heavily decorated with gingerbread accents. The wraparound porch makes me think of lemonade and iced tea and warm summer nights with children chasing fireflies on the lawn. She owns about five acres of land, much of it given over to old-growth trees, and this property serves as a fairly effective buffer between her house and the encroachments of urban development. That level of privacy is essential for a family of shape-shifters. My own bungalow is on a plot of land that backs up to a semi-wooded area; I hunted a long time for a house where my neighbors would have to put some effort into keeping track of my comings and goings. But Christina's house is even more isolated.

Dante pulls into the driveway and cuts the motor. I'm out of the car before I realize someone is on the porch. I didn't notice him a second before; he seems to have materialized from nowhere. It's William, of course. He's wearing a white sleeveless T-shirt and slouchy jeans, and he looks even thinner and stringier than Dante. His hair—a twilight brown instead of Dante's midnight black—is tied back in a ponytail, so I can't tell how long it is, but last time I saw him, it was past his shoulders. He's smoking a cigarette. He doesn't say anything as we come up the walk and climb the stairs.

"You know those things will kill you," I feel compelled to observe as we halt beside him on the porch.

His grin is ferocious. "Doubt I'll live long enough to find out."

He's not kidding. Although he's five years younger than Dante, today he looks five years older. Up close, I can see the heavy streaks of gray in his hair, the slight sagging of the muscles on his bare arms.

"So have you recovered?" Dante asks him.

"Seem to."

I glance at William; he is so thin and so pale that he could have been brought down by anything, from malaria to AIDS. "What was wrong with you?" I ask.

"Got hurt," he replies tersely.

"Badly enough to see a doctor and get a blood transfusion," Dante says.

That must mean William had been at death's door, because I have never seen Dante seek out medical attention for any wound or illness. "How dreadful!" I exclaim with easy sympathy. "But you're better now?"

"Good as ever," he says and gives me a grin. I can't help but think of the word *wolfish*.

Dante gives him a hard look. "And you haven't had any relapses?" He says it in a meaningful voice, as if he's asking something he doesn't want to put into words.

"Nope. I think I'll be just fine."

"Good," Dante says. "When did you get here?"

"Friday. Would have been gone already, but she asked me to stay."

Dante's frown returns. "What's this about?"

William sucks on his cigarette again. His face has lightened to genuine amusement. "You mean you don't know? Oh, you've gotta go inside."

Dante's eyes narrow, but he doesn't pose any more questions, just pulls open the screen door and steps into the house. I'm right behind him. I see William pitch away his cigarette before he follows.

We've stepped into a big, gracious room with windows on two walls letting in copious amounts of cheerful autumn sunshine. To the left an archway leads to a hallway that would take us to bedrooms and bathrooms; directly in front of us, the living room opens into a dining room that is equally sunny and inviting. Some of the furniture is well-worn and old, some is newer and brighter, but every piece works together to create a welcoming ambiance. Lace curtains drift over the windows; a brick-red rug warms the floor. An ebony baby grand piano takes up one corner of the room, even though none of the three of them can play. Their mother was a very good musician, Dante has said, but no one has touched the keys in twelve years or more.

Christina stands in the middle of the living room, holding a sleeping infant against her shoulder.

Dante comes to a hard stop and I have to skip to the side to avoid running into him. "Jesus Christ," he says.

"I have something to tell you," Christina says in a lilting voice.

"Yes, I suppose you do," Dante replies grimly.

William slinks in behind us and slips past Christina on his way to the kitchen or the basement or some other part of the house. If he's been here since Friday, he's undoubtedly heard the whole story, and it's clear he isn't particularly interested in refereeing an argument between his brother and sister. I stand motionless beside Dante, not sure if I should excuse myself so they can fight it out or stay to make sure they don't kill each other.

"I had a baby," she says. She's smiling in a sort of soft, unfocused way. She pats the child's back, clothed in some fleecy item covered with a pattern of ducks and dogs. I can't tell from the design or the color if the outfit is meant for a boy or a girl.

"It's yours, then? You gave birth to it? You didn't adopt it or—or *find* it somewhere and decide to keep it?"

"*Her.* I had *her*," Christina emphasizes. "Yes, she's mine. She'll be three weeks old tomorrow."

Dante is shaking his head. "How could you do this? How could you be so careless?"

"I wasn't careless. I *wanted* a baby," she says.

Dante glares at her. "I thought you realized—"

She interrupts. "I realized that *you* think it's a bad idea for any of us to have children, but I don't ever remember telling you I agreed."

Dante throws his hands in the air and starts pacing. I take the opportunity to edge toward the piano, out of the way. I can't stop staring at the lumpy little bundle pressed to Christina's chest. I'm dying to hold her, but it seems too soon to start cooing and fussing over the baby. Not while Dante is so angry.

"Only an idiot wouldn't agree!" He is ranting now. He's stalking and gesturing and tossing his head, but he never gets too close to Christina. I don't know if he's afraid he'll smack her or if he's afraid he'll take one look at that tiny, new face and fall in love. "You're a goddamn *shape-*

shifter, Christina! You turn into an *animal*! How can you take care of a baby? Who do you think you're going to leave her with when you're in some other form? Do you suppose the neighbors will understand when you want to drop her off for a day? 'Oh, I can feel myself turning into a bat or an owl—I need to have someone watch the baby for a while.'"

"Well, I'm on maternity leave until January, but I've already looked into babysitting services that provide overnight care," she says. Her voice is level, her stance dignified. She seems much calmer than the Christina I'm familiar with. Maybe the pregnancy has changed some internal blood chemistry or recalibrated her brain waves. I've read about that happening to women sometimes after they've had babies. They develop allergies or reverse decades-long psychological problems. Maybe having a child has turned Christina into a serene and focused person.

"Oh, and that'll come in handy once you've shifted and you can't pick up the phone to call them."

Christina shakes her head. "That's not how it works for me. You know that. I can feel the change coming on—I'll have plenty of warning. I'll be able to take her someplace safe before anything happens."

Dante churns to a stop and slams his fist into his open palm. "*God-damn* it," he says. "Even if you could take care of her—even if you managed to keep her safe from *you*, from her own *mother*—how could you do this? She'll be another one. She'll be just like us. We shouldn't *have* kids, Christina! People like us aren't meant to breed."

"I don't know why you think that," she replies in a reasonable voice. "Our parents had children. *Their* parents had children. We have aunts and uncles and cousins who are just like us, and I'm sure some of *them* have given birth by now. You're the only one who seems determined to stamp out our kind."

"Because our kind is an abomination!" he shouts.

For a moment, there is absolute silence in the room. I think all of us are shocked. I know I am; Dante has never voiced such self-loathing before, not to me, anyway. I know he has always been adamantly against the notion of having children, but I thought he simply did not want to make a child suffer through the strange, difficult half-life of the shape-shifter. I had not realized he saw himself as grotesque, misshapen, atrocious.

He glances between us, looking a little shamefaced. I think he is sorry to have said the words—not because he doesn't believe them, but because he wishes he had not revealed that dark secret. He tries to pull himself together. "I suppose it can't be undone," he says now in a quieter voice. "I suppose she's here now, and there's no more to say."

The baby gives a funny little hiccupping cry and scrunches up all her limbs. Christina bounces a little in place, and the girl subsides again, scrubbing her pink face against Christina's shirt. "You could ask me about her," she suggests.

I decide it's safe to speak up. "What's her name?"

Christina smiles at me. "I thought about Jane, but I decided on Elizabeth. Lizzie."

Dante snorts with what might almost be amusement. Even I get the reference. The poet Dante Rossetti had a long-suffering wife called Lizzie, and then a long-term mistress named Jane. Neither of them led particularly happy lives. Lizzie, in fact, died of a laudanum overdose not long after losing her own baby. I think, but do not say, that the name could hardly be less propitious.

"And the father?" Dante asks.

"Stevie was back in town for a few months at the New Year—you remember, I told you that."

"Oh, right, right. Well, you could have done worse, I suppose. Does he know about the baby?"

I can only vaguely recall who Stevie is. Some childhood friend, I think. For some reason I associate him with Juneau. Maybe he lives in Alaska now and only returns to Rolla now and then to visit aging relatives? At any rate, I know I've never met him.

"Not yet. Though I told him I wanted to get pregnant and he didn't seem bothered by the idea."

"That's because he doesn't know what a bunch of freaks we are in this family," Dante mutters.

"I don't think we're freaks," Christina says. "And Lizzie isn't, either."

I step closer to her. "Could I hold her?" I ask. "Would that be all right?"

Christina's smile is blinding. I wonder if she thought none of us would make even that small gesture of acceptance. "Of course you can!"

I take Lizzie in my arms, cradling her so that her head rests in the crook of my left elbow. She is awake, and her muddy blue-brown eyes study my face for an instant and then glance away. Her cheeks are a fat, healthy pink; her pursed lips glisten with tiny bubbles of saliva. The finest, faintest, silkiest streaks of black hair lie like cobwebs on her soft skull, and I see that Christina has managed to gather enough of them to Velcro in a yellow bow.

I am instantly and utterly smitten.

"Hey, Lizzie," I croon, unconsciously beginning a slight, rhythmic swaying motion. "Aren't you a beautiful little girl? I'm Maria, I'm so pleased to meet you. How do you like life here on Planet Earth so far?"

She responds with some inarticulate monosyllable, her little mouth briefly forming what looks like a smile, though I've been told babies this young don't really smile. Still speaking nonsense sentences, still bouncing her gently in my arms, I turn away from Christina and Dante and start a slow circuit through the house. I don't encounter William in the kitchen, the bedrooms, in the hallways; he must have slipped into the basement or out the kitchen door.

When I make it back to the living room, Dante and Christina are still talking, but their voices are quieter and Dante looks much less angry. He shows no inclination to hold the baby, though, so I sit on the worn chocolate-colored sofa and lay Lizzie in my lap. Her head is near my knees and her little legs kick in the general direction of my stomach. Her arms work with a continuous flailing, as if she is a windup toy gaining all of her energy from this particular motion. I take hold of one of her tiny fists and gently pry it open, setting my index finger against her palm. Instantly, her fingers close over mine with a grip that is unexpectedly strong. It is as if they cannot relax from their natural inward curl unless they are forced flat by an external pressure.

The things I love most about babies are the minute fingernails on their littlest fingers. How can there be anything so small, so dainty, so perfect? For some reason, it is the detail that convinces me they are really human, truly miniature versions of the people they will grow up to be.

I know I should be asking all sorts of traditional questions. *Is she gaining weight fast enough? Will she take a bottle? How is she at sleeping through the night?* I should inquire into Christina's own health. *Did you have any complications with the pregnancy or the birth? Are you eating right, getting enough sleep, suffering any postpartum depression?* But they seem like mundane and trivial inquiries for such a magical child, for this gift straight from the capricious universe.

I look up and find Christina smiling at me—pleased, perhaps, at the goofy, besotted look on my face. I burst out, "Do you just love her more than anything else in the world?"

"I really do," Christina says. "I didn't know it was possible to love anything this much."

We stay for an odd and uncomfortable lunch. The baby is sleeping in the other room, so half of Christina's attention is focused on the hallway through which any sounds of distress will issue. She's made some kind of pasta dish and a simple salad. Dante is too annoyed to eat much, and William uses silverware as if it's the first time he's ever attempted the feat. Christina has opened a bottle of champagne, but none of us drink very much of it. We are hardly a festive group.

"You know, if you need to, you can have me come out sometime and watch the baby for a weekend," I say as the meal draws to a close. "Or you could leave her with me for an afternoon if you come into the city."

Dante shoots me a look of supreme vexation, while Christina's face lights with a smile. "That would be awfully kind of you," she says. "But are you sure?"

"Yes, of course I'm sure. You have my phone number, don't you? And my e-mail address?"

"I must have them somewhere, but why don't you write them down for me? And I'll give you mine—I changed my e-mail address last year, you might not have it—"

"Maria's never spent much time with babies," Dante says, his voice overloud. "You might need to give her a refresher course before you leave Lizzie with her for an entire weekend."

"I used to babysit all the time when I was in high school," I reply frostily. "And I kept my cousin Beth's baby for an entire week when she was in the hospital with pneumonia."

I don't need to defend myself; Christina isn't alarmed. "I'd never spent any time around babies, either, before Lizzie came along," she says. "Everybody told me how hard it would be, but it's been easy. She's such a joy."

William looks up from the ruins of his pasta, laying his fork aside as if he's given up trying to feed himself this way. "Has she changed yet?" he asks.

"No," Christina says, her voice ever so slightly defensive.

William gives me that wolfish smile again. "That'll be a fun time for you," he says. "Put a baby to bed in the bassinet, walk in a half hour later to find a kitten. Or worse."

"I guess I'll deal with that when it happens," I say.

"*If* it happens," Christina interjects. "I didn't change shapes until I was three. Mother thought I might never do it."

"Would to God that Mother had been right," Dante growls.

William leans back in his chair and nods over at his brother. "It's getting longer for you all the time, isn't it?" he says. "Your stays in animal shape."

Dante nods curtly, not looking at me. "Twenty or twenty-two days in a row sometimes," he says.

"You ever think it will be permanent?"

"William!" Christina exclaims.

Dante shrugs. He still won't look at me. "Hope not. Can't do anything about it, so I don't lose much sleep thinking about it."

William jerks his chin at me. "You go to Maria's house when you come back?"

"Usually."

Usually? I think. *Where else do you go? Is there some precious moment of your human time that you spend with someone else?* But I think I know why he gave that answer. He thinks it makes him look dependent and weak if he admits that he comes straight to my door. He thinks it makes him look as if he loves me more than he wants his siblings to know.

"What if she's not there?" Now William's restless eyes flick to Christina then back to Dante. "That's what happened to me a few weeks ago. Christina was in the hospital having Lizzie. I had to break into the house. I was afraid one of the neighbors would see me, so I hid out by the old cemetery until midnight. Naked as a baby. If somebody would've seen me, they'd've thought the graveyard was haunted for sure."

"Or they would have shot you," Dante says flatly.

"Well, it didn't happen," Christina speaks up. "He knows I keep a spare key under the stone rabbit in the garden. He just forgot it was there." I can supply the observation she's left out: *William sometimes goes so long without becoming a man that all sorts of human details slip away from him.* I wonder how long William generally goes between bouts of shape-shifting. I wonder how Christina managed to communicate with him and convince him to return here today so that both of her brothers could be present at the same time.

"You should carry a key with you everywhere you go," Dante says, tugging the leather cord out over the neck of his black T-shirt. "That's what I do."

"That's to Maria's house?" William asks.

"It's to a storage locker where I keep clothes and papers and things," Dante says.

"I've *offered* him a key," I feel compelled to say. It doesn't bother *me* if his siblings know how much I love him. "Don't think I haven't."

William has leaned forward a little to examine the sturdy strip of leather looped through the dangling brass and triple knotted at the back. "It's a little long," he says. "Does it ever catch on anything?"

I'm suddenly beset with a whole new class of worries as I imagine Dante strangling to death because the cord has tangled on a fallen branch and he can't get free. He knows what images are in my head because his voice is hard and curt. "I'm taking bigger shapes," he says briefly. "I need the extra room. If you're always turning into something that's the same size, you could make it shorter."

William sits back, satisfied. "I think I'll try it."

"I've got two extra keys," Christina says. "I'll give one to each of you."

William is nodding, but Dante is shaking his head. "I don't need to confuse the issue," he says. "I'll stick with this one."

And your buried cell phone, I think, but do not say aloud.

"So who wants cake?" Christina says.

I'm the only one who has dessert, and then I'm the only one who helps Christina clear the table when we're done eating. William has disappeared again, and this time I think he might have shifted shapes and slipped back into the wild; the house suddenly feels empty of his presence. I would like to hold Lizzie again before we leave, but she's still sleeping when we're done in the kitchen and it's clear Dante is growing restless.

"We better go," I say to Christina, and she nods and escorts us out the door. On the front porch, I pause and hug her, something I cannot remember ever doing before.

"I'm serious," I say. "Call me if you need help."

"I will," she says. "Thanks for coming."

For the first twenty minutes of the drive home, Dante rants about Christina's stupidity and selfishness and sheer wanton stubbornness. "She *knows*, we've *talked* about it, she realizes *none* of us should ever have children," he says in that fast, angry voice.

I mostly don't listen; I've heard this diatribe before. Dante and I had been lovers for a couple of years when I made some offhand comment about having a baby one day. He was very clear on that point: No children. Ever. Not if I wanted him as the father. I had hastily agreed (I was only twenty-three at the time, and not seriously interested in becoming a mother any time soon), but during the last ten years, I've grown more and more wistful at the notion of remaining childless my entire life.

I haven't said so to Dante, but on this subject, he's eerily sensitive, and he's picked up on my unspoken longing for a baby of my own. Five years ago, when he was still human for more than half the month, he had a vasectomy, not telling me about it until afterward. He has no health insurance, of course, so he'd found a city clinic that performs operations for cash or for free, depending on the patient. Then he lay around the house for the next day making self-pitying jokes about being neutered and complaining that the pain was worse than he'd anticipated.

Unexpectedly, I'd been sharply, bitterly disappointed when he told me what he had done. I would never have the chance to change his mind; I would never be able to hold in my arms a small, fragile, enchanted creature who was half me and half the man I loved. It was impossible to explain to him my sense of loss, so I had commiserated and teased him and made bright jokes in reply.

"You could have waited till you were in dog shape and let me take you to the vet," I'd said. "I imagine that would have been even worse, don't you?"

"Cut my balls right *off*," he'd replied. "I don't think *you'd* have liked it, either."

What makes you think I like this? "Well, you'll be feeling better in a day or two. Let me get you more ice."

I am so lost in memories that at first I don't realize Dante has fallen silent. When I do, I assume that he's simply brooding over Christina's sins, maybe remembering all the times in her childhood she showed a similarly disastrous lack of judgment. I'm astonished when he abruptly says, "I'm sorry."

Dante rarely apologizes, and usually only after I've been crying for three hours. "For what?" I ask cautiously.

"I know you want children. I know it–it hurts you to think you'll never have any."

I've relaxed back against the seat and now I just turn my head a little to look at him, not straightening up from my loose pose. "I'll never have any with *you*," I say in a mild voice.

He digests that for a moment. "You'd really get pregnant by another man? What happened to all those 'Oh, Dante, I love you more than life itself' things you're always saying?"

"I could go to a sperm bank. I could adopt." I shrug. "I have options."

He takes his eyes off the road long enough to glance at me. "Do you really think so?" he asks quietly. "Do you really think you can bring up children—no matter how you acquire them—while I'm in your life?"

"I don't know why not," I say. He has no idea how much thought I've given to this subject over the past few years. "It's not like you ever take animal shapes while you're with me. So you're an unusual guy. You show up for a few days every month or so, and Mommy's really happy to see you, and we do fun stuff like go to the park every day. Then you leave, and Mommy cries for a day, but pretty soon life goes back to its ordinary routine. I promise you, there are kids in this world who see their parents entertain much stranger lovers. Well, entertain them on much stranger schedules. I don't know that any of the lovers are actually odder than *you*."

I am still speaking lightly. I don't want to spook him; I don't want him to freak out over the notion that I might bring another life into our small, private circle. But I *don't* think it's impossible. I *don't* see why a child couldn't adapt to Dante's unconventional visits, just as I have. Kids adapt to lots weirder things than men appearing and disappearing frequently in their mothers' lives.

He glances at me again; his face is furrowed and his voice, when he speaks, is uncertain. "I don't think it would be as simple as you make it sound. I don't think—Maria, I don't think it would be a good idea."

"I thought your objection was to passing on your corrupted genes," I say, my tone a little flippant. "So I bypass *your* deficiencies and take on the unknown ones of a total stranger."

"Well, but—I mean—it's got to be awfully hard to be a single parent. I obviously wouldn't be able to help you out much—"

"Who asked you to?"

Now he's a little ruffled. "Well, you didn't, but I assume—I mean, if you still want *me* in your life once you've got this baby, this child—"

I sit up and turn toward him as much as the seat belt will allow. He keeps his eyes fixed on the road ahead, his hands in a death grip on the steering wheel. I see that this is a wholly new idea to him and he doesn't like it. Is it that he resents the idea of sharing my affection with someone else or that he literally can't imagine any part of my life that isn't built around him?

"Dante, I love you," I say, every word heavy with emphasis. "I will love you till I die. I have made ninety percent of the choices of my life to accommodate you, and I will continue to make those choices. But you have made it very clear that you have a life that does not include me and that I will never be invited to share—"

"Dammit, how can you share being an *animal*?"

"And I have started to look at how I can fill the parts of my life that are empty because you're not in them. You're right, I've been thinking how much I want a baby. You're right, being a single mother seems really hard. I haven't made any plans yet. I may never go forward with any of these ideas. But if I do—"

I pause. I had not expected to tear up at this point. Well, I had not expected to be having this conversation with Dante today, though I had rehearsed it many times in my head. But I had not expected to see a baby at Christina's house, and to have all these emotions stirred up, all these questions, all these desires.

"If I do," I repeat softly, reaching out to stroke his face, "I hope you will find a way to stay in my life. I hope you will be—not a father to my baby, but an eccentric friend, maybe. A mysterious but fascinating visitor. An intermittent delight." I stretch the seat belt to the limit so I can lean over and kiss his cheek. "Which is how *I* see you. Every time. Without fail."

He does not answer, but he does not pull away from my hand, which now rests on his shoulder. His face shows an expression that is somewhere between unhappy and resigned, but that's better than I had expected. In my mind, when we've had this conversation, he's sometimes stormed off in a rage and sometimes argued me into tears. Maybe it's the fact that we're in a car and there isn't much room for theatrics that has kept him so calm.

"I'll have to think it over," he says at last.

"You have plenty of time," is my amiable reply. "I'm not planning on doing anything anytime soon."

He nods and, surprising me, twists his head suddenly to kiss the back of my hand. I am unutterably pleased. I think Christina's astonishing secret has proved to be a much bigger gift than I could have hoped for, if it has made it so easy to have this conversation with Dante. It makes me adore little Lizzie all the more—and I had already fallen in love with her the minute I took her in my arms.

I anticipated that the long drive and the emotional upsets of the day would leave Dante moody and withdrawn, but instead, he is extraordinarily affectionate for the rest of the evening. After dinner, we lie entwined on the couch as we start to watch *How to Steal a Million* on cable, but he cannot keep his attention on the screen. His hand slips under my shirt; he plays with my breast when he should be smiling at Audrey Hepburn's madcap plan. I am hardly one to complain. I turn in his arms to kiss him full on the mouth, pressing myself against him with all my strength.

We move to the bedroom and make love with all the desperation of a young wartime couple who realize their honeymoon might be the only night they ever spend together. I know this means Dante feels the animal instincts starting to overtake him; I also know this means he will not be beside me tomorrow night. I cling to him as if he is my only source of light and heat and air; I kiss him as if only the pressure of my mouth against his can ward off my impending death.

He falls asleep a little after midnight, but I don't. I sit up and watch his face, studying its shape, trying to catalog its dreaming emotions. I want to memorize it, in case I never see it again. In case he never comes back. In case this ends up being all I ever have of Dante.

CHAPTER FOUR

Mondays are always bad, but this one is worse than most. I managed to get only about three hours of sleep the night before, and I leave the house knowing Dante probably will not be there when I return. I yawn through the entire morning, despite drinking three cups of coffee before 11 a.m., and I keep my eyes averted from the mirror every time I go into the bathroom. I know I look like hell.

"Seriously, did someone tie you to the back of a car and drag you down a dirt road yesterday?" Ellen asks when she drops by my desk a little before noon.

I manage a wan smile. "I think I got food poisoning over the weekend. I was throwing up most of Sunday afternoon. Didn't feel like the flu, so I don't think I'm contagious, but–I know. I look like shit."

"Marquez and I are going to lunch. You hungry?"

I shake my head. "Not even. I think I'll heat up a can of soup and be miserable."

"Well, drink some 7UP. You need those electrons."

"Electrolytes."

She smiles faintly. "I knew that. I was just checking to see if your food poisoning had damaged your brain."

"I think I'll be okay after I get a good night's sleep."

I'm sitting in the lunchroom spooning up a bowl of soup and paging listlessly through a three-year-old *People* magazine when Kathleen steps through the door, carrying a purple insulated lunch bag. "Oh!" she says when she sees me, so I assume she usually has the place to herself at this hour. There are four tables and only mine is occupied, so I figure it will be easy enough for her to ignore me.

But once she buys a can of soda and tears two sheets from the paper-towel dispenser, she approaches my table in a cautious, sideways manner. "Do you want to sit here by yourself or could you use some company?" she asks in a soft voice.

I muster the energy to smile and turn the magazine facedown. "I'd love some company," I say. "Talking might help me stay awake."

She smiles and sits across from me, arranging her food before her. Her meal is so healthy it almost irritates me—baked chicken breast, fresh cut-up vegetables, and an apple. Kathleen can't be more than an inch or two over five feet and probably weighs less than a hundred pounds, so I can't imagine she's dieting. She's petite because this is the way she *likes* to eat.

While she organizes her food, I have the opportunity to study her. She might be my age, mid-thirties, though her small size gives her a childlike air that subtracts at least five years. Today I don't see any new bruises marring her face—or her arms or any other exposed stretch of flesh—and she's wearing only light makeup over her fair skin. Her hair is a plain brown that she's inexpertly washed with highlights; her clothes are pink and girly. I think this is someone who, pure and simple, loves pretty things and has far too few of them in her life.

She uses a knife and fork to cut off a dainty piece of chicken and, right before popping it in her mouth, asks, "Why are you so sleepy?"

I repeat my story about food poisoning and then embellish it. "I checked with my cousin—she's the one I had brunch with—and *she* was sick yesterday afternoon, too, though not as bad as I was."

Kathleen quickly swallows. "I had food poisoning once when I was out of town at a hotel," she says. "I thought I would *die*. I had the front desk call a doctor for me, and he sent over some pills."

"Wow, it didn't even occur to me that there was something I could take to make me feel better."

She laughs. "I can't remember if the pills did any good." She takes another small bite and then asks, "Did you get to do *anything* fun over the weekend?"

"Yeah, I felt great on Saturday and the weather was beautiful. A friend and I went hiking in Babler State Park."

"Oh, I love Babler!" she exclaims. "Ritchie goes there to train, but I just walk."

"Train? What for?"

"He wants to run the Chicago Marathon next year, so he goes running with some of his buddies."

I rest my chin on my hand; my head feels so heavy I'm afraid it'll pull me over onto the table if I don't give it some support. "No disrespect to Ritchie, but I can't imagine anyone wanting to run twenty-six miles. For fun."

She laughs. "No, I think it sounds dreadful. But Ritchie likes to do hard things, you know? He likes to prove to himself that he's really tough."

I fight to stifle a yawn. "I like to do easy things," I say. "But it's probably more admirable to do the hard ones."

"His brother's a Navy SEAL," Kathleen says.

I nod. "And I guess he feels a little competitive."

"Yeah. He wanted to join the Army when he was eighteen, but they wouldn't take him because of some problem with his feet. It was such a disappointment to him."

I find myself wondering if Ritchie was lying to Kathleen about the reason he'd been rejected from the military. Maybe the recruiters had analyzed his psychological profile and determined he was the type of man who would beat up his wife, and they'd decided to pass. "What's he do now? I can't remember."

"Security work," she says.

Great. He probably has a gun and some martial-arts training. Just the sort of advantages you'd want to give to a violent sociopath with self-esteem issues. "How long have you guys been married?"

"Seven years, but we dated for two years before we got married." She smiles again, looking happy. "I met him at a baseball game. I was there with three of my girlfriends and none of them knew anything about sports. *They* didn't care—they just wanted to drink beer and meet guys. But I was trying to figure out the game. Ritchie was in the seat next to me, and when he saw that I was really interested, he started explaining everything to me. You know, what's a sacrifice fly, what's a ground-rule double, when do you try to bunt. He was really sweet." Now she laughs. "I was the only one of my friends who wasn't trying to pick somebody up that night, and I was the only one who actually found a date."

I'm not really sure what to say in response to that. This is the longest conversation I've ever had with Kathleen, and already I feel it's been extended beyond its natural life. "Well, good for you" is all I come up with, but she looks pleased.

"What about you?" she asks. "I've never heard if *you* are dating anyone."

She could hardly have picked a topic I would be less interested in discussing, though on a normal day I'd have done a better job of dissembling. I have been lying about Dante for fifteen years; it's become second nature to me now. I realized a long time ago, with a certain amazement, that no matter how important something is in your life, no matter how huge it is, how much space it takes up in your heart and in your thoughts, unless you mention it to other people, they have no idea it exists. They cannot simply look at you and realize, *Oh, Maria is in love with a shape-shifter.* They cannot even realize, *Oh, Maria's in love with a strange, unpredictable, unreliable fellow, and he's mysteriously disappeared again, and her heart is broken.* Unless you tell them, they simply don't notice when something is wrong.

That's not entirely true, of course. Ellen has sharp eyes and she can usually guess when I'm moping over Dante, though she doesn't seem to have put together the cause of my moodiness; she just knows I have down days on a recurring basis. My family members, who see me more erratically, have proved easier to fool. I have perfected the art of bright and airy conversation when I'm with them for holidays and birthdays and random outings. I have learned how to conceal my true emotions.

As I say, it has been astonishingly easy. This has led me to wonder what secrets everyone else must be nursing behind cheerful or weary or unemotional masks. If I can hide the fact that half of my waking thoughts are consumed by my passion for a mythological creature, if I never mention his name at all to people who think they know me very well, how big could their own lies be? Are they serial killers, foreign spies, members of the Witness Protection Program? Have they been transgendered, bitten by vampires, kidnapped by aliens? Do they molest their daughters, have affairs with their neighbors' sons, give blow jobs to strangers while their spouses record on video?

No possibility seems too outlandish. And I would not blame any of them for refusing to spill their secrets.

I have hesitated too long in answering Kathleen's question. It's possible my eyes have watered; at any rate, they're burning. Kathleen's delicate face puckers into a worried frown. "Maria?" she says uncertainly. "I'm sorry. Did I upset you?"

"Oh—" I say, and I can hear the thickness in my voice. *Fucking tears.* I'm scrambling to think of a story that will explain my sudden despair while not giving anything away. "There used to be this guy, you know? And every once in a while he—he e-mails me. Or sends a birthday card. And it's hard. Maybe I'm still in love with him, but he's moved on. And for a while I think I'm over him, but then, there it is, another e-mail in my in-box." I rub a finger over my eyelids. "I don't really like to talk about it."

So briefly it's as if it doesn't happen, Kathleen touches the back of my wrist and then drops her hand in her lap. "I'm sorry," she says. "That must be really hard."

"Yeah, well, sometimes life sucks," I reply. I grab my Coke and take a few swallows just to clear my throat. "God, please don't tell anybody I acted like this. I feel like such a loser."

"You're not a loser," she says. "Love is impossible. I mean, even when you have it, it hurts you. So you know—" She shrugs. "You just get through the day."

I nod. "Yeah, that's what I try to do."

She hesitates and then says in a rush, "But if you ever need someone to talk to—you know—I mean, you can tell me anything. I wouldn't repeat it."

Not only is the offer sincere, I think, but it's a good one. Kathleen probably *would* be excellent at keeping secrets, and my guess is that her sympathy would be boundless. I could pick worse confidantes—though I don't want even this one.

"Thanks, Kathleen. I can't tell you how much I genuinely appreciate it. But I really feel better if I *don't* talk about it."

"I know," she says. "That's the way I feel, too."

When the day finally limps to a close, I head out to the parking lot without lingering in the hall to say good-bye to Ellen and Marquez, as I usually do. In traffic, I am impatient and reckless, passing cars when I don't have quite enough room, keeping the speedometer at a good ten miles above the speed limit. I am desperate to get home, almost able to convince myself that Dante will still be there waiting for me, on the verge of leaving, perhaps, but unwilling to melt into the shadows without giving me one last kiss. At the imminent risk of death, I run a red light to make the final left turn into my neighborhood, and my tires protest as I turn too fast into my driveway.

I run up the walk, fumbling for my house key, and waste a good sixty seconds at the door because I drop the key ring *twice* as I try to unlock the door. "Dante?" I call before I'm even across the threshold. "Dante? Are you home?"

Nothing answers me but silence.

He might be sleeping; he might have left to run an errand, to buy another pair of shoes, perhaps, or a snack food for which he had an irresistible craving. But he's not lying in bed; he's not in the bathroom. I can hardly bring myself to take the short walk from the bedroom back to the kitchen.

As always, he has left a note lying on the counter. Apparently, all he could find was an envelope rescued from the recycling bin. *Had to go* are the only words he has written in his thick, nearly indecipherable scrawl. He hasn't even signed the note.

It's as if someone has sliced me in two with a scythe so keen I didn't even feel the blade bisect my body. Yet I am staggering with the knowledge of a pain that will soon be fatal. I open my mouth, as if to wail, but no sound comes out and no air makes its way in. My lungs have shut down, and my heart, and now all my muscles fail me at once. I drop to the floor, still silent, completely unseeing, unable to weep or even breathe. I can feel the cool linoleum against my cheek. The substrata of the floor makes a hard, unforgiving platform against my shoulder and hip. My mouth is still open, still producing no noise. My right hand is stretched out before me as if I am reaching for . . . something. A phone, perhaps. As if I could call for help. A shot of epinephrine to restart my heart. An oxygen tank. Something that will keep me alive.

None of those will help. Dante is gone.

I lie on the floor, unmoving, until all the light is gone from the world.

Tuesday I claim that I'm still feeling the ill effects of food poisoning, but by Wednesday I'm more or less recovered. I always follow this cycle when Dante leaves: a day of mourning, a few days of disorientation, and then I return to my normal routine. As his visits grow shorter, that normal routine has expanded. I have learned how to fill my days.

Over the weekend, I drive up to Springfield, Illinois, to celebrate my cousin Beth's birthday. My mother, my aunt and uncle, and Beth's sister, Sydney, all live in Springfield, which is where I was born and where my mother returned three years ago after my father died. Despite the fact that my father and my uncle were present for every holiday, every birthday, every summer camping trip that my mother and her sister planned, I grew up in a family that was utterly dominated by women. Two of my great-aunts are still living, still characterized by boundless energy and strong opinions. And the only member of the next generation—so far—is also a girl, Beth's three-year-old daughter, Clara. Already she shows every tendency to be as strong-willed and outspoken as the rest of the women in the family.

All of us share a certain olive-toned coloring inherited from my great-grandparents, who emigrated from Mexico, though a certain amount of intermarrying with light-skinned European descendants during the past two generations has definitely modified the gene pool.

We all gather in Aunt Andrea's house on Sunday afternoon, stuffing ourselves on homemade quesadillas and tamales before lighting candles and singing "Happy Birthday."

"I can't believe I'm thirty-five," Beth laments. "In my head I'm still eighteen and I don't have to wear a bra to look good in a tight T-shirt."

Even the older women burst into laughter at this remark, but Aunt Andrea puts her hands over Clara's ears.

"Don't listen to your mommy," she says. "She shouldn't say such things in front of little girls."

"Hell, Clara already spends more time than I do thinking about clothes," Beth responds. "You better believe she'll care what she looks like when she turns my age."

Both of my cousins are tall women with athletic builds and waves of dark curls. Beth, the oldest, wears her hair short enough so that it makes a wild frothing mass around her face. Sydney, who is two years younger, keeps hers long, but ties it back with scarves and scrunchies so that her face is uncluttered and severe. Sydney is the more beautiful and sophisticated of the two, but Beth is my favorite. Always has been. We were born eight months apart and were inseparable as children. As adults, we remain close. Her house is about twenty minutes from mine, so we get together fairly often and rarely go more than a week without talking.

Though naturally there are things we don't talk about.

"I'm getting a boob job when mine start to sag," Sydney announces. "And then a face-lift. Or maybe a face-lift first. Whichever body part needs the most work by then."

"It's the sags and wrinkles that show who you really are," says my great-aunt Vannie. "Don't be trying to smooth those away."

"Well, I won't if I look as good as *you* do when I'm eighty," Sydney says. The easy flattery makes everyone smile.

"Who wants more cake?" Aunt Andrea asks.

"Me!" Clara exclaims.

"Me," adds Beth. "Then I can get a tummy tuck along with my boob job and face-lift."

As we redistribute ourselves for the second round of dessert, my mom settles beside me on the couch. I'm always struck by her serenity. She can be high-spirited in certain moods—a trait that is enhanced when she's around her sister, Andrea—but her default mode is relaxed. When I was a teenager, I found her calm so maddening that it could incite me to hysteria; but as an adult, I find her presence soothing even on my most frazzled day. I wish I could live my life with equal grace, instead of being rocked by transient emotions and hopeless desires. On the other hand, I have often wondered if behind my mother's smooth skin and dark eyes some hidden fire burned. She might be the person who had unwittingly taught me the art of living with secrets.

"How's work?" my mom asks as she balances her cake plate on her knees and sips water from a paper cup.

I shrug. "Fine. Boring some days, actually kinda interesting other days." I take a bite of cake. "Still better than working in a coal mine."

That was what she always said to my father whenever he complained about his job as a delivery driver or to me when I commiserated about her own work as a waitress. I'm not sure she ever knew anyone who *did* work in a coal mine, but the message was clear: *Life could be worse. Don't whine.*

"Well, you look good," she says. "Very pretty."

I bat my eyelashes. "New makeup. I bought a whole pile of new stuff at the Clinique counter a couple weeks ago."

She transfers the water cup to her other hand so she can reach up and rub a thumb across my cheek. "You've got good bones," she says. "You're beautiful even without makeup."

"Oh, way to give yourself a compliment," I scoff.

You have to look for a moment to see how much we resemble each other, because in superficial ways we don't: Her hair is now a coarse gray, while mine is still deep brown and my eyes are dark blue. And, of course, our styles differ, since I tend to favor bright colors and she is most often in black. But our cheeks, jawbones, and pronounced noses—those indisputably prove that we are linked by blood.

"It's true, Maria. All you girls would look perfectly fine without makeup," Aunt Andrea calls from across the room.

"I wouldn't," Sydney says. "I'd look like a hag."

"I wouldn't know," Beth says. "I've never tried to leave the house without lipstick and mascara. And usually blush. And some eye shadow. And fingernail polish."

"And perfume," Clara adds. "*I* want perfume."

After about an hour of the food and the banter and the laughter, Beth and I find a few minutes to slip outside and talk in private on her mother's screened-in back porch. The weather has turned sharply colder for this last weekend in September, and our breath hangs in the air for a second or two as we speak.

"So how are things going with Charles?" I ask. Charles is the man she has dated off and on for the past five years. He's not Clara's father; it was during one of their breakups that Beth met Enrique and had a brief fling. So brief that she had already broken up with him, and decided she never wanted to see him again, before she discovered she was pregnant with Clara. She told him he had a daughter, but made it clear she wasn't interested in his interference or support, and he's been only too happy to keep his distance.

Charles, meanwhile, has two kids of his own, and he shares custody of them with his ex-wife. The divorce was amicable enough that he occasionally still sleeps with his ex-wife, even though she's remarried.

Beth rolls her eyes and leans against one of the flat beams that stand sentry along the perimeter of the porch, holding up the roof. "We had a fight last night."

"Well, that's too bad. On your *birthday*."

"I think that's why we fought," she says humorously. "He thinks if I'm mad at him around my birthday and Christmas, it means he doesn't have to buy me a present. You watch, we'll make up in a week and then break up again right around December fifteenth."

"That's pretty sucky."

"That's Charles."

Which about sums it up. She loves him, despite his childishness, his emotional unavailability, his complicated relationships. Who am I to counsel her to seek out a lover who will treat her better, behave more like an adult, and buy in to her hopes and dreams?

"What about you?" she asks.

I shake my head. "Nothing new on the romantic front." From time to time, just to stave off more questions, I manufacture blind dates, occasional short-term boyfriends, cute guys at the office I have a crush on, just so my family doesn't start worrying that I am completely incapable of normal social interaction. Once I used Marquez as my template, just so I could make the details feel particularly real. I must have been successful because Beth still asks about him once in a while with an intense and knowing tone, as if she suspects he is the real love of my life.

She shakes her head and crosses her arms over her chest, hugging herself against the chill. "Well, aren't we pathetic," she says. "Let's go do something fun! I've been thinking about driving up to Chicago someday. You wanna go with me? Mom or Sydney will keep Clara. We can get a hotel room on Michigan Avenue and spend three days shopping. And drinking margaritas."

"Oh, that sounds great!" I exclaim. "When did you want to go?"

"I don't know, sometime in October? Before it gets too cold. Though, you know. Chicago. There could be snow on the ground before Halloween."

I calculate rapidly. Dante left my house seven days ago. That means he's not likely to be back for two weeks or more. I simply don't want to be gone if there's any chance he will be around. It's really only safe to make future plans when he's actually in my house and I know he'll be gone soon.

"Can we be kind of flexible about it?" I say. "There's this project coming up at work in a couple of weeks—this big client we've been trying to land—and I know we're all going to have to work through the weekend to get a proposal ready. I just won't know which weekend that will be until the project comes through. Can I let you know when I have a better handle on it?"

"Sure. All I know is that I can't be gone *next* weekend, but after that I'm clear for a while."

"I'll call you."

I drive home in a nasty rain, my car loaded with Tupperware containers of food and my heart lightened by conversation with loved ones. I've promised my mom I'll send her a book I enjoyed, given Sydney the name of a website that sells dress pants for tall women, and signed up to sponsor Beth's walk for the food pantry. I've remembered that most of life is about small, essential connections, so unobtrusive, so elastic, that you scarcely realize they're actually holding you together. The big ones—the great, grand emotional bonds—those are the ones that break, the ones that fail you, the ones that give way and send you careening toward the foot of the bleak and jagged canyon. It's the tough, gnarled, unadorned ties that really do bind, that never let you fall all the way down into darkness.

CHAPTER FIVE

I'm getting ready for work the next morning when a news item on the radio causes me to freeze before the mirror. All I'm wearing is underwear and a robe; I've just started to sweep mascara on my right eye when the announcer's voice stops my heart.

"Police are investigating the murder of a woman whose body was found early this morning in the northwest corner of the Mark Twain National Forest, not far from Rolla. She appears to be in her mid to late twenties and she may have been carrying an infant. Police have found a diaper bag at the scene, but no evidence of a baby."

The professional voice pauses to make way for another man to speak, this one in the hesitant and nasal tones of someone not trained for radio. "It's too early to say what might have happened, but there is some speculation that the woman was killed so that someone could steal her child. We'll know more once we identify the body." There is the muffled sound of a reporter asking an indistinguishable question, and the sheriff—or whoever he is—answers. "We haven't determined cause of death yet. No, not a gunshot wound. No, not blunt force trauma. I'm afraid I can't be more specific than that."

I stop listening. I put down the mascara brush, my left eye still unenhanced, and go straight for my purse to dig out Christina's number. When she sleepily answers on the third ring, I almost collapse to the floor. My hands suddenly begin to shake.

"Oh, thank God," I whisper into the receiver.

"Hello? Who is this?" she says, sounding more alert and more annoyed.

"It's Maria Devane. I'm sorry, did I wake you up?" It's only seven in the morning, and she's still on maternity leave; she might not have planned to get up for hours, especially if Lizzie kept her awake all night crying. But I don't care if she's tired, I don't care if I've ruined her morning, I'm just overwhelmingly relieved to realize that she's alive.

"Dante's Maria? What's wrong?"

"There was a story on the news just now. A woman murdered near Rolla and her baby missing. I just thought—I mean, there must be thousands of women in Rolla who have babies, but I—just for a moment I—and it's not like either of your brothers is likely to notice right away if you go missing—"

"You were worried about me? Oh, Maria, that's so sweet. But I'm fine. Lizzie's fine. She's sleeping here in my room in the bassinet."

"I'm so glad. I heard the story and I—Well, I wouldn't have been able to relax all day until I knew you were all right. I'm really sorry if I woke you up."

"What time is it?" Over the phone line I hear the rustle of bedclothes and then her little *eek* of dismay. "Crap, it's after seven! I have a doctor's appointment at eight thirty! I must have slept through the alarm."

I attempt to laugh but the sound is more like a whuffle. "Good thing I called, then."

The timbre of her voice changes. I can tell she's out of bed, moving around the room, probably putting slippers on or sorting through an underwear drawer. "I was thinking about calling you anyway. I'm coming to St. Louis on Friday, and I was wondering if you'd be able to watch Lizzie."

"This Friday? Day or night? I don't have much vacation time left, but I'd love to keep her in the evening for you. I'll even keep her overnight if you like."

"Oh, that would be wonderful, but are you sure? Your very first time with her?"

I hope she can hear the smile in my voice. "Don't listen to what Dante says about me. I'm perfectly comfortable with babies." I pause and then add, "Though it might be a little different if she changes shapes on me. You'd have to tell me how to handle *that*."

Christina's laugh is merry. "Well, she hasn't done it so far for me, so I don't think you have to worry about it," she says. "I'll call you later with more details, okay? Right now I have to get ready."

"Yes, yes, go! I'll talk to you later," I say. "Can't wait to see you on Friday!"

As I hang up, I'm smiling, genuinely excited about the chance to see little Lizzie again. But my body still has that loose, rubbery feel caused by having too much adrenaline dumped too suddenly into the bloodstream. How quickly we can go from nonchalance to terror and then veer in a completely new direction, straight toward anticipation.

How easily the progression could have gone another way. I don't know what I would have done if Christina hadn't answered the phone. I spend the rest of the morning trying not to wonder about that.

The week drags by with all the reluctance of a child going to the dentist. Lunches with Ellen and Marquez are the highlights, since Marquez has new information about Caroline and Grant. They're planning a vacation together; he's seen the travel brochures on Grant's desk. We maintain the website for a travel agency in the building next door, and they keep us supplied with fliers about special deals to Prague and London and Las Vegas. I think we get a discounted fare, too, but I've never used their services, so I don't know for sure.

"He might be going with a friend, or his brother, or anybody," Ellen objects. "That's not proof."

"They're going to be gone at the same time," Marquez replies. "Check the calendar." We all have to fill in our planned absences on a huge wall calendar mounted outside the lunchroom. "He'll be gone for six days, she'll be gone for ten, but they overlap for *all* of his days. I'm telling you, they're planning a trip."

"Where are they going?" I ask.

"Italy, I think."

"Wow, that's romantic."

Ellen frowns at me. "*None* of this is romantic, Maria. It's all sad."

I shrug. "You don't watch enough old black-and-white movies," I say. "*All* grand romance is sad at the core."

"Well, now I'm depressed," Marquez says.

"Have a French fry," I say. "It will cheer you up."

Oddly, I have another meal with Kathleen, too, and not one of those random we-accidentally-happened-to-be-in-the-lunchroom-together encounters. She drops by my desk on Thursday afternoon, seeming nervous and shy as a girl about to ask a boy to the Sadie Hawkins dance, to see if I might want to plan lunch the next day.

"It's just so hard to get through Friday," she offers as an excuse. "It's so much better if I can break up the day."

I'm not sure what we'll find to talk about for an extended period, but I don't feel I can turn her down. "Sure. Where do you want to go?"

"There's a new Pasta Pronto just down the street. We could be there and back in an hour, easy."

"Sounds good."

I don't actually dread the meal, but I can't say I'm looking forward to it. I don't feel like sharing confidences, and Kathleen and I don't seem to have much in common. But our Friday outing is enjoyable enough as we're both cheerful, the food is pretty good, and we have a ready-made topic in discussing a coworker who was fired for insubordination the day before. When that palls, I tell her I'm going to be babysitting overnight for a friend.

"Oh, that will be fun!" Kathleen exclaims. "Sometimes I keep my neighbor's little boy for her. But he's a terror. If he wants something, he will *not* stop screaming until you eventually give in and hand it to him. I'm always worn out by the time she comes to get him."

"Do you and Ritchie ever plan to have kids?"

She looks wistful. "We've been trying for the past three years, but it hasn't happened yet. I think–" She glances around the restaurant, as if people might be listening, and lowers her voice. "I think Ritchie has a low sperm count, but he won't go to get tested, so I don't think he'd be willing to–you know. Donate. So that we could try in vitro fertilization."

This is skating dangerously close to becoming information I do not want to have in my head. "Maybe there's nothing wrong with him," I say.

"I had all the tests done on *me*," she says, still in that almost-whisper. "I didn't tell him, though. I didn't want him to be mad."

For a moment, I consider how exhausting it must be to spend your whole life placating the person you live with–guessing in advance what might set him off, always trying to steer the conversation or the activity into a channel he will find pleasing. I wonder what trade-offs make such an effort worthwhile. "Well, you're both still young," I say, though their window is narrowing if they're both in their thirties. "Plenty of time for the situation to change."

I'm relieved when a glance at my watch shows that our lunch hour is almost over, and we both rise to head back to the office.

"This was fun," Kathleen observes as we step outside. "We'll have to do this every Friday."

I smile but don't answer. I'm pretty sure I have just become Kathleen's new best friend and I don't know what to do about it.

Christina and Lizzie arrive at my door about fifteen minutes after I get home. Christina is dressed mostly in black heavily accented with silver accessories, and she strides through the door with the manic energy I always associate with her.

"Are we too early? I could take Lizzie down to McDonald's for a half hour while you get settled. I wasn't sure how long it would take me to get downtown at this time of day. Is there a Cardinals game in town, do you know? What will traffic be like?"

I ignore her for a few moments while I take Lizzie in my arms and exclaim over her sweet little face. She is just as beautiful as I remember, though even in two short weeks, she looks different to me. More filled out, more defined. More alert. More human. "Traffic will probably be bad for another half hour or so," I say. "Why don't you stay awhile and have something to drink before you go? And tell me everything I need to know."

It turns out Christina has printed out a list of instructions that cover every eventuality she could think of: what to do if Lizzie cries, if she refuses a bottle, if she poops, if she vomits, if she spikes a fever, if she stops breathing. For only a couple of these, I am relieved to see, the advice is *Call 911.* "And I've put my cell phone number there at the bottom, see? And the phone number for my friend Annie's house. That's where I'll be staying tonight. Call me if you have any questions at all."

It is clear she is eager to get out of the house. Traffic or no traffic, she does not want to sit and have tea or a Coke. "Go," I say, waving her toward the door. "We'll be fine. See you in the morning."

In fact, we *are* fine. Lizzie is an amazingly sunny-tempered baby, crying only in short, halfhearted bursts and easily soothed with food or attention or a clean diaper. Shortly after feeding her an evening bottle, I turn on Nickelodeon and pace around the living room, gently bouncing her in my arms. She watches me with an almost unnerving intensity, as if she is memorizing my face, trying to determine how it contrasts and compares with her mother's, what makes me trustworthy, what makes me unique, what makes me safe.

I think she still comes in at less than ten pounds, so I am surprised by how quickly she grows heavy in my arms. Eventually I have to sit down so the armrest of the couch can take some of her weight. "You're a big strong healthy girl, aren't you?" I coo to her in that ridiculous happy voice people use with infants. "You're about to break Aunt Maria's elbow. Yes you are! Yes you are!"

Her face squinches up as she produces a sharp bark of laughter, and her tiny fists wave in delight. I know how she feels. I could laugh out loud; I could punch the air with joy. It is all I can do to keep myself from standing up again and carrying her to the credenza where I keep my phone books. I would page through to the A's, *adoption services*, or the S's, *sperm banks*. I can't believe how happy it makes me to hold a baby in my arms.

I am a little less enamored of motherhood by six the next morning. Lizzie has had a restless night that included a sixty-minute stretch when she couldn't stop crying and I couldn't figure out why. But the intervening hours of sleep have restored her natural good humor, and she wakes up gleefully, kicking her feet and chortling as she anticipates the day.

I am less refreshed but still game. After giving her a bottle, I chance taking a shower, leaving the bathroom door open so I can hear if she starts wailing. As I blow-dry my hair, I wonder how soon she might take a nap and if I'll be able to fall asleep when she does. I've heard new mothers complain about sleep deprivation, but I'd always imagined it took weeks to kick in and that the deficit could be easily erased by a night of uninterrupted rest. Now I realize it must be an ongoing state that not only is *not* cured by a good night's sleep, but no such thing as "a good night's sleep" actually exists when there's an infant in the house. I wonder how Beth made it through Clara's early years. I think I should have offered to help out more than I did. I wonder if the only time she felt rested was when she was hospitalized with pneumonia.

"So what should we do now, little girl?" I ask Lizzie. She is strapped into her car seat, which is perched on my kitchen table, and she is watching me consume my toast and jelly as if she knows it tastes much better than the lukewarm formula that constituted her own breakfast. "If it's not too cold, I could take you out for a walk. Or maybe we should go for a ride. When do you suppose your mother will be coming to get you? Soon? Not that I am not enjoying every minute with you, but I just wonder how many more entertainments I should plan."

As if she knows I am talking about her, Christina chooses that moment to phone. My Caller ID has been erratic lately, but it shows me a number that I recognize as hers before the LED display wavers and disappears. As soon as I answer, Christina asks in a cheerful voice, "Maria? How's it going?"

"Great. She's been an angel."

"How'd she sleep?"

"Mmm, she went down at ten, but then she was awake for about an hour around two, and awake for real by six."

"Oh, that's pretty good!" Christina says. "Sometimes she's awake two or three times in the night. And she's *still* up by six."

"You must be tired all the time."

She laughs. "I've learned to survive on five or six hours' sleep a night. Though I have to confess, it was heaven last night, even though Annie's spare bed has a lump in the middle that's the size of a watermelon. I just curled up around it and never once woke up."

I think there must be a reason she's called instead of just coming to the house, so I ask an indirect question. "I was wondering if I had time to take her for a short walk. It looks like a pretty day outside."

"That's why I'm calling," she replies. "I haven't even taken a shower yet, and Annie wanted to go out to breakfast. I can leave right now if you can't stand it anymore, but if you think you can hold on until noon, I'll come later."

I glance at the clock. It's not quite eight. "Sure," I say a little too brightly. "I'll be happy to keep her another few hours. You and your friend have fun."

"You're a sweetheart," Christina says, sounding like she wants to hang up as soon as possible so I can't change my mind. "See you around noon."

I hang up, yawn, and sink back onto my chair at the kitchen table. Lizzie makes a noise that sounds like *gooh*. "Guess we have time for that walk after all," I tell her, pouring myself another cup of coffee. "I'll show you the neighborhood."

But apparently Lizzie has been worn out by the effort of waking up and eating, because a few minutes later, she is nodding off. The caffeine has already kicked in, so it's pointless for me to try to nap alongside her. I sigh and turn on the computer so I can check my e-mail, pay bills, and make the morning somewhat productive.

By nine thirty, Lizzie is awake, changed, and restless, so I decide we'll both benefit from a walk. I've opened the front door to check the weather and found that the September air is as warm as a cat's fur and scented with cut grass and fallen leaves. In other words, perfect. I'm halfway through putting on my shoes when a knock at the door startles Lizzie so much she sneezes. I hop across the room with my other shoe in my hand to find Beth and Clara waving at me from the porch.

"Too early?" Beth asks a little anxiously. "I know I should have called first, but I was driving right by."

"Not at all. Come on in," I say, motioning them inside.

"I had to drop off some notes to a woman I work with. She's flying out to Denver tomorrow and I was—" She abruptly stops speaking. I realize she's spotted Lizzie. Or rather, Clara has spotted Lizzie, who is lying on a blanket in the middle of the living room floor, and Clara has squatted down to get a closer look.

"You have a baby," Beth says blankly.

"Well, she's not mine," I say, and close the door. I'm thinking fast. Obviously the exact truth won't do, but it shouldn't be too hard to come up with a plausible variation. It's just a question of how much detail to supply. "You want coffee or something?"

Beth drops to her knees beside Clara. "Whose baby *is* she?"

"What's her name?" Clara wants to know. She reaches out a tentative hand and pats Lizzie on the head as if she is a not particularly tame kitten. The baby laughs.

"Lizzie."

"Where did she come from?" Clara asks.

Beth turns her head to give me an inquiring look. "Yes, where?"

I settle on the couch and put on my other shoe. "She belongs to a woman named Christina, who is the sister of one of my college friends," I say. "I met Christina, I don't know, a couple dozen times while I was in school. I didn't really know her that well, but she friended me on Facebook about three months ago."

"I thought you never checked your Facebook account."

"Well, I don't, not very often. Anyway, so, you know, we exchanged a few e-mails, and she told me she was pregnant, and I said, oh, I'd love to see the baby if you're ever in town, and she dropped by a couple weeks ago, which surprised the hell out of me—"

"You shouldn't swear," Clara says primly.

"Right. She surprised the *heck* out of me. But we had a very nice visit, and I thought Lizzie was cute, and I said—not dreaming that she would ever take me up on it—'Gee, if you ever need someone to watch her for a few hours, you should call me.' And so then—"

"Then she called you," Beth finishes up. "Well, that was nervy."

"Kind of what I thought," I agree. "But I *did* offer, so I could hardly turn her down." I shrug. "I know it seems weird, but it's just for a little while. She'll be back by noon."

Beth rolls her eyes. "Oh, it's not weird at all. I know what's going on here."

"You do?"

"You've got baby fever. You're thirty-five—"

"*You're* thirty-five. I'm thirty-four."

"And that clock's ticking, and you're thinking, 'How many years do I have left? How many *eggs* do I have left?' And suddenly everywhere you look, *other* women have babies—the women at work, the women at the grocery store. And all you can think about is how much you want one, too, but you're not dating anyone special and you're wondering if maybe you don't *need* anyone special, maybe you can do this all on your own—"

By now I'm grinning. "Hold on, *chica*, are we talking about *me* here? Who's the one who went off and had a baby just because she felt like it?"

"That's why I know I'm right! Because I did it, too! But let me tell you, it's not so easy to just pop out a kid and then go on with your life. In fact, most of the time it's pretty hard being a single mom."

I drop to the floor so I can cover Clara's ears with my hands. She's used to it; her grandmother and her aunt frequently try to block out some comment of Beth's that they don't think she should hear. "Don't listen to those mean things your mommy is saying," I whisper into the nape of her neck.

Clara shakes her head to dislodge my grip. She's offered her own hand to Lizzie, who has brought it up to her mouth and appears to be sucking on Clara's index finger with great energy. "She likes me," Clara says seriously. "I can tell she likes me."

"She probably does," I say. "She has exceptionally good taste in people."

Beth pokes me to get my attention again. "So? Am I right? Baby fever?"

"A little bit right," I say defensively. "But I haven't gone and done anything irreversible yet. I'm just watching a little girl for a few hours." I don't consider it necessary to say that I've kept Lizzie overnight. Beth would find it hard to believe I would do such a big favor for a casual friend.

"She *is* pretty cute," Beth allows. "So you've got her for a few more hours. Want to go to the park?"

"I was planning to take her for a walk, but I've just realized I don't have a stroller."

Beth jumps to her feet. "I've got one in the car. Come on, let's go."

The four of us pass an exceptionally pleasant couple of hours. I have never paid attention to how many parks there are between my house and the highway, but apparently Beth automatically catalogs public spaces and playgrounds, because she drives us directly to a little park that features a slide, a swing set, some kind of brightly colored climbing bars, and a nicely paved track that circles the mulched play area. Clara goes straight to a sandbox to dig; I push Lizzie around the paved path while Beth strolls along beside me, talking idly.

I don't listen as closely as I should. I am too busy inhaling the perfumes of wet cedar and fading roses, marveling at the brilliant colors dripping off the surrounding trees. The soft September sunshine drapes itself across my shoulders like lace tatted by my grandmother's hand—something made with love especially for me. *This feels right,* I think as I guide the stroller along the path. *This feels happy.*

It doesn't take long for that sense of certainty and contentment to fade. Minutes after we decide it's time to go, just as Beth has gone to fetch Clara from the sandbox, a pickup truck pulls up and a young couple climbs out, a baby already in the woman's arms. Clearly they don't believe in traveling with car seats. They look like they're in their early twenties, or maybe younger, and they're dressed in jeans and sweatshirts and running shoes. She's blond and petite; he's not a big guy, but he's burly, and I imagine that he works construction somewhere. As soon as they're out of the car, he takes the baby from her and tosses it in the air—not high enough to be scary, but high enough to make the child shriek with delight. I think it's a boy; at any rate, he's dressed in blue coveralls with an engineering logo embroidered on the front, and the parents don't, at first glance, appear like the types to ignore gender stereotypes in clothing. The father tosses him in the air again, then flips him upside down and dangles him by his ankles. I can hear the child's infectious laughter from twenty-five yards away. The young mother says something to the father, and he leans down to kiss her on the cheek.

All of a sudden, my heart cramps up; my fingers on the stroller handles turn icy. Beth's right, in a way. I *do* have baby fever. I *do* have an empty sense that my life holds no core purpose. But I don't simply want a child. I want a family. I want a family with Dante. I want to wake up on a Saturday morning—any Saturday morning—and know he'll be lying beside me in the bed, half listening for the baby's cry, half hoping she sleeps another hour so that we have time to make love. My life is incomplete, but it's not just because I don't have a cradle in the spare bedroom. It's because, most of the time, Dante isn't even in the house. It's because, no matter who else I surround myself with, I always feel abandoned and alone.

CHAPTER SIX

Monday seems to arrive much more quickly than usual, probably because I lost so much of my weekend to Lizzie. All morning, I have the sense that I've fallen behind, so I keep myself sequestered in my office, focused on the computer. A knock on the door frame makes me practically jump out of my chair.

"I'm so sorry," Kathleen says remorsefully. "I didn't mean to startle you."

"No, no, it's fine. What's going on?"

She leans against the wall as if she's been told that's a commonly accepted casual pose, but she still looks tense and anxious. I don't notice any new bruises, though.

"I just stopped by to see how your weekend was," she says in a timid voice. It's so odd. I can tell she wants to be friends with me but she's not certain how such a thing is accomplished. It's as if she's never had a friend before.

The thought makes me gentle my voice when I reply. "It was much too fast! Remember I told you I was going to babysit for a friend? I did, and it was great, but it took up, like, hours. So then I spent all day Sunday cleaning the house and getting groceries and answering e-mail and—you know, organizing my life. What about you?"

"Oh, we have bowling league on Friday nights, and then on Saturday and Sunday we did stuff around the house," she replies. "Ritchie is remodeling the basement, so we always have to go to Home Depot a couple of times during the weekends, and then there's all the work to do. Plumbing and electrical and so on."

Still sitting in my chair, I stretch my arms over my head. I should get up and jog down the hallway, or maybe run up and down the stairs a few times. Step aerobics with real steps. "You're doing the remodeling work yourself? I'm impressed. Ritchie must be pretty handy."

"I suppose so," she says doubtfully. I interpret this to mean that he *thinks* he's handier than he really is; and that he hates it when, for example, his faulty wiring technique leads to a power failure or a small electrical fire. "He says it's saving us a lot of money."

Before I can answer, Ellen appears in the doorway, peering over Kathleen's shoulder. "Haven't talked to you all day," she says to me. "What are you doing for lunch? Marquez wants pizza."

They have a veggie option at Pizzeria Plus, one of our standby restaurants, so I nod. "That sounds good. Is it lunchtime already?"

"We'll probably leave in about fifteen minutes." Ellen looks at Kathleen. "Want to come along?"

Even I can't tell if Ellen is merely being polite, since it's rude to plan an outing in front of someone and not issue an invitation, or if she's really hoping Kathleen will join us. I speak up. "Oh, please do," I say as warmly as I can, hoping she'll refuse. "You like pizza, don't you?"

Kathleen glances over her shoulder at Ellen, then back at me. Now she's the one whose expression I can't read. Does she want to decline but can't figure out how, or does she want to come with us but desperately fears to intrude? "I'd like that," she says finally. "Let me close out some files on my computer."

She rushes off. Ellen steps in from the doorway and we both wait in silence—long enough to be pretty sure Kathleen is out of earshot. I lift my eyebrows and Ellen smiles.

"I saw her standing here," she says. "If I didn't want to ask her along, I'd've called you on the phone."

"We won't be able to talk about her," I say in mock dismay.

Ellen snorts. "Plenty of other people to talk about."

In fact, the lunch is more convivial than I expected. It turns out that Kathleen is a little easier for me to take when there are other people participating in the conversation.

It also turns out that Marquez has kind of a thing for her. Oh, he's not romantically interested in her; he doesn't flirt. But he treats her with an odd sort of tenderness, as if she's a beloved sister who's barely recovered from a long illness, or a frail, gorgeous child destined for an early death. He talks her into splitting a meat-lover's pizza with him, almost as if he thinks he has to cajole her into eating more calories or she'll waste away to nothing.

"I like that sweater, it's a good color for you," he tells her, leaning over to fool with the collar. "But I think you need to undo this button and wear a black shell under it—no, navy. And then put on that silver necklace you have—the one with the blue topaz. That would look really good."

I trade a glance with Ellen. I don't remember ever seeing Kathleen wear a necklace with a blue topaz pendant. But frankly I couldn't tell you what any of my coworkers keep in their closets or jewelry boxes.

Kathleen is smiling. "Ritchie gave me that necklace on our third anniversary."

"You should wear more silver," Marquez tells her. "It brightens your hair."

"Maybe you can come dress me up someday," Ellen drawls. "I could use the help."

He throws her a look. "You certainly could."

Kathleen looks dismayed, but the rest of us laugh. "You think he's a sweetheart because he's nice to *you*, but really Marquez is just as obnoxious and mean as the rest of us," Ellen says cheerfully. "Don't let him fool you."

"Yes, you can find my picture up on iambitchy-dot-com," Marquez says, "right next to Ellen's."

Ellen sighs. "Or you could, if my stupid laptop didn't crash five times a day," she says. "I spent half of Sunday on the phone with tech support trying to figure out why I couldn't get to my e-mail account."

"Get a Mac," Marquez says smugly. "All your problems will go away."

"I'd like a Mac," Kathleen says wistfully. "I'd like *any* home computer. But it's not in the budget right now."

I wonder how her expensive diamond-and-star-sapphire ring fit into the budget; it must have cost more than a cheap desktop, unless it's filled with cubic zirconia. Not for the first time, I find myself wondering if Kathleen is the primary breadwinner for the household. Jobs might be scarce for a freelance security guard with a bad temper.

"I have a little netbook you can borrow," I say before I have time to think about it. "I haven't used it since I got a new laptop about three months ago."

Kathleen looks at me uncertainly. She's a whiz with the office equipment, like fax machines and photocopiers, but she has an uneasy relationship with her desktop PC. "Why not? Don't you like it?"

I wiggle my fingers. "I *hate* it. I can't get my hands to scrunch down small enough to hit the right keys. You could keep it till you get your own—or until my laptop crashes, whichever comes first."

"Better make sure you erase all your top secret personal data before you go around handing out old computers," Ellen says.

"Yeah, well, I never used it enough to fill it with personal information," I retort. "And I changed all my passwords when I got the new one. I think I'm safe." I glance at Kathleen. "You still have to have some kind of Wi-Fi provider if you want to get online."

"I could take it to the library," she says. "It's right down the street."

"Perfect," I say. "I'll bring it in tomorrow."

"Are you sure?"

"Absolutely."

She glows. "Oh, thank you. I would like that so much."

Ellen follows me back to my office after we return to our building. "That's how we'll save Kathleen," she says without preamble. "We'll draw her into our circle of friends, we'll lavish her with gifts, we'll make her trust us. Then we'll do an intervention. 'That dickwrinkle you're married to will be the death of you. We'll help you leave him.' Maybe she'll believe us."

I laugh so hard I can barely say the word. "'Dickwrinkle'?"

She shrugs. "He's not even man enough to be a whole prick."

"What's with her and Marquez?"

"She reminds him of his mother."

"That's kind of stereotyping, don't you think?"

Now she grins. "Well, ask him. I bet he'll tell you the same thing. He doesn't talk about it much, but he grew up in a house in Chicago where his father was abusive and his mother was tiny and afraid. But she opened a secret bank account and gave all the money to Marquez when he turned eighteen so he could get out of the house and go to school. Something like twenty thousand dollars. He calls her Saint Joan. I think she must look like our little Kathleen."

"His parents still married?"

"Nah. Soon as Marquez got a job he started funneling her money and eventually she had enough to move back to California and live with one of her sisters. So she left the bastard."

"A rare happy ending to *that* story," I say, shaking my head. "Most of the time, people just depress me."

"That's because you're weak," she says. "They should intrigue you."

I look up in indignation, but she's grinning. "You *are* a bitch," I say.

"But I'm a bitch who cares." She nods in the general direction of Kathleen's desk, a couple of hallways away. "Maybe we'll rescue her yet."

Kathleen is suitably excited to receive my netbook the next day, and over lunch we head to a local coffee shop with free Wi-Fi so I can show her how easy it is to get online. She's daintier than I am; her hands look just right on the undersized keyboard. I admit the observation leaves me a little disgruntled. But she's so pleased by my generosity that I can't hold the uncharitable thought for long.

"The minute you want this back, you just tell me," she repeats for the twentieth time. "Promise."

"I promise. But as long as the laptop is functioning, it's yours," I say. "Have fun."

The act of kindness buoys me for the rest of the day, which holds no other highlights and, in fact, delivers to me a rather nasty bookkeeping tangle that keeps me at the office an hour later than usual. Once home, I'm too lazy to cook, too unmotivated to exercise, so I eat an entire package of frozen vegetables for dinner and spend the whole evening watching the *Moonlighting* DVDs Beth gave me last Christmas. It's hard to conceive of a less worthwhile way to spend my time.

I recognize my mood for what it is: vague depression sparked by loneliness. Dante has been gone for two weeks; he will probably be gone six or seven more days, and the time apart seems so long and dreary. But I remind myself that I have made it past the midpoint of his absence, the winter solstice of our season apart. It is time for me to start feeling hopeful again. Time to begin looking forward to the lengthening of the days, the return of the light, the burst of bright sunshine that is Dante's presence. Soon, I will feel spring move through my blood, full of promise and renewal. As I anticipate his arrival, I will begin to come back to life.

The red LED numbers on my bedside clock proclaim a stark 1:47 when my phone's shrill ring startles me out of a deep sleep. I swim back to consciousness, fumbling for the receiver. My erratic Caller ID is working here in the darkest hours of the night, but I don't recognize the number, so it's not particularly helpful.

"Hello?" I say a little fearfully. Chances are good that any post-midnight call is trouble. Someone's hurt, someone's dead, or an unknown pervert is about to make an unwelcome suggestion.

"Hey, baby," says a rough voice on the other end. "Sorry to wake you up, but I think I only have about an hour."

Just like that, I am fully awake and flooded with happiness. "Dante! Where are you?"

"Sedalia, I think. I'm not sure. I think I found the last pay phone in the entire state of Missouri."

"And you're all right? You're healthy?"

He sounds a little amused. "Perfectly healthy. Don't fret."

I can't help but fret. I fret every single minute that you're gone. He knows that already, but he doesn't particularly like to hear me say it, so I change the subject. "I saw Christina over the weekend."

"Really? Why?"

"She was in St. Louis and asked if I'd watch the baby overnight, so I did."

"That was nice of you."

"Oh, she's the cutest thing. Lizzie, I mean."

He laughs. "I knew who you meant. How did Christina seem?"

How should she seem? "Oh, you know Christina. A little manic but perfectly cheerful. I could tell she was glad to get away from the baby for a night, but I can't help thinking she's a really good mom. Well, Lizzie is just so happy and good-natured, so obviously Christina is doing something right." I can tell I'm babbling, but I can't quite stop. "I mean, I know you were concerned about Christina trying to raise a baby on her own. But I think she's doing a really good job."

"Great, then I won't worry anymore," he says. "What else have you been doing? How's work?"

When we're together, when he's actually in my presence, Dante doesn't ask me many questions. He doesn't seem that interested in my job, and only listens out of politeness to my tales about family activities or shopping expeditions. But when he's gone, when I'm out of sight, out of reach, he's filled with curiosity. *What did you have for breakfast? What did your mom say? Did you get that travel account?* I'm not fooled; I know he doesn't really care about those details. He's just trying to fill in all the colors for the image of me he carries in his head. He wants to make me real. I feel so far away I could be imaginary; he wants to give me weight and substance and flavor. He wants to devour me.

I know, because that's exactly how I feel about him.

I find myself telling him about Kathleen, the fact that she's married to a jerk, the fact that she seems to have chosen me for a friend and I don't know what to do about it, the fact that I gave her a computer. "Well, she'll really want to be your friend now," he says with a laugh.

"I know! I should have kept my mouth shut."

"No, it was nice. You're nice."

During the conversation, I have slouched farther and farther under the covers, and now I'm not even making a pretense of sitting up. I roll to my side, cradling the phone between the pillow and my ear. I never bothered to turn on the bedside lamp, so the room is completely dark except for the fugitive lights that sidle in from streetlamps and passing cars. There is a kind of unmatched intimacy that comes from a phone conversation at night—no noises, no sights, no sensory inputs except that warm voice in your ear.

"Have you really been taking care of yourself?" I murmur. "Have you been safe? Have you been eating right?"

His voice is amused again. He's irritated when I ask such questions face-to-face, but he doesn't seem to mind if they're posed long distance. "Oh, yeah, I had a nice tasty squirrel for lunch, and I found a Dumpster behind an Italian restaurant. That'll make for a good breakfast."

I want to say *Yuck* but then he'll say *Why ask me about food if you don't like to think about what I eat?* and I don't want to end the conversation on a note of exasperation. "Well, doesn't that sound yummy," I say instead. "Maybe I'll have some leftover pasta in the morning and I can pretend like we're having breakfast together."

"I wish we were," he answers. "I miss you."

"I miss you, too," I say. "Every day."

"Sometimes—" he says, and then stops abruptly.

"Sometimes what? What were you going to say?"

"Sometimes I can't figure out why you put up with me at all," he bursts out. "Every time I come back. Every time I show up at your door. I stand there for a minute—usually covered in grime and stinking to heaven—and I think, 'Maybe I shouldn't go in. Maybe it would be better for Maria if I just walked away.'"

My eyes fly open and I stare in horror at the ceiling, just barely visible in the imperfect dark. "Dante! What? No, no, no! Don't say that! Why would you— Don't think that! I *love* you. It would break my heart if you left me."

"Sure, but maybe it would be better for you. Once you got over it.

You'd move on, you'd find a nice guy—a normal guy—you'd live a normal life—"

"I don't want a normal life. I want a life with you."

"You'll tell me, won't you? If you change your mind? I won't blame you, I won't be surprised. I just want you to be happy, Maria. I really do."

"Dante." I make my voice as firm, as certain, as I can. I want him to believe me. "*You're* the one who makes me happy. *You're* the one who puts meaning in my days. *You're* the one I can't live without. If I ever change my mind on that, I'll let you know, I promise. But it's not going to happen. I promise that, too."

"All right," he says, his words muffled. I can't tell if he's speaking against his sleeve, trying to hide the fact that he's crying, or if his throat is roughening, if he's feeling the transformation coming over him and trying to fight it off. "I'll come back as soon as I can. I love you."

"I love you, too," I say. A second later the phone goes dead.

My hands are shaking a little as I place the handset back into the charging dock. I snuggle back under the covers, but I can tell it will be a while before I fall back to sleep. I can feel the energetic sparkle in my veins that I usually associate with too much caffeine; my mind is darting here and there like an overzealous hummingbird.

I'm not upset by the conversation, oh no. I'm excited. It's so rare that Dante admits to weakness or need. From time to time, when we're together, he remembers to tell me that he loves me, but he says it in an offhand way, as if it might not really be true. But alone on some moonless night, isolated, examining his life, he comes to the conclusion that I am the one he loves, and he says so. I recognize this fever in my blood. It's happiness.

What Dante doesn't know is that I've already tried to fall in love with someone else. What I already know is that I can't.

CHAPTER SEVEN

I met Matt Tanaka about eight years ago, before I had the job at the agency. I was doing external auditing for a small private company, traveling all over the state for weeks at a time. At this point, Dante was staying human for longer periods, so I didn't feel such a desperate desire to see him during whatever rare and precious days he could offer me. At the same time, we weren't getting along that well. He was edgy and sarcastic, I was feeling both put-upon and taken for granted. We would generally have one good day together, when he first returned, and then a few days of quarreling, and then he would go off on his own pursuits long enough for me to miss him again. At the time, he was renting a small apartment of his own, so it was fairly easy for us to spend a couple days apart if we were getting on each other's nerves. But generally we liked each other again before our time was up, and so we had another good twenty-four or forty-eight hours together before he had to disappear.

Still, I had started asking myself some very basic questions: Couldn't

I find a nice guy? Couldn't I find a normal guy? Wouldn't my life be better if Dante just walked away?

Matt was a comptroller at a regional bank in Kansas City, an attractive, outgoing man of mixed American and Japanese heritage. As an external auditor, I was used to being ignored by everyone in the offices I visited; sometimes people wouldn't even bother pointing out where the bathrooms and vending machines were. But that first day at the bank, I had to spend a half hour interviewing Matt, and afterward he invited me to join a group going out for lunch.

I was in Kansas City for a week during the month of July, and Matt and I ended up having lunch every day.

He was fun. He told stupid jokes. He described with rueful amusement his attempts to rehab an old house in Overland Park. He loved to play Guess-What-Their-Relationship-Is whenever we spotted odd groupings of people sitting together in restaurants. I was filled with laughter during every minute of our time together, and I always returned to my hotel room grinning a little about some of our conversational exchanges.

Neither of us was sorry when it turned out I had to return to Kansas City the next week to finish the audit.

"Why bother to go back to St. Louis at all?" he said on that Friday afternoon, when I dropped by to say *Good-bye* and *See you Monday.* "Stay for the weekend. We'll go see the Royals. I've got a friend who can get us tickets, even if the game's sold out."

I would have done it, but Dante was human back in St. Louis, possibly enjoying my absence but also very likely to notice if I didn't come back. "Oh—I can't," I said regretfully. I'd already learned how to lie so automatically that I didn't even have to fumble for an excuse. "It's my mom's birthday and *I'm* the one hosting the tea party on Sunday. Kind of hard to break that date. And I don't have any clean clothes with me."

"We-elll," he drawled. "Stay *next* weekend. Pack enough stuff. Cancel all the birthday parties and the movie dates with your girlfriends."

I hesitated. "I don't have enough work to do here to justify staying a whole 'nother week."

"Come up Wednesday," he suggested. "Or, you know, take a couple of vacation days. I assume vacation days are part of your benefits package?"

"You know, I think they are. And I have about twenty of them stockpiled, since I've been too busy to take any time off."

"See? It all works out. You'll stay? I can get tickets?"

We were standing in the doorway to his office, which was little more than a glassed-in cubicle visible from every point in the bank. About twenty people were close enough to hear if they had been trying hard enough to eavesdrop. Even so, it was all I could do to refrain from leaning forward and planting an impulsive kiss on his mouth. His wheedling had made my blood fizz; it was so delicious to have someone flirting with me, someone paying attention to me who so obviously *liked* me. In those days, there were times when it felt like Dante barely tolerated me. He certainly didn't seem to want to spend *more* time with me than our lives afforded.

"You can get tickets," I said.

"Yessss!" Matt exclaimed, slapping a hand against the wall. "Friday night or Saturday night? Or Sunday afternoon? Or all three?"

I was laughing. "Umm, I don't think I like baseball quite as much as you do."

"I don't care about baseball. Let the bastards trip over their bats and their running shoes, I don't care. I just want you to feel obligated to spend all that time with me."

"How about a Saturday night game, and the rest of the time we can wing it?"

"Sounds good. Sounds great. See you next week. Drive carefully!"

I was a little giddy during the whole drive home, a little more than four hours straight across I-70 past cornfields, wheat fields, small towns, and the clump of heavy traffic that marked Columbia at roughly the halfway point of the journey. The house seemed empty when I first got home, so I assumed Dante was at his apartment, but then I found him sleeping in the second bedroom.

"What's wrong? Why are you in here?" I asked, bending down to touch his forehead.

His skin was hot. "I think I have a stomach virus," he said in a miserable voice. "I was throwing up all afternoon."

"Oh—you poor baby," I said. "You want me to get you some Tamiflu? Alka-Seltzer? Tea? Saltines? Gatorade?"

"Yeah, keep talking about stuff I'd have to swallow," he said faintly. "That won't make me want to vomit some more."

I strangled a laugh. "Okay—well—you just tell me if there's anything I can do for you."

"I just want to go to sleep."

"All right. I'll come back and check on you in an hour or so."

He was sick all weekend, and bad-tempered about it, which certainly erased any chance he had of seeming so attractive that Matt paled in comparison. I was never seriously worried about his health, which made it easier to be annoyed with him, though I tried very hard to be a sympathetic nurse. And I never suggested he go back to his own place to convalesce, though the thought certainly did cross my mind more than once.

And I did walk out of the room Saturday evening when he threw a packet of crackers to the floor and growled, "I *hate* this crap!" I walked out of the house, in fact, and drove myself to the mall, where I stayed until it shut down at nine. I seriously considered not returning home at all—I could have gone to Beth's, could have told her there had been a water main break in my neighborhood and asked her if I could spend the night—but I decided that was too petty. Dante would surely apologize as soon as I got home.

He didn't. He was sound asleep, his hair very black against the white of the pillowcase, his eyes creased against a nightmare or some ongoing pain. I stood there for about ten minutes, just watching him in the faint light from the hallway. He didn't look particularly exotic or beautiful or precious or beloved. He didn't, at that moment, even look familiar. I turned away and let him sleep.

I woke late the next morning, alone in my bed, hearing rustling and clinking noises from the kitchen. Wrapping myself in a robe, I stumbled down the hall to find Dante standing at the stove, stirring oatmeal with one hand and eating an apple with the other one.

"Feeling better?" I asked in a neutral voice.

He glanced at me over his shoulder. "A hundred percent. I'm starving."

"Good. Need any help or can I go take a shower?"

He put down the apple, hastily swallowing a bite, and laid aside the spoon. Crossing the room, he took me in a warm hug, wrapped his arms tightly around my waist, and rested his cheek on my head. "I probably need you to kick me in the butt," he said. "Christina always said I was a lousy patient, but I didn't mean to be such an asshole the past few days."

"Asshole? Really? I scarcely noticed," I said brightly.

He kissed the top of my head and released me. "Yeah, I think you did."

I smiled. "Yeah, I kind of did. But I'm glad you're feeling better."

"I'm still a little shaky," he said, "but maybe tomorrow we can go do something fun."

"I have to go back to Kansas City in the morning."

He looked affronted. "What? You didn't tell me that."

"Sorry. I thought I did. I never finished the bank audit."

His face showed growing dissatisfaction. "I've hardly seen you at all this time."

"Sorry," I said again. "Maybe when I get back–"

"I'll be gone by then," he said brusquely, and returned his attention to the stove.

He was contrite again by the time I came fresh-scrubbed out of the shower, and I had managed to soap away some of my irritation. The day was astonishingly cool for July in St. Louis, maybe eighty degrees, so we sat outside on the porch glider, sipped lemonade, and listened to a baseball game. We had our arms wrapped loosely around each other and our heads tilted so that our skulls touched, and that sweet, casual contact filled me again with deep affection. He was like a drug, some powerful opiate that I could absorb through my flesh; just the sensation of his skin against mine was enough to get me high. I sighed with contentment and had a hard time remembering what there was in Kansas City that could justify the drive.

When the game ended, he sighed, unwound himself, stretched, and sighed. "God, I am so *bored*," he said.

I went straight inside and began packing.

The rest of the audit could be stretched legitimately through Thursday morning, so I kept myself busy for most of the week, not hanging out in Matt's glass cubicle for more than a few minutes a day. But Thursday afternoon we had lunch together and then returned to his office so he could finish a story about a bad trip to Mexico.

"I won't drink tequila to this day," he said as a pretty blond secretary came in to drop a pile of papers on his desk.

"Too bad," I returned. "It's my favorite kind of rotgut liquor."

The secretary turned to give me an unsmiling glance. "You know he just broke up with his girlfriend. He *always* breaks up with his girlfriends," she said and walked out.

There was a small, charged moment while Matt and I stared at each other, trying to figure out what to say. His face was full of both chagrin and eagerness, like he couldn't wait to explain everything once he had figured out how to phrase it.

"You just dumped somebody?" I said.

"I did. But I tried to be really nice about it."

"There's no nice way to dump somebody."

"I know but I—See, here's the thing. We'd been dating for almost a year. She was so sweet. Really. Too sweet. I was always hurting her feelings when I didn't mean to, just by being myself, you know? I was always tap dancing when I was around her. Trying to be careful about what I said, and then apologizing because I always said something wrong."

Keeping my face impassive, I merely nodded.

"And she's, okay, she's thirty-two, it's clear she's thinking it's time to get married and have kids, and I'm pretty sure I'm not the right one for her to marry. So if I wanted to be a nice guy, I had to break up with her so she could be available for the right man, you know? But she didn't really hear it that way when I tried to explain."

I nodded again. "And you break up with *all* your girlfriends?" I asked, repeating the secretary's accusation. "Do they *all* want to get married and have kids?"

He made a helpless gesture with his hands. "Sometimes that's the reason and sometimes it's not," he said. "It's just so complicated."

"Boy is it ever," I said.

"But I really don't want you to think I'm a jerk."

"I have a boyfriend," I replied.

He was already poised to say something else, and this stopped him so completely that for a moment his mouth hung open. "Are you about to break up with him?"

"No," I said, and laughed.

He laughed back. "I didn't want you to think I was on the rebound," he says. "So I wasn't going to tell you about my ex-girlfriend."

"I wasn't going to tell you about my boyfriend, either."

We both laughed even harder. I wondered if we were being watched by the blond secretary (who probably had a secret crush on him). I wondered if she found it impossible to believe that I was amused by her revelation instead of unsettled. I wondered if she had any idea how tricky it was to navigate any relationship and what a relief it could be when laughter was one of the first options.

Over dinner that night, I told Matt more about Dante than I had told almost anyone up to that point. It was odd; it wasn't as if I knew Matt so well that I felt I could trust him with the one thing I had hidden from everyone else. It was more like he was a seatmate on a transatlantic flight, someone I knew I would never see again, and the very randomness of our connection made it safe to confide in him.

Even so, I wasn't entirely truthful. "I've been dating Dante for six or seven years now," I told him. "And yet there are all these things I don't know about him. Like, he travels for his job. He's gone about half the time. But he's evasive about where he goes. I've never met his boss or his coworkers. He tells me he's in sales—he sells valve and gear parts for big machinery—but I can't really get a sense of the job."

Matt's eyes were huge; he was suitably intrigued. "Do you think he works for the CIA?"

"I don't know! It's crossed my mind."

"Maybe he's a hit man."

"Something else I've considered."

"Does he carry a gun?"

"Not that I've ever found."

"Have you looked? Like, have you gone through his clothes when he's sleeping?"

To anyone else I would have been ashamed to answer honestly, but with Matt I simply nodded. "I have. And I've looked through his closets when we're at his place."

"So he does let you come to *his* house."

"His apartment. He rents a studio. Yes."

"Well, that's good, because my next thought would be—"

"That he might be married."

Matt nodded. "That was what I was thinking."

"I've wondered about that, too. Hell, he could have *several* wives all over the Midwest, the amount of traveling he does."

"Have you considered hiring a private detective?"

I shook my head. "No. I don't think—well, if he's an assassin, I surely wouldn't want to put a private detective in danger! And if he's married—maybe I don't want to know."

"I'd want to know," Matt said.

I scoffed. "You'd be relieved. Less pressure on you."

He grinned. "You're right. I think it sounds like a good arrangement."

"Anyway, I don't ask too many questions."

A look of unwonted seriousness pulled down the corners of his dark almond eyes. "But you want to be careful, Maria. I mean, if you really think he's leading some kind of double life—and if you think it could be dangerous—"

He's a shape-shifter. Half the time, he roams the world as a wolf, a dog, a bear. His life is dangerous to him, but probably not to me. Unless he is lying about all of it. "How nice of you to be concerned," I said playfully, changing the tone and changing the subject. "And here I thought you were such a carefree guy."

He grinned again. "It's easy to be carefree with a girl like you."

He took off that Friday, and I, of course, was already on vacation. We spent the day wandering through the Plaza, Kansas City's high-end collection of shops and restaurants and apartments. We found a sports bar for dinner—since it turned out Matt was far more than a casual baseball fan—and cheered on the Royals over beers and burgers. When he drove me back to my hotel, we found a shadowy corner of the garage and sat in the front seat, kissing.

"Isn't this the point when you're supposed to invite me up to your room?" he asked finally in a breathless voice. He drove a small European sports car, and it wasn't entirely satisfactory—or comfortable—to lean over the gearshift to make out.

I laughed shakily. I was having a hard time remembering when I'd last kissed anyone but Dante, and I hadn't slept with anyone else since college. It was odd how what was essentially the same act could taste so different, feel so different. Matt's lips were fuller than Dante's, softer. He held back a little more, but I liked that; it made me feel like he wasn't certain of me, or he wanted to explore me slowly, or both.

What was odder still was how the body reacted to two such different men. All the physical symptoms were the same, the breathlessness, the rush of blood, the flood of desire, the building urge to press harder, go farther. My body was fully engaged; my body was ready to go the distance.

But my heart was not. Or perhaps it was my mind. Or whatever part of the psyche that presided over monumental decisions. I could picture Matt in my bed, but I didn't want him there. Not tonight, anyway. I wanted to think about this some more. I wanted to consider whether I was ready to cheat on Dante.

"I don't think so," I said. "I think I'd better say good night and go up to my room alone."

"There's a word for women like you," he said, but he murmured it against my mouth, nibbling at my lips.

"Mmm, I know. Always loved that word."

He laughed and straightened up, pushing me away. "Don't wear anything too sexy tomorrow," he said. "I want to be able to control my lust."

I opened my eyes wide as I resettled my shirt over my jeans. "You mean you don't plan to ravish me in the middle of the Royals' stadium?"

"If we'd gotten box seats, maybe, but we're in the stands, right behind first base. I just don't think there will be much privacy."

I sighed. "And I thought you were getting us *good* seats."

He grinned and patted me on the head. "Scoot," he said. "I'll pick you up at noon tomorrow."

I glided across the hotel lobby and smiled during the whole elevator ride to my room. There is something about amorous contact, whether or not it culminates in sex. It roils through the body like an intemperate liqueur, leaving the brain pleasantly fogged and every inch of skin sensitized. It blunts your irritations and flushes you with well-being. It just damn well makes you feel *good.*

The red light on my phone was blinking, so I sat on the bed and dreamily dialed the hotel operator. "You have a message from Mr. Tay," she said in a voice bearing traces of a Spanish accent.

Mr. Tay? Who was that? Someone from the bank? "What did he say?"

"He said, 'Had to go.'"

"'Had to go'? What? *Who* is this message from?"

"Mr. Tay. Mr. Don Tay."

Don Tay. So fuzzy was I from excited endorphins that I had to run the syllables through my head three times before they clicked. *Don Tay. Dante!*

"Wait—he said what?"

"'Had to go.' He left the message ten minutes ago."

The sense of the words hit me like a punch to the stomach, and all my floaty happiness withered away. "Thank you," I whispered and hung up the phone.

I sat there on the bed for the next fifteen minutes, rocking a little, my arms wrapped around my shoulders, my eyes filling with tears. *Had to go.* It was what he always said when he departed abruptly, impatient of farewell scenes or long, drawn-out good-byes. It meant he wouldn't be waiting for me when I returned Sunday evening, it meant I would go at least another full week without seeing him—maybe two. It meant that by sitting in the hotel garage, madly making out with Matt Tanaka, I had squandered my last chance to hear Dante's voice for days and days and days. For a moment, I burned with anger at Matt—the faithless, irresponsible man who kissed many girls and then cavalierly left them—but almost immediately I was angry with myself. What kind of lover was I, what kind of human being, to play games with one man while the one I truly belonged with was hundreds of miles away, missing me, girding himself for a hard and physically risky transition? I was not steadfast, I was not honorable, I was not deserving of either man's affection.

But soon enough, my anger turned on Dante. Who was irritable, who was secretive, who went to elaborate lengths to make sure I only got so close to him, and no closer. Who might be lying to me every time I saw him. Who might be betraying me every time he left my house. Who did not love me enough to stay, no matter what shape he took, what challenges he faced. Who would not let me love him as much as I wanted to, which was with all my heart.

The ball game was fun. I sipped Cokes since it was clear by the third inning Matt was going to reach my two-drinks-and-you-stop-driving limit. A man at the end of our row caught a fly ball. Some player hit three home runs in three different innings. The Royals won.

"So that was a great game," he said as I drove his car back to my hotel.

"It was. Great seats, too."

"Good enough for you to invite me up to your room tonight?"

I laughed. "Mmm, good enough for us to sit in the hotel restaurant while you drink enough coffee to sober up."

"I'm not drunk." He leered over at me. "But maybe I should spend the night in your room just in case I'm more hammered than I thought."

There was a Starbucks in the lobby. We bought coffees to go and carried them to my room—where they sat unnoticed on an end table while we collapsed on the bed, in each other's arms. I could not have gotten out a pen and paper and mapped a coherent illustration of the confused thoughts in my head. I was still angry with Dante, angry with myself, sad, aggrieved—and yet excited by Matt's presence. My nerves and my skin instantly responded to his touch. I was thinking it would serve Dante right if I slept with another man. I was thinking it might be the best thing that had ever happened to me, curing me of the daft notion that I could never love anyone but Dante. I wasn't actually thinking at all, just reveling in sensation, longing, and heat.

I wanted to have sex with Matt, I really did.

But something went wrong. He was drunker than I realized, maybe, and not able to maintain an erection. I was too tense, too nervous, and not able to open myself to him fully. We tried a few times, kissed some more, tried again, laughed a little, and ended up curled together face-to-face, half entwined, like friendly puppies full of affection but absolutely no sexual desire.

"This doesn't seem to be working out exactly as I envisioned it," Matt whispered against my cheek.

"I expected something a little different myself," I replied.

"I swear to you, it's not because I'm thinking of my ex-girlfriend."

I choked on a laugh. "I'm not thinking of her, either."

He kissed my cheek. "Can I still spend the night?"

"I think you better," I said. "A man who can't fuck has no business trying to drive."

You'd think we would be shy and awkward around each other in the morning, but we weren't. We made fun of each other's bedhead, we took turns showering, and I even let him borrow my toothbrush, though I ostentatiously threw it away once he was done. "I'll buy a new one," I said.

I was doing one last glance around the room to make sure I hadn't left anything behind when he said, "I keep wanting to ask if I'll ever see you again."

I looked over and smiled. "I don't know," I said. "Do you want to?"

"I don't know," he said.

I kissed him and opened the door. "So I guess we have to keep on living if we want to find out."

"You think that's supposed to be a metaphor for life in general?"

"It *is* life," I said. "It's its own metaphor."

He saw me to my car and I drove away, humming along with a song on the radio.

I haven't seen Matt again, in fact. But I do hear from him now and then. Every time I get a new e-mail address, I send it to him, and he always replies. (He's never changed his old AOL account.) He finds a new girlfriend about every two years. He was engaged once but broke it off. Still not ready, he wrote.

Now and then he asks about Dante. It is a relief, sometimes, to be honest on this topic with someone—well, as honest as I can be with anyone. Still seeing him, I reply. Still mysterious.

Still love him. Still not capable of loving anyone else.

CHAPTER EIGHT

The next two days creak past like an old woman clinging to a walker as she navigates an icy sidewalk. There are no more midnight calls from Dante, there is no communication at all. I don't hear from Christina, either, though I half expect to. Half hope to. I would love another overnight visit from that enchanting little girl.

The workdays amble by, enlivened by conversations and outings with coworkers. Ellen has continued with her campaign to incorporate Kathleen into our little circle of friends, so she has lunch with us the rest of the week. One day we are joined by Marquez and one of the copyeditors; another day Grant Vance tags along with Ellen, Kathleen, and me, something I can only remember happening once before in the past three years. I think Ellen is trying to make a point to Kathleen, though it's a subtle enough one that I'm not sure even *I* get it. I think the message is: *Normal people lead a different life than you do.*

What I want to tell Ellen is: *Give it up. There are no normal people.*

Now and then Ellen is more blunt than sly. On the day that Grant has joined us, we're back at the pizza place, which turns out to be his favorite venue, so he's smiling widely. Well, of course he is. He's Grant. He's always smiling.

I wonder if Ellen has decided to try to rescue Grant from Caroline. How many people does she think she can save at one time? Maybe she hopes to promote a romance between Kathleen and Grant. I actually like the idea, since he seems gentle and she seems like she could use some kindness, but I think there are far too many hurdles in the way—primarily the fact that they're both in love with other people.

Ellen is wearing an electric blue blouse that's tight enough to show the lines of her bra. It looks like she's just had her hair touched up, because it's as blond as a Dolly Parton wig. Still, she looks five times better than I do today in my drab black and washed-out pink outfit, which was all I could find in my closet after I got up late because I failed to set the alarm last night. She's holding a copy of the newspaper, and she rustles the pages of the metro section as she reels off the headlines. "'Priest Accused of Sexually Assaulting Four Boys' . . . 'Bank Robber Holds Ten People Hostage for Eight-Hour Standoff' . . . 'Young Couple Killed in Suburban Park.' I mean, each story is more depressing than the last."

"Yeah, I read about those people being killed," Grant says, his cheerful face drawing into an expression of sympathy. "They were mauled by animals."

"And then, here's another one—" Ellen starts, but Kathleen interrupts.

"What? Mauled by animals? In a suburban park? In *St. Louis*? Are you reading the local news?"

Somewhat grudgingly, Ellen turns back to that story. "Well, it's extreme suburban. Out past Wildwood."

"What kind of animals?" I ask. "I know there are coyotes around here. Foxes. I saw a fox at the Botanical Gardens once."

"Hey, I saw that same fox!" Grant exclaims. "It was cool."

Ellen is frowning at the paper now, clearly annoyed at being side-tracked. "No, not foxes. Not wolves. It says—well, it says they still need to do forensics to determine exactly what kind of creature killed them." She reads a little further into the article. "Also, apparently they were dead for a few days before anyone found them. So there's been some decay. We won't know all the details for a while. Like how they were killed or even when."

"I don't want to know the details," I observe.

Kathleen shivers a little. "I don't, either. That's creepy."

"But we know all we need to know about this article," Ellen continues. "'Father of Three Kills Wife, Children, Self.' Boy, seems like every time you open the paper, there's some version of that story in it."

I realize what Ellen's trying to do, so, feeling clumsy about it, I try to support her. "You always wonder if maybe the women in those situations don't realize they have somewhere else to go," I say. "Like, maybe they have a friend who could help. Or there's a hotline they could call."

Ellen taps the paper. "It gives a number right here. But if I were a woman in an abusive situation, I'd tell a friend. Someone who knew the right resources. Hell, if someone came to *me* when she was in trouble, I know I could help her out."

I can't tell from her expression if Kathleen realizes what Ellen is saying. Her eyes are shadowed; it's clear the tale is affecting her. "I feel sorry for that woman's family," she says in her soft voice. "Her mother and her father. Just think. Last week they had a daughter and three grandchildren. Now they don't. How does something happen so fast? Everything wiped out in a minute."

Grant makes a strangled noise. "Can we talk about something else? I'm never having lunch with you guys again."

Ellen raises her gaze and gives him a considering look. "Sure. Let's talk about something more fun. Didn't I see your name on the wall calendar? Aren't you going on vacation pretty soon?"

Grant's smile returns, a bright curve against his dark skin. "Yes, I am! Italy." He waves his hand at the restaurant around us. "Where I can get *real* pasta, straight from the source."

"Have you ever been there before?" I ask.

"No. I've wanted to go my whole life."

"Who are you going with?" Ellen asks innocently.

He doesn't hesitate, doesn't look self-conscious. Either he's practiced this lie a hundred times, or he's telling the truth. "A buddy from college is meeting me in Rome. He lives in England now, and I haven't seen him since—wow, since grad school."

"Oh, I think I'd rather go to England if I was going to travel," Kathleen puts in. "London—and Stonehenge—and Bath—"

We all look at her in surprise. "Bath?" I repeat.

"Haven't you ever read Georgette Heyer?" she asks. The rest of us shake our heads. "Well, if you'd read Georgette Heyer, you'd want to go to Bath."

"I was in Paris once," Ellen says. "Went with some of the girls from the sorority. We—"

"You were in a *sorority*?" I interrupt. "I thought you'd be the type of person who picketed Greek Row because they were so elitist."

She glares at me. Clearly she was about to make another point and I derailed her. "It was a service sorority," she says stiffly. "We did charity work around the city. Let me finish."

"I was in a frat," Grant offers.

"I thought Greek stuff was stupid," I say. "Though now I wonder if joining a sorority *then* would have helped me with my social network *now*."

"I got my associate's degree at a community college," Kathleen says. "I don't even know if they had sororities."

"Well, *my* sorority went to Paris during the summer between junior and senior year," Ellen says, wrenching back control of the conversation.

"And we're standing in line at the Louvre, waiting to see the *Mona Lisa*, when I hear somebody call my name." She glances around at the three of us, making sure we are ready to be impressed by her revelation. "And who is in line about ten people behind me but the guy I went to prom with in high school! In *Paris*. At the *Louvre*. Isn't that the most amazing coincidence? I hadn't even *thought* of the guy in three years."

It takes me a minute to realize the message she is trying to deliver with this story, and then I get it. She is warning Grant that if he secretly meets Caroline in Rome, he is bound to encounter someone he knows. She is telling him that he can run to the ends of the earth trying to keep his forbidden romance a secret, but the most unexpected coincidence will expose him no matter what precautions he takes.

"Oh, I have a similar story," I say, fluttering my hands to show how excited I am to tell this anecdote. "I was on a plane once, flying back from—Boston, I think. It doesn't matter. There was a guy sitting next to me and we started talking and it was all the usual, where are you from, where do you live, what do you do for a living? And at the time I was working for this little accounting firm that no one had ever heard of, but when I named it, he said, 'Oh, my friend Nancy Kelly works there! Do you know her?' And I said, 'Know her? We *carpool* together! What's your name?'"

I take a sip of my Coke and go on. "So he tells me he's Tom Marcus, and I almost fall out of my seat. You know how, when you spend a lot of time with friends, you start talking about other friends, and pretty soon you feel like you know those other people? Well, Nancy had told me all about Tom, and how he and his wife were going through this nasty divorce. I knew everything about him. *Everything.* I knew he and his wife had been trying for years to have a baby, I knew they'd considered in vitro, I knew his *sperm* count, for God's sake. So then when his wife got pregnant, he started to wonder if the baby was really his, and he had her followed, and it turned out she was having an affair—I knew all of it."

Everyone at the table actually looks sort of amused. "What did you say?" Grant asks. "'Sorry about your boys being such low shooters'?"

Kathleen seems confused; Ellen chokes on a laugh. "No, I just said, 'Oh, you know, I think Nancy might have mentioned your name. I'll tell her I met you.' And then we talked about movies for the rest of the flight."

"See, that's exactly my point," Ellen says. I can tell she's pleased with my contribution. "You never know when you're going to run into someone you know. Or someone who knows *you*, even indirectly."

"When I was in summer school my junior year, three of my friends and I cut class to go see a baseball game," Kathleen says. "And my best friend Audrey? She was this really cute blond and she was wearing this halter top and one of the TV guys kept turning the camera over at her. So she'd wave and kind of do a little dance." Kathleen offers a discreet shimmy. Nothing bounces on her tiny frame, but we get the idea. "They showed the footage on the evening news, and we were all busted. My mom grounded me for the rest of the summer."

Ellen points at her. "See? There's always someone watching or a camera pointed at you. You can never be anonymous in today's world."

It is hard to tell if Grant finds this a sobering thought, but I surely do. By this reasoning, dozens of people could have—might already have—spotted me out with my own secret lover. I might run into Beth at a restaurant, Kathleen and Ritchie in the state park. We could be at a convenience store when it gets robbed and be captured on the security camera, our pictures broadcast to the entire world. *Who's that guy you were with, Maria? Why were you holding hands? Hey, do you have a boyfriend?*

Well, in fifteen years no one has spotted us together—or, if they have, they haven't mentioned it to me. And I have a dozen answers ready, ranging from the partial explanation I had given to Kathleen to an assortment of stories designed to fit particular situations or accusations. *He's an old boyfriend who happened to be passing through town . . . He's this guy I've been seeing for a few weeks. Cute, don't you think? . . . He's someone that a friend at work fixed me up with. I don't think the relationship will go anywhere, though. He's kind of moody.*

Lies are easy. It's the living behind them that's hard.

Finally, finally, it's nearing the end of the third week since Dante disappeared. Over the weekend, I feel my heartbeat quicken, my nerves grow taut. By Monday at work, I am so tightly wound that when someone accidentally bumps into me in the hallway, I actually give a little scream. I'm continually dropping things, spilling things, losing track of conversations. Surely tomorrow, or the day after, or possibly the day after that, Dante will be back.

The birthday of my life
Is come, my love is come to me.

It is important every day to look my best, in case he is at the house waiting for me when I return. Starting on Monday, I set the alarm a half hour early, so I have extra time to style my hair and make up my face. I pick my most flattering clothes, red blouses, purple scarves, tight sweaters that show off my curves.

"You're looking good, girlfriend," Marquez tells me Tuesday afternoon. "Did you get your hair cut? Shop some sales? Fall in love?"

I just laugh and shake my head.

When I go home that night, I know Dante is waiting for me. The front door is open to admit the last of the October sunlight—and to let me know he has arrived. Before I go in, I spend a moment indulging in a frequent fantasy: He has stopped to buy champagne, roses, chocolates, bubble bath. I will push open the door to find a path of petals leading from the foyer to the bedroom, where candles paint the walls with warm highlights. Soft music will be playing in the other room, and Dante will be wearing some Chippendales-style outfit—slick black pants, a bow tie, no shirt. "Darling," he will say, and pull me into a gentle embrace. We will slow dance around the bedroom, our bodies drawing closer and closer, as we desperately try to hold back from that first kiss. Finally, there will be no more resisting. Our arms will tighten around each other, he will sweep me against his chest, and we will fall on each other with an unappeasable hunger.

Well, we've managed that unappeasable hunger part often enough. Perhaps I'm greedy for wanting the romantic prelude, at least once in my life. But Dante doesn't dance. He doesn't bother with sexy clothes—he scarcely even notices if *I've* gone to the trouble of putting on black lace or red silk. And he never calls me darling.

Still, I feel my chest tightening with anticipation as I push wide the door and step inside. "Dante?" I call in a low voice.

No answer, and I do pause to consider that the door might have been opened by a thief instead of a boyfriend. But the living room is tidy and the mail has been dropped on the coffee table—an act that seems too considerate for a burglar. The most likely answer is that he's sleeping. I lock the door behind me and creep to the bedroom.

Yes, there he is, sprawled facedown on the bed, his hair a smear of black across my white pillows. He's naked and smells faintly of soap, so he's been here long enough to take a shower and wash away most traces of *new Dante*. But I can still sense the wild creature in him. His hands are balled around the chenille bedspread, his face—turned so his left cheek lies against the pillow—is clenched in a frown. A long, half-healed gash runs all the way down his right arm, from the round knob of his shoulder to the bulky juncture of his wrist.

Sometime in the past three weeks he has been in a fight. I wonder if there are even worse wounds on his chest. I wonder if he has chosen to sleep this way simply so I won't see them, not at first.

But he won the fight, or at least survived it; he is here now. Moving quietly, so I don't wake him up, I lay aside all of my workaday encumbrances—purse, briefcase, phone. I slip out of my shoes, silently pull off all my clothes except my underwear (which, yes, is black and sheer), and carefully crawl onto the bed beside him. He mutters in his sleep and turns on his side, all without waking up. I fit myself against him, feeling the heat rising from his skin, pressing myself even closer to absorb that warmth with my own body. It is as if I am some kind of hothouse flower that thrives only under a rare sun, and now that solar body has made its reappearance in the skies. I slide one set of fingers under his hard ribs, coil the others in his dense hair; they are like questing plant tendrils, twining around some upthrust support as they strive to get closer to that source of light. Only now that the sun shines on me again do I realize how shriveled I had become; only now that I can open up and bask greedily in his light do I realize how dark the days have been. Only now do I acknowledge how close to death I have been without him.

Once Dante wakes up, we order Chinese food and curl up next to each other on the couch to eat it while we watch TV. We don't bother turning on any lights; the whole house is dark except for the flickering colors emanating from the screen. I love these early hours back together, when he is still sleepy and a little inclined to cling. We are always touching; it is like we both know we're floating, and the only thing that keeps us from crashing to the ground is the weird electrical power we generate when we are skin to skin. So while our hands are busy wielding forks and chopsticks, we intertwine our ankles. When he stands up to carry our dirty plates to the kitchen, he places his hand on my head as if he needs to catch his balance. Eventually, of course, we stretch out side by side on the couch, my back to his stomach, his arms around my body, my hands around his arms.

My fingers encounter the red edge of that recent wound. "Looks like you got into a fight or something," I say in a carefully casual voice.

Dante grunts. "Yeah, but I didn't. Got caught in a windstorm and a branch came down. Gouged my front leg. Hurt like hell, but didn't do any lasting damage."

My eyes widen, an expression he can't see. "Wow. That could have been a lot worse."

He lifts a hand to rap a fist gently against my skull. "Yeah, could've hit me in the head and knocked me right out. But it didn't." His voice holds the equivalent of a shrug. *No use worrying about things that might have happened, things that didn't happen. Just deal with what you're handed and forget the rest.*

"So how far do you think you traveled this time?"

The hand that tapped my head is now stroking my hair. "I don't know, a few hundred miles? Distance seems harder to estimate when I'm in animal shape."

"Going to be getting cold pretty soon," I say, although he obviously knows this. "I hope you shift into something warm and furry."

I hear the grin in his voice. "I always have before."

I turn in his arms and now we are face-to-face. "Like, you know, a malamute. A Saint Bernard. A sled dog."

"Sure, because those are pretty common in Missouri."

I lean in to kiss him. "Common enough. If you take dog shape, come around to the house. I'll put out food for you. Good stuff. Canned stuff. You'll like it."

He responds enthusiastically to the kiss and offers me one of his own. It's clear he's losing interest in conversation as a way to pass the time. "How about scraps from the table?" he murmurs. "You could feed me with your own hands."

"I'm a vegetarian when you're gone," I say primly, or as primly as a person can when someone else's hand is toying with the lace of her bra. "You'd probably prefer the canned goods."

"I'd prefer anything you wanted to give me, baby," he says.

We both giggle, and then we snuggle closer. The kissing continues and intensifies and eventually takes over all my senses. I sit up just long enough to unhook and discard my bra, kick off my panties. The lights from the television play across my body, across Dante's, making us glow like space aliens filled with phosphorescent blood. When I lie back on top of him, his skin is hot enough to reinforce the illusion that he is from another planet altogether. Certainly he is foreign enough, rare enough, to have no permanent place in this world.

We writhe on the couch and make love, and I swear, beneath our laboring bodies, I can feel the spinning of the earth.

CHAPTER NINE

The next two days pass in an odd checkerboard of daytime blur and nighttime clarity. I yawn through my working hours, drowse at my computer, but come alive every night as my drive brings me closer to home. Oh, those evenings aren't perfect. As Dante becomes accustomed to being human again, he grows increasingly irritable. It takes more effort to entertain him, more activity to keep him cheerful.

There are frequent pickup basketball games at the high school about a mile from my house, so we go there Friday evening and find about a dozen men of all ages and races playing a sloppy but raucous game. There are even a couple of women on the pitted asphalt court, tossing balls and sinking baskets. I think they might be from a local college team; at any rate, they're better than about half the men. I huddle on the metal bleachers, glad I wore my heavy coat, and talk idly with a teenage girl whose boyfriend is playing center. She's black and so is he. He works construction by day, delivers pizza in the off hours. She's studying at the community college, hopes to get into nursing school next year.

"Health care, always a good field," I say. This exhausts the topics on which we can manage to converse, and we watch the rest of the game in silence. It's hard to tell who has won, but everyone coming off the court looks sweaty and happy. On the way home, Dante and I stop for ice cream and swap cones halfway through. I consider this an excellent end to a pretty good day and a pretty satisfying week.

I am in no way prepared for the turbulence that Saturday will bring.

It's scarcely eight in the morning when the doorbell rings, often enough to seem frantic, followed by repeated knocking at the door. Adrenaline brings me fully awake, and I'm already afraid as I jump out of bed and throw a robe over my nude body. An urgent summons at this time of day cannot possibly be good news.

Dante, of course, is wide awake and coiled on the bed as if prepared to leap up and fight. He's still fully human, but it is impossible to miss a predator's instincts in the set of his shoulders and the narrowing of his gaze. "What do you want me to do?" he says. "Maybe I should be the one to answer the door."

"No, no, it might be Beth or Sydney," I say, slipping my cell phone in the pocket of my robe. "It might be a neighbor who needs to use the phone. Just stay here. Unless I start screaming."

Using my hands to comb back my tangled hair, I leave him in the bedroom with the door half closed and hurry to open the front door. I'm astonished to find Kathleen on my front porch. Her little blue Aveo is parked in my driveway.

She's crying—sobbing, really—and it looks like she has been doing so for a good couple of hours. Her cheeks are so splotchy that I can't tell if any of the marks were caused by a blow to the face. She's wearing a loose sweatshirt over a turtleneck sweater, so I can't see if she's got marks anywhere else on her body. The air outside is so chilly that my bare feet are instantly cold, and I pull the robe more tightly around me as I hold the door as wide as it will go.

"Kathleen!" I exclaim. "Come in! What's wrong?"

"I have to—Ritchie says—here, take it back," she chokes out as she thrusts a canvas grocery bag in my direction.

I take it automatically; whatever's inside doesn't weigh more than a couple of pounds. "What's—Kathleen, come inside. Let me get you something to drink. What's wrong? What happened?"

"I can't," she replies, her voice so distorted from crying that she doesn't even sound like herself. "I just came to drop that off, I have to go home."

I reach out, take her arm, and tug her into the house. She looks like she wants to resist, but she doesn't know how; she has learned the hard way that gainsaying anyone with a stronger temperament will lead to disaster. She is still sobbing and I'm pretty sure she doesn't know how to stop. She stands there with her arms wrapped around herself, her eyes cast down, and her face a mess of tears and snot. I have never seen anyone so forlorn.

I keep a box of Kleenex on a console by the door, so I hand her one. "What happened?" I ask gently. The answer is obvious, though I try to couch it in the least accusatory terms. "Did you and Ritchie have a fight?"

She nods and swipes at her nose with the tissue. She has to gulp for air twice before she can answer. "He said—he said that we don't need charity—that he doesn't want anyone thinking he can't provide for his family—"

For a moment I am wholly bewildered. "But—who said—what charity?" And then I realize what is actually in the canvas bag I'm still holding. "Oh my God. The computer? The one I let you borrow? That wasn't charity. That was me lending you something I don't even *need*."

Now the words are tumbling out of her mouth. "I know, I know. I tried to tell him that, but he said, *'Bullshit.'* And then he said that I knew it was wrong, that I knew I was wrong to take it from you because I tried to hide it from him. But I wasn't hiding it. I mean, I didn't have it set up in the living room, it was folded up on top of the filing cabinet, but it was out in the open, I wasn't *concealing* it—"

My heart twists with pain for Kathleen, pain and horror at the life she must lead every day. I put my hand on her shoulder. "Kathleen," I say in a quiet voice. "I will certainly take the computer back. That's no problem. But I'm a little worried about you going back to the house while Ritchie is so mad. Can you stay here for a few hours? Or maybe even overnight?" I'm not quite sure what I will do with Dante, but I obviously can't send Kathleen back to her husband's unloving care. "I've got plenty of room, and maybe it would—"

Her drowned eyes have gone wide with fright. She backs away from me, forcing me to drop my hand. "Oh, no, no, that would make it worse. He'll be even madder. He'll think I told you secrets—"

Maybe you should *tell me secrets.* "Kathleen, I don't want to pry but—"

"Don't. Don't ask. I'll be fine."

"Can you at least stay and drink a cup of tea or something? You look too upset to even drive home."

"I—thank you, no, I've got to go." She has put her hand on the doorknob, but now she turns back to give me the saddest look I've ever seen. "Please don't tell anyone at work," she says in a low voice. "Don't tell Ellen."

Of course I plan to call Ellen as soon as the Aveo is out of the driveway. "I think Ellen might be able to help you."

"I don't need help," she says.

On the words, the front door is shoved open so forcibly that it hits Kathleen in the shoulder, and she trips backward with a little cry. A small, fierce, dark-haired man charges inside, eyes glaring and hands clenched as if he's prepared to take on a host of adversaries. I do not need Kathleen's cry of "Ritchie!" to guess who this newcomer is. I catch a glimpse of a rusted red truck parked at the curb in front of my house. It takes no great deductive reasoning to guess that he followed his wife to make sure she did what he told her.

"What the fuck are you still doing here, Kathleen?" he demands. He grabs her by the arm and shakes her while she begs him to *Stop. Stop. Stop.* "I told you just to drop off the damn computer and go, but you been in here five minutes, ten minutes. Talking, talking, talking."

"I didn't say anything, Ritchie!" she protests. With her free hand, she is digging at the fingers clenched around her forearm. "Maria asked if I wanted a cup of tea!"

"Well, you *don't* want tea, you don't want *any* charity from these people. Now get out the door and go *home*."

I am flabbergasted, horrified, and more than a little afraid. I have stood mute and motionless, unable to think how to respond, but now I take a tiny step forward on my frozen feet. "Please, I think everyone's upset. Mr. Hogan, I apologize for offending you by lending Kathleen the computer. Let's just talk calmly for a moment—"

Not letting go of Kathleen, he swivels on the balls of his feet and shoves me hard in the chest. I lurch back and slam into the couch, no doubt earning an impressive bruise on the back of my thigh. "Don't you *even* mess with me," he says in a menacing voice.

Catching my balance, I pull out my cell phone. "I'm calling the police," I say coldly. "And Kathleen had better be here when they arrive."

He flings Kathleen aside, bounds over to me, and knocks the cell phone from my hands. I hear it skitter across the floor and bounce against a wall into the kitchen. "You stupid bitch," he says. "Don't you ever call the cops on me."

I am the only one not surprised when a deep voice from over my shoulder growls, "Get the fuck out of this house."

Ritchie freezes; Kathleen spins around to stare. I sense Dante cross the room in a slow, lethal glide. I am gazing fixedly at Ritchie, so I only see Dante out of the corner of my eye. He is still naked, and he looks magnificent—tall, lean, muscled, marked with the souvenir scars of a dozen fights, all of which he has clearly survived. "Get out," he says, "and leave the girl behind."

Ritchie crouches into an antagonistic pose. God, is he really going to launch himself at Dante? Does he really think he can take on a shape-shifter in a fight? Of course, he doesn't know Dante is a shape-shifter, but surely he must see—everyone must see—how powerful Dante is, how wild. It must be obvious from his face and his eyes that he is used to making the most ruthless of life-and-death decisions.

"This is none of your mix," Ritchie snarls.

"I belong in this house and you don't," Dante says. His eyes never waver from Ritchie's face. "Get out."

"I'm not afraid of you."

Dante takes a step closer. "I will take your fucking head off."

I have backed away, trying to get out of the path of violence, should it come. "Should I call the police?" I ask Dante in a low tone. I really don't know the answer. If cops come, there will be a lot of questions, and I'm not certain Dante's life bears investigation. So if he says no, no matter how bad it gets in here, I won't pick up the phone.

"Not yet," he says. "But if things get too rough, you better." *If Ritchie pulls a gun, if he tries to split Kathleen's head open, if it looks like I'm losing the fight . . .*

Kathleen is still sending wondering glances Dante's way, but she's more focused on her husband. She's stopped crying, which I consider a good thing. Tentatively, she approaches Ritchie and touches his arm. "Don't let's cause any more trouble," she whispers. "Let's just go."

It's then I realize that she has suddenly changed course. She's no longer afraid for herself; she's afraid for Ritchie. She doesn't want Dante to hurt him, and she's pretty sure he could.

But it's a mistake for her to let Ritchie know she thinks he's weaker than another man. All of us realize it at the same time—Kathleen, Ritchie, me. With something like a howl, he snatches his arm away from her, strikes her in the shoulder, and launches himself at Dante.

Kathleen screams; maybe I do, too. The fighting is sudden and brutal. The momentum of Ritchie's body slams Dante into the wall, and causes a framed picture to crash to the floor with a shattering of glass. Dante grunts, wraps his arms around Ritchie, lifts him, and then heaves him against the hardwood floor into the middle of the living room. I hear the crack of Ritchie's head, but before he can react, Dante has raced over and dropped on top of him. He begins pummeling Ritchie in the face. Now Kathleen is shrieking.

Ritchie isn't done yet. He bucks hard, punches Dante in the gut, and bucks again, dislodging him. They roll backward and forward, knocking into the coffee table, each trying to land a telling blow. I see blood streaking down Ritchie's face and welts forming along Dante's arms.

"Stop them! Stop them!" Kathleen is crying. Instead, I dash into the kitchen and scoop up my cell phone, checking to make sure it's still operational. But I'm not ready to call yet. As far as I can tell, Dante isn't in any real danger, and that's all I care about.

Kathleen has run over to me; her face is pleading. "Stop them," she begs.

I shake my head. "I don't know how."

They have rolled again, and once more, Dante is on top. He's got his hands wrapped around Ritchie's throat and now he starts banging Ritchie's head against the floor. The sodden thumping sound is terrifying. After about the fifth concussive knock, Ritchie makes a strangled noise and lies still.

"Ritchie!" Kathleen wails, and skids across the floor to kneel beside him, her hands fluttering around his face and neck. "Oh my God, Ritchie!"

Dante comes wearily to his feet and stares down at Ritchie for a moment. I step close enough to touch his arm. His skin is slick with sweat and a few streaks of blood. Some of it is his, but I think most of it isn't.

"Are you all right?" I ask in a quiet voice. When he nods, I say, even more quietly, "Is *he*?"

Dante nods again. He's panting a little. "I don't think he's even unconscious."

As if to prove Dante correct, Ritchie moans and curls onto his side, holding a hand to his head. Kathleen looks up at me, her expression cold.

"I need ice. And some water to wipe away the blood."

Wordlessly I nod and head to the kitchen to ruin two dishcloths. One I line with ice cubes from the freezer before folding and knotting the edges together; the other I hold under warm water then wring out so it doesn't drip. Dante has followed me.

"What do we do now?" I ask in a low voice. "I'd like to keep the police out of it if I could."

He nods. "Me, too. I think we just send them home."

"They came in two cars. And I don't think Ritchie's in any shape to drive."

He curses under his breath. "All right. She drives him home, you follow in her car, I follow in yours. Then you and I get the hell out of Dodge before he recovers."

I glance at Kathleen, who is smoothing the hair from Ritchie's face, bending down to press a kiss against his battered cheek. "I'm afraid for her," I whisper. "As soon as he's feeling good enough, he's going to beat the hell out of her again."

His gaze has followed mine. "That's Kathleen, I take it," he says wryly. "We weren't formally introduced."

"That's her."

"Well," he says with a certain satisfaction, "he won't be hitting *anyone* for a while. Pretty sure I broke his arm."

Part of me is fiercely glad to hear this. It will be good for Ritchie to know how awful it feels to be beaten up by someone you are too small or too helpless to defend against. Part of me is worried. I cannot help but think this humiliation will make him even more dangerous. More dangerous to Kathleen.

"Maybe we should take him to a hospital," I say.

"We'll let Kathleen make that decision."

I give him a look of protest. "She's too afraid of him to make those kinds of decisions."

He returns his attention to me. "She's chosen him," he says gently. "She's still with him. She's making *some* decisions every day."

I want to say, *The only reason she doesn't leave is that she fears for her life.* But I know that isn't true. It might be one of the reasons she doesn't leave. But she loves him. She wants him to love her back. That's the real reason she stays.

"Are you sure you're all right?" I say instead. "It looked like he got in some nasty blows."

He nods and puts a hand to his jaw, then his groin. "Yeah. Hurts like hell. But nothing broken."

I sigh. I'm still holding the ice-filled towel in my hands, and now my fingers are as cold as my toes. "And to think I'm always worried about you when you're gone. I worry about what terrible things might happen to you when you're—you know. Different." I glance at Kathleen and Ritchie. They are too far away to hear me, but I want to be circumspect anyway. "And now it turns out that you only *really* get hurt when you're just hanging around my house, not looking for any trouble."

He smiles, but I think his expression is sad. "That's because there is no safety, Maria. Just living is dangerous. Wherever you are and whatever shape you take."

I push to my tiptoes to kiss him on the mouth. "I'm glad you were here," I whisper. "Now get some clothes on so we can drive them home."

He glances down at his body, as if, until this moment, he didn't realize he was still naked. "Right. I'll be out in five minutes, and we'll go."

It is only as I bend down to hand the dripping towels to Kathleen that I realize I, too, need to dress before we leave the house. I have been so focused on everyone else that I have, for a moment, completely forgotten about myself.

Kathleen does not speak to me or Dante as Dante carries Ritchie to the rusty red truck and none too gently settles him inside. Ritchie is fully conscious now, but in bad shape. His head lolls back against the headrest and he moans as Dante jostles his broken right arm. Kathleen climbs into the driver's seat and then reaches out the window to hand me the keys to her Aveo.

"You might want to take him to an urgent care center," I suggest. "I think he should have that arm looked at."

"Let's get the cars home first," she says in a clipped voice.

We form a strange procession, me following the truck, Dante in my Saturn following the Aveo. I have only been to Kathleen's house once before, when I dropped off some insurance papers, so I would have had trouble locating it on my own. This makes me wonder how she found my place. Then I remember that Ritchie gave her a GPS system for Christmas last year, since she was getting lost so often. I think, *There's another reason to hate technology.*

She does not want our help getting Ritchie inside the house. She does not want my repeated solicitations, and I cannot bring myself to apologize. Dante did nothing wrong, after all; he defended himself against an attack by a home intruder. It occurs to me she might be just as embarrassed as she is angry, but, in any case, she refuses to let down her guard. I sigh, give her the keys, and climb into the Saturn next to Dante.

He hadn't bothered to cut the motor, so we are out of the driveway, out of the neighborhood, in seconds flat. "Well! I've worked up an appetite," he says brightly. "Let's go for breakfast."

The rest of the weekend passes in an oddly companionable manner. There is none of the restlessness and bickering that I usually associate with the later parts of Dante's visits, as if we are trying to build up walls of irritation between us to cushion the blow of the upcoming separation. Instead, we are affectionate, clingy, just a little spooked, as if we witnessed a tornado or barely survived a plane crash. As if we looked straight at the bony face of Death and saw him watching us with a hard, considering stare. We never have much time together, and we always know it could be cut short, but we seldom have such tangible reminders of how frail our existence is. We are kind to each other, these last few days. We remember we're in love.

Naturally, I have tried to call Ellen to tell her the story and to get her take on what to do next, but she doesn't answer her phone. I remember that she had plans to be out of town over the weekend, visiting her sister, I think, and she won't be back until late Sunday night.

"Come in early Monday," I say in the last voice-mail message I leave her. "I'll tell you the whole story then."

So Monday morning I leave Dante half asleep in my bed, kissing him hard on the mouth before I step out the door at seven. I meet Ellen at the office. As soon as I say, "It's about Kathleen," she suggests we find a different venue for our conversation, and we head to the local McDonald's for coffee.

As you'd expect, she's disturbed by the tale, but not even remotely surprised. We debate whether or not I should have called the police to have them check on Kathleen's house as the weekend progressed and Ritchie recovered, but we both decide it would be hard to predict when he might gather his strength for retribution. "I'll talk to her, but I don't have much hope that she'll listen to me," Ellen says in a brooding voice. "But she has to know that there are options. She has to know that if he turns violent, she has somewhere to go."

I blow on my coffee to cool it. "I'm afraid she'll never speak to me again," I say. "It's not my fault and I know that, but she– She'll blame me somehow."

"Well, she's in an impossible situation," Ellen says. "And she has to blame someone."

Ellen has finished her first cup of coffee and gone for her second one before she brings up the topic that I knew would be unavoidable. "So let's get to the only part of this story that includes an element of novelty," she says. "You, and the man who was sleeping in your bedroom when Ritchie arrived."

"You're like a tabloid reporter," I say. "Always looking for smut."

"Honey, I don't have to look for smut. It's always there."

I make an irritable gesture. "Anyway, why is it *you* never talk about your personal life? Why are you always asking questions but never giving out details?"

Ellen laughs. She has two ex-husbands, both of whom she gets along with so well that they come to her house for Thanksgiving and Christmas, and for the past decade or so she's been dating an auto plant supervisor named Henry. They each maintain their own houses and, as far as I can tell, only get together a few times a month. I've met him a dozen times. He's a big guy, heavyset, with a thick walrus mustache and merry blue eyes. He gives the impression of being friendly, capable, and easily amused by the world, but I've always thought he could deck someone with a single blow if he felt the situation called for discipline. "My life is so boring that insomniacs could hire me to come talk about it and they'd fall straight to sleep," she says. "But ask me anything you want. I've got nothing to hide."

"*I* am not interested in all the intimate details of my friends' lives, thank you very much."

She curls her fingers impatiently in a motion that means *give*. "C'mon, tell me. It's been obvious for a while that there's a guy in your life—"

I almost choke on my coffee. "Obvious? *Obvious?* Are you kidding? I never talk about my—my romantic encounters."

She rolls her eyes. "Yeah. Every few weeks you glow like a lava lamp, and anyone who's ever had sex knows you're sleeping with someone you're pretty hot for. And then you mope around for a few days, so it's clear you've broken up. And then you're happy again, so you're back together. I figured you'd talk about it when you wanted to talk about it—but I've decided now's the time."

Oddly, even though I was expecting the interrogation, I haven't put much energy into preparing a cover story. Even now I'm torn between my usual evasions and a strange longing to tell the truth. Share the story. Make the burden easier to bear.

"Well," I say. "His name is Dante."

She makes a face. "I can already tell this isn't going to end well."

I give her an indignant look. "It's a great name!"

"For a cat, maybe. Go on."

"His name is Dante, I've known him since college, we've been involved off and on for years. But he's—mysterious."

She knows how old I am, so she does the math. "You've known him for about fifteen years and he's still mysterious? Honey, any man I've known longer than six months is so predictable I can tell you when he's going to fart and when he's going to shit."

"Well, Dante's different."

She rests her chin in her hand. "How so?"

I give her essentially the story I gave Matt all those years ago. "He travels a lot. When he's gone, I can't really get in touch with him. He's not particularly forthcoming about his job or his circumstances. I only know about him what he wants me to know."

Ellen's eyes are huge. "Well, now, you could hardly have opened up a cookbook and come up with a better recipe for disaster!" she exclaims. "Next you're going to tell me you've allowed him to invest all your money for you and put his name on the title to your house."

I can't help a chuckle. "Nope. In fact, I have access to *his* bank accounts when he's gone, and he trusts me to handle bills and various transactions for him."

This crinkles her forehead. "Have you ever met his parents?"

"They're dead, but I know his brother and sister. I babysat for his niece the other day, in fact."

Her frown deepens. Clearly this description doesn't fit her notion of a con man or felon. "Do *they* seem normal?"

I have to laugh again. "Define 'normal.'"

"Do they have jobs and houses and stuff?"

"Christina does. William—I don't know."

"Do you think they're gunrunners? Drug dealers? *Slavers?*"

"God, no. I think they're—eccentric." I can't say, *I think they're harmless*, because I remember Dante beating the shit out of Ritchie, and I know the word doesn't apply. "I'm pretty sure I don't have anything to fear from them," I say lamely.

She tilts her head to one side. "There's more to this story than you're telling," she says with conviction.

"A little."

"But you're not afraid. You don't think you're in danger."

"Right. I'm really not."

"And the sex is good?"

Again, she's caught me taking a sip of coffee, and again I nearly choke. "Ellen!"

"Well, it would almost have to be to put up with this—mystery crap."

"The sex is good." I shrug and set the coffee down. "I love him. I've loved him for a long time. I've adjusted to his lifestyle."

She's regarding me shrewdly still. "You realize that anytime someone has secrets, there's usually a cold day of reckoning when those secrets are revealed. You could find yourself in love with a terrible man."

I nod. "I could. I don't think so, but I could."

"Well." She drums her fingers on the table. "It's no worse than I thought."

I laugh at her. "Don't worry about *me*," I say. "You've got enough on your plate trying to fix Kathleen and Grant."

She sighs. "Neither of whom, I would guess, can be fixed." She glances at her watch and pushes to her feet. "Shit, we're going to be late. Come on. Let's go see how Kathleen's doing."

I am convinced Kathleen doesn't want to lay eyes on me, so I send Ellen to reconnoiter while I go straight to my office. Ellen appears in my doorway about ten minutes later.

"She looks okay," she reports. "Tense, you know, but not like she's been hit in the face recently. I asked her how her weekend was and she just said fine."

"Should I go talk to her?"

"Sure, why not?"

But I don't have the courage to try until late in the day. At noon, I avoid both the lunchroom and the group outing so I don't accidentally run into Kathleen. Whenever I have to use the bathroom, I skulk around in the hallway first, trying to determine if she's already in the ladies' room. It's no surprise the day drags on as if it is sixteen instead of eight hours long.

Finally, about ten minutes before closing time, I slink to her corner of the building. I've already seen our boss leave early, and I know there are no other desks within hearing range. Unless Ellen is lurking somewhere nearby—a real possibility—we should be able to talk in privacy.

She is hunched over her desk, a pencil in hand as she scans a document. Maybe a piece of correspondence she is editing before typing a clean copy; our boss is a notoriously bad speller.

"Kathleen," I say.

She looks up. Her face is somber, her expression is closed, but at least she meets my eyes. "What," she says, no invitation in her inflection.

I step a little closer. I've gotten over my aversion to apologizing. "Look—I'm not sure what to say. I'm sorry. I wish—I'm just so sorry."

She nods. "I'm sorry, too."

That's more than I expected. "I wouldn't blame Ritchie for telling you that you should never speak to me again, but I hope you won't be mad at *me* for what happened," I say. I think Ritchie's an asshole, but I think she's more likely to talk to me if I take a different approach. "I know Dante overreacted. But he—"

"Do you think so?" she interrupts, wholly surprising me. "A strange man comes into your house and starts calling you names and shoves you and looks like he might punch you—and you think your boyfriend overreacted? I think he did what any man should have done. He protected the woman he loves."

I file that away under *statements I don't necessarily agree with*. Generally speaking, I don't think I need to be protected, but I have to admit I was glad Dante was in the house that morning. "Still, it got out of hand. I hope—I hope Ritchie's feeling okay today."

She shakes her head. "I took him to the doctor. Had a cast put on his arm. He won't be able to work for a couple of weeks, so he's mad about that."

Now I examine her face a little fearfully. As Ellen said, there are no new bruises—visible ones, anyway. "I hope he didn't take his frustration out on *you*."

She shakes her head again. "He didn't feel well enough. He's still got a terrible headache and he's kind of dizzy. Doctor said it was a mild concussion. So he's been pretty sweet to me, actually. Letting me take care of him."

I'm not sure if the appropriate response is *That's nice* or *Run while you can*. So I answer indirectly. "Listen, I know it's awkward, but I hope you and I can still be friends. It wasn't my fault, it wasn't your fault—"

She lifts her eyes and gives me a long sad look. There is so much heartache in her expression that for a moment I just stare. Who could carry such grief and devastation around inside, all the time, and not be ground down to dust and ashes? "I don't know, Maria," she says in her soft voice. "I'm not sure I'm meant to have friends."

"*Kathleen!* Don't say that! Everyone is meant to have friends. You're—I get the impression Ritchie is kind of possessive"—*there's an understatement*—"but it's not good for anyone to be too isolated, too dependent on one other human being. You have to have friends. People to help you through the rough times." I take a deep breath. "And I think recently there have been a lot of rough times."

She shrugs and glances down at her document again. "Yeah. Well, who doesn't have it hard?" she says. "I have to finish this before I go, Maria. See you tomorrow."

Slowly, reluctantly, I walk away, glancing back twice before I'm around the corner and she's out of sight. The conversation has unsettled me, even though it went better than I had expected. Maybe because I was braced for anger—hoped for anger—because anger showed a flash of fighting spirit, a certain will. I had not prepared myself for the blank despair of someone who feels completely and utterly trapped.

I remember something my mother said years ago when one of our neighbors woke up one morning and found her husband dead in his car, a suicide note beside him on the seat. It turned out he'd been embezzling from his company and he knew he was about to be exposed, and he didn't know how to fix his mistake or how to face the consequences. *People always find a way out, when there's no way out,* my mother had said. *They run away. They kill somebody. They kill themselves. People always find a way to leave an untenable situation.*

The implication, of course, was that those desperate measures are always drastic. Effective, but disastrous. Even those who come out alive are horribly scarred.

I know Kathleen is in an untenable situation. How will she get out?

I'm so depressed by my conversation with Kathleen that I can't bring myself to whip through traffic to speed home before Dante leaves. Sunday was haunted by the air of good-bye that usually hangs over us the day before he vanishes, and I know chances are good that the house will be empty when I get home. That knowledge adds to my general sense of misery, but my limbs are too leaden, my mind too numb, to allow me to careen down the roads with my usual missing-Dante mania.

So I am both shocked and dumbly grateful when I arrive at the house and see the door standing open, a light on through the window. Hope lends me strength and I jump out of the car and rush inside.

"Dante?" I call.

He sweeps around the corner from the kitchen, catching me up in a ferocious hug, kissing me till I'm breathless. "I have about an hour, I think," he mutters into my hair. "Then I've got to go."

That's cutting it close for him; he likes to be far outside the city limits before he feels the changes working their way through his body. But oh God, he is kissing me with a hungry desperation; his hands are fumbling at my clothes, trying to push them out of his way. There is something wild in the flavor of his mouth, different in the touch of his fingers. It is like his skin has already roughened, his blood has already heated up. He has not transformed yet, his body is all human, but some internal essence has recalibrated, some element in his body has already alchemized.

I feel my own blood transform, my own cells react. I am as wild as he is. I kick off my shoes, rip the fabric of my blouse as I impatiently discard it. I cannot get naked soon enough, cannot wait to feel his hard, sleek body against mine. We do not make it to the bedroom or even bother dropping to the floor. We clutch and claw at each other, grunting with an animalistic pleasure as we join together and frantically couple. He is gripping my shoulders so tightly that I feel his nails break my skin; I don't want to look, in case those nails have already lengthened into talons or claws. But I am holding him just as close, grinding against him, my open mouth gasping against his skin as if it is *him* I need to breathe in, and not unsatisfactory air. He cries out as he climaxes inside me, and I squeeze him more tightly between my legs, not willing to allow him to slip away from me just yet. He pumps a few more times and my own orgasm shakes me, though I muffle my reaction with my lips pressed against his chest. We are both panting, gulping for air; I can feel the trembling of my legs as my body remembers what the rest of its parts are for.

Suddenly the air around me feels cold, and I cling to Dante for warmth. His embrace has gentled, though he is holding me just as closely. He kisses the top of my head over and over.

"I have to go," he says. "But I couldn't leave yet. Without seeing you again. Without–" He kisses me again.

Now it's not just my legs that are shaking. I'm shivering so much that I'm practically palsied. "I know," I say, the words chattering out of my mouth. "I'm so glad you waited—I'm so glad you were here—but go. Go. I don't want you to be anywhere near civilization when the transformation comes."

"I love you, Maria," he says, his voice more guttural than I am used to, and kisses me hard on the mouth. He breaks free and scoops up a pair of running pants that he must have left at the edge of the kitchen floor. Apparently that's all he plans to wear; he must expect the change to occur too quickly for him to need shoes or a shirt. His pack is at the door and, of course, his key is already around his neck. "I really do. I'll be back as soon as I can."

He kisses me and then he is out the door. I snatch up a coat and run after him, but, as if my lawn has been protected by some invisible electric fence that will incinerate me if I touch it, I stutter to a halt right before the grass gives way to asphalt. Dante is already loping down the street, bent over, as if at any moment he expects to drop into a crouch or go to all fours. It's at least an hour until full dark, but shadows are already bunching up along the road, thrown by houses and garages and old-growth oaks. For a few moments I can make out the pale texture of his bare torso as he flits in and out of those dark patches, and then he disappears. I don't know if he's merely gone too far for my eyes to follow him, or if he has that suddenly transmogrified to another shape, another creature. I do know that, for the first time since I've met him, I absolutely and unquestioningly believe that he has always told me the truth about who and what he is.

I stand there, staring at the empty roadway until night falls, until I am so cold that I can't feel anything, not my frozen feet, not my wet cheeks, not my broken heart.

CHAPTER TEN

As always, it takes me a couple of days to get past my systemic shock at Dante's absence. Ellen eyes me with a knowing look on Tuesday and says, "I suppose he's run off again?" but she doesn't press it further. No one else notices or, at any rate, says anything.

Relations with Kathleen remain tentative and awkward, though Ellen is doing her best to mend *that* situation as well. She makes sure both of us are included in some group lunch outings, so we can appear to be interacting without actually having to speak to each other. I drop by Kathleen's desk a couple of times a day with flimsy excuses, and she always responds with a polite smile; but it's clear that the walls she maintains with everyone else are back in place when I'm around. I had been far from certain I wanted to be Kathleen's best friend, so it's ironic I miss her now that she's pulled away. I chalk it up to just more proof of the contrariness of the human heart.

But there are other people who are plenty happy to spend time with me. The day after Dante leaves, I call my cousin Beth.

"Hey—do you still want to go to Chicago?" I ask.

"Do I ever!" she exclaims. "Can we go now? Tonight? I'll pick you up at seven."

I laugh. "Well—I wasn't thinking *quite* so soon. But I could go this weekend, if you can be that spontaneous. Or next weekend. Probably not the weekend after that." *Because Dante might be back.*

"Let me check with Mom and Sydney to see if one of them can keep Clara. Can you take Friday off? Or Monday?"

I've been hoarding my last remaining vacation days, but suddenly I feel reckless. I'll call in sick later in the year if I need more time off. "Sure."

"Great! I'll get back to you by tomorrow."

It seems all the stars have aligned, because Aunt Andrea can keep Clara, Beth's friend with a condo on Michigan Avenue will let us stay at her place for free, and I have more vacation days than I had thought. As office manager, Ellen is the one who monitors these things, so it's possible she's tweaked something in my favor, but it turns out I've been given credit for a Saturday that I came into the office to straighten out an accounting mess.

"So have fun on the Magnificent Mile," she tells me.

And we do.

It's cold in Chicago, of course—probably twenty degrees colder than in St. Louis, which means the temperature hovers around the freezing mark—and everyone is bundled up in winter accessories. We don't see sunshine the entire time we're there; the sky just frowns down at us, a face full of puffy gray cheeks surrounding the bleary white eye of the sun. Between the skyscrapers, we occasionally glimpse the dark bruise of Lake Michigan, a flat expanse of water that looks as limitless as an ocean. Twice in three days—during this last weekend in October—it snows, but it's only a halfhearted effort. Nothing sticks to the dirty pavement or the marvelously varied architecture. This is a city that shakes off all hindrances and just plows forward.

We fill the days shopping and eating, the evenings in the condo sipping margaritas and watching video on demand. We agree it's been the best vacation ever.

"Let's call our offices and say we won't be back for a week," Beth suggests on Saturday night.

She's probably not serious, but I think about it anyway. Dante won't be home for at least another week, and if he finds himself in human form for an hour or two in the next few days, he knows to call my cell phone. But I make a face. "Not enough vacation days."

Beth sighs. "And surely Clara will have driven Mom crazy by tomorrow night, let alone *next* Monday. I suppose we have to go back."

Still, we stretch out the visit as long as we can, not starting our return trip until about four in the afternoon on Sunday. We're not even halfway home before dark gathers around us and turns Highway 55 into a long, snaking tunnel intermittently illuminated by headlights. Beth has brought her *Honeymoon in Vegas* soundtrack, while I've contributed my old New Kids on the Block CDs, and we sing all the way home. I can't help thinking that it was a more successful weekend than the one before.

It's past ten before Beth drops me off, and I bang a few of my shopping bags against the door frame as I enter the house. Once I've checked to make sure no murderers are hiding in the closets, I turn on the computer to read e-mail and then play back the messages on the answering machine. All of them are junk calls except the one from my mother asking me to let her know when I get back.

"Hey, Mom, sorry to call so late, but we didn't want to leave Chicago until we absolutely had to," I say when she answers the phone. I can tell by her sleepy voice that I've woken her up.

A yawn breaks her next words. "Did you have a good time?"

"It was great. We have to do that more often. How was *your* weekend?"

We chat for about ten minutes, catching up. While she talks, I scroll through the last three weeks' worth of data on the Caller ID, mostly deleting numbers. But just as we hang up, I get to one that catches my attention. It's a 636 area code, just like mine, which means the call was made from somewhere in the St. Louis area, outside the boundary of Highway 270. The number's unfamiliar, which it would be since in place of the name of the caller, the unit just spells out the word PAY PHONE.

Who would be calling me from a pay phone in the western suburbs?

I check the date then calculate when the call came in. Two and a half weeks ago . . . at 1:47 in the morning.

Oh. That was when Dante phoned during the one hour he was human.

At first I smile, remembering the conversation, but then my brows draw together. I had asked him—I think I remember asking him—where he was calling from, and he'd said, "Sedalia, I think." I drop onto my desk chair, flick the computer to life, and do a quick Google search on Sedalia's area code. It turns out to be 660.

He had not called from Sedalia, after all.

I sit there for a few more minutes, still frowning, still turning the matter over in my head. It doesn't mean much, of course. He has always told me—he said it again during this most recent visit, in fact—that it is difficult to keep track of geography and distances when he is in another shape. *Sometimes I think I've traveled for miles, and I'm just a county away. Other times I don't think I've gone too far, but when I turn human and find a highway sign, it turns out I'm in Colorado.* He could honestly have thought he was in Sedalia—he might even have *been* in Sedalia earlier in the week—he might simply have been confused.

Or he might have been lying. If he'd been calling from a 636 number, he'd have been nearby, close enough to come to my door. He might have thought that's what I would have begged for, if he'd told the truth. He didn't want to argue.

Maria, it would take me an hour to get there and by then I'd be ready to transform again. It wouldn't be worth it.

But it would be worth it to me! Tell me where you are! I'll come get you!

He knew he only had time for the call, not the physical connection. The lie was to spare us both.

Still, it makes me unhappy. It brings some of the old bitterness to the surface, the worry that he does not love me as much as I love him, does not so breathlessly treasure our hours together.

It also makes me suspicious. If he lied about this, what else does he lie about? What else have I believed because I have been unable to disprove it? How stupid have I been?

I am exhausted Monday morning, since I wasn't able to sleep Sunday night. I was both too keyed up from the trip to be able to relax and too fixated on the question of Dante's phone call from not-Sedalia.

Ellen takes one look at me and says, "Boy-howdy, somebody had too much fun over the weekend."

I am grateful that she instantly ascribes my peaked condition to overindulgence instead of romantic moping. "Remind me never to travel with my cousin again," I mumble.

"Nah, it's good for you to be hungover a few times once you're past thirty," she says. "Reminds you not to mourn your lost youth."

I get more sleep as the week goes on, but I don't feel much more cheerful, and the fact that the weather has gotten sharply colder doesn't help my mood. I keep thinking about Dante and then trying to think about something else. It's almost a relief to be at work all day because at least I'm forced to focus my mind on something productive.

Through some misunderstanding about times and dates, I end up having lunch alone with Grant Vance on Wednesday. I can tell he's not thrilled by the arrangement. "I could see if Turtle wants to come with us," he offers.

"Turtle?"

He grins. "New guy. His name is Tuttle, but he's bald and he always wears turtleneck shirts that he hunches into like he's trying to make his head disappear." Grant demonstrates by scrunching up his shoulders, shortening his neck, and then peering around with big, blinking eyes. He does not look remotely like a turtle—more like an Ewok—but I get the general idea.

"Sure, if you want to."

But Turtle can't join us, and I'm too apathetic to care if Grant is uncomfortable dining alone with me, so off we go to Pizzeria Plus. He's willing to split a large veggie pizza, extra olives, and the gesture makes me put a little more effort into being companionable.

"So! How's the trip planning going?"

"Great! I've got my tickets and my friend is looking for places to stay."

"And I assume you have your passport already."

He grins. "Got it last December. I knew I was getting to Italy one way or another this year—even if I had to go by myself."

I take a second piece of pizza. "I've never been to Italy," I say. "I've hardly been anywhere."

This is my own fault, of course. Travel is expensive and overseas travel can really tax the budget, but even a middle-income wage earner like me should be able to save her pennies and find a great deal to make it to Europe once in her life. But I haven't wanted to go without Dante. And how can you take a shape-shifter across the ocean?

Well, I suppose you could. It wasn't like we'd be traveling by boat and he'd be changing shapes a couple of times before we got to the opposite shore. Assuming no unfortunate weather or mechanical delays, you could travel from Lambert Field to Heathrow in nine or ten hours, even allowing for plane changes at O'Hare or JFK. Human Dante could fly with me in both directions, and Animal Dante could explore a new continent if he got the urge.

I even proposed this once, back when his stays in human form were much longer. Back when we had a two-week window or better. *Plenty of time to get there and back,* I'd said. *We'll make it a short trip. I just want to see London.*

He wouldn't risk it. *I don't always know what's going to trigger the change. What if it's air pressure? What if it's the chemical composition of the water? What if it's stress? I don't want to be stuck in England because I've changed and I can't change back.*

I had tried to respond lightheartedly. *That's okay. If you're a dog, I'll bring you back with me. I'll buy you an expensive carrier and pay whatever they charge to transport a pet.*

And what if I change in the belly of the plane? What if they quarantine me and I change back to human shape while I'm in some kind of cage?

I wasn't used to thinking of Dante as fearful. Usually he was the one who shrugged off any notion of risk and made fun of me when I worried. But clearly the thought of being out of his environment, away from familiar haunts, out of control, left him nervous and cold. We would never be traveling to Europe together, that was certain.

And I just didn't want to be that far from Dante.

While I've been musing, Grant has been talking. "I've been to Mexico a few times, and Canada—Does that count as a foreign country?—but never across the ocean."

"Are you worried about speaking the language?" I ask. "Or does your buddy know Italian?"

"No and no," he says. "But I've been practicing. I can order stuff off the menu and say things like 'I want another beer, please.'"

Our waitress has come by to see if we'd like refills on soda. She's got curly dark hair and deep olive skin; I imagine she'd be right at home stomping grapes in the old country. "You're studying Italian?" she says cheerfully. "I learned from my grandpa. Say something to me."

Flashing his easy smile, Grant complies. The only word I catch and think I can translate is *amore*. Is he telling this stranger that he's going to Italy with his true love?

"Buon!" she replies and rattles off some complicated sentence that has Grant laughing and waving his hands.

"I didn't get a word of that," he says.

"I was telling you to make sure you eat gelato every day," she says. "I like lemon best."

They talk Italian food for a few more minutes while I consume another slice of pizza. When I have Grant's attention again, I quiz him for additional details on his trip just to have something to talk about. We then debate ideas for the office costume party Ellen has decreed we will hold on Halloween, which is just a couple of days from now. Everyone has to come as some kind of animal.

"So here's the question," I say. "Do you come in a costume that reflects who you *are* or who you're *not*? If we're coming as who we are, you could be a big teddy bear."

He looks affronted. "You think I'm a teddy bear?"

"Is that an insult to the masculine ego? I thought it was a compliment."

"Well, I'd rather be a grizzly bear. Something a little more powerful."

"I think I'll come as a *hibernating* bear," I say. "That way I can sleep all day and no one will bother me."

"Ellen should be a Jack Russell terrier or something that never sits still," Grant says. "That woman has more energy than anyone I've ever met."

We toss out more ideas. *Bob in accounting would make a great snake. Louise in creative should be a cat.*

"Caroline could be a hawk," I say, as if inspired. I'm watching him covertly. "Elegant and dangerous."

"Yeah, or—oh, hey! Marquez could be a, what are those things? They're big and kind of pear-shaped and they don't move too fast. Tapir?"

"Who the hell knows what a tapir looks like?" I demand. He hadn't even reacted to the Caroline comment.

He flashes that smile again. "Saw it on some nature program."

"Well, I don't want to dress up at all," I say, my voice grumpy. "But I know Ellen will insist."

"I think it will be fun."

"You think everything's fun."

"Pretty much." He shrugs. "Why be unhappy?"

Because the world is full of wordless suffering and broken hearts and absent or inconstant lovers. "No reason," I say. I rifle through my purse and pull out a twenty; Grant hands me a matching bill. "Let me go get change."

Our waitress is temporarily working the cash register, so she loads me down with ones and fives. "What did my friend say to you in Italian?" I ask casually.

She looks blank for a second until she remembers. "'I love Italian food. Can your grandfather recommend a restaurant?'" She drops four quarters in my hand. "He didn't say grandfather right, but I didn't bother to correct him."

I am still laughing as I leave a tip on the table. Grant is already at the door, more than ready to go back to the office. Either Grant doesn't have any secrets or he's even better than I am at concealing them. No matter which, I like him even more.

The houses in my neighborhood are widely spaced, most of them sitting on an acre or more of land, some of them set so far back from the road that when trees and shrubs and flower beds are heavy with their summer finery you can scarcely see them through the greenery. We don't get many trick-or-treaters here, but even so, a few of the residents have dressed up their houses for Halloween. After work I stroll down the streets for a half hour, enjoying the displays. One house—with a huge front lawn surrounded by a pointy black wrought-iron fence—has turned its grassy yard into a zombie cemetery. Mummy-wrapped heads break the ground in front of a dozen tombstones; at other sites, hands and feet appear to be kicking and clawing their way to the surface. A few shambling creatures with glowing eyes and outstretched hands are posed on the front porch and under the bare branches of a massive oak. When I walk by, the motion of my body triggers an eerie, menacing laugh.

Not sure this is a house I would walk up to, demanding candy, if I was a small child.

Just as compelling as the artificial displays are the natural decorations of the season. About half the trees still have their leaves, some green, some brown, some flaming with shades of autumn. I am fascinated by the ones that have lost a good portion of their red or yellow leaves to a rainstorm earlier in the week; these lie around their trunks in great uneven circles, their edges fading and curling so that they present a rippled appearance. The leaves on the ground mirror back the colors still on the branches, so that each tree looks as if it is standing in its own individual reflecting pool.

I keep walking and admiring the sights until it's almost fully dark. As I return to my house, there's just a touch of red delineating the horizon line, and the sky overhead is an intense blue that is slowly corrupting into black. The moon is full, yellow, and low in the sky. It looks too heavy to rise—more likely to sink as if drowning under greedy waters. The first evening star glitters, cold and haughty, against the gathering darkness. A faint wind stirs a sound like ghostly footsteps into the fallen leaves. I can't help shivering a little and hurrying the last few yards back home.

There is a shape sitting on the sidewalk leading to my house.

Surprise and uneasiness bring me to a full stop. A moment's study tells me it's a dog, and a rather large one. In the insufficient combination of moonlight, porch light, and streetlight, it looks all white except for its nose; even its eyes are pale, possibly a sky blue. It's watching me with a fixed stare that seems oddly intent. My breath catches; I go a step closer, though I am a little afraid.

"Dante?" I ask in a low voice.

The creature doesn't respond, just continues to watch me. Moving slowly, I drop to my knees on the hard sidewalk and extend my right hand. The dog comes to its feet and cautiously approaches, sniffing at my fingers. In the uncertain light, I can see that it's too thin and it has a few partially healed wounds along its ribs. They don't correspond to anything I've seen on Dante's body, but that doesn't mean they couldn't have been acquired sometime in the past week.

I don't see a key around the dog's neck, no small pack of supplies. Both could have been lost in a skirmish, in a mishap.

Neither do I see a collar or anything to mark this dog as domesticated. If it's not Dante, I need to be careful. There's no telling what its temperament is, what diseases it might be carrying.

"Who are you, huh?" I say as the dog's tongue finally darts out to lap across my knuckles. I carefully reach up with my other hand to scratch the top of the white head. The fur is matted and dirty; it's been weeks since this animal has been bathed or groomed. Less likely to be Dante, then. "Are you hungry? Are you thirsty?"

The dog closes its mouth and watches me again, settling back on its haunches. Its eyes are so bright, so focused, so expressive. I almost believe it has the ability to talk, or at least communicate clearly.

Could this be some other shape-shifter? Maybe it's not Dante, but a wild friend of his—with a common secret? Might Dante have told this person, over some shared campfire late at night, that my house would be a place of safety and haven should the need ever arise? My skin prickles with another thought. Is this the shape William takes when he's out roving? Could it even be Christina?

"I'm going to get some food," I say in a quiet voice. "You stay right here."

I step calmly until I'm inside the door, then I practically run to the kitchen. I don't have dog food, of course, and I don't know how my visitor would feel about leftover salad and pizza. But I keep thinking about those thin legs, those bony haunches, those sad eyes. This is a creature in desperate need of nourishment.

I throw some frozen hamburger in the microwave, fill a big mixing bowl with water, and dig through my closet to find a stained old comforter that still has plenty of puff to it. I flip the meat over, set the timer again, and carry the other items out the front door.

The dog is still waiting for me, its mouth open in a slight pant. I've brought a flashlight, too, so as soon as it comes to its feet, I shine a beam down between its legs so I can determine gender. Female. I feel disappointment knock through me, but I'm not really surprised. It didn't *feel* like Dante.

But she still feels human.

"Come on over here under the carport," I say, as if the dog can understand me, which maybe she can. "I'll make a little bed for you out of the wind. I don't think it's going to get too cold tonight—no worse than forty. You look like you're dressed for zero." I'm not an expert on dog breeds, but I think she looks like a Siberian husky. Her fur is definitely warm enough to see her through a St. Louis October night.

She follows me to the side of the house, where light from the kitchen window provides a certain amount of golden illumination. As soon as I set down the water bowl, she pads over and laps up most of its contents. Then she watches with interest as I shake out the comforter and bunch it up to make a structure that's half cave, half mattress. "There.

That ought to be nice and soft," I say. I pick up the water bowl. "I'll be right back."

Five minutes later I've returned with more water and another bowl holding the half-cooked hamburger. She's already trampled a space for herself on the rumpled comforter, and her tail beats a light rhythm against the side of the house when she smells the meat. I set both bowls in front of her, and she buries her nose in the mounded ground beef, gulping it down.

I get the sense that she doesn't want me too close, so I take a few steps back and watch her. If it had been colder out, I would have had to consider bringing her into the house, but I'm reluctant to do that, and she doesn't appear interested in coming inside, anyway. A blanket and some scraps seem to be exactly what she wants.

She licks the bowl clean and takes in a little more water before turning to give me one long, deliberate stare. She offers a single bark—I cannot help but consider it an expression of thanks—then paws at the comforter again, shaping it how she wants. With a sigh, she drops to her belly and curls around so her head lies on her paws. I think she falls asleep while I am still watching her.

In the morning, the husky is gone, but I have the notion that she might return again at nightfall. I skip Ellen's outing at lunch to go to a nearby PetSmart and pick up a hefty bag of dry dog food that claims to come enhanced with all the nutrients your pet could ever need. I'm not sure what else to buy—toys, collar, leash, rawhide bone all seem inappropriate. Anyway, there's no guarantee she'll be there when I get back. I'll probably have to donate the food to the local shelter.

But she is waiting for me when I return, sitting up on the folded blanket, her big eyes on my face the minute I step out of the car. I don't even go into the house first, just rip open the bag of food and pour it into the bowl with a clinking sound. She's on her feet and nosing my hand aside as soon as the first bits drop. The water bowl is dry again.

I refill everything a couple of times and then sit and wait as she settles back onto the comforter. She turns to her side, exposing that injured flank, and I creep close enough to take a look at the wounds. They were deep and ugly not too long ago, but, from what I can tell, they appear to be healing cleanly.

I wonder if I should call a vet anyway. I wonder if I could find one who would come to the house. I wonder if the dog would get in the car with me if I tried to explain where I wanted to take her.

I decide I will wrestle with those questions if she stays a few more days and appears to be in some kind of pain.

"Well, let me know if there's something else I can do for you," I say, rising to my feet. She lifts her head and meets my eyes, her mouth slightly open. I swear she's grinning. "Right," I say. "I'll just leave the bag of food here against the house and you can help yourself if you get hungry in the night."

I gather my purse and a few other items from the car and head inside. From time to time, over the next few hours, I peer out at her from the kitchen window, but she seems perfectly comfortable. I wonder if she really is human. I wonder if there is someone much like me, in some small house on the edge of civilization, worrying about her, hoping she's safe, hoping she's still *alive*. If she had tags, I could find a number and call. *Hello, this is Maria Devane, you don't know me but I've found your dog. Oh, it's your daughter? Well, she's been at my house for a couple of days and I wanted to let you know she was fine. A little thin, a little beat up, but healthy enough. You can go to bed tonight—this one night of the year—and not be worried about her.*

It occurs to me that I might finally have gone completely insane.

CHAPTER ELEVEN

Halloween is a cold, wet, nasty Friday that shows every sign of turning into a cold, wet, nasty night. I can just imagine all the children across Missouri pleading with their mothers not to make them wear coats over their carefully assembled outfits.

It is, of course, the day of our costume party at work. I am going as a cow. I'm dressed in a brown turtleneck and brown cords, and I've sewn irregularly shaped white patches all over my clothing. I'm wearing a headband adorned with paper ears that don't look much like a cow's, and over my neck I've slipped a leather cord holding a bell. My udder will be represented by a surgical glove filled with water and attached to my belt, but since I can't figure out any way such an accoutrement will survive contact with the seat belt, I save that final piece to add once I'm in the office. A quick duck into the women's bathroom and my ensemble is complete. I glance at myself in the mirror and say out loud, "You look ridiculous."

So does everyone else, which is something of a comfort. Many of us roam the halls for the first hour of the day, considering coworkers for a few moments before asking, "What are *you* supposed to be?" Marquez is the most puzzling. He's dressed in a washed-out two-piece shapeless gray velour tracksuit that is not particularly flattering on his paunchy frame. When I ask the inevitable question, he snatches up a clear plastic umbrella and snaps it open to reveal long dangling strips of gray ribbon attached all around the outer perimeter.

"I still don't get it," I say.

"I'm a jellyfish." He tosses a handful of brightly colored candies at me. "And I'm giving out jellybeans."

I throw back a couple squares of milk chocolate. "I have a joke," I offer.

"Is it funny?"

"Sure. Knock, knock."

"Who's there?"

"Interrupting cow," I answer.

"Interrupting—"

"Moo!" I shout before he can finish.

He shakes his head. "It's *not* funny."

"Well, do you know any jellyfish jokes?"

"I didn't know that was one of the requirements."

"It's not a requirement. It's just, you know, reasonable to expect."

He doesn't even answer. He just shakes his head again and goes back to work.

At lunchtime, all twenty-two of us gather in the "major function room" on the ground floor of our building, where decorations have been hung from the ceiling and a luncheon has been laid out. The punch is orange, the sheet cake is covered with chocolate frosting so dark it looks black, but the rest of the food looks like relatively ordinary pasta and salad. Cats and reindeer mingle with dogs and alligators and one impressive dragon. There are tables set up around the edges of the room, and some people are sitting down to eat their meals, but most of us are trying to wield our silverware while simultaneously holding paper plates, plastic cups, and themed napkins. Before the luncheon is ten minutes old, three people have dumped the entire contents of their plates on the floor.

Ellen has come as a parrot, wearing an astonishing weave of bright fake hair pieces in her own brassy blond curls and a great hooked beak over her nose. She is telling a series of filthy jokes related to her costume to anyone who will pause to listen.

"An old man is sitting on a park bench, waiting for a bus, and there's this punk kid sitting next to him. The kid's cut his hair in a Mohawk and dyed it blue and red and yellow and green, and the old man is giving him this long cold stare. Finally the kid says, 'Hey, didn't *you* ever do anything stupid in your life?' And the old man says, 'Yeah, I fucked a parrot once. I was wondering if you were my son.'"

She invariably gets a laugh, even from Kathleen, who doesn't much appreciate obscenity. It's hard not to smile when Ellen is trying to be entertaining.

I'm getting a second glass of punch when I practically run into Caroline at the food table. She is dressed in a long, sweeping, belted black dress, with sleeves that cover her wrists and a skirt that brushes her ankles. Her feet are hidden by black leather boots and her hands by black lace gloves. A mask of blackbird feathers covers the upper half of her face; beaded black earrings swing just below the severe edge of her black hair. It's annoying that even in costume she retains an assassin's cold elegance, while the rest of us look like particularly clownish children.

"Oh! Caroline!" I say as if she's startled me, because she always *does* startle me. "You must be a—a bird. Or, well, a crow."

"A raven," she says.

"Nevermore," I say brightly.

She gives me one long, puzzled inspection. Behind the mask, her eyes glitter with malice. "And you are—?"

"A cow."

She glances down at my stomach. "I think your teats are leaking," she says. With a swirl of fabric, she spins and strides off.

I glance down to see that, yes, water is dripping from the imperfect seal at the top of the glove. There's a little puddle at my feet and a spreading stain across my midsection. "Shit," I say.

There's a laugh behind me, and I turn to see Grant dressed as some kind of feline. A snow leopard, maybe, all in white except for dozens of small black circles. He's affixed whiskers to his face and rather more successful ears to his head. Like Caroline, he has managed to not appear ridiculous; he looks both attractive and amiable, another combination that none of the rest of us have managed to pull off.

"When costumes go bad," he intones in a TV-announcer voice.

I unfasten the faulty udder, attempt to squirt him with the contents but end up just getting more water on the floor, and toss the half-filled bag into the nearest trash can. "I hate Halloween," I say.

"Oh, man, I love it!" he exclaims. "All the cute little kiddies coming to your door and telling you stupid jokes! I won't give them candy unless they perform."

"I have a joke," I say. "What do cows do on Saturday night?" He raises his eyebrows in inquiry, so I answer the riddle. "They go to the mooooovies."

"That's good. I'm going to tell that to the trick-or-treaters."

The Halloween party is only supposed to last over lunch, but once you've started chatting with leopards and lemurs, it's awfully hard to go back to balancing accounts and answering calls from vendors. Ellen hangs out in my office for the last hour of the day, perching on my big worktable and kicking her legs like a girl on a swing. I'm not sure parrots have red feet, but her scarlet shoes seem like the perfect complement to the rest of her garish outfit. She is pleased by the success of the party and looking forward to the weekend.

"You doing anything interesting?" she asks as quitting time finally rolls around and we step out with everyone else.

"No," I say with a sigh. "It will probably be the most boring weekend of my life."

"Sometimes those are the best ones," she says.

I laugh. "I agree."

The husky is gone when I get home and I worry about her. The rain has cleared up, but the heavy air is so damp and chilly that the slightest breeze sends ice skittering across bare flesh. It will be a cold night to sleep outside unprotected. And it could be a dangerous night, if tough kids roaming the neighborhoods decide to torture black cats and stray dogs. Will she be safe? Does she know she can come back to me if she feels threatened? I leave the blanket, water bowl, and food outside, just in case.

I've done nothing more than remove my headband and cowbell before the doorbell rings and a voice calls, "Trick or treat!" I grab the candy bowl on my way to the door, but it's no small ghost or vampire awaiting me on the porch.

"Christina!" I exclaim, holding the door wide enough for her to come in out of the miserable weather. "Oh, and Lizzie! Look at you, you're a little jack-o'-lantern!"

Christina smiles brightly as she carries Lizzie across the threshold. The baby is, indeed, dressed like a carved pumpkin, with a yellow face stitched onto the belly of her orange jumper and a green-stemmed hat on her little head. She waves her hands and chortles when I bend down to give her a kiss.

Christina is wearing tight blue jeans, a gold-sequined top, and flat gold shoes with big buckles. Clearly she's heading to a party, though it must not require costumes. She says, "I know, isn't she adorable?"

"Are you going somewhere? Do you want to leave the baby with me?" I ask. Though I am a little taken aback by her bold assumption that I would be available, I'm more than delighted at the prospect of spending an evening with Lizzie.

Christina laughs. "How rude would that be to just show up at your door and demand that you babysit! No, I'm heading into town and I thought I'd swing by and show you her outfit. I just bought it yesterday."

I hold out my arms and Christina willingly gives me the baby. I fancy I can tell that she's gained a pound or two since I held her last. "Are you sure? I wouldn't mind. I'm not doing anything except handing out candy."

"I'm sure. There's a whole group of us getting together, and everyone has children, and we've hired three girls to babysit for the night. It ought to be a lot of fun."

I jostle Lizzie in my arms. She reaches out curious fingers and pokes at my nose, my chin. "Does Mama let you have candy yet, little girl?" I ask. "Would you like some nice, juicy Baby Ruth candy bars? Or how about a Snickers? No? Just wait a couple of years. Right now you think formula is pretty awesome, but chocolate is going to rock your world."

"It will, if she's anything like her mother," Christina agrees.

I turn toward the cluttered console table that sits just inside the door and holds everything from my car keys to my phone books to a week's worth of mail. "I think my camera is here somewhere. Can you take a picture of me with the baby?"

"Sure. Actually, can you take a picture of *me* with her? I don't have any recent photos of the two of us."

So we pass Lizzie back and forth while we snap a few shots, and I promise to e-mail them to Christina.

After they've been here about twenty minutes, I offer food and drinks, but Christina shakes her head and says, "Gotta run. It seems like *years* since I've gone out with my friends and I'm dying to get to the party."

I hold the door open and a battalion of cold marches in. "Have fun."

She steps outside, but then turns back. "Have you talked to my brother lately?"

"Not since he was here last. About ten days ago. Do you want me to give him a message?" *Do you know where he is? Is he nearby, pretending to be far away? Is he human, pretending to be an animal?* God, it's been so long since I've had these doubts about Dante, and now they're crowding back. I brush my hair from my face, trying to brush away the thoughts.

Christina answers, "No, I just wanted to thank him. He sent Lizzie a present. I think that means he might not be so angry about her anymore."

I shrug, wrapping my arms around myself to stay warm. I keep my voice neutral as I say, "You can't worry about Dante being mad. He has his own rules and his own secrets. And they're not always easy for other people to live with."

Christina rests Lizzie against her shoulder and absently pats the back of the orange jumper. "Well. Next time he's around, if he wants to get to know his niece a little better, tell him I'd be happy to see him." She smiles at me. "To see both of you."

"I will. Talk to you later."

She leaves, and I take a few moments to strip away the rest of my cow costume and put on normal clothes before anyone else comes to the door. During the next couple of hours, I'm visited by two pirates, a caterpillar, and a girl in some catchall costume that probably started out as princess but ended up as gypsy, and then I lose track. I give everyone handfuls of miniature candy bars in an effort to get rid of as much as possible.

By nine o'clock, I figure all the traffic is past, so I turn out the porch light, eat a Snickers bar, finish a Sudoku puzzle, and go to bed. It's Friday and since I have nothing planned for the weekend, I don't have to set the alarm clock. That seems like the biggest luxury I've indulged in for the entire month.

I'm deeply asleep a couple of hours later when the shrill ring of the phone jerks me awake. My first reaction is panic—*Someone's dead*—and my heart pounds as I fumble for the lamp and check Caller ID on the bedside phone. It's one of those times when the erratic service isn't working and the LED readout flashes NO DATA. The clock on the side table shows a few minutes past midnight.

"Hello?" I say fearfully.

"Happy Halloween," Dante answers.

Instantly, joy routs uneasiness; it overpowers the uncertainties that have dogged me all week. I sit up in bed, practically bouncing. "Dante! How *are* you? It's so nice to hear your voice!"

"Yours, too," he says. "Hey, are you all dressed up in some sexy costume?"

I giggle. "I went to a Halloween party today at work, but I didn't look too sexy. I was dressed as a cow."

"Do you think maybe you could find something a little more enticing than that? A French maid outfit, maybe?"

For a moment, hope squeezes the air out of my lungs. "Why?" I manage. "Are you likely to see me wearing it?"

"Yeah. I'm at the gas station down the street, actually. I thought I'd call instead of just coming over, you know, in case—"

"What, in case my boyfriend was spending the night for Halloween?"

I hear the grin in his voice. "Something like that."

I'm already on my feet, throwing on a robe, stuffing my feet into slippers. "He left before midnight, so no need to worry. I have to hang up to get to the front door."

"See you in a few minutes," he says, and cuts the connection.

I'm at the door before he is, and I stand there, shivering in the nasty night air and not even caring how cold it is. Soon I see him loping up the street from the direction of the crossroads where the gas station and the Quik Mart rule opposite corners. As soon as he gets close enough for me to make out details, I see that he is barefoot and wearing nothing but the slick running pants that he keeps in his pack. He has not been human long enough to buy better clothing; he doesn't expect to stay human long enough to require any additions to his wardrobe.

He plunges through the door and throws his arms around me. I squeal at the iciness of his bare skin. He burrows his face under the fall of my hair and shivers elaborately. "It's *freezing* out there," he mumbles. "I didn't realize it until I changed shapes, and then I thought I'd *die*."

"Well, come in, come in, let's get you warmed up," I say, pulling him inside, shutting the door, and rubbing my hands briskly up and down his back. All this time he still has his arms around me and his face pressed against my skin, greatly impeding my movements. "Do you want a blanket? Do you want me to make you some hot tea?"

"I want to climb under the covers," he whispers against my throat. "With you."

I pull back enough to force him to raise his head, and then I kiss him. "Gladly," I say. "How much time do you have?"

"I don't know. Maybe an hour. Maybe an hour and a half."

"How long have you been human?"

"About fifteen minutes."

I kiss him again. "We better hurry."

We race each other to the bedroom and burrow under the blankets. At first we do little more than cling together, while he warms his body against mine, and I continue to chafe his shoulders and his arms. He is not quite *new Dante*; perhaps he has not been an animal long enough, or he won't be human long enough, for the transformation to wreak its usual havoc. He seems more like *dazed Dante*, someone woken unexpectedly from a hard sleep and still not certain how to function outside of dreamland.

"What have you been this time?" I whisper, putting my face so close to his that our noses touch.

"Some kind of cat. Mountain lion, maybe."

"And did you have any adventures? The kind where other creatures tried to kill you?"

He grins; his face is so near that I can see every crease that the expression folds into in his cheeks. "Not that I remember. It's been a most boring transformation."

"Good. Those are the kinds I like."

"How about you? Any adventures?"

"Mmm, I went to Chicago with Beth. That was fun. Oh, and we had a Halloween party today at work."

"That's what you said. You were a cow." He squeezes in closer to kiss me. "I hardly think that was the costume that best illustrates your real personality."

The quality of our intimacy has instantly changed. He's no longer huddling close to me to steal my body warmth; he's suddenly eager for a different kind of contact. I wriggle a little closer.

"Oh yeah?" I whisper back. "What kind of costume do you think I *should* have worn? We all had to dress like some kind of animal." I kiss him. "Would have been easy for *you*."

That makes him snort in amusement. He's tugging at my nightgown, trying to get it over my head without actually letting go of me. "Let's see. I'd have dressed you as a peacock. Something beautiful. Or, no, maybe a koala bear. Something cute."

I am choking back laughter. Both suggestions seem ridiculous and ill-suited for me. "No, no, I would be a beagle or a collie," I say. "Faithful. Reliable. Willing to do anything for someone I loved."

He pushes me away, yanks off the nightgown, and then pulls me close again. I can feel the urgent shape of his erection through the thin material of his pants. "Maybe a sheepdog," he suggests, "all your hair always falling in your face—"

I swat him on the shoulder, then grab his ears and pull him close. "I don't know how many girls you have lined up across Missouri, just waiting for the one night a month you come to their bedrooms in some kind of reasonable human shape," I mutter against his mouth. "But assuming I'm the only one, you better say something awfully nice to me right now, or you might find yourself going back to your feral state without having your animal appetites satisfied."

I am trying to deliver it in a low, sexy growl, but I can't help giggling toward the end, and Dante is laughing outright. I am giddy with the euphoria of seeing him so unexpectedly; I don't know what his excuse is. Perhaps the same as mine. He pulls me with him as he rolls to his back and wraps his arms around me, tightening his embrace so dramatically that all the air *whuffs* out of me in one noisy exhalation. "Oh, I do love you, Maria Devane," he exclaims, covering my face with sloppy kisses. "I don't know how I ever got so lucky as to find you."

"God, I love you, Dante," I say, my voice suddenly choked up, my heart suddenly seized up. "I wish I never had to spend a day apart from you."

Those are the last words either of us speaks for the next twenty minutes. We have gone from playful to poignant in the space of a pulse, and our foreplay has turned purposeful. He slides himself free of the thin pants, slides himself into me; I press my body against his with utter abandon. I can't explain the chaotic images that form in my head as I strain against him, as I clutch his hair, as I drop manic kisses on his face, his cheeks, his throat. It is like I am beating on the outside of a huge, metal-strapped door, trying to break through to whatever is inside. I am pounding on the timbers, flinging the full weight of my body against the wood, gouging out splinters with my fingertips, and still I cannot get inside. What do I think is on the other side? How do I think the act of sex will crack the seal?

Why do I think there is anything hidden from me when Dante's passion, Dante's desperation, match my own?

We are scarcely finished, still lying against each other, still taking in great ragged breaths, when he says in a hoarse voice, "I have to go."

I tighten my hands; my fingernails bite into the rounded muscles of his arms. "Not yet," I beg.

"I have to. I can't—I barely had time for this," he says.

He shakes himself free of me, not cruelly but without negotiation, and swings out of the bed. In the room's faint light, I can see the sheen of sweat on his chest. As he pulls on the running pants, I think idiotically, *He'll really be cold now.* I suppose the condition won't last for long. It's been close to an hour since he called; there must be very little time left.

Feeling woozy as a drunk, I follow him into the living room. I'm so unsteady that I stumble and slam my hip against the table at the door. "Be careful," I say, clinging to the door as he pulls it open. "Come back to me."

"Always and always," he says. He bends down to plant a rough kiss on my mouth, holding it for a second longer than I anticipated. He has not said so, but I am suddenly certain of it. *He does not want to go.* He is, for this brief moment, anyway, furious at the fates that have fashioned his strange existence. "You give me something to live for."

And then he's gone.

I sleep so late the next day that what wakes me up is the postal carrier dropping mail through my door slot a few minutes before eleven. For a while I just lie in bed, feeling the blank disorientation that usually holds me in thrall any morning I'm not wrenched from sleep by the hateful buzzing of the alarm clock. It takes me a moment to remember what day it is and reconstruct all the little details of the day before. Halloween party, Christina, trick-or-treaters . . .

Dante.

Smacked by revelation, I come fully awake, though I don't leap up from bed or even sit up. Was he really here last night? Did I dream his presence? I glance around the portion of the room I can see while still lying flat on my back, but there are no physical reminders . . . no dropped pieces of clothing, no extra glasses of water on the nightstand, no exotic gifts left where my eyes will see them first thing in the morning. I roll to one side and grope for the phone, but since the Caller ID is on the fritz, I can't even reassure myself that he called.

Surely he did. I pull the covers to my chin and imagine I can catch his scent in the cotton fibers of the sheet. My body remembers the love-making. I stroke my hand down the corrugated slope of my rib cage, the curved saucer of my hip. When I step out of bed, when I examine myself in the mirror, will there be marks on my skin—bruises the size of a thumb on the inside of my wrist, the faint indentation of a bite at the join of my throat and shoulder? Will there be any proof of his visit except my conviction of his existence?

I curl into a tight ball, still clutching the covers beneath my chin. Is there ever any more proof than that? Isn't my unreasoning faith in him the only reason he exists at all?

CHAPTER TWELVE

Once I manage to pull myself out of bed, I discover that the first day of November is as beautiful as the last day of October was miserable; it is the Cinderella to Halloween's ugly stepsister. It is replete with sunshine, generous with blue skies, and it tempts me not to stay inside and clean the house as I ought to. So, when Beth calls ten minutes later and proposes that we go to St. Charles for the day, I gladly agree. I barely have time to shower and dress before she and Clara arrive in a big blue SUV, but I'm out the door before she's cut the motor. I hear the house phone ringing, but I don't even look back. It won't be Dante calling; anyone else can wait.

"Sunshine!" I exclaim breathlessly as I climb into the front seat. "Who knew such a thing existed?"

"I want a hot dog," Clara says from the backseat.

"Coming right up," Beth tells her. "Well, in about thirty minutes."

We head for the historic district of St. Charles, an old community right on the banks of the Missouri River, and spend a couple of hours strolling up and down Main Street. Most of the stores have already started putting out their holiday decorations and merchandise, though the full-scale Christmas programming won't start until closer to Thanksgiving. Main Street is paved with uneven red brick and lined with two- and three-story buildings, most of them well-preserved examples of the town's eighteenth-century roots. I love the ambiance of the place, though I rarely purchase any of the candles, dolls, crystal light-catchers, and other tchotchkes for sale; they don't really fit my stripped-down decor. Beth buys a pattern in Patches, the quilt shop, and I pick up a novel at Main Street Books.

"Big spenders," Beth comments as we head back to the SUV. Clara has gotten tired and cranky, so Beth is carrying her while I push the stroller, empty except for our purses and our two small packages.

"We'll have to come back before Christmas and see the carolers," I say.

"I mean, I can't believe it's less than two months away," she replies.

Clara stops whining long enough to say, "I want an American Girl doll for Christmas."

Beth smiles at me over her daughter's head. "And so it begins."

It has just now occurred to me that I can buy presents for Lizzie. That will make the upcoming holiday season even more fun. Maybe I'll buy some on Dante's behalf, too, so I can get twice as much stuff. "Next thing you know she'll want cell phones and navel rings."

"What's a navel ring?" Clara asks.

Beth gives me a mock scowl. *See what you've done?* "Something you won't have any knowledge of until you turn eighteen."

Clara turns her head on her mother's shoulder so she can look at me. "What's a navel ring?"

I reach over to flick her little nose. "Jewelry for your belly button. Doesn't that sound cute?"

"I want one," she says instantly.

"We'll get you one when we go for your tattoo," I say.

"Maria!" Beth exclaims.

I shrug. "Hey, aunts are supposed to be bad influences."

We've reached the car by this time, and Beth hands me Clara so she can unlock the door. "I never heard that before. Sydney's not a bad influence."

"She's just sneakier than I am. She's bad when you're not around to see her."

As Beth snaps the seat belt in place, Clara announces, "Aunt Sydney lets me drink champagne."

"What?" Beth demands, while I succumb to uncontrollable laughter.

"I like soda better," Clara adds.

I'm still laughing as Beth and I climb into the front seat and she pulls out of the parking lot. "This is why you were lucky you never had a sister," Beth says.

"Oh no," I say. "This is why I'm lucky I had *you*."

It's close to three before I'm back in the messy house and I begin a halfhearted cleaning effort. I have forgotten to check my answering machine for messages, and not until the phone rings thirty minutes later do I remember that it was also ringing when I left with Beth. The erratic Caller ID system decides to reveal that Ellen is on the line.

I have a sudden dark premonition that whatever reason she has for calling will not be good.

"Hey, Ellen," I say as I pick up. "What's going on?"

"Ritchie's dead," she says in a flat voice.

For a moment I am absolutely blank. "Ritchie?"

"Ritchie Hogan. Kathleen's husband. He's dead."

I press my hand to my heart like an actress in a community theater production. "*What?* What happened? How did you find out?"

"I don't know the details. She's hysterical. She called Marquez and he called me. He's with her now, but he says I shouldn't come over, she doesn't want more company."

The phone cord is long enough for me to reach the living room and sink onto the couch. I'm still in shock, still not processing information. "But–what happened? Did he have a car accident?"

"I don't think so. It might have been a heart attack. Apparently he was running in some park–he was training to be in a marathon–and that's where he collapsed. Some park rangers found him."

"A heart attack? But–he's so young. And he was in really good shape."

"Well, I'm just guessing about that. Maybe it was something else. I guess he could have had an aneurysm."

"Or an allergy attack. Maybe he's allergic to bees or something, and he got stung. She wasn't specific?"

"Marquez said she wasn't too coherent."

"This is dreadful. What do you want me to do?"

Ellen sounds tired, she who has boundless stores of energy. "I don't know. I don't know what *I* can do. I hate feeling so fucking helpless. This was *not* the call I was expecting from Kathleen's house, you know? I always figured she'd be the one who was dead."

"Maybe she killed him," I say, morbid humor forcing its way past my imperfect sentinels of compassion and decency. "Put poison in his coffee this morning and it didn't take effect till he was out of the house."

"I'd be okay with that," Ellen says. "I mean, *I* don't think it's a terrible thing that he's dead but, holy God, Kathleen does not seem entirely equipped to take care of herself."

"Does she have family in the area?"

"I think the closest relative is a sister in Little Rock. Marquez said someone was on the way and he planned to stay there until this person arrived."

"Well, we can take shifts—if she's willing to have us there. I could go over tonight or tomorrow or—anytime, really."

"Yeah. I think I'll go over tomorrow, no matter what Marquez tells me. I won't stay if it seems like she wants me gone."

"Want me to come with you?"

"Yeah," Ellen says on a sigh. "Might be easier on everyone. I'll pick you up at eleven, how does that sound? We can bring her some lunch."

"See you then."

After we hang up, I sit on the couch for another ten minutes, just staring at my interlaced hands. That's the phone call I always dread, always expect, the information brought by indifferent strangers. *Ms. Devane? I'm afraid I have bad news. We found a man dead this morning, I'm sorry to say, and he had your name and number on a piece of paper in his pocket.* Would that call come to me or would it go to Christina? Is she filled with twice as much fear, worried over two brothers, both of them constantly exposed to risks that they do not bother to try to mitigate? Did she resign herself long ago to the idea that their lives would be short, their ends probably brutal? Is she amazed they've survived this long, grateful for every additional week or month or year that she can turn around one unexpected morning and find them standing on her front porch, hungry and gaunt and edgy, but alive?

I cannot get to that place. I cannot surrender myself to fatalism where Dante is concerned. I cannot endure the knowledge that his condition practically guarantees an early death—may, in fact, lead to him dying alone somewhere, far from me, in a spot where his body is never found. So he might not just die, he might vanish from my life, simply fail to show up again, and I will never know what happened to him. I will first be frantic, then despairing, then lost, lost, lost in a deep well of impenetrable darkness, and I will *never know*. Did he starve to death? Lose a battle with a vicious opponent? Simply wear out, his body too depleted by unnatural stresses to maintain itself another day?

Decide he did not love me after all? Might he be alive still, back in human shape, but tired of my nagging or my possessiveness or my unimaginative personality?

"If it happens, Dante, if you fall out of love with me, just tell me," I pleaded once a few years ago, when I had become a little obsessed with the topic of Dante's death. "Break up with me—I'll make it easy for you, I won't cry and beg—just don't leave me wondering. I'd rather know that you'd fallen in love with someone else than think that you're dead when you're not."

He had rolled his eyes in exasperation. "All right, I'll tell you," he said. "I'll send you an e-mail. 'Hey, Maria. Babe! Tired of you, girl, so I'm dumping you now. But don't worry. I'm fine. Not dead yet.'"

He was being facetious, of course, but I answered, "It would be a comfort."

He'd pulled me into his arms and dropped a rough kiss on the top of my head. "It's not going to happen anytime soon. You're more likely to dump *me*."

I'd stared up at him. "You must be joking."

"Hey, you put up with a lot more shit from me than I do from you," he said. "You're the one who settled. I'm the one who got lucky."

I patted him on the cheek. "You keep on believing that."

"I always do."

I don't entirely put my faith in that declaration, but I do believe that he will keep his promise; he will let me know if he plans to abandon me. So I am back to a single fear, but it's monstrous: One day he will be gone from my life. One day he will die.

There is nothing I want to do less than go to Kathleen's house the day after her husband's death. I spent the morning making spinach lasagna and dividing it into freezer containers to create handy single-serving meals. Food is a cultural substitution for love, and cooking offers a hedge against an overwhelming sense of helplessness, but in my heart I know my efforts are wasted. Kathleen will likely never want to eat again.

Ellen arrives a few minutes late in her red Miata, and we head to Kathleen's in almost total silence. Once I've asked, "Any more news?" and she's replied in the negative, we don't have anything else to say. I am relieved to see two cars already in the driveway, one of them belonging to Marquez, one with Arkansas plates. We will not have to attempt to carry on conversation with Kathleen, just the two of us. I can't think of anything to say to *her*, either.

Marquez answers the door, and instead of berating us for coming over uninvited, he embraces us one at a time. He makes it a real hug; I find it comforting to be momentarily squeezed against his soft, substantial frame.

"How is she?" I ask.

He shakes his head. "Not good."

"Who else is here?" Ellen wants to know.

"Her sister and her husband arrived about three in the morning. They're both sleeping right now."

"You planning to go home anytime soon?" she asks him.

"When her sister gets up, maybe. She seems to like me to be here, so—" He shrugs.

I glance around the house, which I have only ever seen from the outside. The front door leads directly into the living room, which is furnished in a sort of amped-up country style—lots of ruffles on the curtains, lots of blue hearts patterned on everything from crockery-style flower vases to stenciled lamp shades. To my right I can glimpse a darkened hallway leading toward what I assume are bedrooms. The hallway walls are hung with framed family photos that appear to cover generations. There is a sweetness that pervades the whole setting; it is possible to imagine Kathleen happily choosing each flounced valence, each stitched doily, each separate mat and moulding. Something inside my chest twists with pain.

"Where is she?" Ellen asks.

"In the kitchen. I was trying to convince her to eat something, but she—" Now he shakes his head. "I don't think she's consumed a thing since yesterday morning, and I know she was throwing up last night."

"We'll get her to eat something," Ellen says, striding purposefully down the hallway to our left. "*That* I can do."

The kitchen is small and bright, decorated with copper molds of roosters and cheery yellow accents. Kathleen is sitting at an oak table, her arms lax before her, her hair lank, her face a ruin. She looks up when we step in, but I can't read any expression. She's not angry we're here, not surprised, not grateful. She simply doesn't care.

Ellen marches over, bends down, and takes the limp body in a hug. "It's so terrible that I don't even know what to say," she says, "so I'm not going to try to make stuff up. Maria and I came by just to help you fill the time. We'll sit here for a little while, and then there will be another two hours gone by."

I see Kathleen sort of nod over Ellen's shoulder, then Ellen releases her and I step in to offer my own awkward embrace. I know it's impossible for anyone to lose significant weight overnight, but somehow she feels like she is nothing but bones, jostling against each other inside a thin bag of flesh. "Hey," is all I have to offer. She nods again.

Ellen turns brisk. "So what would you like to eat?"

"Nothing," Kathleen manages in a faint whisper.

Ellen rests her fists on her hips. "Well, you're going to have *something* before I leave today, so you'd better figure out what you're most likely to keep down."

"One of the neighbors brought over some chicken noodle soup," Marquez tells her.

"And I brought spinach lasagna," I say, though even I realize someone who's been throwing up all night will not be interested in pasta.

"Oh, can I have some?" Marquez asks. "I'm starving."

"Anyone who wants it can have some."

"I'm just going to heat up some of this soup," Ellen says. "Where do you keep your pans?"

In a few minutes, the four of us are seated around the table in an uncomfortable travesty of one of our workweek lunches. But perhaps the familiarity of the ritual, the group of friends, works benignly on Kathleen's mental state. She takes the bowl of soup from Ellen and obediently begins spooning up the broth. She also drinks half a glass of 7UP that Marquez has poured for her. I can't help but think of these as "sick foods," since they're part of the diet my mother would always prepare for me when I had a stomach flu. Then again, I suppose Kathleen has fallen ill with one of the most calamitous diseases there is—grief—and she will be a long time recovering, if she ever does.

Kathleen, while she might be managing food, is not up to conversation, so Ellen and Marquez and I talk softly on the most neutral topics we can identify. I mention my trip to St. Charles yesterday. Marquez tells us he saw a movie Friday night with friends. He wouldn't recommend it, though; too many plot holes, not enough action. Ellen says her tomato plants are still yielding fruit. "One year I was getting tomatoes almost through Thanksgiving, but I can't imagine that will happen again anytime soon," she says.

We have been sitting there for nearly an hour when Kathleen suddenly begins to speak. "I didn't want him to go yesterday morning," she says in a soft, exhausted voice. She is not looking at any of us; she's watching her hands crumble one of the saltines that Ellen insisted she eat along with the soup. "I said, 'It's such a pretty day and there's so much work to do in the yard. Go running when it's cold and cloudy out and I don't feel like working in the garden.' I said, 'You've still got a cast on your arm. What if you trip? You'll really hurt yourself if you fall.' But he wanted to go."

Nobody responds with anything like *It was his time* or *God has a plan and you can't know what it is* or *Everything happens for a reason.* "He loved to run," Marquez says, and that seems to satisfy her.

"He really did," Kathleen answers. "He was good at it and it made him happy. There were a lot of things he wasn't good at, and that would make him mad, but he could run really fast." She shakes her head; big tears fall from her eyes but she doesn't appear to notice. "That's why I don't understand. Why couldn't he just have kept running? Why couldn't he get away?"

The three of us exchange startled, puzzled glances. We have no idea what she's talking about, but will it make it better or worse for her if we press for an explanation?

"Honey, we're still not quite sure what happened to Ritchie," Ellen says. "Don't tell us if you don't feel like talking about it, but if you do—"

"He was running. In Babler State Park," Kathleen says, enunciating with great precision. "And some—some *creature* caught up to him and attacked him. *Mauled* him to death. *Killed* him."

Ellen and I stare at each other in horror. This is far more gruesome than any of the ordinary demises we had speculated about. "'Some creature'?" Ellen repeats faintly. "Do you know what kind?"

Kathleen shakes her head. The tears are still dropping from her eyes, steady as a drip from a leaky faucet. She doesn't seem to care. "They said—the police said—they would have to do some forensics. They couldn't tell if it was a dog or a coyote or something else—they didn't know yet. They're going to do tests."

"Can coyotes kill a grown man?" Ellen asks. "Aren't they too small?"

Marquez makes an abrupt motion with his hand to cut her off, as if to say, *Consider that question some other time.* "I'm sure they'll figure it out," he says.

"They think they have a witness," Kathleen says in a hopeless voice. "Oh, but maybe they don't. They aren't sure. But they found human footprints at the scene—right by Ritchie's body, they said—footprints that had to have been made after he was attacked. But no one called the cops to report the crime, not until a couple of park rangers happened to find him."

"Well, that's cold," Marquez observes.

"So there's a sociopath *and* a dangerous animal on the loose, but I'm more worried about the animal," Ellen says. "You'd think the cops would make an announcement. Or maybe even close the park until they can catch it."

"Even if they do," Kathleen says softly, "Ritchie will still be dead."

Ellen lays a hand on her arm. "I know, baby," she says. "I'm sorry."

It's clear Kathleen isn't going to choke down another bite, and the rest of us have long ago finished our meals, so Marquez stands up and begins clearing the dishes. Ellen clears her throat. "I don't want to sound heartless, but I have to ask practical questions," she says. "Have you thought about funeral arrangements?"

"Kelly's going to help me with that," Kathleen says. "My sister."

"Good. Make sure to take someone with you when you—when you pick out a casket," says Ellen. "Sometimes you're not thinking clearly and you end up with something way more expensive than you planned."

From the sink, Marquez says, "You let us know if you want any help writing up death notices or anything like that."

"When do you think you'll have the funeral?" Ellen asks. "Ritchie has family, doesn't he—a brother, maybe a mom still living? You'll probably want to wait till they get here."

Kathleen's hands clench, her face flushes, and she speaks in a voice that is suddenly frenzied. "I'll *wait* until the police are done with the *autopsy*," she exclaims with a sort of singsong emphasis. "They're cutting him open—they're *examining* him, they're trying to figure out what exactly *killed* him. But I don't *care* what killed him. I don't want him to be *dead*."

Then she breaks down, sobbing in long, hysterical wails, pounding her fists against the table, knocking her forehead against the wood. Marquez spins around from the sink, but Ellen is quicker. She leaps up, pulls Kathleen out of her chair and into a tight hold, rocking that fragile body against her own. Kathleen can't be comforted, of course; she continues to sob, to flail, to beat her small hands against Ellen's sturdy back. Ellen strokes the disordered hair, makes soothing *shh* sounds into Kathleen's ear, and eventually pulls Kathleen down so they are both sprawled on the kitchen floor. And still Ellen holds her, and still she rocks her, and still she offers proof with her own body that the world has not ended, that it still holds life, it holds love, it holds real and physical connections that cannot be severed all at once.

I sit unmoving; I have not said a word for ten minutes. My stomach is a burning knot of suspicion too dark to examine and horror too awful to endure.

Ritchie was killed in Babler State Park—by an animal police have yet to identify.

What if the killer is not an animal at all?

What if the murderer is a man with a grudge against Ritchie? A man who is certainly familiar with the park and happened to be within its general vicinity Saturday morning when the attack took place?

What if that man can take the shape of any animal in the world?

What if he suddenly finds himself back in the shape of a man? What if he stands there, staring with terror or disbelief or even satisfaction on the carnage he has wrought?

We have been at Kathleen's for two hours when her sister comes out of the bedroom, looking scarcely more rested or cheerful than Kathleen. There's a family resemblance between them, but

Kelly is darker and more robust; I can't help thinking that if her husband tried to beat her up she'd haul off and knock him straight to Sunday. Then again, statistics show that women of all types are abused by their domestic partners. She might not be as strong as she seems.

Kelly thanks us all profusely for coming to see Kathleen and promises to call if there's anything else we can do, but it's clear she wants us out of the house so she can start imposing her own brand of order. Once we say our farewells and exit, Marquez and Ellen and I stand in the driveway a few moments, shivering, and confer about what to do next: whom to call, how much information to give to everyone else at the office.

"Well, anybody with a TV set will hear this story by the end of the day," Marquez predicts. "I don't see any point in trying to conceal the circumstances of his death."

I feel like I have to contribute something to the conversation or risk snagging Ellen's restless attention. "What about her finances?" I ask. "Do you think Ritchie had life insurance? Can she afford the funeral? Can she afford this house on her own?"

"Yes on the life insurance, because they got that through us. And they both had health insurance through the company, too, so that's good," Ellen says.

"She's used up all her vacation time for the year. And sick time," Marquez puts in.

Ellen waves a hand. "Company policy officially allows for a three-day bereavement absence, and unofficially people can take at least a week," she says. "If she needs more than that, we'll be able to work something out."

"I don't know how she'll get through this," I say in a low voice. *I don't know how I will.*

Ellen gives me a short, sharp nod. "She'll get through it the way any of us would," she says. "Because she has to."

Do I have to? I don't think I can.

On the drive back, Ellen is talkative, mostly going over plans to ease Kathleen's next few days. We'll take up a collection at work, we'll implement a schedule of calls and visits, we'll organize meal deliveries. I manage to offer a few ideas when they seem called for, and make sounds of approval when that's sufficient. Ellen doesn't seem to notice that I have turned to stone or ash or liquid fear—the states I pass through sequentially as we make the trip home.

"Come in early tomorrow morning and we'll talk some more," she commands as she pulls in front of my house.

"All right," I say as I climb out. "I can't imagine I'll be able to sleep tonight, anyway."

"We need to get Kathleen some sleeping pills," she says, "and keep some for ourselves."

I step inside the house and then slump against the door, not even having the strength to walk across the floor.

Ritchie is dead. Did Dante kill him? Ritchie is dead. Did Dante kill him? Ritchie is dead . . .

It cannot be true. Dante could not have done such a terrible thing. He had no cause, no *reason*. The altercation at my house surely was not enough to inspire a killing animosity.

Does he need a reason? What instincts govern him when he is in his animal state? He has often said his memories of those days are indistinct, though he makes no secret of the fact that he regularly hunts and eats small creatures to sustain himself when he's in the wild. Is it much different to slay a man? Can his beast's brain tell the difference?

Still leaning my spine against the door, I press a hand to my forehead. I can't think. It's too complicated, and my questions contradict each other. Am I afraid that, even in the form of a wild creature, *animal Dante* is human enough to hate Ritchie and deliberately kill him? Or am I afraid that *animal Dante* is so lost to civilized instincts that he doesn't even realize he's capable of slaughtering a man?

I realize I am afraid of both possibilities, though the first one is infinitely worse. The first one speaks to rage and premeditated murderous intent; it bears the whiff of *evil*, and that scent is intensified when I imagine the animal shifting back to human shape so he can view and judge his handiwork.

The second possibility is appalling, too, but it's tragic more than terrible. You would have to believe that the soul who took human form after his bloody rampage stood beside his victim and wept in remorse and fear. You would still have to find a way to contain him in his incarnation as a mindless marauder, of course. You would have to cage him up, keep him off the streets, and make sure he never had the chance to harm another person.

But you would have to *hate* any creature that could deliberately kill a human being. You would have to destroy it.

My breath breaks out of my body in a single hoarse gasp. I cannot hate Dante. I cannot see him destroyed. It doesn't matter what he's done.

Am I crazy to even think this way? Is there any reason to believe that Dante is Ritchie's killer? Yes, he was at my house late Friday night; yes, he could have been in Babler Park Saturday morning when Ritchie went for his run. But it's just as likely that he was miles from the St. Louis area by daybreak. He could have gone north toward Hannibal, west toward Columbia, or south toward Cape Girardeau. He could have crossed the river and headed for the open land of southern Illinois.

And even if he *was* in the park, so were dozens of other wild creatures, some far more dangerous than Dante. Rabid dogs could have been roaming those paths, or hungry bobcats, even coyotes—surely a pack of them could bring down a man, even one as fast as Ritchie. And those footprints hardly prove that a shape-shifter was responsible for the crime. Any number of people could have stood by that mangled body and decided not to call for help. A sociopath, as Ellen suggested, or a developmentally delayed adult who did not comprehend what he was seeing. Perhaps an escaped convict with worries of his own.

What nags at me is Kathleen's frustration at the ignorance of the authorities. *The police said they would have to do some forensics. They couldn't tell if it was a dog or a coyote or something else.* What if they couldn't tell because the creature was unfamiliar to them: something unique, a strange hybrid chimera that borrowed characteristics from three or five or seven animals?

Dante has always been so vague about the shapes he takes, the process he undergoes, that I have sometimes thought he doesn't really know what animals he becomes when the transformation overtakes him. What if his conversions are always jumbled and incomplete? What if he is a griffin or a harpy, a wyvern or a sphinx, some crossbred creature? Wouldn't such an animal leave behind baffling tracks, some sort of unidentifiable spore?

The longer it takes the police to determine what caused Ritchie's death, the more I will worry that it was Dante.

Shuddering and now nauseated, I push myself away from the door and take a few tentative steps deeper into the house. I think I might, like Kathleen, spend the night vomiting and weeping, made physically ill by the manifestation of a reality that cannot be borne. But hers is solid, a hard granite wall of starkness. Mine is misty, formless, populated by specters too frightening to contemplate.

I simply don't know yet if my world has ended.

How will I survive if it has?

I force myself to keep moving, to walk around the living room, picking up discarded shoes, straightening piles of magazines. I wash the breakfast dishes, put away laundry, and iron a few shirts that I might wear in the coming weeks. I am just trying to find tasks that will occupy my hands and give the outer edges of my mind some slim, pitiful distraction. I turn on the television and tune in to a football game. I don't know who is playing and I don't care. I just want to hear voices other than the ones screaming unanswerable questions inside my head.

I am not thinking clearly enough to switch channels before the local news comes on at five o'clock.

Ritchie's death is the lead story, of course. The reporter is a young woman with a suitably solemn face; she wears bright red earmuffs and a puffy white coat as she broadcasts her story from one of the RV lots in the park.

"Authorities are still trying to determine what kind of animal killed Mr. Hogan," she says. "And they're trying to determine if his death can be linked to the three similar deaths that have occurred in public spaces in recent weeks."

Three similar deaths?

What?

My legs are shaking as I cross to the computer and turn it on, waiting with feverish impatience during the seconds it takes for the screen to come to life. It is a matter of a few clicks to get to a Google page and begin searching for HUMAN DEATHS + ANIMALS + ST. LOUIS + OCTOBER. A handful of stories immediately come up, most of them describing the still-unresolved case of a man and a woman killed in some park in Wildwood. I vaguely remember discussing this one day over lunch with Ellen and Grant, but it didn't really register with me at the time.

Now I read three of the stories, but don't glean much useful information. The victims were youngish, in their twenties, and they'd been missing for nearly two weeks before they'd been found slashed to pieces by some kind of creature the police still haven't identified. Time of death has been tricky to establish, but the coroner eventually estimated that they were killed on or around September twenty-fourth. The police have noted that they "have reason to believe" someone may have seen or overheard the attack, and they ask that this witness come forward with any descriptive information. They don't say exactly why they think someone else was on the scene, but I'm guessing there was a dropped glove, an empty soda can, or another set of footprints nearby.

I do the math and shiver. Dante had been staying with me for the days just prior to that. He would have left my house sometime on the twenty-second.

At the bottom of the third story is a paragraph that states:

> *Rodgers and Stemple are the second and third people to be slaughtered by wild animals in eastern Missouri this fall. On September 29, a young woman was found mauled to death in a public area in Mark Twain State Park, not far from Rolla. The animal that killed her has never been found, either.*

My hands freeze on the keyboard.

A young woman killed in Mark Twain State Park. I remember that event. I had called Christina the morning I'd heard the news, terrified she'd been the one attacked. But the report hadn't specified a cause of death, not that I can recall, anyway.

Had Dante been in the St. Louis area when this other death occurred? Surely not—if he'd left my place on the twenty-second, he would have been gone nearly a week by the time this woman was killed. He could have been miles away from St. Louis, possibly not even in Missouri.

Or he could have lingered, drawn to familiar haunts or disinclined for the effort of travel. I remember that late-night call from the pay phone in my very own area code. Maybe, despite what he has always told me, he never strays more than a hundred miles from my house. Or maybe, at this particular time, he had simply decided to spend a few days in Rolla—either to visit his siblings or to take shelter in an area he knows so well that he can, perhaps, let down his guard a little. He might have holed up in that park for days, for weeks, enjoying the good weather and the easy hunting.

He could have killed that woman. He could have killed all of them.

Oh God.

Oh God.

Absolutely no work gets done the next day at the office. The only conversations revolve around where people were when they got the call, or saw the news on the television, and what they thought, what they said, who they told. Those with a wider circle of acquaintances are able to supplement these reports with stories about people they know who died bloody or mysterious deaths. It is possible, before noon, to wonder if anyone ever expires of natural causes.

I try to keep myself occupied, sitting at my computer, opening spreadsheets and checking figures, but my brain is such a frantic jumble of fear and worry that nothing my eyes take in has a chance to register. Every twenty minutes or so, someone drops by my office to ask for news or speculate some more. I find these interruptions to be both a nuisance and a relief. Every time someone says, "Kathleen must be devastated," I want to shout, *My world has ended, too!* But of course I don't.

Our boss, Frank, who has spent half the morning in consultation with Ellen, is genuinely trying to be useful and sympathetic. He has announced that anyone who wants to help Kathleen in some way—by running errands on her behalf or visiting her during the day—can do so without being charged for personal time. He also has taken money from petty cash to buy ten pizzas to be delivered at lunch, so that we can all gather together to continue our endless conjecturing. People wander through the hallways for the rest of the day, slices of pizza in their hands, the same topic on their lips.

By the time I go home, I have a raging headache.

It is impossible to imagine that tomorrow will be any better.

I have no idea how I will even get through the night.

The evening stretches ahead of me, blank and endless, and I'm pretty sure television sitcoms won't be able to hold my attention. I've never been much of one for exercise, but I think maybe physical exertion will slow the ceaseless, jangling adrenaline rush that makes my veins feel as though they're filled with ground glass. I head to a nearby community center that has a handsome set of gym equipment, and I pay the guest rate to go in and use the machines for the night. I don't understand how most of them work, so I settle for the ones that seem to make sense—the treadmill, the stationary bike, a weight-and-pulley contraption that works my arms and back. I am covered with sweat, my muscles are rubbery with exhaustion, and still I go for another rep. I might force myself to walk the indoor track before I go home, just to squeeze the last drop of energy from my body. I do not want to lie awake tonight, as I did last night, thinking, thinking, thinking. I want oblivion.

It is past nine by the time I shower and get home and force myself to eat some soup and crackers. *Sick food.* I feel mentally and physically depleted, so unable to concentrate that I could believe I'm drunk, but I swallow some Benadryl, anyway, before I go to bed. I don't want to take any chances.

Still, it's close to an hour before the drug kicks in, and I spend that whole time lying flat on my back, eyes wide open, staring at the patterns of light that chase each other across my ceiling whenever a car drives by. My thoughts are circular, hopeless, endlessly repetitive.

Dante couldn't have killed Ritchie. Not the Dante I know. He would fight Ritchie, he might hurt him, but he would never kill him. Dante would never kill anybody. I would know if he was a killer. I wouldn't love him. But I love him. But I can't love him if he killed Ritchie. But he didn't kill Ritchie . . .

Over and over again, I find myself astonished that Kathleen didn't turn to me yesterday and howl accusingly, "Your boyfriend killed my husband! This is all your fault!" Over and over again, I have to remind myself that Kathleen knows an animal killed Ritchie, but she doesn't know that Dante can become an animal. Exhausted, depressed, and hardly able to form a coherent thought, I think, *Thank God we didn't have to call the police that day Ritchie came here and started a fight. Or Dante would be the first one they'd suspect now that Ritchie has been murdered.*

Then I remember. *Of course they wouldn't suspect Dante. They think an animal killed Ritchie.*

Then I realize what I have just revealed, silently, to myself: I am glad the police will not connect Dante to this crime. Though I suspect him, I am not willing to turn him over to the authorities; even if I had proof of his guilt, I would not show it to anyone. I will not betray him, no matter what he has done. If he has killed a man—or several people—I will shield him, I will protect him, I will keep him safe.

After all, I shielded a murderer once before, and Dante knows it.

That's why he picked me.

CHAPTER THIRTEEN

I was twenty when I fell in love with Dante.

I was in my junior year at the University of Missouri-Columbia, a school I had chosen because a good friend from high school wanted to major in journalism and I wanted to be just far enough from Springfield that I couldn't commute but I could get home quickly if I had to. My friend and I almost instantly drifted apart as we settled in different dorms, made new friends, and realized we didn't have that much in common after all, but I loved Mizzou.

Dante and I lived in the same dorm, and during the past couple of years, we had occasionally run into each other in the hallway or on the front walk. I thought he was flat-out gorgeous, in a dark and dangerous way, but it never occurred to me that he would ever ask me out. I didn't seem like the kind of woman who would catch his attention, and he wasn't really my type. Up to that point I had dated guys who were nerdy and smart and disarmingly goofy—engineering students, math geniuses, guys who collected comic books. I was comfortable around them. Dante

Romano didn't seem like the kind of man I would ever be at ease around. It didn't seem worth the effort to develop a crush.

Now and then I would spot him with some girl or another—beautiful and bitchy-looking, mostly blond—exactly the type I would have expected a broodingly handsome guy like him to hook up with. His roommate was a pre-med student named Gary who fell exactly into my category—intelligent, dorky, funny, and wry—but he had a girlfriend back home whom he eventually married, so we were never more than friends.

Other girls in the dorm would pester Gary with questions about Dante. "Is he still dating Nadia? Is he into sports? What kind of music does he like? How can I get him to talk to me?" But Gary always laughed and put them off.

"He's kind of an odd dude. He keeps to himself and he's gone a lot. I mean, I think he's gone home for the weekend at least once a month since freshman year. But he's a great roommate, man. He never makes a mess and he never complains about anything."

"Does he have girls over very often?" We lived in a co-ed dorm and there was plenty of mingling between the sexes. My own roommate and I had come up with a complicated unspoken communication system for asking and granting permission to host an overnight guest. The study lounge on the ground floor was where dispossessed individuals usually spent the night when their roommates were entertaining company. I'd encountered Gary there a few times, but never Dante.

"Oh, you know, he sees girls now and then, but I don't think he's too serious about any of them," Gary would say diplomatically.

"Let me know if he's ever looking for someone new. Let me know if you think he'd like me."

Whether or not Gary ever passed these messages along, I don't know. He and Dante were roommates for three of the four years we were all in school. By senior year, Gary's girlfriend had moved up from Cape

Girardeau and they were sharing a house. I'd moved into an apartment about six blocks from campus—and Dante was there as often as he was anywhere else.

By then I had known for more than a year that Dante claimed to be a shape-shifter. I had already convinced myself that he was telling the truth.

I first heard him say the words one winter day so filled with snow that the university canceled classes—an occurrence so rare that no one could remember it actually happening before. The blizzard didn't keep the students inside; in fact, about half my dorm joined in an epic snowball fight that involved hours of planning and building forts, and another hour of actual combat. Another contingent fashioned an articulated sled from trash can lids and bathrobe ties and dragged this through the drifts to the nearest liquor store. When these adventurers returned, they sold beer and assorted other spirits for about twice their retail value, and by nightfall pretty much everyone in the dorm had scattered to attend one party or another.

Gary invited me to a small get-together in the dorm room of two girls who lived next door to him and Dante. The cafeteria had never opened that day, so we were all subsisting on the snacks we had squirreled away in our rooms, and we made a dinner by combining our resources—bagel chips and peanut butter and trail mix and Oreos. Needless to say, on such an insubstantial meal, the alcohol went to work on us even more quickly, and I, at least, was drunk within the hour. I declined to take a toke when the joints were passed around, but everyone in the room was pretty mellow by the time one of the other girls proposed a truth-or-dare sort of game.

"Everyone has to tell a story that they've never told to anyone else—ever," said Janine. She was a bossy brunette with a great figure. I always assumed she'd been an eldest child and was used to ordering people around *and* getting lots of attention because of her looks. A heady combination. "And it has to be true."

Her roommate, Rochelle, demurred. Rochelle was Janine's opposite, small and delicate and fair, but she was stacked, too. Between the two of them, they always had guys hanging around. "I don't want to tell secrets."

"You have to. Everyone has to," Janine said.

"You go first," Gary said.

Janine pouted at him, obviously not used to following other people's instructions, and then she smiled. "All right. When I was twelve I stole a hundred dollars from my dad's wallet. He was so mad. He thought one of the workers in the mailroom had taken it, and he got the guy fired. I hid it in an old pair of shoes and every once in a while when I really, *really* wanted something, I'd sneak out a twenty and go buy it. Like games and clothes and makeup. It lasted me almost a year. No one ever caught me."

"What happened to the guy who got fired?" Rochelle asked.

Janine shrugged. "I don't know."

There was a short silence, and then Gary said, "All right, I'll go next." He blew out a puff of breath. "I cheated on my SAT tests."

"Wow, how'd you even do that?" Janine asked. "Security was tight when I took mine."

"I knew someone who knew someone who had copies of the tests and I paid, like, fifty bucks to get them."

"I thought those were always scams," I said.

"Nope. These were good. About half the questions and answers that were actually on the test were things I'd seen on these copies."

"So what were your scores?" Janine demanded.

"Over seven hundred in everything. The funny thing is, I probably would have done just as well even without cheating. I didn't learn that much that I didn't already know."

"Do you feel bad about it?" Rochelle asked in her soft voice.

"That's the worst part," he said. "I should, but I don't."

"Well, don't cheat on your boards after you get out of med school," I said.

Gary laughed. "Okay. For you, I'll be honest."

Now Janine was looking pointedly at me. "Maria? What's your secret?"

"When I was in high school, my best friend, Karen, killed her father," I said. That riveted everyone's attention; every other story suddenly turned trivial by comparison. "He was always beating her up—her and her sister. And one day she grabbed a baseball bat and just *slammed* him over the head. He dropped to the floor and didn't move again and she was pretty sure he was dead. No one else was home. She didn't know what do to, so she came running over to my house and we figured out a plan. We decided she could hide in the women's bathroom of the gas station by our high school, because it had an outside entrance and it was never locked. I'd bring her food and money until the police stopped looking for her."

I paused a moment, remembering those terrifying, chaotic days. The police had come to my house three times looking for Karen, and my mother and father had asked me searching questions when the cops weren't around, but I never told anyone anything. I had a bank account with a few thousand dollars in it—money I'd saved from summer jobs—and I used my debit card to take out small sums and smuggle them to her when no one else was around.

"Well, of course, the police *didn't* stop looking for her, so one day she just decided to split. I gave her as much money as I could scrape up, and I took her to the train station, and she bought a ticket to Chicago. They never caught her."

There was a moment's stunned silence. "What happened to her?" Rochelle asked. Practically the same question she had asked Janine.

I gave the same answer: "I don't know. She was seventeen when she left. We were afraid that if she wrote or called, the cops would find her.

She did send me a postcard once to say she was all right, but, of course, she didn't include an address and I didn't know how to get in touch with her. I keep thinking maybe one day I'll figure out how to track her down."

"So I guess her father really was dead," Gary said.

I nodded. "Oh yeah. Blunt force trauma. She left the bat beside the body so everyone knew she did it, too."

"Didn't you feel bad about hiding a *murderess*?" Janine asked in such a judgmental tone that I was sure she'd been a hall monitor and all-purpose snitch from grade school on.

I gave her a fierce look that was only slightly blunted by the smudging effects of alcohol and secondhand marijuana. "No. I'd seen her bruises. We were in gym class together, and when we'd change clothes, I'd see the marks on her back. He broke her arm once—took it between his hands and *broke* it. He was a *terrible* man."

"My stepfather raped me when I was fifteen," Rochelle said.

Her soft voice cut across my outraged tone, silenced me and sucked all the air out of the room. The rest of us stared at her, having no idea what to say.

"I wish someone would have killed *him*," she added.

Gary was the one who managed a response—not Janine or me, the two women, the ones you might have expected to speak up. "What happened after that? Did he—did he try to do it again?"

Rochelle shook her head. "I was never alone in the house with him after that. If he was the only one there, I wouldn't go in. I'd go wait at the library or at a friend's house until my mother got home."

"Did you tell her?" Janine asked.

Rochelle gave her a scornful look. "I thought these were supposed to be secrets we'd never told anyone before?"

"Yeah, but—I mean—"

"I never told her. I didn't think she'd believe me. It doesn't matter, they're divorced now."

"Well, it still *matters*," Janine said. "Have you—"

Rochelle kind of scrunched her shoulders together. "I don't want to talk about it anymore."

She looked like she might start crying. I cast about desperately for something neutral to say, and I could tell by his expression that Gary was doing the same thing. That was when, in a rich and idle voice, Dante began talking. Up until this point he had scarcely said a word, though he'd swallowed his share of booze and taken more than a few hits off the joints that were passed around.

"I was born to a family of shape-shifters," he said. "The past ten generations in my mom's family have been able to turn into animals. At least that's what my mom always told us. She could take any shape she wanted to, whenever she wanted to. I've seen her do it a hundred times."

"Shape-shifters," Gary repeated. "You mean, like werewolves?"

"Sort of," Dante said. "Except not just at the full moon and not true werewolves. Normal wolves, sometimes. Other animals, lots of times."

"That's ridiculous," Janine said. "People can't turn into animals."

Gary shrugged. "Lots of legends about it, going way back in history."

"Selkies," I said helpfully. "Seals that turn into people."

"Oh, and polar bears!" Rochelle said. When Gary and I looked at her doubtfully, she defended herself. "In my class on the histories of native people, we studied Inuit tribes. And some of them believe they can turn into bears and—and other animals. I mean, they *believe* it."

"But that doesn't mean they *can*," Janine said.

"I can," Dante said. "I do. Two or three days a month."

"Show us," Janine commanded.

Dante shook his head. "I can't do it at will. It's just something that comes over me and I can't stop it."

"What kind of animals?" I asked.

"Dogs. Deer. Foxes. Cougars. Mostly animals native to the Midwest."

"What's it like?"

"It's *made up*, that's what it's like," Janine said.

Rochelle gave her a frosty look. "Did any of us say we didn't believe *you* when you said you stole money from your dad?"

"This is hardly the same thing!"

"Yeah, this is a lot more interesting," Rochelle muttered. It was the first time I had seen the dainty blond girl challenge her more forceful roommate.

"So all those weekends you say you're going home to visit your mom—" Gary said.

Dante grinned. "Yeah. Sometimes I go see her, but I'm not human."

"That is so cool," Gary said. "I wish I could see it sometime."

"I don't like to be around people when I'm in animal shape. Except for family."

Rochelle's pale blue eyes were big. "Why? Are you *dangerous*?"

"I don't think so. No. It's just that—the way I think is different. My instincts aren't the same. I react like an animal instead of a person. It's hard to explain."

"Do you remember everything?" Gary asked. "Like—what you did and what you ate?" His face changed. "What *do* you eat?"

Dante grinned. "Just what you think I'd eat."

"Gross," said Janine.

"And you remember all that?" Gary pressed.

For a moment, Dante's handsome face looked uncertain. "I remember most of it," he said. "I think. But it's fuzzy. Time doesn't feel the same, and different things are important. Some of it doesn't stick in my memory."

"This is so *awesome*," Gary said.

Dante glanced around at the four of us. I thought I saw regret on his face. "I've never told anyone else before," he said.

Gary nodded. "Hence the rules of the game."

"I'd appreciate it if you didn't mention it to anyone else."

Janine snorted. "Anyone else would laugh us out of the room, so you can be sure *I* won't talk about it."

"I won't tell anyone," Rochelle promised.

"Me, either," Gary said.

Dante turned his gaze on me. I think it was the first time those divinely dark eyes had ever fixed on my face and actually *looked* at me. I was suddenly and deeply smitten—so much so that I forgot I was supposed to be making a vow. "Maria?" he asked.

"What? Oh, no, I'll never tell a soul. I swear it," I replied hastily.

Little did I know that making that promise would ensure I turned into one of the world's best liars.

Oddly, there wasn't much fallout from that stoned and drunken night of revelations. I never heard Gary or the girls question Dante about his amazing claim, none of us reported Gary to the school board for cheating, and no one turned me over to the cops for aiding a fugitive. No one much cared about Janine's confession, so the woman who instigated the whole event didn't have much to worry about.

I did try to talk to Rochelle once about her painful admission. We were in the cafeteria and ended up being the only two people seated at a small table during lunch. To my discredit, the first couple of times I'd seen her after the party, I had quickly turned the other way or pretended to be absorbed in another conversation. I wasn't able to cope with the knowledge I'd gained about her; it had changed her so much I was almost afraid of her—or maybe I was afraid of how awful I would feel if I learned more details. This was way worse than the beatings Karen had suffered, and until that point, Karen's father had been my standard for awfulness.

"So," I said as we sat there spooning up our mac and cheese, "have you written your paper for Russian lit yet?"

"I haven't even finished Solzhenitsyn yet," she said glumly. "Thanks for asking."

I mentally took a deep breath and shook my shoulders back. "Hey, I wanted to say something," I said, trying to pitch my voice exactly right between sympathy and admiration. "I thought you were really brave the other night at the party. Saying what you said."

I would never have thought such soft blue eyes could muster such a cold stare. "I was drunk," she said sharply.

I wasn't sure how to interpret that. *I was drunk, which is the only time I'd ever want to talk about such a thing.* Or *drunk, which means I can't remember what I said.* Or *drunk, so I made shit up.* "Yeah, we all were," I said. "But it was still pretty powerful. And I just wanted to tell you–"

She hunched a shoulder. "Don't."

"If you wanted to talk about it–"

"I *don't*."

"I mean, I'll listen, if you want, but maybe you should find a therapist, a professional. Something that traumatic can stick with you–"

"Jesus, Maria, what does it mean when someone tells you they don't want to talk about something?"

"Well, I think it might be important that you do," I finished. "As your friend, I just thought I should say that."

"Great. As my friend, just finish your lunch."

I held up my hands, palms out, conceding defeat. "Okay. I have the study guide for *The First Circle* if you want to borrow it."

She nodded but didn't look up. All of her attention was focused on her macaroni and cheese. "Yeah, that'd be great. I'll be down in the study lounge tonight."

"Okay, I'll bring it by."

We labored through another fifteen minutes of conversation before Rochelle declared herself done with lunch and carried her tray away.

I sat there by myself ten minutes more, worried that I had said too much, worried that I hadn't said enough. When do you trust people to solve their own problems, when do you force them to take your help? When can you trust yourself to have a clearer view of their pain, their danger, than they can from inside the maelstrom? And why would you ever believe you have the power to reach out your hand and stop the bitter winds from their poisonous swirl?

I hadn't wrestled with those questions often and I couldn't come up with satisfactory answers. I would discover, over the years, that I never could. I never believed that excused me from the obligation of trying.

There was one unexpected and monumental side effect of the party held on the night of the blizzard. Dante asked me out.

Snow was still on the ground a week after the storm, and I was getting pretty tired of wearing boots everywhere, not to mention gloves and the ugliest hat in the history of winter. I always found it so hard to look cute in cold weather. My eyes would tear up, my face would splotch with red, and I would swath myself in so many sweaters and scarves and socks that I looked like one of those children stuffed into a snowsuit and sent out to the backyard to play. Even more than I did in summer, I resented beautiful girls who seemed to float effortlessly through the season. They wore chic-heeled leather boots and white parkas with a fluff of fur that framed their faces, and their skin took on a healthy rosy glow. I trudged. I coughed. I blew my nose. I fell on the ice. I spent three months feeling clumsy and oafish and monstrous.

Dante didn't seem to notice either my unattractive attire or my grumpy expression when he came across me sitting just inside the front door of the dorm, trying to repair a broken bootlace by knotting the frayed ends together. "Hey," he said. "On your way to or from?"

I glanced up at him, so startled he actually noticed me that for a moment my hands lay lax on my laces. "Uh, to. I have a three o'clock Ancient Egypt lecture."

"I'll walk over with you," he said casually.

He would? Really? *Dante?* "Great," I said, my voice just as casual. I finished the knot, tied a sloppy bow in the shortened laces, and grabbed my backpack as I stood up. "I haven't been out yet," I said. "Still as cold as yesterday?"

He didn't exactly hold the door for me, but he pushed it open and made sure I'd stepped out behind him before he let it go. I squealed as the frigid air hit my face, and he laughed. "Maybe colder," he said.

"I keep looking for the forsythia," I said with a sigh.

He glanced down at me in amusement. I was tall for a girl, not quite five-nine, and my boots added another inch and a half. But I was still an inch or two shorter than Dante. "You'll have to explain that to me."

"Forsythia," I said, waving a gloved hand. "It's one of the very first signs of spring. You see it in mid-March. Sometimes it blooms and there's another snow, so you have these bright yellow flowers in a patch of ice. But at least you know winter is *almost* over."

He shrugged. "I don't mind winter that much. I like to ski and snowmobile, and I like to hike in the woods. It's a totally different experience on a winter day. You hear different things. You see animals you don't notice in spring." He pointed to the thin, interlaced branches of a bare oak looking like a crosshatched woodcut against the ancient vellum of the overcast sky. "You see bird nests left behind—things you'd never see on a summer day."

True, in this particular tree there were three dark clumps of coiled leaves and twigs that might have been home to robins or sparrows on warmer days, though I couldn't say the ability to locate them gave me any greater appreciation for the dreary weather. "Well, I guess you get points for seeing the beauty in the season," I said, trying to be fair, "but I still hate winter. I always have."

"What's your favorite season?"

"Autumn," I answered without hesitation. "And October is my favorite month."

"Let me guess. Your birthday is in October."

"*No*, it's in the spring. I just like the colors. And the weather. Cool enough to wear a light jacket, but not so cold that you have to take ten minutes to put on all your extra layers before you step out the door."

"I like autumn, too," he said.

I noticed he hadn't asked me *exactly* when my birthday was. He wasn't really investigating me; he was just making small talk as we walked together along a common path. "And I like Halloween," I added.

He was silent a moment. I couldn't tell if he was trying to think up a reply or if he was sorry he'd initiated this conversation because I was turning out to be the dullest woman he'd ever encountered. I tried to come up with a new topic but my mind was as blank as a field of freshly fallen snow.

When he spoke, he surprised me. His deep voice was slow and serious; he seemed to be sharing a thought he hadn't put into words until this moment. "I like Halloween, too," he said. "It's the one day I don't feel so much like a freak."

"A freak?" I repeated reflexively. *What?*

He nodded. "This whole shape-changing business. It makes me weird. But on Halloween, everyone dresses up. Everyone tries to be someone or something they're not. I feel a little more like I belong."

I couldn't decide if this was sad or endearing. I certainly didn't know how to answer. So I just said, "I don't think you're a freak."

We had reached the semicircular patch of sidewalk that formed a sort of landing pad right outside the building where my history class was held. I was sorry to realize my conversation with Dante was almost over, but really excited I would soon be in a warm place, out of the wind. I shivered a little as he came to a halt and seemed to expect me to pause alongside him.

"What do you think I am?" he asked.

When in doubt, go with the truth. "A really cute guy who dates a lot of hot women."

A smile brushed his full lips and was gone. "Just because they're hot doesn't mean they're nice."

"Yeah, guys always *say* things like that, but I've noticed they still like the beautiful girls."

"That wasn't what I meant, though," he said. My confusion must have showed on my face because he clarified. "When I asked you what you think I am. If you don't think I'm a freak."

Fighting back another shiver, I regarded him for a moment, trying to figure out what was behind the question. What did he want from me? "I don't know you that well," I said slowly. "You always seemed like someone who was sure of himself, not too worried about what happened around you. Maybe not too connected to other people, but not afraid of them, either. Just living your own life without being bound by what other people thought. But I don't really have any idea."

"I'm not," he said. "Too connected to other people, I mean. You got that right."

"You have friends, though, don't you? I mean, you seem to get along with Gary just fine."

"Yeah, Gary's cool. He takes people for what they are and doesn't get too worked up about things. But in general—" He shrugged. "I'm not always sure what other people are thinking. I'm not always sure what to say to them. I don't know if it's okay to ask them questions."

Was that what this was all about? "You can ask me questions," I said.

His dark eyes darkened even more with some passing thought; his eyebrows drew together as if he was working through a puzzle. "Did you really hide your friend in the gas station and never tell anyone where she was?"

I stared up at him. I could no longer feel my toes and my cheeks stung from cold, but I knew we had to finish this conversation—and we had to finish it outside, where no one was close enough to overhear. "I really did," I said.

"She knew she could trust you with her life," he said.

"She was my best friend."

He lifted a hand and for a moment I thought he was going to touch my face. He wasn't wearing gloves; I imagined his fingers would feel like icicles tapping the frozen surface of my skin. "I have a feeling most people know they can trust you," he said. "Even if they're not one of your best friends."

That sounded embarrassingly melodramatic, but I was pretty sure he was sincere, so I just said, "I hope so."

"I've seen you around the dorm," he said. "You're usually talking to someone, like you're in some deep, serious conversation. Except, you're always the one listening. The other person is always the one talking."

I opened my mouth, shut it, tried again. "Yeah, well, that's just girls, you know? We always think everything's a big dramatic event in our lives, and we have to tell someone else about it. I do my share of talking, too."

"I just have this feeling about you," he said. "Like I'd be safe with you."

Everything else fell away from me—the cold, my various physical discomforts, my ongoing wonder at the notion that *Dante Romano* was bothering to have a conversation with me at all. "That's kind of a weird thing to say," I replied in a quiet voice. "Why don't you feel safe with other people?"

He was staring back at me with those intense eyes, dark as a collie's. For a moment I flashed on the notion that he was some highly intelligent alien creature attempting desperately to communicate, attempting to *will* knowledge and understanding into my head since he was unable to formulate the words. "I think a lot of people would try to hurt me if they knew," he said. "I think people would like to experiment on me, or lock me up and see what happens when I take different shapes. Maybe I'm crazy, maybe I'm paranoid, but I just feel like, if people knew, they would put me away somewhere."

"That's what happened to the Dionne kids," I said.

My digression wholly confused him. "What?"

"They were the first set of quintuplets that survived birth, and they were put on display so people could walk by and stare at them. Like zoo animals."

A corner of his mouth twisted into a half-smile. I could tell that my comment had derailed him a little, but that he didn't entirely mind. He thought I was kind of funny, and not in a bad way. "Right. Just like that. I don't want people turning me into a tourist attraction. Or worse. And I've always thought that if I wasn't really careful, it could happen." He blew out his breath on a sigh of exasperation. "And I can't believe I was so drunk the other night that I told *four* people the truth about me."

I was backhanded by a curiously strong slap of disappointment. "Oh. Are you making a point of talking to each of us separately and asking us to keep your secret?"

His eyes were fixed on my face again. "No. I'm hoping everyone thought I was just making up stories. I mean, that's what Gary said to me the next day when we woke up—hungover as hell, I might add. He said, 'You just invented all that shape-shifting crap on the spot, didn't you?' I said yes."

I cheered up instantly. "That's probably what Janine and Rochelle thought, too."

"But you didn't," he said.

Again, my first answer died on my lips. For a long moment of silence, I met his gaze squarely. I was searching his eyes, searching his face, looking for truth; I was opening up my own soul to him, hoping he could read it through the medium of expression. I was asking and answering with one long stare. *Will you promise never to lie to me? Will you promise to share all your secrets with me, all your heartaches, all your fears and all your sorrows? In return, I will believe in you, I will support you; I will be your safe haven and your source of strength. If you trust me, I swear that your trust will never be broken.*

"I didn't," I said at last. "I thought you were telling the truth."

"It didn't make you afraid," he said.

I shook my head.

"It didn't make you—*excited*—like, in a creepy way," he added.

I couldn't help a giggle. "No."

"What did you think?"

"I thought, 'No wonder Dante is so interesting.'"

He reared back a little, as if that wasn't the answer he was expecting and he wasn't sure he liked it, but then his face relaxed. "Right," he said. "You just figured it's what makes me *me*."

"Part of what makes you *you*," I corrected. "There's got to be a lot more to you than changing shapes two or three days a month."

He wore an arrested expression. "I guess so," he said. "But mostly that's what I figure controls my life."

"If you let it, I suppose. But—what about the other twenty-eight or twenty-nine days? I mean, you're taking classes, you're holding down jobs, you're dating girls, you're seeing movies and reading books and skiing and hiking and *living*. You're not just the person who changes into an animal now and then. You're a person who does a lot of other stuff."

He was smiling broadly. I wasn't sure why he thought my comments were so funny. "That's right," he said. "So can I date *you*? While I'm doing all this other stuff?"

I wasn't sure I'd heard right. "Are you asking me out?"

"Well, duh."

"I don't seem like your type."

Now he laughed out loud. "You're kind of in-your-face honest, aren't you?"

"When I'm not keeping secrets," I amended dryly. "Yes."

"So will you? Go out with me, I mean?"

Suddenly I felt fluttery and nervous. "Sure. If you, you know, have a specific thing in mind you'd like to do."

He laughed again. "How about dinner? How about tonight?"

Now my frozen toes felt like they were floating several inches off the unfriendly ground. "That sounds great."

"What kind of food do you like? Pizza? Burgers? Seafood?"

"Yes."

"All right. I'll come by your room around six thirty, does that sound good?"

"Yes."

He bent down to peer at me in exaggerated concern. "Are you going to be able to say anything but 'yes' during the whole meal?"

My mouth shaped the word again and he shook his head warningly. I laughed. "Depends on what you ask me," I substituted.

"I'll see if I can come up with some interesting topics," he said. "See you later."

He nodded and took off, striding back toward the dorm. Cold as I was, dumbfounded as I was, I just stood there staring after him. It was hard to determine which part of our conversation I had found most astonishing.

The fact that he asked me out, I decided at last. As if in a trance, I turned slowly toward the door and finally stepped into the heated air. But it was as if I no longer cared or noticed that my toes were frozen, or that my hands were blocks of ice. Like Dante himself, I had transmogrified into some magical nonhuman state where common concerns of the flesh ceased to matter. I thought it was likely that I would never feel ordinary again.

The truth is, I never have.

CHAPTER FOURTEEN

The rest of the week stumbles by like a drunk on a bender, but most of us manage to get a little work done. I have a series of end-of-the-month reports to finalize, and they take a clear head and reasonable concentration, so I am forced to shut down the buzzing in my brain in order to get them finished. I contribute to the fund-raiser held on Kathleen's behalf, dutifully ask Ellen and Marquez if they have any news, and shake my head like everyone else when it turns out the police still haven't identified the animal that attacked Ritchie in the park.

"But I watched the news last night on Channel 5," says a woman from the marketing department, speaking in a meaningful tone of voice. "And one of the reporters—that good-looking guy, you know, Brody something—he was saying that all sorts of questions were being raised by the media. Is there a dangerous animal on the loose? Can all these deaths be tied together? He said the police will have no choice but to close the parks down until this thing is caught. And if the police won't do it, maybe the governor will."

"Well, it's about time," says a girl from the mailroom. "I'm afraid to leave my house these days! I mean, don't they care about public safety? I can't believe the families of the dead folks haven't sued the state over this."

On Wednesday, I run into Grant in the lunchroom. I haven't seen him since he was wearing his snow leopard costume on Halloween. He greets me with a quiet "hey" as I head to the hot water dispenser to make a cup of tea.

"Have you talked to Kathleen?" he asks.

"Not since Sunday. Ellen's going over there this afternoon, though."

He nods and then just stands there, stirring creamer into his coffee. This is the first time I can ever remember seeing Grant without a smile on his face. "I just can't stop thinking about her," he says. "She was so happy at the party. She was wearing this kitten outfit, you know, with these paper ears and whiskers painted on her face. She was saying how much she loves Halloween, that Ritchie would dress up like a mummy and hide behind one of the bushes, and when kids would come up and ring the doorbell, he'd walk out with his arms in front of him, stiff, like he was dead—" He shakes his head, not able to finish the sentence.

"Yeah," I say heavily. "The whole thing just sucks."

"It makes you think," he replies. "You never know. You think you have all the time in the world and then—" He snaps his fingers. "Gone."

I feel certain Marquez and Ellen would want me to take this opportunity to do a little spy work, so I force myself to make the monumental effort of an inquiry. "You mean, like, chase the dreams you've put off? Or tell people you love them? Or stop living a lie?"

He nods. "All those things."

I find that even knowing how ephemeral life is does not make me any more inclined to start sharing certain truths about myself. I'm already pretty good at telling people I love them—some people, at least. So Ritchie's death, while it is having a profound impact on my existence, doesn't make me want to modify my behavior.

I know I should ask, "Who do you love?" but instead I go with, "You've been living a lie? Do tell."

Now his face takes on its more accustomed contours as he grins. "I'm really a white man," he says.

It's so unexpected that I choke on my tea. And then I laugh. I had thought laughter was a thing of the past. "God, I never would have suspected," I gasp.

"I've been meaning to confess for a long time now."

"I won't tell anybody," I promise him.

"I know you won't. Everybody knows they can trust Maria."

Right before the day ends, my mom calls. She and Aunt Andrea drove down from Springfield this morning to go shopping, and they've decided to spend the night in St. Louis. Would I like to have dinner with them?

"I'd love to," I say. God, yes, undemanding and affectionate company to fill the nightmare hours. "Do you want to stay at my house? One of you can have the spare room and one of you can sleep on the couch, unless you'd rather share a bed."

"No, Andrea has some AARP discount at a hotel in Clayton and she wants to use it. And she has some frequent-flier miles she wants to apply before they expire. I couldn't follow it all, to tell you the truth, but anyway, that's where we're staying."

"I'll meet you at six."

I pick them up at their hotel and we head to the Delmar Loop, a funky little area close to Washington University, crammed with shops and restaurants. Delmar Avenue is impassable on weekend nights, but since it's Wednesday, we don't have much trouble finding a parking spot or a table. As we stroll by Iron Age, my mom and Aunt Andrea dare each other to go in for tattoos, and then start giggling like teenagers.

"You ought to do it," I say a few minutes later as we study our menus at Blueberry Hill. It's a restaurant/bar/live-music venue where Chuck Berry still performs from time to time. Mostly college students hang out here, but my mother likes hamburgers, which the place is famous for, and Aunt Andrea likes any place with a lot of color and noise. "Get tattoos. I think it would be cool."

"Yeah, mine would say, 'Older than dirt,'" Andrea replies with a snort.

"I could get a dinosaur," my mom says. "Low on my back, where all the girls have them. What do they call that?"

I am dissolving with merriment. "A tramp stamp."

"Right. I want a dinosaur tramp stamp. A triceratops."

"Bet they'd do it," I say.

"I think I'll get a nipple ring instead," Andrea says, which sets me off again. "I think their sign said they do body piercing, too."

My mom frowns in my direction. "You don't have any tattoos, do you?"

"No, and no nipple rings, either."

Beth has a tattoo, though I don't say so, of course. Clara's name, in a small heart, inked over her left breast just low enough that a reasonably cut neckline or swimsuit will cover it. I went with her when she had it done—here at Iron Age, as a matter of fact—and I seriously considered getting one of my own. I would have, if I'd been able to settle on something that I wanted to be branded onto my skin forever. I've never been able to come up with a slogan I wanted for a vanity license plate, which could be easily discarded; it's even harder to decide on a permanent ornament for my body.

Well, Dante's name, of course. That has occurred to me. But do I put it over my heart, where it would make him laugh every time he made love to me? On my butt, which seems somehow disrespectful and a little offensive? Around my wrist like a lacy bracelet, where anyone could ask me what it meant?

If he had some definitive alter ego. If he were always a fox, always a bear. I could have opted to have a small stylized creature etched into my flesh, would have come up with some explanation that would satisfy Beth and Ellen and anyone else who noticed. But Dante changes too much to be captured by any kind of indelible medium.

And now. Now he may have morphed into a murderer.

Determined to shut off that line of thinking, at least for the evening, I glare at my menu. Blueberry Hill has a decent selection of vegetarian items, and I settle on red beans and rice, along with a salad. My mom and aunt order burgers and beers, which for some reason amuses me.

"So what did you buy, since you came to town to shop?" I ask.

This elicits a rather long story about the stores they visited at the Galleria and the West County mall. Andrea has a niece on her husband's side who's getting married next month, and she's searching for a dress to wear to the wedding.

"The bridesmaids are wearing a color called mermaid," she says, looking mystified. "What do you suppose that means?"

"Mmm, something kind of watery-looking, I suppose," I reply. "You know, blue or green or a mix of the two. Sea foam."

"In my day, we called it aqua," my mother says.

"So did you find something to wear when you swim out to the wedding?" I ask.

"I *did*," Andrea answers. "It was on sale, too."

Our conversation continues along much the same lines for the rest of the meal, which is very good. Neither of them likes to stay out late, even when they're not far from home, so I return them to their hotel by eight thirty. Andrea climbs out of the backseat as soon as the car comes to a halt. She's already on her cell phone, since Sydney called just as we arrived in Clayton. My mother pauses with a hand on the door.

"You look tired," she says.

I smile. "It's nighttime. You can't even see my face."

"I was noticing as we sat in the restaurant. Is everything all right?"

Everything is as far from all right as it could be, but I do not want to burden her with that information. "It's been a rough week," I admit. "I told you about Kathleen." I had phoned her Saturday night, shortly after I'd gotten Ellen's initial call but before I had learned the cause of death. Back when I could still be rational about the whole thing. "It's had this horrible effect on everyone in the office. No one can concentrate on work, but no one knows what to do for her and—well, it's been sort of awful."

She reaches up to pat me on the cheek. For a moment I lean my face into her hand, deriving more comfort than I would have expected from that simple touch, so familiar, so reassuring. This is the woman who saw me through the first unbearable calamities of my life, whether she was required to kiss away bruises or stay up till midnight as I sobbed about the breakup with my latest boyfriend. This is the woman who taught me that grief can be endured, faced down, and left behind, sometimes with grace, sometimes with scars, always with stubbornness. The potential disaster looming before me is greater than any of those that have come before, but her touch reminds me that the same skills and strategies must come into play.

"You'll be fine," she says.

I lean over to give her a hug. "I know I will," I say. "I'm glad you guys called. Have a good day tomorrow."

"We will," she says as she gets out of the car. "You, too."

I think that is far less likely.

In fact, at first it seems as if Thursday will be indistinguishable from the rest of the week, just as dreary and unproductive, though I do my dogged best to churn out the most essential reports. Ellen calls around eleven.

"I have to drive down toward St. Clair and drop some stuff off this afternoon. You want to ride with me and have lunch somewhere?" she asks.

"Sure. Anything for a distraction," I say.

"Let's leave around one. See you later."

It feels good to get out of the office, good to be in motion. Activity always makes you feel like you're making forward progress, even if the activity itself is circular and meaningless. I watch the scenery as Ellen goes west for about ten miles on I-44. This far from the city proper, we're practically in farmland; there are great tracts of open fields, visible humps of forested foothills, hunched up along either side of the highway. Here in early November, most of the autumn color has given way to flat brown and sandy beige, but now and then a lone tree flames against the sere countryside as if it's bearing a message from God.

Ellen pulls off the highway, swears under her breath as she makes two wrong turns before finding the office she wants, some featureless one-story clapboard building with six cars in its rutted parking lot. She leaves the motor running as she goes in and drops off an envelope. She's back in less than a minute.

"I'm *starving*," she says.

I glance around. We're in some small town that squats alongside the highway, but I can't imagine it offers too many opportunities for fine cuisine. "Do you think they even *have* restaurants around here?"

"Oh, yeah, I've been here a dozen times. There's a place down the street that has pretty decent food."

Five minutes later, Ellen pulls up in front of a hole-in-the-wall pub in a strip mall that also features a hair salon, a used bookstore, and a pizza parlor. It's high noon, so we're not surprised when our skimpily clad hostess, who barely looks old enough to work in an establishment that serves liquor, tells us the only seating left is in the bar.

"Works for me," Ellen says, and we follow her to a small table crammed against a wall. From where I sit, I can see five neon signs advertising different beer products and three high-def television sets broadcasting sporting events. None of the patrons are paying much attention to the games, so I assume they're reruns of the past weekend's matchups.

I know St. Louis County has been debating ordinances that forbid smoking in public areas, but either the rule doesn't hold in bars or the folks in this corner of the world have decided the law doesn't apply to them. At any rate, the bar half of the restaurant is foggy and pungent with cigarette smoke. Ellen takes a deep breath as if inhaling a bouquet of lilies.

"*Love* that smell," she says and flips open her menu.

It turns out the pub doesn't have much in the way of vegetarian selections, but I manage to put together a meal of French fries, an iceberg lettuce salad, and fried mozzarella sticks. Ellen orders a Bud Lite, so I do, too. What the hell. It's not like I'm getting much work done at the office anyway.

Our conversation is pretty desultory until the meal comes, and we only talk about Kathleen for ten minutes, which has to be a speed record for the week. Over the meal itself, Ellen relays an anecdote about her most recent visit to the vet with her ancient and ornery Maine coon cat. Between the easy conversation and the beer, I find myself smiling and relaxing as I have not done in days.

So I am caught completely unprepared when Ellen shoves away her empty plate and says, "So what's been bugging you?"

For a moment, I think it's generic. *Enough about me—what's up with you?* But I can tell, by the narrowed intensity of her eyes, that she's being far more specific. *Why the fuck are you moping around these days? It's not like* your *husband is the one who died.*

Nonetheless, I try to look innocent and uncomprehending. "What do you mean?"

She makes a gesture. "You've been—like this *haunted* thing for the past week. You hardly talk. You hardly eat. It's obvious you're not sleeping, 'cause you look like shit. I just want to know why."

I attempt a patronizing little smile. "I know you want to, but you can't fix everybody's problems. So worry about everyone else, and take me off your list."

"I didn't say I could fix it, I said I wanted to hear what it is," she replies. "And you're my friend. You're always gonna be on my list."

"That's sweet," I say. It seems pointless to deny that there's something wrong, so I shrug and add, "But I don't really want to talk about it."

She shrugs, too. "Well, I've got time." She signals the waitress and says, "We'll have two more Bud Lites."

Now my eyes widen. "What—you think we can sit here the rest of the day? You're going to ply me with alcohol until I crack?"

"Something like that."

"We both have jobs—or we *did*, when we left an hour ago."

"Yeah, I told Frank we might not be back. I said we were taking some stuff to Kathleen." She grins. "He said fine."

My mouth falls open. "I can't believe you would take advantage of somebody else's tragedy to suit your own personal agenda."

"Yeah, well, I figure you're having a tragedy, too, so it all seemed kind of karmically appropriate."

"It's not a tragedy," I said. *Maybe it is.*

"So tell me."

I just shake my head. Ellen reaches for her purse, pulls out a pack of Kools, and lights one up. She takes a drag as if she is sucking on oxygen in the cargo hold of a compromised spaceship, and without it she will die.

"Put that out!" I exclaim. "You quit!"

"Bought a couple packs this weekend once we left Kathleen's," she says. "Went straight to Walgreens when I dropped you off."

"Oh, just like Grant," I say in a scoffing voice. "Ritchie's death has made you rethink all your priorities. 'If I die tomorrow, what will I regret having done or not done?' And what you regret is *cigarettes*?"

"No, what I regret is not sleeping with Kurt Armstrong in high school because I thought good girls waited till college," she says. "But it's a little too late to go back and change that one."

She's made me laugh, so when the waitress arrives a moment later with our beers, I start drinking mine, which I had initially decided not to do. "Seriously. The cigarettes?"

"I bought two packs. I'm gonna finish them and then quit again."

"You better."

She smiles, takes another puff, and blows a smoke ring. She hasn't touched her second beer. "So. What's going on?"

"You wouldn't believe me if I told you."

"Honey, at this point if you told me you were being abducted by aliens on a regular basis, I would believe you. I know there's *something* happening. I'm guessing it's got to do with that sexy guy who shows up at your house now and then. Maybe he dumped you. But I don't know, it seems worse than that."

"Though that would be bad enough," I say.

"So tell me. We're not leaving until you do." She makes a vague motion. "You're too far away to walk back to the office. I don't imagine they have taxis in this town. You gotta stay here till I take you back. So talk."

I start picking at the label painted on my beer. The waitress has brought us each a glass, but neither of us has bothered to use one. I can't quite explain it, but I've always liked the sort of breezy confidence you seem to show when you guzzle booze straight from the bottle. Sipping is for nerds and people pretending to be refined. Swigging is for the cool kids.

It's not the alcohol. It's not the empathy. It's not the venue, smoky and gritty and so ground down that you know every single person sitting there has troubles too big to handle alone. It's the terror, the worry, the great gaping uncertainty that has become my life, and presses down on me so hard I feel it squeezing out the words I thought to never say aloud. I *want* to tell Ellen, and I have never wanted to tell anyone before. I want someone else to know, someone to stand beside me at that dark portal into oblivion and clutch her fingers in my belt loop and haul me back when I begin to fall.

Still, it's hard to know how to begin. I start by asking, "You watch any of those TV shows about vampires and werewolves and stuff like that?"

Ellen lifts her eyebrows but doesn't seem unsettled by the seeming non sequitur. "Some of them. I think they're pretty stupid. Oh, but I liked *Dark Shadows* when I was a kid."

"So you understand the concept of a—a shape-shifter. Someone who can take animal form when he or she feels like it."

I expect her to say *What the fuck?* or *Girl, you are even crazier than I thought.* Some sort of reasonable response wrapped in Ellen-speak. But she sits there a long moment, just watching me. She's holding the lit cigarette so that the smoke drifts across her face, but it's the only thing that moves while she thinks this over.

When she answers, it's with her own non sequitur. "When I was fifteen, I used to babysit this kid down the block. Little girl, six or seven years old, blond and skinny. She didn't like me very much. She lied all the time—even her mama knew that. You'd say, 'Sammie, did you break this glass?' and she'd say, 'No, the dog knocked it over,' even if you'd seen her do it. Even if she *saw* you seeing her do it. Little shit."

She pulls on the cigarette again, blows out the smoke in one long, even stream. "She used to tell me she could turn into an animal if she wanted to. So I'd say, 'Fine, then, show me,' and she'd say, 'I don't want to do it *now*.' And, of course, I didn't believe her. But every once in a while—"

Ellen pauses to remember something, and I see her shake off the slightest shiver. "I'd go look for her and I couldn't find her. I'd think she was in the basement, so I'd go down there, and she wouldn't be there. So I'd come back upstairs, look around, go downstairs again—and there she'd be. Big as life. It wasn't a real large space, there weren't closets or boxes big enough to hold a child. But a hamster? Or a mouse? Sure. There were little nooks and crannies where something that size could hide."

Now she takes a few swallows of her beer. "Once she was out in the yard—or I thought she was—but I couldn't find her, and I checked under the bushes and behind the garage. There was a stray cat sitting on the woodpile, watching me, but it jumped off and ran into the neighbor's yard when I told it to go scat. I went back in the house, checked the front yard—Sammie wasn't there. Out to the backyard again—and she was there, climbing over the neighbor's fence."

She fixes her eyes on my face. They're wide with remembered disbelief. "Well, you know. I still didn't *really* believe she could change shapes. I mean, that's impossible, right? But it spooked the hell out of me."

"Did you ever tell her mother what she'd said to you?"

Ellen shakes her head. "I figured, why bother? Either it was *true*, and her mama knew, and her mama was a shape-shifter, too. Or it was a lie, and I'd look like a fool for even asking about it. So I never said anything." She sips her beer again. "In fact, I'm not sure I ever told anybody until right this minute."

I barely smile. "I'm honored."

"So? Is that what you're telling me? You can change shapes?"

"Not me," I say. "Dante."

I've only told her his name once, but, being Ellen, she recognizes it instantly. "That's your mysterious boyfriend's big scary secret? How come he finally told you now after fifteen years?"

I shake my head. "No, I've always known he was a shape-shifter. That hasn't changed."

"Really? And you've *still* slept with him all this time?" Her face lights up as a new thought comes to her. "Hey, do you ever do it with him when he's, like, a dog?"

"Ewww! Ellen, that's disgusting! Why would you even think that?"

"Well, why wouldn't I? I mean, I'd guess that would be one of the perks of—"

I wave a hand. I think she's kidding—though, I don't know, Ellen doesn't really have that many boundaries or taboos. "Stop. No. Never."

"Fine. Whatever." She sucks on her cigarette one last time, then stubs it out. "Prude," she mutters under her breath.

Weirdly, this exchange has the effect of loosening the band of pressure that has circled my ribs for the past week. I have a moment where I can actually take a deep and unrestricted breath. "Sometimes it's impossible to have a conversation with you."

"Sorry," she says. "So. Dante can change shapes, not that it ever benefits you, and you've known about it forever. So why are you suddenly acting like you're standing under the world's biggest rock and it's about to land on your head? *Did* he dump you?" She can't repress a snicker. "For a tiger? Or a chimpanzee?"

"No. No, as far as I know, we're still good."

She reaches for her pack of cigarettes again, hesitates, and puts it back in her purse. I notice there are only three left. Maybe she's saving them for a time she really needs one. "Then what is it?"

"Maybe you can figure it out," I say evenly. "What's happened lately that might make me worry about a boyfriend who can turn into almost any kind of animal?"

She makes a face—*Fine, make me answer riddles*—and rather ostentatiously assumes an expression of fierce cogitation. But it doesn't take her more than a minute to put the pieces together. *Kathleen. Ritchie. Mauled to death by a still unidentified creature . . . who might also have left human footprints behind . . .*

"Oh, shit," she says, and pulls out that smoke after all.

"Exactly," I say in a very dry voice, and gulp down the rest of my beer.

Not until she's taken a couple of drags on the fresh cigarette does she speak again. "What did he say when you asked him?"

"I haven't seen him since it happened."

"So you don't *know*—I mean, you just suspect—"

"I can't believe it's true and I tell myself that every minute, but then this little voice in the back of my head says, 'But it *might* be true,' and I can't shut that voice up," I say. "And I don't know what I'm going to do when I see him again. I don't know what I'm going to ask him. I mean, how can you look at someone and say, 'So! Kill any human beings since I've seen you last?' I mean—if he hasn't, he'll be so hurt and offended he might never speak to me again, and if he has . . ."

My voice trails off.

"If he has," Ellen says quietly, "your own life is in danger."

Mutely, I look at her. All the reasons I have had for keeping silence so long suddenly rush back at me, clamoring, gibbering, screeching out my stupidity. God, how could I have told her this story? I have betrayed Dante as surely as if I threw a net over his head and dragged him to the nearest police station. *I* will never turn him in, but *Ellen* will. She'll have to. She's not a priest or a lawyer, someone sworn to secrecy no matter how heinous the confession she hears. She is more like a social worker, a teacher, someone trained to look for the burned hand or the broken wrist. The person who must call the hotline, confront the perpetrator, expose the abuse.

So long. I have been faithful for so long, have lived in silence and shadows. I was prepared to take this secret with me to the grave. I have woven the most complex and skillful webs of lies, have spoken them—unblushing and unremorseful—to the people I care about most in the world. And now all my carefully constructed fabrications have been yanked from their flimsy supports. I have been undone by grief, fear, and suspicion, all adding their own impossible loads to a burden that had already become almost too heavy to carry. But it does not matter why I have slipped and fallen; all I can see is the ruin I have caused by crashing down.

"Don't tell anybody," I whisper.

Her eyes are compassionate. The hand that is not holding the cigarette reaches out and brushes my arm. "Only if I have to," she says. "Only if it's true."

CHAPTER FIFTEEN

I don't say much as we drive back to the office, don't accomplish much before the day ends at five, don't allow myself to think much until I get home. When I step inside, I collapse on the couch and drop my face into my hands.

What have I done? What have I done? What have I done?

How can I repair it?

I can't think straight, and the disastrous events of the past week have seriously disrupted my internal sense of time. I can't remember when Dante is likely to reappear. Is it next week, or the week after that? I drag myself to my feet, cross to the kitchen to find the calendar hanging on the side of the refrigerator, the one that shows vintage travel posters for every month. If Dante's last significant length of time in human shape ended on October 20—if he's been staying in animal shape about twenty or twenty-one days—then he should be back very soon. Monday or Tuesday of next week.

Normally, this knowledge would make me wild with anticipation,

but now I stare at the stylized steamship with mounting horr
Dante returns I will have to conceal my doubts and inner turm
him, and simultaneously make sure he is safe—from Ellen, fro
body. I'm not sure I am up to these tasks.

But I have to be.

I boot up the computer, delete about forty-five e-mails ab
erectile dysfunction cures, then compose a cheery little message
Christina.

> I'm so glad you brought Lizzie by last week! She's the most adorable little girl, and I'd be happy to watch her for you again sometime. Listen, if you hear from Dante over the weekend, can you tell him to call me before he comes over? I think one of my neighbors is spying on me—long story!—and I just want to make sure everything goes smoothly next time I see him. I'll drop him an e-mail, too.
>
> Thanks!
> Maria

I don't know what the likelihood is that, in the next few days, Dante will be human long enough to call his sister, but if I *can* get a message to him, maybe I can avert catastrophe. Or, at any rate postpone it. In case he checks e-mail but doesn't make any phone calls, I also send a note to him.

Hey lover, I write, since that is how I always start my letters to him.

> Call me if you get a chance. There's a situation here and I want to avoid it if I can. Maybe we can meet in Columbia or Kansas City next time you're available? Let me know. Miss you miss you miss you love you miss you.
>
> M

/ he is. He has an animal's instincts for dan- sixth sense will warn him that trouble awaits house might no longer be a haven. Surely he choose, I would rather have him abandon me

ng when I arrive at work, there is a white van emblazoned .ocal NBC affiliate's logo and sporting what looks like a .a from its back door. Standing on the path that leads from g lot to the front door are two men: One is a sort of scruffy ating a professional-quality video camera, the other is an actor- ome man dressed in a neat trench coat and holding a microphone. t looks like the local media has come to call.

I'm a little early, so the parking lot has only about half the usual num- ber of cars, though more are turning in as I sit in my front seat and try to figure out what to do next. At the moment, none of the employees are actually speaking to the reporter, but I have no doubt that some of them will be only too happy to share their impressions with him. I am certain he has come to ask about the murder. Unless something really spectacu- lar has happened overnight, there is nothing about our little company, or our neighboring tenants, to interest a news-gathering organization.

I stare a little harder at the reporter. No, he's not here about the mur- der per se. He's here about the *murderer.* This is the guy who has been publicly demanding that the mayor or the public safety commissioner or the governor disclose information they might be withholding about the marauding animal, and further calling for them to close the parks until the animal is killed or captured. It takes me a moment to remem- ber his name. Something Brody. No, Brody Something. Brody Wester- brook. I'm guessing he made the name up because it would sound good when intoned by an announcer on CNN. He's a slim brown-haired man who appears to be just under six feet tall. He looks bigger on television, but I suppose the camera always bulks people up. His face is handsome, with regular features and an attractive smile. I suddenly hate him more than I have ever hated anyone in my life.

This is even worse than me telling Ellen about Dante. A pushy investigative reporter trying to make a name for himself might try all sorts of stratagems. For instance, he might stake out the houses of Kathleen's coworkers, hoping they're so rattled by his ambush that they make unguarded comments about what a terrible job the authorities are doing protecting the good people of Missouri. Obviously, he wouldn't be *looking* for shape-shifters who magically appear in the middle of the night, but he would be pretty damn excited if he happened to catch one on camera.

I see Caroline stalk by Brody Westerbrook with a contemptuous expression and a swirl of black skirts. Not two minutes behind her comes Grant, who doesn't pause, either, though he offers up his usual friendly smile. The girl from the mailroom, though, *she* is willing to stop and talk. I see her wave her hands, pause to point at something invisible across the street, and then continue relating her story with great animation. Brody Westerbrook keeps his expression serious and his eyes on her face, nodding several times as if she is confirming something he has always suspected. I see him mouth the words "thank you" before she resettles her purse on her shoulder and trudges on toward the front door.

No one else is immediately available to talk to the newsman, and he says something to his cameraman and rubs his gloved hands together. No doubt he's freezing. It's barely thirty degrees this morning, and he has probably been standing out here for at least a half hour. I'm already cold, and I just turned off the motor five minutes ago.

I still don't get out of the car. I am afraid that if I try to hurry past Brody Westerbrook, he will block my way, he will stop me. If he does, I am afraid I will shove him or kick his cameraman or start screaming maniacally in his face. And then *I* will become the interesting story; I will be the one Brody Westerbrook follows home. It is much too dangerous for me to catch his attention.

It is, no surprise, Ellen who comes to the rescue. I see her red Miata spitting gravel as she wheels into the parking lot. She no doubt spotted the NBC van from the road and instantly figured out why it is here. She is fighting mad as she leaps from the car and practically runs up to confront the reporter. I see the cameraman swing his lens around to capture her tirade, but Ellen doesn't care. She is literally shaking her finger under the reporter's nose, and once she actually shoves him in the chest. Though she is probably seven inches shorter than he is, and at least forty pounds lighter, I would put my money on her in a physical contest; you just know Ellen can fight dirty.

They're far enough away that I only catch pieces of the altercation.

"Get the hell off this parking lot! You have no right to be here unless you have permission—"

"It's public property and I have every right—"

"It's *private* property, and I'm calling the cops!"

"Ma'am, I am a member of the news media, and under the Constitution I have the right to speak to anyone who is willing to speak to me—"

"Fine! Then do it from the other side of the road, because this is private property and I swear I will have you arrested!"

I wait until Brody Westerbrook and his colleague climb back into their white van and, slowly enough to show they're doing it under protest, pull out of the lot and park across the street on the shoulder of the road. Then they disembark and continue filming, as Brody speaks into the camera and gestures toward our office building. I can only imagine what he's saying now about freedom of the press and uncooperative citizens.

I take a deep, shuddering breath, and finally get out of the car.

As you might expect, the office is in a shambles again this morning. Everyone mills around the break room, sipping coffee or pouring a second cup just because they can't bring themselves to go back to their own offices and sit in silence. I hear the frequent refrain—"Did *you* talk to the reporter? What did you say?"—and a mishmash of replies. A fair number of people think Brody Westerbrook is using the power of the press to ensure the safety of the city, and they're damn proud of him; the cynics say he's mounted this campaign merely to boost his own career. I'm in the latter camp but I don't offer an opinion. I don't want to speak to reporters and I don't want to speak to my fellow employees. I just want to get through the day with as little damage as possible.

Accordingly I huddle in my office, stare at my screen, and actually manage to produce a few of the more urgent reports. I decline the offer to have lunch with Grant and Ellen and a new girl in the creative department; I can tell Ellen is not surprised by my refusal, but she doesn't push it. She's strolled by my office a few times today and glanced in, but she's kept her distance. She must know I feel like one single exposed nerve and that she's the one who cut me open. But I know Ellen; this unaccustomed restraint won't last long. By next week, she'll be badgering me again. *Have you talked to him? What did he say? Are you all right? How can I help?*

A friend like Ellen is both a blessing and a curse. I'm convinced that even if I quit my job tonight, never came back to the office, moved to a different house, got an unlisted phone number, changed my e-mail address, she would still find a way to track me down. *Are you all right? How can I help?* There are days I know I am lucky to have won a friend who is so steadfast, so insistent. Today is not one of those days.

A little after three, I hear the muffled sound of my cell phone singing inside my purse. It's a scramble to dig it out before the music stops, and I sound breathless when I say, "Hello?"

"Hey, baby," says Dante's voice, and I feel my whole body spike with emotion. Elation and terror, equally fierce. "Got your message. What's going on?"

"Wait, let me close the door," I say. After I've accomplished this task and sunk back into my chair, I say, "Dante, it's been so awful here. Kathleen's husband, Ritchie, was killed, and so everyone feels terrible for *her*, and no one's getting any work done, and now the reporters have started hanging around the office, interviewing anyone who will talk to them. So first it was depressing but now it's scary, because I don't want any reporters following me home and accidentally getting a glimpse of *you*."

I have deliberately left out any mention of how Ritchie died. I have, with some calculation, allowed myself to sound so stressed and worried that I am not entirely coherent. My hope is that he won't ask for too many details—and he won't come to the same conclusions I have. *Hey, this sounds like he could have been murdered by a man who's sometimes a beast. Does Maria think I had anything to do with this?* But, of course, my account is so vague that I am braced for a few questions.

"He was killed? That's terrible. How did it happen?"

"The police haven't been very specific." I have a sudden inspiration. "He was in Babler one morning pretty early. I've heard speculation that it might have been a drug deal gone bad."

Drug dealers. They use guns, or so I think. They're unlikely to be shape-shifters. At any rate, if you think the cops are looking for a drug dealer, you won't waste your time wondering if they're looking for *you*.

If you think everyone else, even your girlfriend, believes that drug-dealer theory, then you can relax, even if you know the story isn't true.

Half my life, I've been lying *about* Dante. Now I'm lying *to* him. I find, to my dismay, that it's just as easy.

"Well, I'm sorry," he says, and he sounds sincere. "How's Kathleen holding up?"

"Not too well. She hasn't been at work all week. We've taken turns going to visit her and bringing her food and stuff, but—It's just so awful. Nobody's getting any work done."

"Sounds like you need a weekend," he says. "Today's Friday, isn't it?"

"Very good! You must have seen a newspaper." I try to take a bantering tone.

His voice matches mine. "I glanced at CNN.com when I checked my e-mail at the library."

"Wow, so, you've been human for a while, huh?"

"Not quite an hour. I don't think I have much time left."

"I've been trying to figure out when your next long stretch will be. I think maybe Monday or Tuesday of next week."

"Feels about right," he agrees.

"Listen, what do you think about what I said in my e-mail? Meeting up in Kansas City or Columbia? Can you get that far? I just–I think I need to get away from here. A little vacation sounds nice. And I *don't* want that stupid reporter snooping around my house."

There's a smile in his voice. "Oooh, hot vacation spots–Kansas City or Columbia! How will you choose between them?"

"If you were closer, I'd smack you," I inform him. "I will *choose* based on what's easiest for *you*."

"Right now I'm in the Blue Springs area," he says. "So Kansas City would be easy. But how do you want to work this? I can't figure out the logistics."

All the time I've spent *not* thinking about work has been spent wrestling with just this problem, so I have my answer ready. "You know where the Marriott is in the Plaza?"

"Sure."

"You call me the minute you turn human for the long haul. I'll phone the hotel, reserve a room, give them my credit card, say you'll be checking in first. I'll have my bags packed already, and I'll just hop in the car five minutes later. I can be there in about four hours."

"That'll work," he says. "But it's a lot of effort for you."

"Effort I am happy to expend on your behalf, silly."

"But if this happens, say, next Tuesday—you don't have much vacation time left, do you? Is this really how you want to spend it?"

Still holding the phone to my ear, I close my eyes and prop up my head with my other hand. I feel as if I have shut out the world, as if nothing exists but this small private cocoon of sound, my voice, Dante's voice. "Yes," I breathe into the phone. "I want to spend it with you."

I can tell he still feels a little doubtful—on my behalf, not his—but he doesn't have the time right now to probe or argue. "Okay. See you then. I'll skulk around Kansas City and call you the second I can."

"Love you. Can't wait to see you."

"Love you more," he says, and hangs up.

I slowly fold the phone shut, then slowly bow my head to the desk and pillow my forehead on my arms. Good. For the moment he is not at risk. He's in the western part of the state and he'll stay there, at least for the next week or so. He has not yet realized that I suspect him of murder—and if I am any kind of actress, he will *never* realize it.

For the moment, nothing has changed. All is well. Like the tightrope walker I am, I have achieved a moment's stasis; I am perfectly poised above a jagged chasm, perched on the narrowest possible support. The smallest miscalculation—a weighted gesture, an incautious tilt of my head—could cause me to overbalance and tumble, spinning, to the bottom of the rocky gulf. There is no safety net to catch me if I fall, nothing to intervene between me and ruin.

I must be very, very careful.

According to the informal lottery we have set up at the office, it will be my turn to go to Kathleen's on Sunday. On my way home from work Friday night, I swing by a Schnucks grocery store and pick up some beef. I figure if Dante was in Blue Springs this afternoon, there's no chance he's been captured and slaughtered in time to be turned into hamburger at my local butcher's counter by this evening.

When I arrive at my house, the white husky is sitting on my front porch, waiting for me. "Hello, sweetie," I say, bending down to scratch her head with one hand while I hold the straps of the canvas grocery bag in the other. "Are you hungry? Thirsty? Give me a minute to put everything away and I'll be right back out."

She licks my fingers, then settles on the concrete as if she's understood my words. Maybe she has. In the kitchen, I hurriedly stuff grocery items in the pantry and the refrigerator, depending on where they belong, and then I haul out the dog paraphernalia. It takes me multiple trips to carry out the bowl of water, the bowl of food, and the old blanket for her to sleep on. She has taken up her old place, under the carport, against the wall of the house that borders the kitchen. There's a small toolshed situated at the end of the driveway, and it helps block out most of the evening wind.

But I'm worried. I stand and watch while she devours the food as if she hasn't eaten in three days. She looks relatively healthy, and I don't immediately spot any fresh wounds, but it's supposed to get cold tonight—dropping into the low twenties at least. She looks built to withstand an Alaskan winter, but I can't shake the idea that she isn't really a dog, and maybe not suited for outdoor living.

"Would you like to come in the house to get warm?" I ask her. "You'd have to stay in the kitchen because, pardon me, you're a little dirty, but I swear I'd let you out again in the morning."

She glances up at me and wags her tail a little; again, I'm convinced she caught the sense of my words. But when I open the side door that leads to the kitchen and try to lure her inside, she won't cooperate. She refuses to budge when I make coaxing noises, and when I approach her, she dances away, uttering a short bark. She might be playing. She might simply be saying, "Stop it, Maria. I'm not coming in the house."

"Well, hell," I mutter, and ponder for a moment. I ordered a new dishwasher last year and it arrived in a huge shipping box, which I broke down and folded flat and stored in the basement in case I ever needed it. So I fetch that, along with a couple more blankets, and I fashion a padded nest for my stubborn visitor. She knows exactly what it's for. The minute I crawl back out of the box, she trots in, tramples a circle in the pile of blankets, and drops down with a sigh. Resting her pointed nose on her paws, she regards me from her haunted blue eyes.

"Yes, but that's still not exactly *warm*," I tell her. I'm too afraid of fire to run an extension cord out the side door to power a space heater, and I don't really know what else I can provide her. Maybe a hot water bottle filled with steaming contents. Swap it out at midnight if I happen to wake up. "Though I suppose you've been sleeping out in the cold for the past few nights and you seem to have managed just fine."

I refill the water and food bowls before finally going inside. I'm already chilled to the bone, which makes me worry even more about the husky.

I make myself a light dinner, check my e-mail, talk to Beth, try to read a book, try to watch a television show, convince myself that I'm tired enough to sleep. First I carry a hot water bottle out to the husky and debate where to place it near her body to do the most good. Eventually I wrap it in a fold of the comforter and snug it up against her stomach. Her mouth is stretched in what appears for all the world to be a laugh.

"Sleep well, my friend," I tell her, patting her on the nose. "Let me know if you need anything."

Then I go to bed and toss and turn for hours, catching snatches of sleep in short, unsatisfying intervals. I do get up once around three and head out in the frigid cold to retrieve and refill the hot water bottle. The white dog stirs when I approach, but doesn't sit up; when I return with the bottle wrapped in a towel, she looses a sigh that sounds like contentment. I'm probably projecting my emotions on her, but the whole interlude makes me feel a little better.

As I turn back toward the house, I glance toward the shadows of the front lawn. I'm standing in the broken patches of light spilling out of the kitchen window, so my eyes can't adjust quickly enough to penetrate the deep darkness of the yard. But there's a shape there—a silhouette against the empty road—and two amber refractions at about the height of my knees. Before my brain even consciously analyzes what I'm seeing, I experience a visceral spurt of fear that has me scrambling for the door. I'm inside and slamming the lock home before I've even realized I'd better run. My stomach churns with adrenaline and my arms feel weak.

Wolf. Lean body, pointed ears, hunter's eyes. Focused on me.

There are no wolves in Missouri, I remind myself, but I know what I saw. And anyway, the police haven't yet identified the animal that attacked Ritchie. Wolf or not, what if this is the beast that has developed a taste for human blood? It would be an incredible coincidence, yes, but why couldn't it have wandered by chance to my house and happened to pause in my yard just at the moment I stepped outside? Even if this particular beast is not a killer, surely I am justified to feel afraid of it. Primitive instincts, primal fear, would have urged me to flee the minute such a creature stepped into my sight.

Of course, it's just as likely that the wolf is not an animal at all. I believe there's one shape-shifter sleeping under my carport. Who knows how many others might be wandering the countryside while the rest of us carry on with our familiar, oblivious lives?

Or it could be Dante.

He told me he was in the Kansas City area, but I have no way to verify that's true. After all, last month he told me he was in Sedalia when, in fact, he was near enough to call me from my own area code. He might be curious about my sudden aversion to having him in my house; he might have recognized the falseness in my voice and guessed I was lying about something, even if he couldn't guess what. He might have come by tonight to see if I was entertaining a much more interesting guest than a lost dog.

If we have started distrusting each other, lying to each other, I don't know how much longer this relationship can survive.

CHAPTER SIXTEEN

It is close to five in the morning when I finally fall into a heavy sleep filled with fleeting, stressful dreams that leave my shoulders cramped and my hands clenched. The sound of the doorbell startles me out of bed about three hours later. I actually leap to my feet, staring around wildly, until I realize what the insistent ringing means. I grab a robe and stumble to the door, not even bothering to glance in the vanity mirror as I pass. I know I look dreadful; whoever is at the door deserves to know they woke me up and that I'm not happy about it.

I'm expecting Beth, maybe my mother, possibly some overzealous deliveryman who doesn't know to just leave packages on the porch and drive away. A tiny, rebellious corner of my brain thinks—hopes? fears?—it might be Dante, human and on my doorstep even though he's been warned away. But the face looking back at me through the small window in the front door is not one I've ever seen at my house before.

"William," I say blankly as I open the door. The tone of my voice supplies the unspoken words: *What are you doing here?*

"Christina said she was worried about you and I came to check up on you," he says.

I open the door wider and gesture for him to enter. Cold air rushes ahead of him like a playful puppy. "There's some weird stuff going on here and I'm not sure it's safe for—" I give him a look, not certain how to phrase it. "Unusual people to be hanging around," I end lamely.

He appears amused but steps inside. "You look like shit," he says pleasantly.

"Thank you, so do you."

He does, too. As always, he is lean to the point of emaciation, wearing clothes so thin and ragged that I can hardly guess where he got them and why he keeps them. Maybe they're items he's owned for twenty years and only wears a few days a month when he happens to take human form. They aren't particularly dirty or stinky, so Christina—or someone—has kept them clean for him. He's not wearing a coat. His shoes are disreputable old Nikes that can't possibly have any support left. His hair, in a ponytail, hangs almost to his waist, and his stubble looks like it's at least three days old. I spare a moment to wonder how fast stubble grows on a man who's in animal shapes most of his life.

Then I wonder if he was the wolf I saw in my yard last night, and if he's been here checking up on me for longer than I realize.

I decide not to ask. I jerk my head toward the kitchen and say, "Go make yourself comfortable. Give me five minutes to get presentable, and I'll come out and make you breakfast."

"Sounds like a plan," he says, ambling across the floor.

It's more like ten minutes before I've brushed my teeth, washed my face, combed my hair and pulled it back into a clip, and thrown on some sweatpants and a T-shirt. I still don't look great, but at least I feel human. *More human than William does, I bet,* I think with a silent snicker. The touch of humor makes me more cheerful than I've been for days.

William's started the coffee—which surprises me somehow; he

doesn't seem like the type to develop familiar addictions or know how to operate household devices—and is enthusiastic about the idea of eggs and bacon. He sets the table while I cook, though he handles the plates gingerly, as if afraid he will break them.

"So what's going on here that's got you so upset?" he asks as he pours orange juice. I notice he's used wineglasses as juice glasses, and I decide I like the touch of elegance. William has always seemed the most mysterious of the Romano siblings to me; maybe he's got a poetic streak. Or maybe he doesn't know the difference.

I try to remember what I said in my e-mail to Christina. *I think one of the neighbors is spying on me . . .* "Jeez, what has happened *since* makes what I told her seem tame," I say with a slight laugh.

He looks over at me with an arched brow. "So?"

I'm scrambling the eggs while the bacon cooks in the microwave and the bread browns in the toaster. I concentrate on the pan before me. "Last week, I thought the guy down the street was way too interested in my life. Every time I turned around he was out in his yard, watching me, *filming* me. I don't know, maybe he got a new video camera for his birthday or something, but it was giving me the creeps. And I didn't want Dante just showing up and—and—transmogrifying on my front porch while this guy was pointing a camera in my direction."

I glance at William and he seems suitably impressed. "That would make an interesting bit of footage for the evening news," he says.

"Funny you should mention the evening news," I say. The microwave beeps just as the bread pops up. "Can you get that? There are hot pads on the counter."

William fetches the bacon and toast and arranges them on the table while I spoon eggs onto our plates. In a couple of minutes we're sitting across from each other, munching. I'm not a great cook, and I don't usually have an appetite first thing in the morning, but even I think everything tastes pretty good.

"We've had this awful event at my office. A woman's husband was murdered," I say around a bite of toast. I figure I don't have to be too specific; I don't think William watches much TV. "Which was bad enough, but yesterday some Channel 5 reporter and cameraman showed up at work and started interviewing people about the murder. Our office manager kicked them off the property, but they went nattering on about freedom of the press, and I have this terrible suspicion they might start coming to people's houses to ask them questions. And that would be even *worse* than having neighbors spying on me! If some reporter got shots of Dante changing shapes, it would be disastrous."

William is licking jelly off his fingers. I notice that his hands are clean enough but his nails are dirty. "I don't tend to panic, myself, but you seem to be showing a reasonable amount of caution in this instance," he says. When I give him an indignant look, he grins. "I'm serious. It wouldn't be so great for Dante to get caught on film."

"Or *you,*" I say pointedly. "So I hope you were careful about how exactly you materialized on my front lawn this morning."

He's still grinning. "I'm always careful. Don't live too long as a shape-shifter if you're not."

You don't live too long as a shape-shifter even if you are, I think. "So you've seen Christina lately?" I ask.

He nods. "Yeah. I don't usually stray too far. Don't go more than a hundred miles from St. Louis, as a general rule. So I go by her place once a week or so."

I tilt my head. "And turn human?"

He smiles again. "Not usually."

"So she—what?—she talks to you while you're in animal shape, and you understand her?"

"Something like that."

That's evasive enough to make me wonder if the Romano kids have other supernatural powers: telepathy, ESP, mind-reading abilities. If so,

Dante has never mentioned them. I decide I wouldn't believe it if even William claimed it was true, so I just drop that line of questioning. "How's Lizzie? Did you see her?"

"Yeah." He shakes his head admiringly. "She's something special. Cutest thing I ever saw. And not afraid of me at all."

I decide not to follow *that* opening, either. "Well, you can tell Christina I got in touch with Dante and I'm going to meet him in Kansas City next week. So neither of you has to worry."

"Good to know," he says, nodding. He doesn't add aloud the thought that is clearly visible on his face. *I wasn't worried to begin with.*

I've now pretty much exhausted any conversational topics I have in common with William, so the sound of the doorbell is almost a relief. Except . . . the same question arises that I asked myself the first time I got an unexpected summons this morning. Who would just show up at my door before nine o'clock on a weekend morning? I give William a considering look.

"If this is my mother or my cousin—I have no idea how I'm going to explain you."

He shrugs. He's not worried about my reputation any more than he's worried about Dante's safety. "Tell them I'm the neighborhood homeless guy and you take turns feeding me breakfast on Saturdays."

"You certainly look the part," I retort, "but they would consider the behavior out of character for me."

"What, you don't take in stray *people*?" he asks. "You're willing to take in stray *dogs*."

Which is the first time this morning I remember the white husky sleeping in the dishwasher box alongside my house. The husky that I am half-convinced is just as human as William. "Shit," I say under my breath. The doorbell rings again and I come to my feet. "This better be someone trying to sell me magazine subscriptions so he can finance his way through college."

It's not, though. It's Brody Westerbrook.

And his cameraman.

For a moment, I am too dumbfounded by the sight of them to do more than stare through the layer of glass, the layer of screen, that separate me from disaster. I hadn't *really* thought they would come to the house; that was just one of those stories that you tell yourself to whip up a level of fear that's already beyond the level of sanity. Brody is on the porch, a microphone in his hand. His colleague is a few paces behind him, standing in the grass, his camera pointed straight at me. A red light is blinking above the lens. I don't know for sure, but I think that means the camera is recording.

"Good morning, Ms. Devane, I'm Brody Westerbrook from Channel 5 news," he rattles off, speaking loudly enough that his words will penetrate through the storm door. "I'm doing an investigative piece on the series of murders we've had in the St. Louis area over the past six weeks, and I understand you're a coworker of the woman who recently lost her husband—"

"Go away," I say.

He steps a little closer, although he's already close enough that he could fog the glass with his breath. "Wouldn't you like to share your thoughts on—"

"No, I wouldn't. Please go."

He raises his voice. "You do realize that all these murders—and possibly more that we haven't been informed about—have been committed under mysterious circumstances by wild animals—"

"If you don't go away *right now*, I'm calling the police," I say, hoping I sound threatening instead of hysterical, which is how I feel.

I sense a shape materialize behind me, and suddenly William is at my side, sliding my cell phone into my hand. "You heard her," he says. "Get out."

Brody's attention instantly shifts William's way. He opens his mouth to ask the same set of questions, but I see him hesitate and reconsider, taking in William's ragged appearance and subtle aura of menace. Even I feel a sudden prickle of unease at William's proximity; he radiates a cold, coiled danger that was entirely absent as we shared our breakfast.

"Sir—" Brody begins, but William whips the door open and knocks the microphone out of Brody's hand before the rest of us have even reacted. Then he punches Brody in the chest, hard enough to make him stumble backward. He moves so quickly that the cameraman doesn't even think to come to his colleague's aid. He just stands there, staring, the camera blinking its red eye.

"I said, get the fuck out of here, asshole," William spits out. "And don't come back."

Brody straightens up and stands still for a moment—proving, I suppose, in some macho way, that *he is not afraid*—and then he nods once, short and sharp. He bends to retrieve his microphone, then jerks his head toward his cameraman. They cross the lawn to where the white NBC van is parked in the street. William steps inside and through the glass we watch in silence until they've climbed in and driven away.

Then he closes the door and turns to me with an amiable smile. "And here I thought you were exaggerating," he says.

That quickly, he is the old William, loose and relaxed and ever so slightly amused. But my head is suddenly filled with images from that fight between Ritchie and Dante, three weeks ago, right here inside the front door. *I will take your fucking head off,* Dante had said, and he'd meant it. I have no doubt at all that, if Brody had provoked him, William could have done some major damage to the reporter.

Why have I never seriously entertained the idea that shape-shifters might kill a man? These two incidents have made it chillingly obvious that they *could*. The only question left is whether they *would*.

"Yeah," I reply, making no attempt to erase the shakiness from my voice. "I kind of wish I had been."

"I don't think he'll come back," William says. "But if he does, call the cops. He has his rights and all, but so do you."

I nod. I'm still so unnerved by the whole brief exchange that I can't think of what to say. "Okay. I'll do that."

He sticks his hands in his worn pockets and glances around, as if looking for any items he might need to collect before he goes. "Well, I guess I found out what I came here to find out," he says. "Let Christina know if you need me for anything, and I'll be back."

"I'll do that," I say. We both pause for a moment, as if debating whether or not we should hug each other, and then he just shrugs and goes out the door. He shuffles off the porch, along the driveway, down the street. I stand pressed against the glass, feeling its icy smoothness against my bare skin, and watch him until he's out of sight.

This has been one of the strangest hours of my recent life, which has been filled with odd incidents.

Not until I turn back to the breakfast table and think, *I could feed the scraps to the dog*, do I remember that there is, in fact, a dog to be fed. With a muttered curse, I throw on a coat, stuff my feet into boots, and hurry out the side door to check on the husky.

But she's gone. The food bowl is empty, though there's about an eighth of an inch of ice at the bottom of the water bowl. The blankets remain piled inside the box and I am gripped by the ridiculous notion that the dog did her best, with teeth and claws, to fold them neatly so as not to leave a mess behind.

I glance from the makeshift doghouse to the spot where I saw the wolf's eyes in the middle of the night. When did she leave? This morning before I woke up? Last night, when the presence of a dangerous predator made her cede this territory without a struggle? When William arrived this morning—or last night? I wonder again if William was the creature I had spotted on the lawn, if he stayed to guard me through the dark hours of night. Could he have told me, if I'd thought to ask him, whether the white husky was a shape-shifter like himself?

Am I romanticizing all of this, seeing magical creatures and terrifying monsters where none truly exist? Perhaps even Brody Westerbrook is harmless.

Perhaps I am losing my mind.

Lost it a long time ago, I think. Wearily, I pull the blankets out of the carton, then fold it down to a manageable size, and lug all the dog gear back to the basement. But I leave all the pieces—the box, the blankets, the bowls, the bag of chow—at the foot of the stairs. That way I can get to them quickly in case I need them again.

The rest of Saturday holds no other excitement. I should be grateful for that, but instead the hours pass with a sort of sticky, unendurable slowness. I find it hard to concentrate, hard to settle, hard to function. But I do manage to get the house clean and finish off piles of laundry that have accumulated. I also pack two suitcases—one filled with my clothes, one filled with Dante's—and leave them in the trunk of the car. I top off my gas tank; I make up an emergency ration pack of bottled water, soy bars, and apples, and this goes on the front seat for easy access. I have looked up the phone number of the Marriott in Kansas City and programmed it into my cell phone, which I obsessively recharge every few hours. I want to be ready to leave the moment I hear Dante's voice.

When I've completed all my preparations for travel, I chop up ingredients for beef stew and place them in the Crock-Pot so they can simmer overnight. This is what I plan to bring with me to Kathleen's tomorrow. Also some rolls and a small carton of strawberries that was ridiculously expensive. But strawberries always make me feel better, so I hope they will have a cheering effect on Kathleen as well.

I do all of this with a nervous, jittery intensity that feels like the manic alter ego of depression. Once all my chores are finally done, I try to sit and relax, but neither books nor television shows can hold my attention. I spend a lot of time solving Sudoku puzzles and playing Scrabble against the computer. I wish I knew how to knit. I wish I could bring myself to take up smoking. I think if I could occupy my hands, then perhaps I could occupy my mind, or at least distract it.

Sunday morning I head to Kathleen's, arriving a little before noon. It is hard to think of a place in the world where I would less like to be. At the door I am greeted by her sister, who looks a little more rested but not much happier than she had last week. "Thanks for coming by," she says, taking the Crock-Pot from my hands. "I hope you'll stay and eat with us."

"Sure," I say. "How is she?"

Kelly just shakes her head. "She's in the living room," she answers, and moves toward the kitchen.

I make my way to the room of blue hearts and ruffled curtains. Kathleen is sitting in a denim-covered recliner, wrapped in what appears to be a homemade afghan in a zigzag pattern of blue and white and seafoam green. *Mermaid,* I correct myself, and almost smile. The television is on, though the sound is almost down to zero. Her eyes are turned toward the screen, but I don't have the sense she's really watching the program, which appears to be an old *Law & Order* rerun.

"Hey," I say. I seat myself on the corner of the couch that's nearest her chair.

Without lifting her head from the back of the recliner, she turns to look at me. I can tell her hair has been washed and she's put on mascara, so she has at least made a little effort this morning, or Kelly has bullied her into it. "Hey," she replies.

"I brought you some beef stew. And some strawberries."

"Thanks. Ellen was here yesterday and she brought chicken chili."

"Mmm, sounds good."

"People must think I'm about to waste away. They keep trying to feed me."

I make an uncertain motion with my hands. "Well, they want to do something useful, but they don't know what. Cooking makes them feel like they're *doing* something. It helps *them*, even if it doesn't really help you."

A faint smile touches her lips and fades. "It's kind of weird," she says. "I always felt sort of–left out–at the office. You know, like I didn't really have too many friends there. I mean, everyone was polite, it was just . . ."

Her voice trails off. I nod instead of speaking, since I think she's got more to say.

Her voice picks up strength. "But everyone's been so *kind*. I mean, people I didn't even think would recognize me in the hall have sent me cards and flowers and come by with food. Part of me wants to say, 'Where were you *before* all this happened?' But mostly I'm just amazed at how nice people can be."

"That's good to hear," I say. It's hard to think of an appropriate response.

"Even Caroline," she goes on. "I mean, have you ever had a real conversation with her? I haven't. But she sent me this note. About her father dying when she was twelve. He was murdered in a robbery, did you know that? And she was there. He ran a corner liquor store when she was growing up, and he was shot five times during a holdup. She and her mom were in the storage room in the back when the men came in–they heard the whole thing. She says that to this day she can't go into an independent liquor store. If she wants alcohol, she buys it at the grocery store, or she sends someone else to get it."

I am blank with surprise. "No. I never heard that story. That's awful."

"But she said I'd get through it. She said I might never get *over* it, but I'd get better. Like she did."

"That was—wow. I wouldn't have expected that from Caroline." I wonder if Ellen knows this story. I wonder if Grant knows it. "I guess the only thing good about going through a tragedy yourself is that you can tell other people how to make it to the other side when it happens to them."

Kathleen stirs and then straightens up, pushing the chair around on its swivel base so she is facing me more directly. "I think I'm coming to work tomorrow," she says.

"Really? Are you ready for that?"

"I think it would be better than just sitting here all day, thinking. I keep having the same conversations in my mind, over and over again. Asking Ritchie not to go. *Insisting* that he not go. Or going with him. Maybe if I'd been there, too, I could have picked up a branch and beaten it off—or called for help—or something."

My heart in my throat, I ask, "Has the coroner been any more specific about what kind of animal attacked him?"

She shrugs. "They've tentatively decided it was a wolf, though they're still investigating."

"I thought we didn't have wild wolves in Missouri anymore."

"That's what I said. But Kelly did some Internet searches and she found a few reports about timber wolves wandering down from Minnesota and Michigan. Apparently every year or so some bow hunter sees one when he's out looking for deer." She shrugs again. "Or, I don't know, maybe it escaped from one of the wolf sanctuaries. I know there are a couple across the state."

Or maybe it was a man who just happened to take wolf shape that morning. "I guess it doesn't really matter to you where it came from," I say softly. "I'm just sorry it happened to be there the same day Ritchie was."

"Yeah," she replies on a long sigh. "But at least the police are releasing the body now. I can have the funeral."

"Oh, that's good," I say, though *good* seems like the wrong word to apply to any part of this situation. "When will it be?"

"Wednesday."

Unless something goes very wrong, I won't be anywhere near St. Louis on Wednesday. "Oh, no," I say, infusing my voice with regret and effortlessly conjuring a cover story. "I've already promised my mother I'll take her in for a colonoscopy on Wednesday. I'm probably going to be spending Tuesday night in Springfield with her, too."

"That's okay," Kathleen says. "You've done so much for me already."

Including protecting the man who may have killed your husband. "I'd be there if I was in town, I really would."

"I know," she says.

A moment of silence falls between us. She drops her head back against the chair, and I can tell, by the way her eyes lose focus, that she's watching some internal memory play out. I cast about for something else to say, but she's the one who speaks again, her voice low and dreamy. "We had a huge fight two days before he got killed. I told him I wanted to leave him. I told him I wished he was dead."

I'm in shock. In part because I'd thought Kathleen never stood up to her violent husband—in part because I don't remember her sporting any new bruises the week before he died, and I can't imagine Ritchie responding in a reasonable manner to such statements. Of course, he was still wearing the cast on his right arm; maybe that limited his ability to punch her. Though I suppose he could have bludgeoned her with it. I stumble through a response. "We all say things when we're mad or upset—things we don't mean. Just because you said it out loud doesn't mean it was true."

She's still viewing the rewind of that fight from a week and a half ago. "I meant it when I said it," she replies. "I really wished he was dead."

"And what did he say?" I ask a little fearfully.

She's silent a moment. "He said," she finally answers, "that I was the one who'd be dead if I ever tried to leave him. He said he would kill me if I tried to go."

We're both quiet after that. As far as I know, Kathleen has never told anyone that Ritchie threatened her and beat her up. I had been under the impression that she hadn't admitted, even to herself, what a scary and dangerous man he could be. I wonder if this is the first time she has ever said the words out loud. "I'm sorry," is all I can think to say. "I'm sorry that that's one of the last memories you have of him."

"I know he loved me," she says, her voice dropping to a whisper. "He *did*. He just didn't always know how to show it."

"I believe you."

Now her eyes focus, suddenly and with unnerving intensity, on my face. "But when they called? The police? To tell me he was dead? Maria, it's terrible. But for a minute I was glad. I was glad he was dead."

It is as if the words have been scraped out of her by a sharp, serrated tool. Her voice breaks as she speaks the final sentence, and then she starts sobbing, great, rough, bitter sobs. I leap to my feet, thinking to take her in an embrace, but she has pulled the afghan up over her head and huddles under it, still weeping loudly. Kelly comes rushing in from the kitchen, her hands covered in soapsuds.

"What happened? What set her off?" she demands.

I am not about to repeat what Kathleen said. I shake my head, feeling even more useless—worse than useless, harmful—than I did when I came in. "She was talking about Ritchie, and then she started crying," I say helplessly. "I'm sorry—I don't think I said anything—maybe it's better if I go—"

Kelly wedges herself into the chair beside her sister and wraps her arms around Kathleen. Muffled sobs are still issuing from under the bright woven yarn. "Sometimes they blow over really fast, these crying jags," Kelly says. "Please stay. At least for a while. It's easier sometimes when someone else—"

She doesn't complete the sentence, but I know what she's going to say. It's easier when someone else is here to bear some of the burden of conversation, to help shore up the barricades against grief. "Of course," I answer. "Why don't I go set the table? Call me if you need help in here."

A few minutes later, I gather around the oak kitchen table with Kathleen, Kelly, and Kelly's husband, Tim. Tim is thin and bespectacled, serious and quiet. I think he earns major points for staying here a week with his grieving sister-in-law and still looking like he has stores of patience to draw on. Kathleen doesn't even try to make conversation, so the three of us struggle through various discussions of our jobs, our recent electronics purchases, and movies we've seen. Tim's a software guy, a computer geek, so I ask him about problems I've been having with my printer at home, and that fills ten minutes. Kelly and I compare notes on vegetarian diets, since she's considering going meatless "when all this is over." I ask when they plan to go home.

"Not anytime soon," Kelly says, eyeing her sister. "Tim and I can both work remotely, so we've been able to keep up with our jobs since we've been here."

"Oh, that's nice. I'd like to work from home."

Tim speaks up. "Your kind of job, I'd think that would be a real option."

"Well, I've done it from time to time—when we had bad weather or I was home sick but there was a report I had to finish—but my company doesn't really want to set that kind of precedent. They like us to all *be* there, under their watchful eyes."

Kathleen stirs herself to speak. "I'm going in tomorrow," she says.

Kelly looks concerned. "Honey, are you sure—"

"I can't just sit here for the rest of my life, feeling terrible," Kathleen says with a little more energy. "I'm going in."

Kelly glances at me, and it's easy to read her expression. *Will you make sure she's okay?* I offer up a false smile and say, "Hey. It will be good to see you there. Everybody's missed you."

Kathleen nods and answers a statement I didn't make. "Yes. It's time for me to get on with my life."

I would curse the arrival of Monday morning except I think it brings me that much closer to seeing Dante. Despite everything—my fear, my worry, my grief, my confusion—whenever I think that I will soon be holding him in my arms again, I am filled with a building sense of excitement. He is dawn, he is Christmas morning, he is the promise of spring, the baby's birth, and the return of troops at the end of the war. He is everything you look forward to with such intense longing that your body actually clenches with desire.

Because the birthday of my life
Is come, my love is come to me.

Perhaps he will call today. *I'm here, I'm in Kansas City. Come find me.* Or surely tomorrow. *Hey, lover, I'm human for a little while . . .*

I cannot wait to see him.

Even so, Monday is not a particularly easy day. Kathleen has, indeed, showed up for work; I had called Ellen last night to warn her that this was on the agenda. To make sure we are there to greet her, Ellen and I both get to the office early, and we share three cups of tea before another soul arrives. We don't bother making much conversation. We can't think of much to say that isn't pocked with pitfalls, and we're both too tired to try.

Kathleen walks in, Marquez at her side. It's clear they've carpooled or, more probably, he's picked her up on his way in. It's an act of such kindness that Ellen mutters, "I just love him."

"I know," I answer. "I do, too."

It's hard to know what to say to Kathleen, impossible to pretend that this is an ordinary day, so no one really tries. Most of the day, there is *someone* standing at her desk, making awkward but earnest conversation, and it's obvious she's not going to make much of a dent in the filing that's piled up in her in-box. But she'll get through the day, which is the main point, supported by the dogged goodwill of her coworkers. I envision us providing the emotional version of the "chairlift" carrying configuration we were taught in Girl Scouts, where two eager and determined young Scouts would intertwine their hands in such a way that their forearms provided a seat for a wounded comrade. They would then shuffle along for twenty or thirty yards, jostling their unfortunate passenger, tripping over their own feet, eventually collapsing in a giggling pile. The efforts we make on Kathleen's behalf this morning seem equally amateurish but equally hopeful. We are all trying to carry her for at least a short distance through the day.

I myself attack chores with an enthusiasm I haven't been able to muster for the past couple of weeks. If I'm about to take several days off, there are certain things I *must* get done, and I feverishly type up reports as the hours skid by. Naturally, Ellen has gathered a group to take Kathleen out to lunch and, naturally, I join them, but I take my own car and leave early, apologizing, so I can race back to my desk and keep working.

But the day ends sharply at five, and Dante hasn't called.

I go home and move aimlessly through the house for the next few hours, picking up and putting down books, turning television shows on and off and on again. I make sure I wash every dish as soon as I use it; I take out the kitchen trash as soon as I am done with dinner. The house is as neat and unlived-in as one that's on the market, ready for potential buyers to arrive unannounced at any moment. I want to be able to walk out as soon as the phone rings. I want no unfinished business to delay me for even five minutes.

The evening drags by and it's finally bedtime, and Dante still hasn't called. I brush my teeth, wash my face, and change into a lightweight tracksuit instead of pajamas. If he calls at three in the morning, I can just jump out of bed and wear this in the car.

But the night limps past, and I lie awake for half of it, and still Dante doesn't call.

Today, I think, once the clock reluctantly admits to midnight. *Today I'll hear from Dante.*

Tuesday is not much different from Monday, though I'm yawning a little more often and Kathleen seems to be getting a bit more work done. I see her in Frank's office, making notes on a steno pad while he talks. He's always been a good boss, in that he sets a general tone of civility, makes it clear what his priorities are, and then gets out of our way so we can get our work done. But he's never been particularly adept at the interpersonal skills of motivating employees or offering sincere praise, and he's abysmal at delivering negative feedback. His management style seems to be a dogged hope that all employees will simply do their best, but he's basically a nice guy. While Kathleen was gone last week, I noticed that he took all the plants from her desk into his office so he would remember to water them every day. It was a small gesture, but a kind one; it made me like him better than I already did.

I run into Ellen in the lunchroom and she gives me a knowing look. "Here's something that never occurred to me before—Frank and Kathleen," she says under her breath. "He's been divorced for five years. Maybe it's time he started dating again."

"For someone who can't claim the most successful love life *herself,* you're awfully eager to pair other people up," I say, pouring myself a cup of coffee.

She laughs. "I just like to meddle, and love lives are the most visible places to do it. If you had a child looking for a job, or a sister trying to buy a house, I'd be just as happy to jump in and start mucking around, offering my advice and doing a little networking for you."

"I'll keep that in mind."

Pleading a deadline, I skip the group lunch and manage to get my most essential weekly report done by three thirty. Just in time, too. My cell phone rings and I claw it open to breathe a hopeful greeting into the receiver.

"Hey, baby," says Dante. "You still want to come to Kansas City?"

I'm flooded with a tide of tingling adrenaline. If I wasn't already seated, I would have to drop to a chair, I feel that unsteady. "Yes, yes, *yes*," I murmur into the phone. "Give me five minutes to make the reservation, five minutes to tell someone I'm leaving, and I'll be on the road."

"Don't be careless," he says in a warning voice. "Don't drive too fast. I'd rather wait another half hour to see you than—than have you get in a terrible accident."

I laugh shakily. "All right. I'll be good. Are you someplace you can hang out for a while? Can you wait twenty minutes or so before you go to the hotel and ask if I've made a reservation?"

I hear the grin in his voice. "Yeah, longer than that, probably. I need to find a store where I can buy a sweatshirt or a T-shirt so I can look just a *little* more respectable before I walk in and claim a room."

"All right. See you soon. Love you."

"Love you, too."

I e-mail my report to Frank, turn off the computer, make sure nothing in the office looks like it's going to fall over or catch on fire, gather up my coat and purse, and head down to Ellen's office.

"I'm leaving for the day," I say baldly. "And I probably won't be back for the rest of the week."

She lays down the paper in her hand, which appears to be an invoice for furniture or office supplies. She's seated behind her desk, which is laughably huge for such a small person, and she's wearing her reading glasses, which add a touch of professional sobriety to counterbalance her bright blond hair and her vivid pink blouse. For a moment, she says nothing, just looks up at me over the rims.

"All right," she says finally. "Would you like to inform me what you'll be doing or where you'll be going? Inform me as your friend, not your coworker," she adds.

That *where you'll be going* is a shot in the dark, I'm sure, but it catches me off-guard and so I tell her, though I didn't plan to. "Kansas City. I'll have my cell phone with me if you need to text me. Or you could call me, of course," I finish lamely, making it clear which option I would prefer.

She takes off her reading glasses and tilts her head to one side, still watching me. "Is that where he is right now? Kansas City?"

"Ellen, I don't want to talk about this."

"But that's where he is? You're going to meet him there?"

I fold my lips and don't answer.

She nods. "Well. You're a big girl. And you're a smart girl. Don't do anything stupid. And if you're afraid—if you start wondering what this man is capable of—"

"I don't wonder," I interrupt. "I'm not worried. I'll be fine."

She nods again. "I hope you will. Have a good trip." And she puts on her glasses and picks up the paper again.

I walk out, part of me annoyed with Ellen, part of me mad at myself for telling her anything—and part of me, a teeny-tiny traitor part, grateful and relieved. Grateful that someone cares enough about me to worry about me and not hide the fact.

Relieved that, if I disappear, someone will know where to begin to look.

I push that thought down, bury it, stomp on the dirt till it lies flat, and cover it with leaves and dried branches so that no one will ever know it was there.

I'm in the car and on the road twenty minutes after Dante has called. I take 109 up to 64-40, and 64-40 until it intersects with I-70 and I can merge into the steady stream of traffic that endlessly runs east and west across the state.

Four hours from now I will see Dante again. It seems like a lifetime.

CHAPTER SEVENTEEN

I haven't been on the road more than ninety minutes when the early dark of mid-November lays its inky hand over the highway. The world shrinks down to the curve of red taillights racing ahead of me, the sweep of white headlights bearing down on me. I set the cruise control and grope for the snacks laid out on the passenger seat. My hope is to stop only once for gas, after I'm well past Columbia; I don't want to stop for food at all.

The intimacy of nighttime also enhances the poignancy of the music playing on the radio, and somewhere past Kingdom City I realize every station on my route is broadcasting songs that could be featured on the soundtrack of my life.

It doesn't start off so badly. Some oldies/top-forty station offers the Celine Dion version of "I Drove All Night," which seems eerily appropriate for the time and place. I sing along, dropping down an octave on the high notes. I can also appreciate Melissa Etheridge's "Come to My Window," a meditation on forbidden love and the reckless decision to pursue it anyway.

But then comes a whole stream of songs filled with loss and longing, and though none of them exactly matches my circumstances, the emotions are so raw and so spot-on that they resonate as if they had been written for me just this morning. Whitney Houston's "Saving All My Love for You," Phil Collins's "Can't Stop Loving You," Alicia Keys's "Fallin'." I punch buttons, but it doesn't matter which station I find, whether it's pop or rock or country or indie. Emmylou Harris sings "Boulder to Birmingham." Linda Ronstadt and Dolly Parton duet on "I Never Will Marry." Leona Lewis suffers through "Bleeding Love."

In desperation, I switch to CD mode, not even remembering what album I was last playing, but figuring it has to be an improvement. Oh, but it's not. Beth made me a compilation she titled *Great Love Songs from Broadway Musicals*, so first I get Ella Fitzgerald doing her version of "Can't Help Lovin' Dat Man of Mine," and then Shani Wallis performing "As Long as He Needs Me." If I remember correctly, the character singing that second song is later killed by her abusive boyfriend; there's a scenario that hits a little too close to home. With an inarticulate sound of irritation so intense it borders on hysteria, I punch back to the radio, then turn off the stereo system altogether.

It doesn't really matter if music sends me messages of warning, if friends gaze at me with worry and concern. I am rushing headlong through the darkness to fling myself into my lover's arms, and I don't believe even the apocalypse could stop me.

When I pull over to get gas, I find that Dante has texted me. (He disapproves of people who talk on cell phones while they drive, which is why he didn't call.) The message merely reads ROOM 1415. He's got the key, he's got the room, and he's waiting for me.

It is all I can do to remain reasonably close to the speed limit for the remainder of the drive.

It's almost eight thirty by the time I arrive in Kansas City. I get lost trying to find the Plaza, but finally make my destination. I sling a bag over each shoulder and practically run through the lobby to the elevator bank, and then I am almost insane with impatience as the maddeningly slow cage creaks its way to the proper floor. By the time I am finally knocking on the room door, I'm breathless from exertion or excitement or both.

Dante pulls the door open and I stumble into his arms, the luggage thumping at my feet. I clutch him to me and mold myself against him, lifting my face to be kissed even as I inhale the pleasing scents of soap, new clothes, and Dante's skin. He seems a little surprised at the intensity of my greeting, but he responds enthusiastically anyway, gathering me up in a hug that lifts me off my feet, and theatrically kicking the door shut behind us.

"I guess you missed me," he murmurs against my mouth.

I kiss him and then kiss him again. "You don't know the half of it," I say. Not that I'm about to tell him.

"Well, then," he says, carrying me deeper into the room. "Let's make up for lost time."

I spend most of the next thirty-six hours lying to Dante.

We don't leave the hotel room for the first twelve of those hours. After that passionate kiss in the doorway, we head straight for the bed, where we remember, in exhaustive detail, all the pleasures of each other's bodies. Even when our lovemaking has ended, I cannot bring myself to move more than three inches from his side. I want to feel the length of his body against mine; I need the constant reassurance of his steady heat, his untroubled breathing. I need to know that he is alive and, at least for this brief time, out of danger. It is not enough to merely be able to see him across the room. I must be able to press my hand against his chest, feel the swell of muscles, catch the faint rhythm of his heart, and read on his skin the story of his soul as if it were written in Braille.

He is always most willing to snuggle during his first few hours back in human form, and so my clinginess does not annoy him, at least not right now. We order room service, turn on the cable TV, and climb back into bed. I'm not really watching, but I can see familiar actors flickering across the screen, and once in a while I hear Dante's low chuckle. I don't care that he's actually watching the show instead of paying attention to me. His arms are folded around me from behind, his chin rests on the top of my head. He envelops me, he surrounds me, and I experience the most profound sensation of contentment. *If I could die now,* I think, wrapping my fingers around his forearms, *I would die happy.*

A commercial break prompts him to mute the volume. "So what's going on back in St. Louis?" he asks.

I don't allow my body to tense; we are so entwined he would surely notice. "Not much. Same old boring routine. I work, I come home, I wait to see you again."

"No, I mean—with your friend. Kathleen. Isn't she the one whose husband was killed?"

I turn a little in his arms, so I'm sprawling back on the pillows, looking up at him as he lies on his side. "Yeah. She's doing better. She came to work on Monday and seemed to make it through the day okay. Everyone dropped by her desk every five minutes to check up on her, of course."

"Have they found out yet who murdered him?"

For a moment my brain is empty; I can't remember what I told him. "They're still investigating," I say cautiously.

"But the cops still think it was drug dealers?"

I'm swept with relief. Of course! My inspiration. Drug deal gone bad. "Last I heard," I say, nodding. "One of the girls in the office said there was heroin found at the scene, but I think she made that up, since I never heard it on the news."

Dante strokes my hair, but his eyes are looking back at that Saturday morning when Ritchie made his memorable appearance at my house. "I can't say he struck me as the type," he says. "He was pretty fit. Sort of guy who works out every day and treats his body like a fine machine. I wouldn't think someone like that would use street drugs."

"Well," I say, "people will surprise you, even when you know them very well."

"I suppose," he says. "Did you ever hear any more from the reporters?"

I widen my eyes. "*Yes.* One of them came to my house over the weekend and wanted to ask me questions about the murder and didn't I think there should be better policing in the parks and stuff like that. It's really kind of spooky to think that a guy with a camera can just walk up to your front door and start filming you and anything you say."

Dante lifts his brows. "Good thing I wasn't there, changing shapes and looking suspicious."

"Yeah, but you know who *was* there? Which made it almost as bad. William!"

He looks only mildly surprised. "Really? What did he want?"

"To see if I was okay, I think. I'd told Christina I was looking for you, and I guess she told William, and he wanted to know if something was wrong." Dante doesn't say anything, so I add, "It was awfully sweet, but a little surprising. I didn't even know he knew where I lived."

"Of course he does. He knows it's a safe place. If anything ever happens to him and he needs help." The corner of his mouth pulls up in a half-smile. "You know, if he ever gets shot by a farmer and he needs a corner where he can hole up and heal."

I put my fist very gently under his chin. "Don't even say things like that," I tell him sternly. "What happens to *you* if you get shot by a farmer? And you're all the way in Kansas or Nebraska or Colorado or Montana or however far you roam? Where's *your* safe place?"

He narrows his eyes as if considering whether or not I will react favorably to a piece of information he could share. I sit up straighter in bed and lean my back against the headboard. "*You* have safe places," I say accusingly. "All over the state! All over the country?"

He waggles his head back and forth. "Not as many as you might think," he replies. "But there are a couple in St. Louis—a few in small towns along the major highways. A few in every state."

Part of me is upset, imagining warmhearted animal-loving beauty queens running boarding homes for alpha males who shift into human shape and once again are subject to all sorts of hungers. But part of me is relieved to think if he's ever in serious trouble, Dante has someplace to run, no matter where he is. "How do you find out about these havens?" I ask. "Do you have shape-shifter conventions out in Las Vegas every year where you can swap addresses of the new places you've discovered?"

He grins. "Not exactly. But there's a network. There aren't that many shape-shifters in America, and a lot of us are related. So we know where this aunt lives, or this cousin—or this girlfriend of that nephew. Someone who knows. Who understands."

Although Dante has mentioned that his mother had siblings with the same shape-shifting tendencies, he has never wanted to talk about them before. I've never been able to get a sense of how many there are, where they're located, how closely they all stay in touch. I don't want to pry too hard, which might cause him to clam up on the topic, but I can't help but be fascinated. I'm convinced more than ever that my visiting white husky is a supernatural creature, perhaps sent my way some weary afternoon by William or Dante. *You can take shelter with Maria if you ever need to . . .*

"So these other shape-shifters," I say. "Do you know the whole genealogy? Do you keep track of each other?"

"Hardly," he says. "I can scarcely keep track of William and Christina."

"Then how do you recognize each other? I mean, if you're in the wild and you see a bear that looks—different—do you have some secret signal you make to ask if it's really a human?"

He shrugs, slightly irritable. He's already tired of this topic. "You just know," he says.

"But—"

"Seriously, Maria, I can't explain it."

I blow out my breath in a very audible sound of resignation. "Fine. Let's go on to a new topic." I reach out to tug on the key around his neck. The longer cord seems to be working out just fine; he hasn't lost it and he hasn't strangled on it, and I don't notice any signs of fraying. "How's your life been?" I ask. "What's your last week been like?"

He shrugs and pulls the key out of my hand. He hauls himself up to a seated position beside me. "As always. I just keep moving and try to stay out of trouble."

"You were human a bunch of times during this last stretch of time," I prompt. "You came to see me on Halloween, you called me, and I know you checked e-mail. It seems like you changed more often, back and forth, these last three weeks. Or am I wrong?"

He's silent a long moment, regarding me with those unreadable, dark eyes. Finally he nods and rests his head back against the wood. "You're not wrong," he says. "A few months ago—after he got hurt—I hung out with William for a few days. He's always been able to shift more easily than I have, more or less at will, and I wanted to see if I could pick up some of his techniques. Direct the process a little more."

I feel a kick of excitement. "And could you?"

He shrugs and nods. "A little. A half hour here, an hour there. I think maybe if I keep practicing I can extend those periods." He glances at me, frowning down my mounting elation. "But it's really hard. I feel pretty beat up after I've been working on it for a while."

"Still. I know how much you hate being at the mercy of—of the whims of your body," I say. "If you could get some control over the whole thing—"

"Right. I might feel less like a freak."

I lean over to kiss him hard on the mouth. "You might be a freak," I say fiercely, "but you're *my* freak. And I will love you forever. Even if you're only human an hour a month. Even if you're only human an hour a year."

Even if you're a killer.

We spend Wednesday walking hand-in-hand around the Plaza. If you don't feel like eating or shopping, there's not too much to do, but all we require is the slightest bit of structure upon which to hang our day, so the eating and the shopping suit us just fine. We pause for coffee, browse for books, try on clothes at a couple of sporting goods stores, where I also buy Dante two sweaters and two pairs of jeans. We try out couches, sniff at candles, and buy chocolates, which we chase down with wine during happy hour. I admire rings in the window of a jewelry store; Dante is intrigued by computer games and software selections. The weather is cold but sunny, perfect for moving in and out of heated showrooms.

We are together, perfect for making me happy.

We return to the hotel and put on nicer clothes—well, Dante's nicest pair of new jeans—and go out for an expensive dinner. Candlelight, steak, more wine, dessert. We are laughing so much and touching hands so frequently across the table that our waiter asks if we're on our honeymoon. I feel more like a brave young woman who is about to send her fiancé off to the front lines. *Create a special memory to treasure always in your heart. You don't know if you'll ever see this man again.*

I close my mind to the thought. I do not voice it to Dante. I do not tell him a single one of my most pressing fears. I lie with my smile, I lie with my words, I lie with the touch of my fingers on his. I tell him *Nothing has changed*, when, in fact, everything might have changed.

Of course, I cannot escape the knowledge that he might be lying to me as well.

When we return to our room, we make love with a surge of passion, and then with a heartbreaking tenderness. We fall asleep face-to-face, our hands linked, our knees touching. Every time I wake in the night to alter positions, I make sure that some part of me is still in contact with Dante. He must do the same. For in the morning, when I open my eyes, we are lying back to front; his arm is across my waist and my fingers are laced with his. I don't believe we have been parted for a second during one of those dark hours.

It takes me a moment to realize that what has nudged me out of slumber is the sound of my cell phone alerting me that I have a text message. Glancing at the clock, I see that it's scarcely seven in the morning. Way too early for social calls. I don't want to get out of the warm bed—I don't want to leave Dante's side—but I have a feeling I'd better see if there's a crisis brewing before it becomes a full-blown catastrophe. I had told both my mom and Beth that I would be heading to Kansas City this week ("It's a business trip, I'll be there a few days"), but I haven't talked to them since I arrived. Neither of them is above calling me this early in the morning just to make sure I'm alive.

I roll over, kiss Dante on the cheek, then slip out of bed and pull on a robe. I take my cell phone to the bathroom and close the door so I don't disturb Dante if I have to call someone. First I use the toilet, then I put the lid down so I can sit on it like a chair.

The text message is from Ellen, simple and to the point. MURDER IN FOREST PARK THIS A.M. SAME ANIMAL. TIME SET @ 3.

It takes me a moment to absorb this. My first thought is actually for Kathleen, who buried her husband yesterday after the funeral that I missed. *This will just remind her of Ritchie's death.* Belatedly I think I should feel sorry for the victim, and the victim's family, whoever they might be.

And then I realize.

A murder in St. Louis. Four hours ago. While Dante lay sleeping beside me, his hand always grazing my body, his breath sometimes mixed with mine.

He could not possibly have been the killer.

A single harsh sob is punched out of my body. I cover my mouth, which is gaping with so many emotions that I cannot contain them. Horror and grief and shame, that I could ever have allowed myself to distrust him. And over them unutterable relief, that Dante is not, could not have been, would never be a killer.

One-handed, I type out a reply. R U SURE?

The answer comes almost immediately; she must be sitting somewhere with her iPhone in her hand. YES. U IN KC?

YES. YES. YES. OMG OMG OMG.

I KNOW. TERRIBLE NEWS BUT MAKES ME HAPPY 4 U.

THANK U, I type and then I can't think of anything else to say. I hold the phone a moment, balancing it on my knee, and then I finally add, I HAVE TO GO. I LOVE HIM.

CALL ME LATER, she writes.

I shut the phone and lay it very, very carefully on the marble counter surrounding the sink. And then I lower my face into my hands and begin crying. I am biting my lips, I am pressing my palms against my cheeks, I am doing everything I can to muffle the sound, but the tears pour out, unstoppable, inexhaustible. They must be laced with acid; they burn against my face, against my hands. But they are sweet as well as bitter. I taste one against my tongue and I swear there is sugar mixed with the salt.

There is a knock on the bathroom door and Dante's voice outside. "Maria? Are you all right? Maria?"

"Yes," I choke out. That's one lie he recognizes because he comes in to see for himself. His face, already concerned, creases in real alarm, and he drops to a crouch beside me. He is naked, his dark hair loose around his shoulders and tousled from sleep, and he is utterly beautiful.

"What's wrong?" he asks, his voice fearful. Balancing himself on his toes, he wraps an arm around my shoulder and insinuates his face under the fall of my own heavy hair. "Maria? Did I hear the phone? Did something happen to your mom or your cousin or somebody?"

"I can't–" I start to say, but the sobs obstruct my throat. I try again. "They're fine. Everyone is fine."

"Then what's wrong?"

"It's too terrible," I say around a hiccup.

"Is someone dead?"

Yes, but not the way you mean. Not someone I know, not someone I love. "No, no, nothing like that," I choke out.

"Then what is it? Tell me."

I don't even want to answer that, but the words come out in a rush. "You'll hate me," I say. "You'll never forgive me."

His eyebrows shoot up, and then he frowns. Before I quite know what he's planning, he straightens, scoops me up, and carries me out to the couch. Then he pulls a blanket off the bed, bundles me up in it, and fetches me a glass of water. Finally he sits beside me, puts one arm around my shoulders, and takes hold of my hand.

"Whatever it is, I won't hate you," he says. "I swear. Now tell me what's wrong."

I sip the water to force my throat to open, and I will myself into a state of semi-calm. But I cannot look at him as I begin to speak. "When Ritchie died–when he was killed," I stammer. "Before we knew *how* he died. My first thought was, 'Good thing we didn't have to call the police when he had that fight with Dante, or they'd be here asking questions now. And maybe they'd find out that he and I go to Babler State Park all the time, and that wouldn't look good.'"

I feel him nod. "Yes, that makes sense. But since it was drug dealers—"

I shake my head. "It wasn't. I lied about that. There was no heroin at the scene."

"Then—hold on—are you saying they don't *know* who killed him?"

"They have a theory," I whisper. "But it's not who. It's what." I risk a quick glance at his face. He looks puzzled, a little alarmed, but not angry. "They think it was a wolf. Or some kind of wild animal."

He gets it immediately. His whole body stiffens; his arm turns to iron across my back. But he doesn't pull away from me. "And you wondered—"

Now I can't speak fast enough. "At first they didn't seem sure what kind of animal. Wolf? Dog? Mountain lion? And I couldn't help thinking, 'What if it was more than one kind of animal? What if it was something that shifted back and forth between shapes?'"

"It doesn't work that way," he says in a muffled voice.

I can't read his tone, but I stumble on. "And then. At the crime scene. They found human footprints, right there, like someone was watching or someone arrived practically the minute Ritchie was killed—"

"Or a shape-shifter committed the murder," he says in an even voice.

"And I didn't think it could be you. Not you, not *human* you. But I thought maybe—when you're in animal form—you see the world differently, wilder instincts kick in and I—Dante, I'm so sorry, I never wanted to tell you this. I never wanted you to believe that for one moment I doubted you—"

He lifts the hand that was holding mine and places it against my cheek, his fingers hooking behind my ear. He pulls me close enough that our foreheads touch. "And even thinking I might be a murderer, you wanted to be with me? You wanted to meet me here? You wanted me to stay out of St. Louis so that *I* would be safe?"

My eyes are filling with tears again, the big quiet kind that just keep forming and spilling over. "Yes," I whisper. "I will protect you with my life, no matter what you do."

He kisses me softly on the mouth. "I don't think much of your morals. Or your instincts for self-preservation."

I free my hands from the blanket so I can wrap my arms around him. His skin is smooth against my palms. "I love you," I say. "That changes the shape of everything else."

"You love me more than I deserve," he whispers back, "and I can't even tell you how much that means to me."

He closes his eyes and we rest that way for a moment. I feel hollowed out, riven, as if I have just survived a brush with death or surfaced after too long under water. My breath makes a thready sound when I inhale.

"So what changed?" he asks, and opens his eyes again. "This morning. What upset you?"

I probably shouldn't be lying to him quite so soon after this gut-wrenching confession, but I don't want him to know that I have told Ellen his secret. So I offer a partial truth. "Ellen texted to say there had been another murder this morning in Forest Park. Someone else killed by the same kind of animal. We've all been so obsessed with this case that we can't talk about anything else, and she knew I was out of town and probably wouldn't see the news. And I realized—you couldn't have been in Forest Park this morning. You couldn't have done it. And that means you didn't do *any* of the killings."

He pulls away so suddenly my head snaps back. "*Any* of them?" he asks sharply. "How many have there been?"

Suddenly I feel nervous. I don't think he's mad at me, but something has clearly upset him. "With this murder, there have been four. Well, five, because two people died at one scene."

"And they were all at Babler? Or Forest Park?"

"No," I say uneasily. "One was out near Rolla."

Now he looks thunderous, and then sick. "Dear God," he says, and drops his head in his palms.

My hands flutter around his ears, pick at his shoulders, his covered face, like little birds seeking a way past a closed door. "What? Dante, what? Do you think—who do you think—"

He lifts his head and then sags back against the couch. His face looks lined, weary, limned with darkness. He endured with equanimity the news that his lover believed him capable of murder; what thought could turn him so grim, so miserable? "William," he says.

Now I collapse next to him, my thoughts in a whirl. To comfort him or myself—I'm not sure—I take his hand in both of mine. "Why would you think that?"

He hesitates, but I can tell whatever the reason is, it's a pretty strong one. Finally he says, "I told you he got hurt a while back. Needed a blood transfusion." I nod. "What I didn't tell you is that people like us—shape-shifters—we can't always tolerate other people's blood. A transfusion can have terrible side effects."

"What kind of side effects?" I whisper.

His shoulders lift in a helpless shrug. "Madness. Violence. Basically, an entire breakdown of someone's personality."

I open my mouth but struggle to frame a question. "And you think—you've seen this kind of change come over him? I don't know him that well, but he didn't seem out of character when *I* saw him."

Dante rubs his forehead. "Yeah. Mostly he seems normal. No wild mood swings, no crazy talk. But he's been a little—erratic—lately. I've been thinking he was hiding something. I can usually find him hanging around Christina's when I want him, but lately he's gone more than he's there, and he's vague about where he's been." He gives a tired shrug. "Hell, I can't always account for my whereabouts, and we all might have things we want to hide from our brothers, but—William has never been like that. I asked Christina and she said she'd noticed it, too, but with the baby, she hasn't had much attention to spare for anyone else."

My thoughts are racing, tripping over themselves like runners with their shoes untied, and struggling to rise again. "But—would William have reason to kill Ritchie? I mean—I suppose all the murders could have been completely random, it's just that—it never even would have *occurred* to me that you might be involved except that you had a reason to dislike him—"

He nods slowly. "I'd told him about the fight." He looks over at me miserably. "We went by Ritchie's house. It made sense at the time. He said, 'I ought to know where he lives in case he tries to intimidate Maria while you're out of town.' I just didn't think—" He spreads his hands. "This is terrible," he breathes.

I wrap my arms around him and pull him over so that his head rests against my shoulder. "Now you know how I felt when I suspected you," I whisper. "Awful. So awful. And there's probably equally little reason to suspect William. You'll feel wretched when you realize he couldn't possibly have done anything so dreadful."

Not lifting his cheek from my shoulder, he tilts his head back to gaze up at me. "Five people killed by a shape-shifter. Who wasn't me. William is a prime suspect."

"You don't know they were killed by a shape-shifter," I argue. "Maybe there really is a rabid wolf loose in the city."

"Covering that much ground? Between Rolla and Forest Park?" he asks derisively. "I don't think so."

"So maybe it's someone else. You said there are a lot of shape-shifters in the state—"

"I said there are *some*. Not a lot. And I don't know any others who might live in the St. Louis area."

"But then, if it's William—" I say, and stop cold. I remember him showing up at my front door, cheerful and smiling, sitting down with me at the breakfast table. I remember him taking a sudden aggressive swipe at the news reporter, exploding into an instant ferocity that had the potential to be so much more brutal. I remember the amber eyes staring at me from the darkness in the middle of the night. If William turns out to be a killer . . . "Oh, God," I say. I am lucky to be alive.

I feel him shake his head against my shoulder. "I don't know. I don't know what to do," he says very quietly. "But he's my brother. I have to take care of this."

I don't know what that means. I am afraid to ask. I scoot my butt closer to the edge of the couch cushion, so my face is down at the same level as Dante's. "Not just yet," I say in a small voice. "Give me one more day. In case something happens to you. In case—just in case. One more day. And then we'll go back to St. Louis and you can do whatever you need to."

I see the words hover on his lips: *What if someone else dies while we're taking the time for some long, selfish good-bye?* But he doesn't say them. His dark eyes are as vulnerable as I have ever seen them, his face is bruised with emotion. Dante has so few people he feels safe enough to love, and he might have just lost one of them in the worst way possible. At this moment, he needs me as much as I need him, and he shows it. I meet his desperate kiss with one of my own; I gladly submit to his crushing embrace. Only love can make up for the defection of love. No other substitutes exist.

CHAPTER EIGHTEEN

We spend Thursday in Kansas City, but we are no longer the carefree couple so in love that people smile to see us. Our waiter from last night would not mistake us for newlyweds today; he would guess we are in town to bury our only child. We don't talk much. We catch a couple of movies, holding hands as the films play out. We buy newspapers and cheap novels and sit together in the coffee shops, reading in near-total silence. We sit at adjoining computer terminals in the hotel's business center. I check e-mail while Dante surfs news sites, looking for more details about the murders. He doesn't share with me anything he learns.

Unexciting activities, even a little grim, but I treasure these hours nonetheless. It is impossible not to realize that change is in the air. We might never have such a day again.

I cannot bear to think about it.

Friday morning we check out and drive back to St. Louis with Dante behind the wheel. He expects to be human at least three or four more days, but he wants to begin the hunt for William right away. He doesn't think the search will take very long. *I know where he goes to ground. Unless he's off on one of his mysterious excursions, I ought to find him in a few days.*

And then he will say what—?

For much of the time, we ride in silence. I rest my left hand on his leg, just to reassure myself that he is near, but I keep my eyes on the view alongside the road. Once we get clear of the city, the landscape is mostly composed of farms and open prairie, with rolling tree-covered hills in the middle distance. Here in mid-November, most of the trees are wholly naked, and their dense, contorted branches appear to have been flung up to protect them from the ill humor of a gunmetal sky. Here and there, against the fawn-colored grasses and the dull brown tree trunks, brilliant spots of color leap out, marking a few stubborn trees just now surrendering to red. I can't tell what they are, maples maybe, burning with rebellious color. Twice along the highway I spot weeping willows whose long, trailing branches still clutch handfuls of green leaves, though the color has faded like an old woman's hair, bleached pale by time.

There isn't much more to see except billboards advertising Meramec Caverns, factory-made wooden bowls, adult video stores, restaurants, hotels, fireworks, and lawyers. Now and then a sign will simply offer the word JESUS in giant letters. I wonder what I would put on an oversize outdoor ad if I were allowed a single word. *Love,* I think. Both a noun and a directive. Find it, offer it, and make it the guiding principle of life.

We are not far from Wentzville when I stir. "Will you tell Christina?" I ask.

He shakes his head. "Not if I don't have to. I want to talk to William first and see what I can find out."

I'm not sure how to phrase my next question. "What if he—if he takes exception to what you say." *To you asking him if he's a murderer.* "Will he start a fight? Will you—who would win?"

He shakes his head again. "I don't know. In human shape, I'm bigger than he is, and stronger. But—"

I try to still the acid surge of fear that rises to the back of my throat. "But he can turn to animal shape at will. And you can't."

He glances at me, then stares straight ahead again. "I know William," he says quietly. "The *real* William, the one whose mind hasn't been poisoned by madness. If he really is—If he really has killed people, it's something that would horrify him. He would want to be stopped."

I turn my eyes his way. "Would *you*?" I say. "Want to be stopped?"

He nods without taking his eyes from the road.

"Even if it meant your death?"

He risks another quick look at me. "Even then. And I expect it would."

After that, we don't say another word until we arrive at my house.

In the morning, Dante is gone.

I thought *last* weekend was impossible to endure, but this one is even worse. I can't even distract myself by going out with Beth or leaving for the movies, because I know Dante is still human, and I don't want to miss any moment he might have to spare for me. He has taken his cell phone with him, and he calls me every few hours, just because he can, even though he has no progress to report. He is in Rolla, but he has not made contact with William. He has dropped in on Christina and questioned her casually, but she hasn't seen their brother for several days.

"Keep your doors locked," Dante cautions me. "And if he comes to the house, don't let him in."

"Oh, great. What do I say to him when I answer the door? 'Uh, sorry, I'm suddenly afraid of you. Go away'?"

"I don't know. Pretend you have the flu or something. And then call me the minute he leaves."

"Come back to me," I whisper. "Before you change out of human shape this time. Come back for one more night."

Silence on the phone for a moment, then the promise. "I will."

Monday arrives like an immigrant, bedraggled and apprehensive. I haven't been in my office more than three minutes before Ellen strides in. I've already turned on my computer, knowing my in-box will be stuffed with e-mails that require immediate attention, but I spin around to meet her keen, inquiring gaze.

"So did you tell him?" she asks.

It is the strangest thing in my life—of all the strange things—to think I can actually discuss Dante with someone else in cold, literal terms. "Yes," I say. "Right after I got your text."

"Was he furious? What did he say?"

"He said—Oh, God, this could only be worse if Dante really was the killer. He said maybe it was his brother."

Ellen snaps her fingers. "That's right! I forgot he had a brother. And a sister, too, right?"

"And a niece."

"And they're all—" She glances over her shoulder toward the hallway, though so far we appear to be the only two people on our floor. "You know."

"Yes. Well, we don't know yet about the baby."

She leans against my bookcase. "Well, that must have been a bad morning," she remarks. "First he finds out his girlfriend thinks he's a killer, and then he starts thinking maybe his brother is."

"Right. Pretty much set the tone."

"When did you get back?"

"Friday night."

She appraises me. "So you stayed a few days. Managed to make a little vacation out of it. Despite everything." She nods. "Good for you."

I smile weakly. "I didn't know if we'd ever have another chance."

"What happens next?"

"He's looking for William. His brother. But I don't have any idea how that—that conversation might go."

She mulls that over for a minute and then sighs. "I can't think of a single thing to say about any of this," she offers before straightening up and heading for the door. But just as she steps into the hall, she turns back and says softly, "I'm glad it wasn't him." She leaves before I can reply.

Dante is at my house when I get home Monday night. "William?" I ask breathlessly as I hurry through the door and hang up my coat.

He shakes his head. "I haven't been able to track him down yet. I'll keep looking."

"How much time do you have?" *How much longer before you're back in animal shape?*

"Not long. But I can keep hunting for him after I've changed. Once I find him, I'll just stick with him until we're both human again." He shrugs. "I told you, I've been practicing. Maybe I'll be able to shift right away and have the conversation as soon as I find him."

"Well, if you find yourself back in human shape, with no brother to beat up and time heavy on your hands, give me a call. Or hey, drop by."

His smile is fleeting. "I'll definitely call. Not sure I'll have time to visit."

I nod. I am trying to seem calm, not overly concerned, not listening to the wailing voices crying that I may never see him again, this man I love so much. "So you'll be leaving again tonight?"

"In a couple of hours. I just came by to—" He pauses. He doesn't want to utter the words. *To say good-bye.* Now his mouth twists in a smile that is far more sad than mirthful. "To see you."

I don't even bother trying to stumble through a maze of words. I just plunge across the room and throw myself into his arms. They close around me and we kiss as if we are stealing breath from each other to stay alive. I think, *This must be how people feel when they're in a submarine or a spaceship that's running out of air. They can see the dial winding down; they can see that their time is almost up. They are alive now, they are perfectly fine, and yet they know that in a matter of hours they will be dead. And there is nothing they can do, no miracle they can perform, that will change the outcome by so much as a second.*

I kiss him, I make love to him, and then I let him go.

Impossibly, the rest of the week is even worse. I bury myself in work—which, fortunately, there is plenty of—and distract myself with friends. Every day, Ellen organizes some kind of luncheon outing, gathering me and Kathleen and any other wounded soul she can round up. Well, neither Grant nor Marquez seems to be particularly injured at the moment, but I am not fooled. They have secrets; they have scars. It's just that their infirmities are not visible at this moment.

On Thursday, Ellen announces that she's having us all over on Sunday afternoon to watch the football game. "What football game?" Marquez asks.

"The one where the Cardinals play the Rams. The true team plays the usurpers."

Grant laughs. Besides Ellen, I'd guess he's the only one of the five of us who might be a sports fan. "Dude, the Big Red moved out of this city more than twenty years ago. Get over it."

"I can't get over it," Ellen says. "My heart belongs to the Cardinals."

"I think I'm busy Sunday," Marquez says. "I have to do laundry. Or, wait. I have to iron my underwear."

"Bring your ironing over to my place and do it while you watch the game," Ellen invites him. "I've got a board you can borrow."

"I think it sounds like fun," I say. I've been dreading the weekend, actually. How will I fill up all those deserted and endless hours? Mindless television watching in the presence of people I like seems to be the perfect answer. I'll have my cell phone with me, of course, in case Dante finds time to call.

"I do, too," Kathleen says in her soft voice. "Kelly and Tim left yesterday and it's been so quiet at the house."

Ellen glances at Marquez with hooded triumph. Kathleen was her trump card, and that card just played itself. Marquez's grin is a silent acknowledgment of the fact, but he goes down fighting. "Yes, but *football*," he says to Kathleen in a pleading voice. "It's so *boring*. And those *outfits* they wear. At least when it's basketball you can appreciate their fine bodies."

Grant makes a loud groaning sound and covers his ears. "I do not want to hear you saying that crap." I think the straight-male response is just posturing; Grant seems perfectly comfortable with Marquez's sexuality.

Ellen ignores Grant and addresses Marquez. "So bring a Scrabble board. I'll tell you when to cheer and when to boo. You don't even have to pay attention to the game."

"I hate Scrabble," Marquez says.

"We can play Monopoly," Kathleen says, but all of us cry out in horror at that.

Marquez tells her, "I'd play Clue before I'd play Monopoly. I'd play *charades*."

"Great, so I'll expect everyone around eleven thirty. Game starts at noon," Ellen says. "I'll grill some burgers, you all can bring whatever you like." She glances around the table and adds casually, "I might invite some of my neighbors, too, or folks from church."

No one else seems to notice this comment but I feel certain it's significant somehow. Kathleen is already volunteering to make deviled eggs and Marquez says he'll bring baked beans.

"Beer," Grant says. When Marquez makes a rude noise, Grant says, "Hey, it's a football game. You gotta have beer."

"I'll make a salad," I say.

"Of course you will," Marquez replies in a polite voice.

"It will be a really creative salad," I promise him. "With cranberries and pears and gorgonzola cheese. Even you will like it."

Ellen's hand has frozen halfway to her mouth and I see her working her mind around a new thought. *Maria's a vegetarian except for a few times a month. She's in love with a guy who sometimes turns into an animal. Hey—could those two facts be related?* Then she gives me a brilliant smile. "Great," she says again. "It'll be fun."

CHAPTER NINETEEN

I spend what seems like most of Saturday on the phone with various family members, trying to decide who is bringing what to Thanksgiving dinner at Aunt Andrea's on Thursday. This process would be much simpler, Beth and I moan to each other, if either of our mothers would bother to get computers and learn how to send e-mails. But eventually we've all agreed not only on a menu but also on which food items we're willing to bring. I am looking forward to spending the holiday with my family, though I know part of my attention will be straining back toward St. Louis, hoping for news from Dante.

He might even phone me while I'm in Springfield, because he has managed to turn human and call me at least briefly every day this week. He sounds tired and discouraged, and he still has not managed to find William, but he is alive and he misses me. Those are the two things I care about most.

"I'll be over at Ellen's till about four or five today," I tell him Sunday morning when I hear from him. "I'll have my cell phone if you need me."

"All right. But listen. My own cell phone is almost out of juice, and I haven't had a chance to recharge. So don't worry if you don't hear from me."

Don't worry if I don't hear from you? Are you kidding? But I don't say it. "Where are you?" I respond instead.

"Back in Babler. I keep thinking that's where he'll go next."

"Well—be careful." I try not to say the words as often as I think them, or our conversation would consist of nothing else.

"I will. You, too. Love you."

And he's gone again. Before I cradle the phone, I take a deep breath over the receiver, as if some portion of his spirit has wafted through the wires and I can inhale it, internalize it, make it part of my own soul. Then I hang up and return to the job of chopping up lettuce and fruit.

There are about nine cars in front of Ellen's house when I arrive a few minutes before noon. I recognize a few as belonging to my coworkers—Grant, Kathleen, Marquez, Frank, and the new girl in creative—but the rest belong to mystery guests. Well, I'm pretty sure the Jeep is owned by Ellen's boyfriend, Henry, and the blue pickup might belong to one of her ex-husbands. I tuck my head down against an insulting wind and hurry inside.

Ellen lives in an old two-story farmhouse that she's slowly rehabbed during the past ten years. Most of the ground level is now one open space—kitchen, dining room, family room all unfolding into each other, delineated by different floor coverings, some half-walls, and a few weight-bearing pillars. The back wall of the family room is primarily weathered gray stone, brightened by a roaring blaze in a huge fireplace and the big flat-screen TV above it. The adjoining sidewall, made entirely of sliding-glass doors and tall windows, overlooks an enormous redwood deck and a wild backyard that quickly gives way to tangled woodland. I see Henry hunched over the gas grill on the deck, cooking burgers outside in the cold. He's all bundled up and his gloved hands are a little clumsy on the tongs, but he doesn't look at all unhappy. Ellen says he'll barbecue in a blizzard, so he certainly won't be slowed by a little chill.

The rest of Ellen's house, like Ellen herself, is brassy, colorful, and charming. The furniture tends to be a little worn and thickly cushioned, chairs and sofas you feel like you could sink into if you wanted to spend a whole day reading. Most pieces are upholstered in red and rust and dark purple, with gaily patterned throws adding spots of vivid color. The living room is covered by rich chocolate carpet, the dining room gleams with honey-colored hardwood, and the kitchen floor is white ceramic tile speckled with black and red. An enormous black Maine coon cat patrols the family room, investigating strangers and their interesting plates of food. I know Ellen has at least two more cats, but they're nervous or antisocial, since they're nowhere in evidence.

There might be ten or twelve people milling about in these three rooms, some standing and talking, some sitting and munching, and I do a quick scan to see who I know and who I don't. Turns out I'd correctly identified the cars out front. I feel a moment's disappointment when I realize Grant hasn't brought Caroline—not that I thought he *would*, I just figured it would be pretty entertaining if he had. But no, he's talking to Marquez, gesturing with a little more energy than he usually displays, and I think maybe he's already started on the beer.

Then I realize it's not Grant talking to Marquez, it's an African-American man I don't recognize. *Huh,* I think. *I wonder if this is one of the guests Ellen invited from her church or the neighborhood. I wonder if she's trying to fix Marquez up with somebody she knows.* Then I spot another stranger, also black, a pretty young woman sipping a margarita and listening with polite interest to something Frank is telling her. I'd guess she's five or six years younger than I am, tall and slim, with short springy hair that makes the most adorable cloud of curls around her face. She's wearing jeans and an old Cardinals jersey with Kurt Warner's name on it, so I have no doubt that she and Ellen first bonded over football.

I also have no doubt that Ellen has invited her over to meet Grant. I can hardly hide my smile as I carry my salad over to the kitchen counter where about a dozen side dishes have been lined up in their Crock-Pots and Tupperware containers. Ellen is putting out paper plates and plastic forks, and she gives me a quick harassed look.

"I don't suppose you brought any ice, did you?"

"No, do you want me to go get some?"

"Nah, I'll send Henry out when he's done with the burgers. Or you can drink your soda warm."

I nod at the woman patiently listening to Frank, not the world's most gifted conversationalist. "Even by your standards, this is hardly subtle," I say.

Her eyes follow mine and then flick to Marquez. She seems annoyed. "Well, I thought she'd be perfect for Grant, because she loves sports. And she's funny. And look at her—she's hot! But he hasn't even glanced in her direction. But that rat Marquez. He glommed on to her brother the minute they walked in the door, and they haven't stopped talking since."

"See? You *are* a matchmaking genius. At least someone may get a phone number out of the afternoon."

"That's fine, but that's not the way it was supposed to work."

"People love who they love, Ellen," I say softly. "Even when they shouldn't."

Now she frowns at me, but her heart isn't really in it. "Not if I can help it."

"That's the point," I say. "You can't."

There's a surge of sound from the living room, and we realize we've missed kickoff. "Hell and damnation," Ellen says. She tosses the last of the paper goods on the counter and pushes through the press of people so she can stand in front of the television. The Cardinals have elected to be the receiving team, but they don't make it to the twenty-yard line on the return. A few people laugh, and Ellen frowns, then looks around the room for support. "Come on, Jazz!" she calls, waving to the African-American girl. "Someone has to help me cheer them on."

I hurry to catch up with her as I head toward Ellen's side. "Your name is Jazz?" I say. "That's about the coolest thing *ever.*"

She laughs. "It's Jasmine, actually, but you can see how I got the nickname."

"I'm Maria. I work with Ellen."

"I think she's talked about you."

"That wouldn't surprise me at all."

Fairly quickly, the partygoers separate into two camps, those who love football and those who have no idea why we curse when the Cardinals' first possession ends at fourth and three. Secretly I am rooting for the Rams, but truthfully, I don't really care who wins. I touch the cell phone tucked into my back pocket, which I have set to vibrate. Nothing really matters except the news I might learn through this medium. Everything else is just trumpets and timpani, the circus, the parade, the distractions that escort you through the day.

Henry steps through the sliding-glass doors, bringing in a blast of cold air. "Who wants burgers?" he asks, carrying a platter to the kitchen.

The groups realign a little as some people fill their plates right away and others wait for the next commercial break. Grant has drifted into the living room with the sports fans and settled on the floor not far from me, but he still doesn't show any interest in Jazz. Her brother and Marquez, on the other hand, have drawn into a little alcove off the dining room and taken seats in a couple of ladder-back chairs. If anything, they seem more absorbed in each other as the hours go by, and even less interested in the event that ostensibly brought us all together. I think I'll be really pleased if Marquez, and not Grant, is the one who gets a relationship out of this afternoon. But then, I was never particularly outraged by the notion that Grant might be involved with Caroline.

And I certainly don't want him to express an opinion about the person *I* have chosen to love.

The afternoon filters by pleasantly enough—certainly more pleasantly than it would have if I was at home staring at the clock. I divide my time between the sports enthusiasts and the socializers and eat about seven times my body weight in calories. For a time, I sit at the dining room table with Kathleen and Frank and the new girl, doing a solemn taste test on the five separate desserts that have been supplied. All of us rate the chocolate-dipped strawberries as the best, but opinions are sharply divided when it comes to the chocolate chip brownies, the lemon meringue pie, the raspberry gelato, and the fudge. I have to admit that fudge and raspberry gelato, when consumed simultaneously, almost supersede the strawberries for excellence.

By halftime, a few people start to trickle out, and when the game ends around three thirty, only Jazz, her brother, and I are left. Even Henry had to go during the third quarter, but since the Cardinals were leading the Rams by twenty points, Ellen couldn't come up with an argument that would convince him to stay.

"That was fun—thanks for inviting us," Jazz says as she stands by the door, buttoning her coat.

Her brother waits beside her and, for the first time, I get a closer look at him. His features are stronger than hers, not as pretty, but he has an easy smile and a relaxed slouch that give him an agreeable air. He's wearing what might be a full-carat diamond in his right ear, and it's a striking mirror-white against his dark skin. He's about a foot taller than Ellen, and he reaches out to flick her on the nose as if she's a child. "Next time those Arizona boys won't have it so easy," he says.

She shoves him playfully in the arm. "You just wait," she says. "Cardinals will be back in the Super Bowl."

After a little more joshing, they're out the door. "I'll help you clean up," I say, already beginning to gather plates and cups and napkins.

"That would make you an angel," she says, putting her hands on her hips and glancing around. "You'd think I had a bunch of refugees here, instead of civilized folks who know how to use trash cans and bathrooms."

I snort with laughter and continue gathering up debris. This is the reason I don't have parties. Well, this and because I never want people to be hanging around when Dante shows up unexpectedly. I pull out my phone and check it to see if, in all the noise and commotion, I missed a call. But no. No messages.

Ellen busies herself in the kitchen, organizing the mess in there, while I make a more determined attack on the dining room. Once that's in order, I'll move on to the family room, and then break out the broom and the Swiffer. Or the shop vac. I hear the sports commentators dissecting the game and offering predictions on the one that will shortly follow. I'm too lazy to look for the remote control, and I figure Ellen might want to watch the second game anyway, so I don't bother to turn off the TV.

I'm kneeling in the living room, trying to retrieve a beer bottle from behind the red sofa, when urgent music from the monitor presages some change in programming, and a dead-serious anchorman's voice comes on. "We're here with breaking news from Babler State Park," he says.

I whirl around so fast that I slam my hip into Ellen's metal coffee table and yelp with pain. The television has jumped to the bright hues of the news set, and a generically handsome man is frowning down at me. "Police say there's been another attack in Babler Park, where there was a death just three weeks ago," he says. "Investigators determined that the death in that first attack was caused by a wild animal, though they have not yet located the animal in question. And now we learn that there's been another incident today—less than a half hour ago—although fortunately this time, the victim was merely wounded. Reporter Brody Westerbrook is on the scene at Babler. Brody, what can you tell us?"

I come slowly to my feet, mesmerized, terrified, as Brody Westerbrook's features fill the screen. He's standing outside in the sunny but chilly-looking park, wearing an overcoat and a pair of earmuffs, and holding a microphone.

"Mike, yes, a forty-six-year-old woman was attacked here in the park around three p.m., but this time the news is good. She's a lifelong jogger who always brings safety gear with her, so when the animal leapt at her, she was able to shoot pepper spray in its face. She also activated the siren function of her keychain. She said she was surprised when it didn't run right away—it came after her again, and this time it was successful in grabbing hold of her left arm and giving her a pretty deep wound. But fortunately she was able to snatch up a large stick and fend the animal off until help arrived."

"And help did arrive?" the newscaster asks.

"Yes—there were two marathoners nearby who heard her siren and came to investigate. They also called the police on their cell phones. Not until they arrived, they say, did the creature slink away."

"Brody, you keep saying 'the animal' and 'the creature.' Do we know what kind of animal it was?"

Brody glances at a sheet of paper in his hands, though I can't imagine he needs a refresher to answer this question. On any other day, with any other newscast, I would be annoyed by the self-important, overly dramatic quality of the anchorman's questions and Brody's answers. But with this story, I am utterly rapt. If I had plates or bottles in my hands, I have dropped them. I am frozen to the carpet in Ellen's living room, aware of nothing except those faces and the words they are producing.

"Mike, we don't," Brody answers. "The victim was understandably distraught, and police say she couldn't provide any detailed information about her attacker. The man and the woman who came to her aid offered somewhat conflicting descriptions. One of them said it was a wolf, the other one said it looked more like a bear—"

"A bear," Mike repeats incredulously. "I wouldn't think it would be possible to confuse the two animals."

"Right, but you have to understand it was pretty chaotic, with the victim screaming and the rescuers yelling and swinging sticks that they'd gathered along the way."

"What's the status of the woman who was attacked?"

"Her left arm was pretty badly mauled and she seems to have lost a lot of blood. A paramedic team arrived a few moments ago and she's being taken to an area hospital. We'll definitely keep viewers apprised of her condition."

"What about this animal?" Mike says. "Wasn't it a wolf that killed a man there at Babler Park just a few weeks ago?"

"Yes—at least, that's what medical examiners ultimately concluded," Brody replies. "Again—and I admit it seems strange—there seemed to be some confusion over what kind of creature was actually responsible for that death."

"I assume police and park rangers are on the scene," Mike says. "Do they believe that they'll finally be able to find and contain this animal that's responsible for so many attacks?"

I stiffen and put a hand to my mouth. This, after all, is the question that I dread. Or really, the answer.

"Yes, in fact, there are whole teams of rangers and animal-control specialists fanning out from the attack site even as we speak. There are at least three K9 units on hand, and I saw a dozen other officers, some on foot, some on horseback. I think they've got a real chance at catching this creature, whatever it is, this afternoon."

I suck in my breath so hard it sounds like I've been punched. *Dante, Dante, get out of there now,* I think, willing my words to fly through the cold, indifferent air and magically fill him with enough unease that he abandons his search for his brother. I think about calling his cell, but he is surely in animal shape by now, and either nowhere near his phone or incapable of answering it if it rings. *They are hunting William down, they will find him, they will kill him, and if you are anywhere near him, they will kill you, too.*

"I assume they're armed with rifles and other hunting weapons," the announcer says.

"Yes—some of the animal-control people are carrying tranquilizer guns, but realistically—" Brody breaks off and turns his head to listen to the barely audible sound of someone else speaking in a rapid voice. When he whips back toward the camera, his face is filled with excitement. "Mike, we just learned that the rangers believe they've located the animal a mile or so from here. We're going to follow in the news helicopter and see if we can bring you live footage of the capture."

For a moment, the television goes black, presumably as Brody's cameraman shuts off his equipment and goes scampering after the reporter. The anchorman's face snaps back onto the screen a second later.

"There you have it, Channel 5's exclusive coverage of the events at Babler State Park, where police and other officials believe they have tracked the wild animal responsible for several area deaths—"

I must have made a sound. I might have been making sounds for the past ten minutes—choked, desperate noises somewhere between grunts and wails. I am absolutely incapable of gauging what I'm doing, where I'm standing, what else in the world might be happening. All I can focus on, all that exists, is that brightly colored screen hanging on the wall, my portal into hell.

A hand on my forearm makes me scream aloud and whirl around like a trapped animal. It takes me a second to identify Ellen's face, to remember I am in Ellen's house.

"Maria, what the hell is going on?" she demands. The concern in her voice softens the words.

I shake my head and try to come up with words. "On the television—they said—"

She glances at the screen, but it's gone to a commercial featuring some inane piece of dancing candy. "They said what?" she says.

"In the park—there's this woman—Brody is there, Brody Westerbrook—"

Her face sharpens. She knows that name, and she can put it together from there. "There's been another attack? And the news guys are there? They're at Forest Park?"

"Babler."

"Live?" When I nod she says, "Did it just happen?"

I nod again. "They're going to chase it down. The animal. In their news helicopter."

"Jesus H. Fucking Roosevelt Christ."

She's dropped my arm, but now I clutch at hers. "Ellen—if it's William—and Dante is there, trying to find him, trying to help him—I just don't know, I don't know, what if he gets *shot*, what if both of them get shot?"

She pats my arm. "I don't know, either. Do you want to watch or do you want to turn it off?"

"I don't want to watch," I whisper, "but I have to."

She nods and then pushes me toward the couch. We both sit, but it hardly matters. I am as stiff and upright as a telephone pole, my shoulders hunched so tightly that my muscles ache, my hands grasping each other so remorselessly that my knuckles burn.

When the commercials finally give way back to news programming, we are instantly taken to a wavering, noisy view of Babler State Park as seen from the Channel 5 helicopter. We hear Brody Westerbrook's voice, but we no longer see his face. The camera is trained on the ground, where packs of dogs and men and horses make irregular black lines across the tired tan and russet autumn landscape.

Brody shouts over the pumping of the rotary blades. "For those who are just joining us, we're above Babler State Park, following police and other officials as they search for an animal they believe has carried out several fatal attacks in the St. Louis area over the past few weeks. We're currently above the southeastern portion of the park, heading west and slightly north, as searchers with trained dogs track the route of the animal–"

His voice continues, but it's hard to hear him over the grinding of the motor. Anyway, I am too focused on the images on the television to have patience for words. Autumn has stripped every tree in the park down to its skeletal frame, but even so, the landscape is a dense, cluttered brown of tree trunks and undergrowth. The terrain looks difficult for anyone on foot to navigate, and the interlaced weave of branches ensures that watchers from overhead get only a partial view. Even so, my eyes flick from corner to corner of the screen, looking for some hunched, desperate creature running for its life, too winded or too terrified to summon the energy to change back into its human shape. You would think I would feel some sympathy for the mauled jogger, the unfortunate dead; you would think I would *want* the cops and the rangers to find the rogue animal and put it down. But part of me is hoping William escapes the net, saves himself–and all of me is afire with fear for Dante, who might forget to flee if his brother gets captured, who might fall into the trap as well.

"There it is," Ellen says suddenly, jabbing her finger toward the screen.

Brody sees it a second later, a midsize, brownish shape weaving through the jumbled landscape of bushes and bare trees. It is running in a strange fashion, an awkward lope, as if it sometimes falls to all fours and sometimes rises to two feet, and it constantly swivels its head back as if trying to gauge the closeness of the pursuit.

Brody is speaking so fast–or my brain is so frozen–that I can't really comprehend his words until he says, "Roy, let's get a closer look," and the camera zooms in on the fleeing animal.

"What the hell is that?" Ellen demands.

Indeed, it's hard to tell. The creature might be about the height of a small man, if it would stand upright, but it continues its mad forward scrabble in a half-bent posture. It appears to be covered with long, dingy fur the color of baked mud. Its paws are the size of Ellen's paper plates, but its nose—which we see as it swings its head back one more time—is long and pointed, like a dog's. It looks like a Halloween outfit put together by someone grabbing mismatched parts from a costume shop. Now I can understand why someone would say it looked like a bear and someone else would think it looked like a wolf.

Brody has echoed Ellen's question. "I can't definitively identify what kind of animal we're looking at," he's shouting into his microphone. "It doesn't correspond to any of the breeds I'm familiar with—"

The canine trackers have either broken free of their handlers or been released, because suddenly there are eight or ten dogs circling the strange, terrible creature, baying and darting forward to nip at its heels. It draws itself taller and fights back, swiping at its attackers with those big, clumsy paws. Except those paws seem smaller now, more articulated; the fur is receding from the claws and knuckles.

"What the fuck is going on?" Ellen breathes.

"He's changing," I whisper. "He's becoming human."

"Well, this is the wrong-ass time to be doing that!" she exclaims. "He needs to turn back into an animal and *fight* if he's gonna get out of this!"

Trust Ellen to always take the side of the underdog.

Brody has just now noticed the transformation occurring in his quarry. "Mike, can you see this back in the studio?" he asks, his tone incredulous. "It almost looks—from here it seems like the animal is changing shapes—turning from one thing into another. It's—it looks more *human* than it did a few minutes ago."

Human enough, at this point, to snatch up a fallen stick and swing it hard at the nearest dog, connecting with its ribs and sending it yelping to the ground. The other dogs rush forward, but they seem confused, uncertain. I'm guessing that the transmogrification under way is changing the scent of their prey, and they're not sure this is what they're supposed to be tracking. At any rate, they fall back, and the creature staggers forward, falls to its knees, gets up again, and begins an ungainly run. It's clear he's winded, maybe wounded, very close to the end of his resources.

But determined to be taken dead, if at all.

"It's on the move again!" Brody calls out, as if we can't see that for ourselves, as if the searchers might not have noticed. Briefly, the camera pulls back to give us the whole scene again, and I hear myself utter a cry of alarm. The pursuers are closing in; the nearest one can't be more than thirty yards away. At least two have raised their weapons, and I can't tell if they're carrying tranq guns or rifles. Two shots are fired simultaneously, a third one immediately after. I shout in pain as if the projectiles have landed in my body.

The creature jerks, stumbles, jerks, falls, tries to rise, then collapses in a strange twitching frenzy of skin and fur. "Closer! Closer!" I hear Brody urge, and the camera swoops in on the spasming body. Its hands—definitely hands now—claw at the air; its mouth works as if it is starving for oxygen. The shape of its face is becoming clearer as the brushy hair recedes, but it is still impossible to tell who or what will be revealed when the fur gives way to flesh.

"This is simply incredible," Brody mutters. "Folks, I'm telling you, this was an *animal* when we first caught sight of it, and now it looks like a person—"

Someone, either the anchorman in the studio or the cameraman in the copter, asks, "What's that around its neck?"

I shriek and leap to my feet, trembling so hard I almost fall over. Ellen scrambles up beside me. "What? Maria, what is it?"

"Oh my God," I whisper. "Oh my God."

The camera is zooming in even closer, narrowing in on a glittering object tied around the animal's throat.

"I can't tell what that is," Brody says. "A necklace of some sort?"

A key. The camera can't quite get the object in focus, but I know what it's supposed to be, so I can recognize it, even from such a distance, half obscured by the slowly thinning hair. A key, hanging on a leather cord . . .

Brody is still speaking. "Maybe an identification tag? Could this animal be part of some government project?"

I cannot breathe. I can only stare at the screen, where the camera is still so tightly focused on the key that it's hard to tell what condition the animal is in now. We can see it thrashing, but I think it's still stretched out on the ground. I think I see blood kicked up by its incessant flailing, but I can't tell how badly it's injured.

Was William wearing a key?

I stare outward at the television, and I stare inward at that memory from two weeks ago. William, slouching at my kitchen table, dressed in jeans and a worn shirt. Were the frayed ends of a knotted cord poking out from the collar? I can't remember. I can't remember. He had said he liked the way Dante wore the key to his storage locker, he would get a leather necklet of his own, but had he bothered to do it? Is this really William, panting and straining and growing gradually weaker, shifting from animal to human state as his blood seeps out and the whole world watches?

Or is it Dante?

I whimper and fling my arm out; I am so dizzy I think I might fall. Ellen's hand closes over mine, warm and reassuring. I cling to her with enough force to break a bone.

Brody's voice sounds again. Even above the whirring of the blades I can hear the stupefaction in his voice. "Mike—all you viewers out there—I can't believe what I'm seeing."

The camera pulls back again, and again we get the whole scene. It is a strange hunting tableau, the trophy animal on the ground in the center, a ring of dogs crouched around it, a ring of humans drawing near enough to touch it. But no one has extended a hand; no one is even poking at it with a rifle. Some are standing, some are kneeling, all are staring, as the creature lies before them on the dead grass and slowly makes itself over.

The fur turns from a muddy brown to a battered gold, then suddenly transmutes into cold white flesh wrapped around limbs that have drawn into a fetal position. Masses of dark hair spill all around the animal's head, obscuring its face, but it is possible to see, beneath the rough tangle, a smooth cheek and the angular jut of a nose. Someone reaches out with a very long stick and pushes back the hair. The creature sighs and flops over, its mouth open but its eyes closed.

Its whole face is visible, recognizable, and it's a face I know.

Christina.

CHAPTER TWENTY

Beside me, Ellen takes a hard breath. "That can't be Dante," she says, her voice loud with relief. "*Or* his brother. That's a girl."

"It's his sister," I say very quietly.

She jerks around to stare at me. "I forgot he had a sister. And you said she's a shape-shifter, too?"

I nod and sink to the couch. I am shaking so hard I really think I might vibrate through the furniture, through the floorboards, and into the earth itself. "Yes, but she—she was always the one who could control it. She said. She only became an animal a day or two a month, and she could hold off the transformation if she needed to." I put a hand to my forehead. My fingers are like ice. I wonder if I'm in shock. "This is terrible."

Ellen sits beside me and takes my hand again. Her fingers are warm enough to remind me what a real person should feel like. "But it's not Dante," she says firmly. "You have to be grateful for that."

"I am but he—he'll be so upset, and he—I mean, *Christina*. It didn't even occur to either one of us. She was always the sane one, the normal one. It was William that Dante was worried about, especially after the blood transfusion . . ." My voice trails off as I consider a new thought. "Although, I suppose, maybe she had a blood transfusion, too, when she had the baby? She never mentioned it, but—"

"Baby?" Ellen says sharply.

Suddenly I snap back to alertness, a fresh surge of adrenaline coursing through my body. I turn to meet her big eyes with mine, wearing an expression that's equally appalled. *"Lizzie."*

"Where's this baby now?" Ellen asks.

I shake my head. "Christina lives in Rolla. Surely she got a babysitter if she was going to be gone. If she knew she was going to be gone—"

"How old is Lizzie?"

I rip my hand free and run across the room, where I left my purse under an end table near the sliding glass door. Pawing through it for my address book, I say over my shoulder, "Three months, I think. Something like that." Kneeling on the floor, I pull my cell phone from my pocket and punch in Christina's number. "None of the attacks happened more than three months ago. Jesus. How can this *be*?"

Ellen snorts. "How can *any* of this be?"

Christina's phone goes straight to voice mail. Still on the floor, I slew around to stare at Ellen. "No one's answering," I say. "Maybe she left the baby with a neighbor."

Ellen looks straight back at me. "Or maybe she didn't."

In my heart, I know she didn't. In my heart, I know that whatever primitive, feral imperative had Christina in its grip, it didn't allow her time for rational thought. I have absolutely no doubt in my mind that Christina loved Lizzie. She loved her brothers, and she probably had a whole circle of friends that she genuinely cared about. But the affectionate, goofy, odd Christina I knew wasn't the one who had shifted into a grotesque, imperfect animal shape and gone lumbering through the world wreaking mindless mayhem.

"I have to go to Rolla," I say. "I have to see if Lizzie's all right."

Again, Ellen makes that snorting sound. She's already on her feet. "*We* have to go to Rolla," she says. "I'm not about to let you drive there on your own. You can't even stand up."

"But—"

"Just give me time to bank the fire and feed the cats, and we're outta here," she says.

While Ellen locks up the house, I call Dante's cell phone. He doesn't answer, of course, and I cannot bring myself to tell him this devastating news in a message. So I just say, "It's me. It's really important that you call me as soon as you can. No matter when you get this message. I love you."

Five minutes later, we're on the road and heading for Highway 44. Ellen's driving, but we're in my car. *She's* the one who said, "We can't take the Miata. No room for a baby seat."

I hadn't been thinking that clearly or that far ahead. But of course I'll be bringing Lizzie home with me. At least temporarily. At least until we can figure out what to do next.

That is, if we can find her. If Christina has left her with an acquaintance—what then? How do we locate her? It's not like Dante or William can sit patiently at her house, waiting for someone to bring the baby home. Do Christina's friends and neighbors even know she has brothers? Would they willingly turn over that small, sweet, fragile life to anyone who looks as unkempt and unsafe as Dante or William?

I close my eyes. There are too many questions.

Ellen has tuned my radio to KMOX, where all the talk is of the dramatic capture in the park. The word "capture" yanks my eyes open and has me staring at the dashboard, but the next few exchanges make it clear that the creature under discussion did not survive the hunt.

"Unfortunately, the perpetrator died at the scene," one commentator says. Another one jumps in, "Unfortunately? This is an animal that is responsible for at least four deaths." The first one responds, "Yes, but there's great confusion about what exactly this creature was. Animal? Human? Ladies and gentlemen, if you haven't watched the live footage of the pursuit, you will be astonished at what you see . . ."

"They'll be talking about this for weeks," Ellen says abruptly, her eyes fixed on the road. She is driving at least fifteen miles over the speed limit, and we are passing cars as if they are all being driven by octogenarians out for an afternoon of sightseeing. I didn't know my Saturn could go this fast. "It'll be in all the papers. 'Half-Animal, Half-Human, All Killer.' Stuff like that. Your Dante and his brother might be exposed after all."

I rub my forehead. The second adrenaline rush has dissipated, and I'm getting a headache. But I can also feel my body marshaling its reserves, using this brief period of comparative calm to recharge, preparing for the next onslaught. This is a day when I will have to survive multiple assaults on my emotions; I will have to be ready for extended battles.

"Maybe," I say. "But if they can't identify Christina's body, they won't be able to trace her back to Dante and William. Or Lizzie."

"What about that key?" she asks. "What's it to?"

I shake my head. "I don't know. I didn't even know she wore one. She didn't until recently." I'm silent a moment before adding, "Until a couple months ago, only Dante wore a key like that around his neck."

She gives me one quick, marveling look as she now comprehends some of the anguish I went through back at her house. "Jesus."

"But if it's, say, a key to her house." I shrug. "How will they track that down? Unless she's in the system for some other crime—which I don't think she is—I don't know that they'll be able to identify her."

"Okay, but her friends. The people at her office. Won't they notice that she's missing? Won't they start to put it together? And if any of them saw the footage today—or reads a newspaper or checks the Internet *ever*—"

"There's a chance someone will recognize her," I admit. "But—I don't think I would have if I hadn't been expecting to see William or Dante. And—seriously—would *you* think it was possible that someone you know could turn into a monster? I mean, this is like something out of a comic book. No one's going to look at photos of her face and say, 'Hey, she looks like Christina Romano.' I just think they won't credit it."

"Okay, maybe, but she's still missing," Ellen points out. "So the timing is going to make them suspicious. And if you suddenly say, 'Oh, how sad, Christina died,' and you don't produce a body—I just think people will start adding up the pieces."

I nod. I'm trying to think it through. "She's still on maternity leave, so we have a little time where her coworkers are concerned," I say. "I know she has friends in St. Louis, but I don't know how many. I don't know how close they are to her, how often they keep in touch." I ponder for a moment. "If someone can get me into her e-mail account, I can send all her friends a few messages, as if I'm her. Maybe I'll say I'm going on a trip down to—Florida or somewhere. I'll be gone for a few weeks. And then she'll conveniently die in a car wreck on the way home, and I'll have Dante or William send *that* message out to all her friends. That will change the timing between the deaths."

I'm concentrating on concocting the scheme, so I'm staring out the window, but I feel Ellen give me another quick glance. "You sure have a fertile mind for lying," she says.

I give a hollow laugh. "Years and years and *years* of practice."

"So what about the baby?" Ellen asks. "Can her brothers realistically raise her, or will you need to turn her over to the state?"

"I'm keeping her," I say.

I expect her to exclaim with disbelief or dissent. *Oh, no, girlfriend, do not even* think *you are keeping that baby.* But this is Ellen; she's usually a few steps ahead of me in anticipating emotional developments. "That's the trauma talking," she says quietly. "That's the body revving up to do whatever it takes to survive an emergency. You haven't thought it through."

I turn toward her as much as my seat belt will allow. "But I *have* thought it through," I say. "I told Dante just a couple of months ago that I wanted a baby, and if he didn't want to contribute to the process, I'd find another way to get one. He wasn't keen on the idea, but he didn't shoot me down. And Lizzie—I've only spent a couple days with her but I just adore her. I can do this, Ellen, I know I can. I *want* to." I take a deep breath. "I'm just not sure, legally, how to make it all work. I mean, what happens to an orphaned child?"

She risks a quick look at me then returns her attention to the road. "Orphaned," she repeats. "Who's her daddy?"

"Some old high school friend of Christina's who lives in Alaska now and only comes home once every five years, or something like that," I say. "She didn't even tell him about the baby. I don't think he's a factor, but that still leaves a lot of questions. How can I get custody of an abandoned baby? Does the state have to get involved? Will Dante or William automatically become her guardian? I don't know any of this."

"I can help you through it," she says. "I have friends who are social workers and lawyers. People who know the system. But I'll have to be convinced it's the right thing for her *and* for you."

I manage a soft laugh. "Well, it's the right thing for her, no question," I say. "She's a shape-shifter's child, Ellen. Chances are good that one day pretty soon she's going to turn into something else. A kitten. A rabbit. How do you think a foster parent would handle *that* little wrinkle?"

Ellen groans. "You're right, but—hell. Well, that's a little ways down the road. First we have to find her. Then we can think about keeping her."

A momentary silence falls between us, filled by the ongoing sound of the radio. The special news report has ended; now we're listening to the comments by listeners calling in to offer their opinions on everything from the police department's latest scandal to the newest baseball trade. Some, of course, still want to talk about the bizarre "wolf-woman" caught and killed on live television this afternoon. I don't want to listen, but I can't bring myself to change the station.

One caller instantly catches my attention. "I can't believe how gullible all you people are!" he exclaims. "That was the fakest newscast I ever saw. That stupid reporter is just trying to land himself a job in a big city like New York. Or maybe Channel 5 is just trying to boost its ratings, 'cause we all know it's the suckiest station in the city. I mean, were there *other* news helicopters out there taking pictures? *Noooooo.* Well, isn't that convenient for Channel 5!"

I straighten in my seat and stare at the radio dial, which Ellen reaches out to tap with her right index finger. "There it is," she says. "That's what's gonna save us. Redneck conspiracy theorists, who believe everyone is trying to trick them in one way or another."

"But I think there were a lot of cops and park rangers and other people who were on the scene and actually saw her change," I say.

"Yeah, maybe," Ellen replies. "But some of them were too far away to get a good look at Christina's face until she was dead, and others will say they thought they saw her throw something to the ground as she was running—a mask, maybe?—and all of them will feel like idiots swearing that they actually saw an animal turn into a human. I think the sheer suspicious nature of the average American will work to your advantage. People can't believe this story is true, therefore someone's lying to them. And no one investigates. And Lizzie and Dante and William are safe."

"I hope so," I say. "Let's hear it for fear and ignorance."

The bleak November sunset is layering icy white, tundra blue, and refrigerated pink on the western horizon as we exit the highway and begin winding through the countryside near Rolla. I had been sitting slack in my seat for the final twenty minutes of the drive, but now I'm upright and tense again, filled with an edgy energy. Prepared for anything at Christina's house. I hope.

Following my directions, Ellen pulls into Christina's driveway and cuts the motor. I've already got my door open when she grabs my left wrist. In the gathering dark, I can barely see her face.

"You realize this might be very bad," she says quietly. "If Christina was so lost to herself that she was killing total strangers—"

I wrench free. "She didn't hurt Lizzie," I say and jump out of the car without another word. But my heart is pounding; my brain is providing me with horrific images of nightmare slaughter. Thank God Ellen kept this speculation to herself until the moment of arrival. I don't think I could have endured the ride with those pictures in my head.

The house key is exactly where Christina had said she kept it, under the stone rabbit in the raised garden, surrounded by stripped winter bushes. Ellen has already climbed the stairs to the wide, gracious porch and is pressing her face against one of the windows, trying to peer into the living room.

"I think I hear something inside," she says.

I turn the lock and open the door. I hear it, too. A baby's voice, lifted in a long despairing cry, ragged and thready as if it has been sobbing for days but has not quite lost its hope of succor.

"Lizzie," I breathe. I *run* through the house for the baby's room, hitting wall switches as I go; it is as if an illuminating fire springs to life in the wake of my passage. The overhead fixture blooms into light as I rush into the baby's room, and I take it all in with one quick glance.

Everything is tidy—a blanket folded neatly over the back of the rocking chair, diapers and onesies laid out on top of the changing table, photo frames and cute little carved animals set out lovingly on the dresser—except for the crib itself. There, all is a tangle of wadded up bedsheets and regurgitated formula and streaks of liquid brown that I have to assume has seeped from a Huggies diaper. Lizzie lies in the middle of the mess, hands balled up, feet kicking at the air, her face red from shrieking. One bootie has come off, it looks like she has scratched her face, and the odor of poop and urine is powerful, but she does not look injured or abused. Angry, afraid, hungry, miserable, yes, but whole. Healthy. Alive.

"Thank God," I whisper, and burst into tears.

The tears don't impede me as I hurry to the bedside and lift Lizzie out of her crib, leaky diaper and all. "Shh, shh, it will be all right," I whisper as I cradle her against my chest. "I'm here, Aunt Maria is here. Everything will be okay."

Ellen is only a step behind me; she assesses the situation with one comprehensive look. "Good," is her pronouncement. "You want to bathe and change her or do you want to prepare a bottle? She's probably starving as well as filthy."

"I'll bathe her," I say. The truth is, I don't want to let her go, even to move the short distance to the kitchen. Lizzie is still crying softly, but she calmed down almost instantly once I took her in my arms, and she is nestling her little head against my chest. Her thin dark hair is sweaty from the effort of screaming; her face is red and strained with remembered fury, but it seems to me she is no longer afraid. It seems to me she trusts me. She knows she is safe.

"Sometimes when they're this dirty it's just easier to get in the shower with them," Ellen advises. "And you're going to need a clean shirt."

"Maybe you can find something for me in Christina's closet," I say. It won't bother me to wear a dead woman's clothes. After all, I'll be caring for a dead woman's child.

Ellen has no qualms about it, either. "Sure thing. Let me mix up a bottle and then I'll go look."

I follow her down the hallway toward the bathroom, still snuggling Lizzie tightly against my body. Her hands have fisted in my shirt; she hiccups against my chest. All the tension is leaving her small, clenched body—I think she might actually fall asleep before I get her clean. I leave the bathroom door open as I step inside and kick off my shoes. It is quite a trick to undress yourself when you're holding a baby in your arms, but I manage to struggle out of my clothes without ever putting her down.

She is mine now, and I am never letting her go.

Within a half hour, Lizzie and I are both clean and wearing fresh clothes, and I am sitting in the rocking chair feeding her a bottle. She wants to close her eyes but I have no idea when she ate last. I feel that food is more important than sleep, at least for the moment, so I keep cajoling and insisting until she has almost finished the last ounce.

Ellen comes in and drops to the floor in front of me, seating herself on a hooked rug featuring an illustration of "Hey Diddle Diddle." It's clear she's been busy. "I cleaned the potentially smelly stuff out of the fridge and took out the trash," she says. "Put the laptop by the door so you can take it back to your house and start going through e-mail. But two things I can't find—a purse, and a set of car keys."

That catches my attention. "She probably drove to Babler," I realize. "Her car is still there. That means—shit, at some point the cops will find it, and investigate it, and trace it back here."

"So we need to go get it," she says. "You know how to break into a car? And hotwire it?"

I shake my head and then lean back against the sturdy wood of the rocker. Suddenly I am so weary I can hardly think. I'm not sure I have the energy for one more adventure today. "No, do you?"

"No. But Henry does."

"Oh, let's not drag anyone else into this if we don't have to."

"Well, we might have to. But we might have a couple days. I don't know when the police start getting nosy about cars that have been left at the park too long."

"Then let's not worry about it right now. Let's just go home. I'll think about that tomorrow."

"Fine with me, Scarlett," she says, coming to her feet. "Let's gather the baby's stuff and get out of here."

It's while we're packing grocery bags with diapers, clothing, bottles, and formula that I hear my cell phone ring. I leave Lizzie sleeping on the rug in her room and race through the house to grab my phone. "Dante?" I say. I don't recognize the number on Caller ID, but I'm sure it's him.

"Hey, baby," he says. He sounds tired but not particularly stressed. I think his day must have been better than mine. *So far.* "Guess what I'm calling you on? That cell phone we buried here in the park a few months ago. My own's completely dead."

"I knew it would come in handy," I say, while I'm thinking, *Let's ease into this.* "Did you get my message?"

"No, but I think I only have about fifteen minutes, so let me tell you my news first. I found him. I found William."

"Yes? And he said?"

"It's not him, Maria. He's been gone so much lately because of a girl. I believed him anyway when he said it, but then–it was so crazy–we were here at the park, and all these dogs and cops started running past us. It was obvious they were hunting something, and we wondered if it might be the killer. William shifted to human shape and found some hikers to talk to, and they said there'd been another attack. The cops tracked the animal down and destroyed it. Do you know if it's true?"

"It's true. We saw the whole thing on live TV."

The breath whooshes out of his body in one long unvoiced expression of relief. "And it wasn't William," he says again. "I can't tell you, Maria—I hated asking him more than I've hated anything in my life. And you know what he said to me? He said, 'I was afraid it might be *you.*' And I told him, 'Yeah, Maria thought the same thing.' And he said, '*That's* why she was looking for you! Now I get it!' Smart guy, put it together right away."

"I thought William didn't even follow the news," I reply. "How'd he hear about the murders?"

"Christina told him a couple weeks ago. She's always pretty up on current events."

"Dante," I say, "I have something terrible to tell you."

I can't see him and he makes no sound, but I can feel him go into high alert, a predator poised to pounce, a prey animal tensed to flee. "What is it?"

"The creature they tracked in Babler Park. The one they killed. It was Christina."

There is a silence so long that I would think the connection has failed except that I can still hear him breathing. I am not surprised he has no words. If someone told me my cousin Beth had become a brutal murderer, I would not be able to make sense of the accusation. "I think it was Christina all along. She killed all those people," I say gently. "I'm guessing that she got a blood transfusion when she had the baby, and she just didn't bother to tell you guys because she didn't want you to worry. And then something—something went wrong in her body or in her head. I'm so, so, so sorry to have to tell you this."

"You're sure?" he says, his voice shredded.

"I saw the broadcast. I saw the animal change to a person. I saw her face."

His next words are so faint it is like they have been drawn on a sidewalk with chalk and all but washed away by the rain. "What about Lizzie?"

"I've got her," I say. "I'm in Rolla right now at the house. She looks like she's been left alone all day, but she hasn't been hurt. And I've fed her and changed her and I'll bring her home with me tonight."

Another moment of bleak, empty silence, and then the phone transmits a sound I have never heard before—Dante softly weeping. If only he was not so far away. If only I was close enough to cradle him to my heart, as I cradled Lizzie, close enough for me to whisper the same lie into his ear, *Shh, shh, it will be all right.*

But he is not, and all I can do is offer the eternal promise, the eternal invitation. "I love you. I will always love you. Come home to me as soon as you can."

CHAPTER TWENTY-ONE

The following week unfolds in such an unfamiliar fashion that I might almost be living someone else's life. The first thing I learn is that an infant in the house changes everything—what you eat, when you sleep, what every minute of your life holds. Ellen has told me she will not expect me at work for any of the three days leading to the Thanksgiving holiday.

"I'm out of vacation time," I say.

She waves a hand. "I know. Maybe we can get you FMLA days. We'll work it out."

I have to find a day care or a nanny, and soon, but Lizzie and I need this first week to get to know each other. She is still a beautiful child, alert and easily engaged, but I think I can sense a tension in her that was not present before. She cries more easily, she wakes more fretfully in the middle of the night, and more often. I have to wonder how Christina's accelerating madness played out in their house—how often she left the baby alone for hours, failed to feed her, or simply allowed her to cry. I have to wonder how long it will take before Lizzie knows I will never fail her.

I have to admit, I am thrilled—and sometimes, moved to tears—when she responds to me, when my touch or my voice is enough to comfort her in the night. When I bend over her, first thing in the morning, she smiles and lifts her arms to me, and every time I am struck in the heart. She is so precious, so pure; if she loves me, I have been approved by angels.

But Lizzie does not represent the only change that has come to my life. She is not the only new addition who looks to be a permanent fixture in my house.

Sunday night, shortly after I have put Lizzie to bed in a makeshift crib constructed of a hastily emptied dresser drawer, I hear a scuffle on the front porch and the sound of a throaty bark. It is close to ten o'clock and I am exhausted beyond description, and yet a prickle of anticipation shoots a burst of energy into my veins. Flipping on the porch light, I open the door to find two large dogs standing just outside, their ears perked up, and their tails straight behind them. One is a German shepherd, mostly black with a little white; the other is some kind of setter, a fluid golden brown. I have never seen either one before, and yet I know, I *know*, that these are Dante and William.

Wordlessly, I open the door and let them in. The shepherd pauses to nuzzle my hand and—when I stoop down—to lick my face, but the setter trots directly to the guest room where Lizzie lies sleeping. Careful not to wake her, he sniffs her face and touches her balled fist with his nose. Then, with a long doggy sigh, he shakes himself and settles on the floor beside her, resting his muzzle on his forepaws. The shepherd also investigates Lizzie, then sinks to his haunches and watches me in the dim light thrown in from the hallway.

Dante has never allowed me to see him in his animal state, and so I am not sure he will permit me to make any contact now. But he doesn't pull away when I reach out my hand, and I can't resist ruffling his fur and scratching the top of his head. He responds by licking the inside of my wrist.

"I don't know exactly what to do now," I tell him. "I don't know if you can understand me. I've got a bag of dog food in the basement—long story—so I'll put out a couple bowls of that and some water. Lay down some blankets. I guess you want to sleep in here with the baby? And then maybe in the morning, if you're human, we can talk." I glance at William. "All of us can talk. Figure out what to do next."

I haul the dog paraphernalia from the basement and set food out in the kitchen. For tonight, I'll let Lizzie's uncles watch over her in her bedroom, but I don't think that should be a long-standing practice. It doesn't seem like it would be good for her *or* them to be so dependent. I spread out the blankets near the dresser drawer and pat them invitingly. William stays where he is, but Dante ambles over and drops down with a noise that sounds like relief. I ruffle his fur again and then lean down to plant a kiss on the silky fur on the top of his head.

"Love you," I whisper. "Even like this."

In the morning, I wake to the smell of coffee brewing and the feel of Dante's arms around my waist. It takes me a second to remember exactly how the situation stood last night when I collapsed into bed, but as soon as I do, I squeal and flip myself over.

He's awake, he's watching me, and he kisses me hard for a long moment. I am so happy to see him—days before I could have expected to have him back—that for a moment joy crowds out all other emotions, all other memories. I hug him as hard as I can and return the kiss with abandon.

When he pulls away, he's smiling, but his face has been etched with a permanent sadness that suddenly reminds me of everything that has transpired in the past twenty-four hours. "Don't get too enthusiastic," he warns. "William's in the other room making breakfast."

I kiss him again, just to prove I'm not afraid of William, and then drop my head back to my own pillow. "There's so much we have to talk about, the three of us," I say. "But I don't want to get out of bed as long as you're in it."

"Well, in about an hour or so, you'll be in bed with a dog, so unless you want to start getting kinky—"

I flick him on the nose. "Fifteen years, you've managed not to make bestiality jokes, and now all of a sudden—"

"Lot of stuff has changed overnight," he replies, suddenly serious.

I sigh. "It certainly has."

He pats my cheek. "Come on. Let's get up, get dressed, talk to William. Figure out everything we need to do next."

It is a strange convocation at my kitchen table that morning. We take turns holding the baby on our laps as we eat breakfast in shifts. I notice that Lizzie is perfectly at ease with William, catching at his fingers, pulling at his long hair, giggling at the sound of his voice; she has been around him fairly often, I think. By contrast, when she's in Dante's arms, she's a little more reserved, but a little more fascinated. She keeps her head turned so she can watch him, so she can memorize him, so she will know him by sight and scent and sound when she encounters him again.

I outline my ideas for delaying the news of Christina's death, and they are in absolute agreement. Like me, they believe only disaster could result from the authorities discovering her identity and taking Lizzie into custody. Some of my legal worries melt away when William reveals that he is executor of Christina's estate and named in her will as Lizzie's guardian.

"No offense, but we still might need a lawyer and a social worker to help us make this a smooth transition, because you might not strike people as the most . . . mmm . . . obvious person to be caring for a baby," I say.

They both laugh. "Hey, I have a Social Security number," William says. "I pay taxes. My only income is in the form of a few investments that don't yield too much, but I'm not a total derelict."

It turns out that their names are on the house, along with Christina's, which will make it much easier to dispose of it, if that's what we decide to do. "Or keep it for Lizzie to inherit when she turns twenty-one," Dante suggests.

"I suppose we could rent it out for the next few years but—ugh. I don't feel like being a landlord," I say. "Well, that's not an urgent problem for today. What's urgent is retrieving Christina's car, creating a plausible lie about where she is, and then in a few weeks letting everyone know that she—that she died."

Dante's face tightens; William looks away. Dante is the one to speak. "What we really need to do," he says, "is figure out what to do with Lizzie."

I tell them what I told Ellen. "I'm keeping her."

"For now, maybe," Dante says. "But you—"

"Forever," I interrupt. She's currently sitting quietly on my lap, playing with the top button of my sweater. "Dante, you know I want a baby. I told you that a couple of months ago. And I adore Lizzie. And she's *yours*, she belongs to *you*. I can't possibly give her up, turn her over to strangers. I'm not going to. Don't even bother arguing."

"You need time to think it through—" Dante begins, but William looks over at him with a sweet smile.

"She told you not to argue," he says.

Dante turns on him. "This is our mess, not hers," he says. "She shouldn't have to fix it for us."

William shrugs. "She loves you, so she thinks it's her mess, too. I think it's a good solution. It feels right."

"It feels like we're taking advantage of Maria."

I lean over to put a hand on his arm. "If it will make you happier, I'll say I'll keep Lizzie for a month and decide then what I want to do," I tell him. "But I already know I want to keep her."

He stares back at me. "I can't help you," he says in a low voice. "Or not very much. I think I've learned how to be human an hour or two a day, but that leaves all the other hours for *you* to have to deal with her."

"Hey," says William. "I'm not completely useless, you know."

I smile at them both. "See? Lizzie will have me *and* both of you. More family than she knows what to do with."

"I'm just not sure," Dante says.

"Well, I am," I reply.

William tilts his head at me. "Of course, your own family might start wondering how you ended up with a baby all of a sudden."

I laugh. "I know. I'm already trying to decide how to spin that story. Beth's met Lizzie, so I have to start with a version of the truth, I think. And I need to come up with a story line pretty soon, because I want to take Lizzie with me on Thanksgiving, and that's just three days away."

"We can watch her while you're visiting your family," William says.

"I *want* to take her with me," I reply. "She's part of my life now. She's mine." I lift my hand from Dante's arm and wave it to indicate the three of them, Lizzie on my lap, Dante and William at the table. "You're *all* mine. More than I ever could have hoped for."

Of course, that one conversation doesn't end the debate, but I'm not too worried about it. Once Dante believes I am utterly committed to keeping Lizzie, he will give in.

I love having him around at least briefly every morning, although I do wonder if all these single hours of being a man will cut into the extended period he will spend in human shape when it is time for him to transform again. I decide not to worry about it. I decide I like having him in the house, or near it, when he is shaped like a dog, and I secretly hope that, because he is spending so much time in a populated neighborhood, his body will realize he must continue to shift into this generally acceptable form. No more bears, no more deer, no more wild creatures foraging through the night. Just man's best friend, a stray who has found a welcoming home.

I'm less certain how I feel about William's continued presence in my life. But then, I've never been sure how to take William, and I am still learning what he's like. It's quickly apparent that he prefers to be in animal shape, and his default creature is that rangy golden setter. He is not always at the house when I get up in the mornings, but he usually checks in every day. It seems he's always told the truth when he's said that he can shift between forms at will. This comes in handy when, for instance, I need to run to the grocery store on Wednesday afternoon and I don't want to bring Lizzie with me. William is more than happy to resume his human body and watch over her while I'm gone.

My guess is that, as we all get used to the new parameters of our lives, William will be around less and less. I will have to find some way to let him know when I need him, or we will have to devise a schedule for when we expect him to appear. For now, I am thinking of asking Ellen's boyfriend to install a doggy door for me so William and Dante can come and go at will. And then I will have to find some way to childproof it before Lizzie is old enough to crawl.

Funny—for so long, it has been just me in this house. Yes, I was joined at intense and satisfying intervals by Dante, but it was still *my* house, *my* life. I fit myself to him when he was here, but he was absent from so many of my daily calculations. And now my life has grown exponentially more complex. I am constantly juggling the requirements and contributions of three other souls, and I cannot make a single decision that does not take their needs into account. I am no longer a strong but lonely woman with a part-time lover; I am the head of a most unconventional family.

Sometimes I'm bewildered and sometimes I'm overwhelmed and sometimes my temper snaps or my mood plummets or my weariness sends me to bed on the edge of tears. But mostly I'm energized, I'm entertained, I'm constantly thinking and planning and solving a problem or easing the way. Mostly I really love my life.

Thanksgiving at Aunt Andrea's comes and goes more smoothly than I could have hoped. Everybody loves Lizzie. Aunt Vannie and Clara fight over who gets to play with her the most, and all three of them settle on the floor after the meal to bat around small soft toys free of any choking hazards. Beth drags me out to Aunt Andrea's back porch to demand more details about this sudden addition to my life, but I've rehearsed my cover story, down to my pauses and gestures.

I wasn't entirely honest when I told you that her mom got in touch with me over Facebook. The truth is, her mother is the sister of this guy I dated for a while in college—Dante, remember him? Yeah, the sort of dark mysterious one. Well, he resurfaced a year or so ago and we've been dating ever since—I know, I know, I should have told you, but I didn't know how long it would last and—anyway. I'm still crazy about him. And he's really worried about Lizzie's mom, he says she's so wild, she's always going off with guys she doesn't know, and he asked if I'd help out with her from time to time, so—here we are.

As I anticipated, she's so intrigued by Dante's reappearance in my life that she doesn't pay too much attention to the details about Lizzie. That may change in the future if I formally adopt Lizzie, but for now I am able to skate by with a minimum investment in the truth.

My mother's reaction is the most matter-of-fact—but also the most insightful. First she tells me they're having a rummage sale at her church this weekend, and she can buy clothes and other baby accessories, perhaps even a high chair if I'd like one. Later she asks if I'll have Lizzie during Christmas.

"It's possible," I say. "Christina's been traveling a lot. And she's very—unreliable."

My mother nods serenely. "Good. Then I'll start looking for Christmas presents for her." She smiles. "I love buying gifts for little girls. And for my big girl."

I think this over as she helps me load up the car, a task that takes forever. Not only are there cartons of leftovers and a stack of books Aunt Vannie has saved for me, there is all of Lizzie's stuff. And Lizzie. It seems my mother has realized, when no one else has, that I intend for Lizzie to be a permanent part of my life. She hasn't figured out why that should be, but somehow she has recognized in me a certain resolve, a certain possessiveness. She knows from long experience that once I find a toy, a friend, an idea, or a house I love, it takes an act of God to make me let go.

I kiss her, climb in the Saturn, and head home. Lizzie is already sleeping in the backseat. I have tears in my eyes for the first five miles of the return trip, but I'm smiling.

Friday we all head down to Christina's house. Dante conserves his energy by staying in animal form for the ride, so William does, too. I never thought I would be the kind of person who drove down the highway with dogs in the backseat, sticking their heads out the window, but, in fact, that is exactly the kind of person I am this chilly November day. I have bundled Lizzie up in several layers of blankets, so I'm pretty sure she's not too cold as she sleeps in the car seat with her uncles on either side of her. I'm probably the only one who's uncomfortable, but

I just turn up the heat and slip my gloves back on, and then I'm just as happy as the rest of them.

There is too much to do at Christina's house to finish it all in one day, but we go through the mail, pay the bills, and thoroughly clean the house. Dante and I disassemble the crib and manage to get it in the trunk; I think I might need to borrow someone's truck to get the rest of Lizzie's furniture to my place. At some point we'll need to go through everything else—Christina's clothes and jewelry, the furniture, the dishes, the idiosyncratic accumulations of a life—but that won't be a quick or easy process. We still haven't decided what to do with the house; we still haven't told her friends that Christina is dead. It is as if—by not making these final decisions, saying these irrevocable words—we can hold back the truth. It is as if, by not acknowledging her death, we can pretend she is still alive, just missing. Just traveling somewhere, visiting her friends, staying a little longer than she planned. She might be back tomorrow, or one day next week. All we have to do is await her call.

"I think I'll stay here a few days," William says as we load the final bag of Lizzie's toys into the car. "Maybe start going through her things. Maybe see if any of the neighbors come around looking for her. Most of them know me, at least by sight, so they won't be too alarmed when they see me."

Dante nods. "All right. I've probably got another ten days before I'm human again for any length of time. We can come back then and get some serious work done."

"Sounds good." William kisses Lizzie on the forehead and smiles at me. "See you later."

I think Dante might want to sit beside me for the drive home, but he climbs in back beside Lizzie's car seat without a word of explanation. "Put on some music," he says as I pull onto the street. "She seems to like classic rock."

"*You* like classic rock," I retort, but I obligingly punch stations until I find one that suits.

I still have never seen him in the act of transformation; I still don't know how long it takes, how unnerving it is to watch, if it is accompanied by the preternatural creak of expanding bones or the eerie pant of resizing lungs. But I am pretty sure Dante requested the music to cover any sounds that might occur during the process, and he has chosen to sit in the backseat so I cannot watch.

At any rate, when we arrive back at my house an hour later, he is curled up on the seat beside Lizzie in the shape of the now-familiar German shepherd. She is awake; her fingers are knotted in his fur. Both of them seem content.

Over the weekend, I try to put some order back into my own life, cleaning the house, buying groceries, doing so many loads of laundry I expect my washer to break down in protest. Beth has given me the name of a friend of a friend who runs a day care in her house and only lives about three miles from me. Lizzie and I go check her out. We both like the proprietor, a cheerful fifty-something woman with curly brown hair, wide hips, and powerful forearms. I approve of her setup, two playrooms in the house, hard plastic climbing walls in the yard, and a thirty-year-old daughter who works alongside her every day.

"I only take two infants at a time, but right now I'm down to one, so I've got room for your little girl," she tells me. She's holding Lizzie against her shoulder with all the practiced ease of someone who has spent her life around babies. She's already told me she raised seven children of her own, something that makes me view her as almost superhuman. I've already told her that Lizzie's uncles are authorized to pick her up whenever they're available. "She's a real cutie. I'd be glad to have her."

"I'll bring her by Monday morning, then."

The following week goes *much* less smoothly than I had hoped. It is just so difficult to get yourself and a child ready to leave the house by seven in the morning. I begin every day feeling frazzled and tardy, and end every day almost too exhausted to stand. I can tell Dante is concerned about me—even when he is in animal form, he watches me with worried brown eyes—but I am not complaining. I am simply adjusting. I still love my new life. Or I will, once I am rested enough to appreciate it.

The first Thursday of December, Dante is back.

I mean Dante the man, Dante my lover, Dante who is standing at the stove, making dinner, when I get home from work. Lizzie is in her punkin seat on the kitchen table, chortling and waving her hands; she looks like a baby who's recently been changed and fed and doesn't have too many other worries at the moment.

"Ooh, well, isn't this a charming advertisement for the new world order," I say, coming up behind Dante and slipping my arms around him. I rest my cheek against his broad back. His ponytail is long enough to tickle my nose. "The brilliant female executive goes off to work while the house-husband stays home with the baby."

"Careful, the pan is hot," he warns, but he pats my arm with a hand encased in an oven mitt.

"*You're* hot," I say into his shirt.

He laughs. "No ripping off my clothes until our little audience of one has gone down for the night."

"Mmm, even better. Anticipation will build the excitement."

It would, of course, except that I am so worn out from the unfamiliar exertions of the past four days. Dressed in my silkiest nightgown, I fall asleep in bed while I wait for Dante to get Lizzie settled in her room. I don't wake up until the clock radio goes off an hour late Friday morning.

Dante laughs away my instant panic. "I reset the alarm last night. All you have to do is get yourself dressed. I'll take Lizzie to the day care today. I'll get groceries while you're gone. All you have to do today is work. And exist."

I kiss him on the mouth. "And love you."

"And love me," he agrees. "The most important part of all."

By Saturday morning, I almost feel rested, and we have a spectacular day. It snowed two inches overnight, but the morning is so sunny that the brightness actually hurts our eyes. We bundle Lizzie up in a snowsuit and romp around outside for a couple of hours. When I hold her in my arms and kneel on the shoveled sidewalk, she reaches for the nearest drift and shoves a fistful of the white stuff in her mouth. I am probably a terrible mother, but I let her do it. Who doesn't want to eat snow? I'm sure there are way worse things she'll try to consume if I'm not constantly vigilant.

We spend the afternoon going out for lunch and getting caught in a parade that seems to be celebrating some high school's football win, and it is past two by the time we get home again. For a change, I'm not the one yawning, but both Dante and Lizzie look sleepy. I tune the television to a cartoon station while the two of them get comfortable on the couch, then I turn to my own chores. Once I've started dinner, I head to the bedrooms to change sheets, gather up overlooked socks, and put away an astonishing miscellany of items that have gotten misplaced in less than a day.

It is far more work, I have discovered, to take care of a household than an individual. But I am two full weeks into my probationary month as Lizzie's caretaker, and I have not wavered for one second on my decision to keep her. If anything, my determination has grown stronger. If Dante were to tell me he and William had concluded that she was better off turned over to someone else, I think I would steal her away from them. I would wait till they were both in animal shape, and I would take her, leaving behind no clues to our whereabouts.

I have not figured out exactly how I would manage this, though I have pictured myself withdrawing thousands of dollars from an ATM while I looked furtively over my shoulder, expecting pursuit.

In my heart, I do not believe it will come to this. In my heart, I am certain that Dante, William, and Lizzie all realize what I have known from the start. Lizzie belongs with me; like Dante, she is mine, and that will never change.

It is nearly four thirty before I am ready to call it quits for the day. Time to check on dinner; time to check on my loved ones. The casserole is bubbling nicely in the oven, but no one is stirring in the living room. I steal across the floor and turn off the TV, then tiptoe up to the couch, expecting to find both Lizzie and Dante asleep. He's stretched out full-length, Lizzie curled up on his chest; he has one hand on her back to make sure she doesn't fall. The fading afternoon light washes the walls with shadowed gold. The room is filled with such a deep sense of peace that I inhale it as if I am inhaling incense.

I pull an old afghan from the rocking chair and carefully arrange it over their bodies. Lizzie doesn't move, but when I glance at Dante's face, I am surprised to see his eyes are open. He's watching me with an expression so intense I cannot read it.

"I didn't mean to wake you up," I whisper.

He shakes his head, the slightest motion against the cushion of the couch. "I wasn't sleeping," he whispers back. "I was thinking. Sit down a minute."

I don't want to disturb the baby, so I settle on the floor beside them.

Dante reaches for me with his free arm, and I nurse his hand against my cheek. "She looks so content," I say. "She certainly loves Uncle Dante."

He nods, but absently. I can sense his mind working furiously, trying to order his thoughts. His hand has closed over my fingers, hard. He has something he wants to say, if only he can figure out how.

"Hear me out," he says at last, slowly. "Don't interrupt."

I try to keep the astonishment and wariness from my face. What's this about? "All right."

He hitches himself a little to one side, enough so that he is facing me without dislodging Lizzie. She waves her arms and makes a little cooing sound, but resettles on his chest. "For most of the past fifteen years, I've had it in my head that you could hardly do worse for yourself than to be in love with me," he begins.

"Dante! How could you—"

"Shh. You promised not to interrupt."

"But—"

"Shh." I subside and he goes on. "What kind of life could you build for yourself with a man who is gone half the time—or more—who leads this strange inhuman existence—and who will probably be dead before he's fifty?"

"Dante!"

This time he just ignores me and keeps speaking. "I always thought you would find someone else—someone *normal*, someone who could give you what you wanted and what you deserved. I hoped you wouldn't, but I was prepared to step out of your life if you did."

"Dante, I never wanted anyone but you—"

"And so that's always been the reason I didn't ask you to marry me. Because I thought you could do better," he finishes up.

Now he falls silent, still staring at me. Suddenly, when it's my turn to speak, I am mute. I stare back. The color of the room shifts gradually from gold to rose.

"But now," he says, his words coming even more slowly, his hold on my hand so tight I can feel my bones protest, "now I think this is the way it's supposed to be. We're together for a reason. It wouldn't be selfish of me to ask you to marry me. It would—it would make us a complete family. A strange and bewildering family that doesn't bear close examination, true, but a family nonetheless."

He pulls me toward him, or maybe I'm leaning that way; it's hard to tell. "I think we belong together, Maria," he whispers. "If you'll marry me, I'll find some way to make it work. I'll fight the changing as hard as I can. I'll—I'll stay as close as I can, like I've done this week, so that you know you can rely on me. Maybe we need to get a place out in the country, where it's safer for me to be in animal form. Maybe we should move into Christina's house. Or maybe not. I've got money, we could afford to move anywhere you liked—"

I stop him with a kiss before he can offer any more desperate, hopeful, unnecessary incentives. I press my mouth against his with all the strength I can muster; I have wrapped my arms around his head like some kind of manic turban. He has released his death grip on my hand to slip his palm against the back of my head and pull me even closer for the kiss. If people had told me that *this* is what happiness feels like, I would not have believed them. It is as much pain as it is euphoria, as much tenderness as elation. I am crying so hard that I break the kiss so I can grope for a Kleenex.

"Dante—yes—of course. Oh God, yes, I want to marry you," I sob. I have no tissues in the pockets of my jeans and there's no convenient box on the end table, so I wipe my face with the sleeve of my sweatshirt. "I never thought you—and I didn't want you to feel trapped, caged—Jesus, I don't mean to keep using animal metaphors. I always wanted you to know that I loved you no matter what you were, who you were, no matter how much or how little you could give me. But I—oh, I mean, if you're sure—and not *just* because of Lizzie, but because of me—"

Now he is tugging at my shoulder as he inches his body toward the back of the sofa. "Get up here," he says. "We'll make room."

"I don't want to wake the baby—"

"She'll fall asleep again. I need to feel you here beside me."

He scoots back a little farther and I lift the afghan and squeeze myself next to him on the slice of sofa that makes a narrow ledge beside his body. We kiss frantically for a few moments, but then we pause to catch our breath, to smile at each other, tremulously, through a mist of hope and wonder and tears. Yes, he is crying, too, just a little bit, but he laughs as he lifts a hand to dash away the wetness.

"You didn't see that," he said. "Where's a damn tissue when you need one?"

I lean in to kiss his damp cheek, and then I scrub my sleeve across his face. "I couldn't find one, either. And I did, too, see you cry. I'll never let you forget it."

"So you'll marry me?" he says.

"I would love to marry you," I reply.

He leans in to kiss me again, but it's one motion too many. Lizzie comes half awake with a fretful cry, and I instantly begin to pat and shush her. Dante takes the opportunity to shove himself farther back and resettle her against his stomach. After a moment, she quiets down again. I feel her small warm restless shape between our bodies, and I know she will not sleep for long.

But for now, the world is perfect. Dante and I lie face-to-face on the couch, arms draped across each other, foreheads touching. From time to time, when we think of it, one of us leans forward to press our lips against the other's mouth, but we are too tired to kiss much or talk much or even dream much. It is enough, for the moment, to simply *be*, to simply be *together*, to fit against each other like puzzle pieces that only form a complete image when their wildly disparate edges interlock. For the moment, I can think of nothing else that I might ever want. Sunset fades around us, turning the room to peach, to azure, to violet, to black, and the three of us lie together, unmoving except for our breath, safe, content, satiated with love.